# DEN OF THIEVES

**Books by David Chandler**

*The Ancient Blades Trilogy*
DEN OF THIEVES: BOOK ONE

*Coming Soon*
A THIEF IN THE NIGHT: BOOK TWO

*and*
HONOR AMONG THIEVES: BOOK THREE

# DEN OF THIEVES

## THE ANCIENT BLADES TRILOGY:
## BOOK ONE

# DAVID CHANDLER

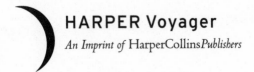

HARPER Voyager
*An Imprint of* HarperCollins*Publishers*

**HARPER Voyager**

*An Imprint of* HarperCollins*Publishers*
10 East 53rd Street
New York, New York 10022-5299

Copyright © 2011 by David Wellington
Cover art by Richard Jones
ISBN 978-1-61129-915-1

*For F.L., M.M., and R.E.H., the Grand Masters*

# Acknowledgments

I didn't think you would ever see this book. I wrote it for myself, for therapy, for fun. I wrote it intending to put it in a desk drawer (well, the back of my hard drive) and forget about it. Nobody else was ever supposed to see it, but Alex Lencicki stood outside my cave shouting insults and dire threats until I threw some pages at him to make him go away. After that it was out of my hands. Russell Galen saw it next, and he beat me over the head with a club until I let go of the manuscript. Diana Gill and Will Hinton took it from there and made it into something better, something I'm proud to show the world. Without these people it could never have happened, and I'm very grateful.

DAVID CHANDLER
New York City, 2011

THE FREE CITY OF NESS

# DEN
## OF THIEVES

# PROLOGUE

Nearly one hundred thousand people lived in the Free City of Ness, stuffed like rats in a sack too small to contain them all. The city was less than a mile across and filled every cranny of the hill encircled by its high defensive wall. At midnight, seen from a hill two miles to the north, it was the only light in the nighttime landscape, a bright ember smoldering in the midst of dark fields that rolled to the horizon. It looked, frankly, like all it needed was one good gust of wind to stir it up into a great whoosh of flame.

Bikker grinned to see it, though he knew it was only a trick of perspective. He was a giant of a man with a wild, coarse beard and a magic sword on his belt. He did not know how the other two members of the cabal felt, but for himself, he'd love to watch the Free City of Ness burn.

The lights he saw came from a thousand windows and the forges of a hundred workshops and manufactories. The city supplied the kingdom of Skrae with all the iron and steel it needed, most of the leather goods, and an endless river of spoons and buckles, as well as lanterns and combs made of horn. The guilds worked through the night, every night, filling the endless demand. Streamers of smoke rose from every chimney, rising like boiling columns of darkness that obliterated the stars, while half the windows in the city were illuminated by burning candles as an army of scribes, clerks, and accounters scratched at their ledger books.

On the near side of the river, gambling houses blazed with light, while whores marched up and down long avenues carrying lanterns to attract passersby. Half the city, it seemed, was still awake. "D'you suppose any of 'em know what's coming?" Bikker asked.

"For the sake of our scheme, I pray they do not," his

employer said. Bikker had never seen the man. Even now the mastermind of the cabal was ensconced in a darkened carriage pulled by two white horses that pawed at the turf. The horses bore no brands or marks, and the driver wore no livery. The coach might have belonged to any number of fine houses—all its insignia had been removed.

A slender white hand emerged from a window of the coach, holding a purse of gold by its strings. Bikker took the payment—the latest of many such—and shoved it inside his chain mail shirt. "For your sake, I advise sealed lips."

"Don't worry, I can be discreet when I choose," Bikker said with a laugh. "Though what a juicy tale I could tell! In a month the city will be torn in half, and the streets will be lined with the dead. How many lights do you think will show then? And no one will ever know what part I played in it all."

"No, they will not," the third member of the cabal said. Bikker turned to face Hazoth, whose visage was covered in a thick veil of black crepe. As much as Bikker disliked this business of unseen associates, he supposed he was glad for that veil. It was not good to look on the naked face of a sorcerer. "If you cannot maintain silence, I can enforce it on you. Don't forget your place. Your part in this is minimal."

Bikker shrugged. He knew that perfectly well. He'd been hired to perform a variety of small services, but mostly because he was probably the only person in the city who could stop these two, if he so chose. When he'd agreed to meet with them—and then agreed to their tentative, secretive offer—they'd been comically grateful. His reputation preceded him, and they didn't dare offend his vanity. But they never truly let him forget that he was their lackey. "I do what I'm told . . . when I'm paid. Gold has a way of stifling the tongue. I know better than to ask of him," Bikker said, jutting one thumb toward the occupant of the coach, "but what are you getting out of this, wizard? What could he pay you that you can't just magic up on your own?"

"I've agreed to turn a blind eye to Hazoth's . . . experiments," the coach's occupant said, "once I rule the city. Does that trouble you?"

There had been a time when that would have given Bikker pause, indeed. Sorcerers could be dangerous. Hazoth stank of brimstone and the pit, and he was capable of things mortal men should never try. Sometimes sorcerers made mistakes and the whole world paid. The sword at Bikker's side was a testament to how high the price had once been—it was sworn to the defense of the realm against the demons a sorcerer could summon up but couldn't always control.

There'd been a time when Bikker was sworn to that same defense. But the world had changed. Times had changed. He too had changed. Any belief he'd had in nobility or service was ground down by a mill wheel that moved very slowly, but never stopped. Once, he'd been a champion of humankind.

Now he only shrugged. He peered down at the city. From here, it might have been a nest of termites clambering over themselves and their dung heap. "Slaughter 'em all. Feed 'em to your pets, Hazoth, if you like! By then I'll be far enough away not to care."

"Indeed. The gold in that purse will take you far. And there is more to come, once you have fulfilled your part of our design. You know the next step?"

"Oh, aye," Bikker said. He spat in the direction of the city as if he would put out all those fires with one gob. "Next thing to do is find our unwitting fourth." A fool was required, someone who would have no idea what he was doing. Without such a pawn, the plan could go nowhere. "I need to scare us up a thief."

# PART I

# A Thief's Ransom

# CHAPTER ONE

There were evil little things skulking in the shadows, their eyes very bright in the gloom. In every burned-out shell of an old house, Malden could hear their tiny footsteps and the occasional whisper. No lights at all showed in this part of town, and the fog hid both moon and stars. The lantern Malden carried could paint a crumbling wall with yellow light, or show him where the cobblestones had been pried up and deep pools of mud awaited an unwary step. It could not, however, pierce the darkness that coiled inside the ruined houses and stables, nor show who was watching him so intently.

He didn't like this.

He didn't like the time of the meeting, an hour past midnight. He did not like the location: down by the wall, near the river gate, in the wasteland called the Ashes. In the same year he was born this whole district had been consumed by the Seven Day Fire. Because the doss-houses and knackeries down here belonged to the poorest of the poor, no effort was made since then to rebuild or even to tear down the gutted remains. No one lived here if they had any choice, and the Ashes had been abandoned to decay. Now limp weeds were sprouting from between the forgotten cobbles, while vines strangled the fallen roof timbers or slowly chewed on the ancient smoke-damaged bricks. Eventually nature would reclaim this zone entirely, and Malden, who had never set foot outside the city since he was born, found this distinctly uncomfortable—the concept that part of the city itself, which was his whole notion of permanence, could rot and die and be effaced.

Behind him something dashed across a forgotten street. He whirled to catch it with his light. Despite well-honed reflexes he was still not quick enough to see what it was, only that it disappeared through the gaping hole where a window had once looked out on the street. His hand went to the bodkin he kept at his hip but he dared not draw it. You never showed your weapon until you were ready to strike.

Malden stopped where he was and tried to prepare. If an attack was coming, it would come quickly, and being braced for it would make all the difference. His eyes showed him little—the scorched beams and the soot-stained street were all of a color by his little light. So he turned to his other senses in his search for signs. He heard nothing but the creaking of old, strained wood, the sifting of ash. He could smell the smoke of the fire, so many years gone.

Behind him he heard soft footsteps. The sound of bare feet slapping against charred timber. Only for a moment, before the sound stopped and he was left in silence again. Silence so profound—and so rare in the clamoring city. It sounded like a roaring in his ears.

He turned slowly on his heel, scanning the empty door frames on every side, the twisting little roads that curled between the buildings. He longed to get his back against something solid. There was a brick building up ahead, or at least the husk of one. Its roof was gone and one wall had come down. The other three still stood, however, and if he could get inside them, at least he would not have to worry about being attacked from behind. He hurried forward, his lantern held high—and then a noise from quite close by stopped him in his tracks.

One of the watchers had stepped out into the street behind him. He heard its feet splashing in a puddle. This time, however, it did not rush off as he turned to see it. This time it held its ground.

Even before he completed his turn his hand was on the hilt of his knife. He hesitated to draw, however, when he saw the creature he faced. It was a child, a girl no more than seven years old. She wore a stained shift of homespun and had rags wrapped around her feet in place of shoes. She also had a hammer clutched before her in both hands. Her eyes stayed on his face and they did not blink.

Malden spread his own hands wide, showing her they were empty. He took a step toward her, and when she did not flee, he took another. He reached down toward her—

—and suddenly the street was full of ragged children. They seemed to emerge from the mist as if generated spontaneously from the cold and the damp, like fungus from a rotting log. They were of both sexes, and varied in apparent age, but were dressed all alike in torn shirts and tunics too big for their skinny frames. And they all held makeshift weapons. One had a carpenter's saw. Another held a cobbler's awl. Bits of wood with protruding nails. A length of iron chain. One of them, a boy older than the rest, had a woodsman's hatchet that he held down against his thigh as if he knew how to use it.

A gang of orphans, Malden thought. A band of urchins joined together in their poverty to waylay any traveler foolish enough to come here by night. A ragged little army. There were dozens of them, and though he was certain he could best even the older boy in a fair fight, he could see in their eyes they held no concept of fairness or justice, such things as impossible and mythical in their experience as the continents the sages claimed lay beyond the sea. They would be on him in a heap, slashing and hitting and pounding and mauling him until he was dead. They would offer no quarter or mercy.

They were waiting for him to make the first move. To try to run, or fight. Not because they were afraid to attack, but because they wanted him to make some mistake, to calculate the odds incorrectly. They would take advantage of whatever weakness he showed and make short work of him.

Malden licked his lips and turned slowly this way and that, looking for an opening. There was no way out, it seemed. Unless . . . unless there was another reason for their silent waiting, for their constant unblinking stares.

"You want some password or sign," he said, "but all I have is this." He reached inside his cloak. They moved toward him, closing the circle they formed around him. They were ready to attack at the first sign of aggression. But he was not reaching for his bodkin. Instead his nimble fingers reached into his purse and drew out the scrap of parchment that had beckoned him to this dreadful place at this beastly time. He unfolded it carefully—the old paper cracked down the middle but he held the pieces together—and showed them the message he had received:

> This house is ONE OF OURS,
> and its owner under my protection.
> At next *Witching Hour* come ALONE
> to the Ashes hard by Westwall—or
> you're DEAD before next *Dawn*.

"I found it tacked to the windowsill of a house I was in the process of burgling. This is what you want to see, yes?"

Could they read it? he wondered? But no, of course they couldn't. It was foolish to think these children had ever been tutored or given even religious education. And yet they seemed entranced by the brief missive. Ah, he thought. They recognize the signature, a crude drawing of a heart transfixed by a key.

He did not know what that sign meant, not for certain, but its power on these children was intriguing. One by one they came close and touched the paper, as superstitious merchants will sometimes touch a statue of the Lady before sitting down to some tricky negotiation. When they had seen the sign for themselves and perhaps decided it was no forgery, they filed away, back into the darkness. All except the girl with the hammer, the first one he'd seen. She still held his eyes with her own. When they two were alone again, she finally broke his gaze and started walking toward the brick ruin he'd thought to shelter in. She led him right up to a doorway and then gestured inside with one hand. Then she made a perfect curtsy and ran off to join the others.

Clearly this was the place. Holding the scrap of parchment before him like a talisman, Malden stepped through the door.

# CHAPTER TWO

Inside the ruined building three old men dressed in rags sat on a long wooden box. Two of them had long white beards, while the other was bald and clean-shaven. Age had withered their muscles but their eyes glinted with cunning—no dotards, these. Malden had the sense there was a great deal more to them than what he saw.

He nodded to the men but did not speak yet. First he studied the interior of the building—its fallen and shattered roof beams, the piles of scorched plaster in the corners. The floor was covered in a thick layer of debris. There did not seem to be anywhere an assassin could hide, though between the lack of light and the tendrils of mist that coiled around his lantern, it was hard to be sure.

"What if I had brought the city watch with me?" Malden asked, because he felt there was no need for polite small talk. He had, after all, been threatened with death.

The bald man smiled wickedly. "We would not be here. You would have never found this place. And before morning your throat would be slit."

Malden nodded in understanding. "This isn't a bad setup. The children out there keep an eye on the place for you, right? Make sure nobody gets in uninvited. I'm guessing that even now if I tried something, you'd be ready for it."

One of the whitebeards raised a long, crooked finger and pointed into the air. With his eyes, Malden followed the direction of the finger until he could just see a spire looming out of the mist two blocks away. Most likely it had been the steeple of the local church, made of stone, so it survived the fire. While he was staring through the gloom, something whistled past his cheek and slammed into a charred wooden plank behind him. He glanced sideways and saw the shaft of an arrow there, still quivering. The arrow was as long as his arm and it had struck the wood so hard the iron point was completely embedded.

For a while after that Malden did not breathe. His lungs clamped shut and every muscle in his body went rigid. He waited patiently for the next arrow, the one that would find his guts or his throat. But it did not come.

He understood rationally what had happened, and why. The arrow was a message—a reminder that here not all was what it seemed, and that he was still in mortal danger. It was not a reminder he'd truly needed.

"I'll pay you the courtesy of noticing you didn't flinch," the whitebeard said. "That's good, lad. Very good."

Malden gave him a brief bow, once he could move and breathe again. "I think I understand where I am. I'm not sure who you three are, but I assume you aren't the ones I'm supposed to meet. Yet you can show me the way to my meeting. You're the guardians of the doorway, yes? And more than that, certainly."

The bald one touched his chest. "I am called 'Levenfingers. These," he said, gesturing at the whitebeards, "are Loophole and Lockjaw."

"Well met," Malden said. "Wait. Wait . . . I've heard of him, of Loophole. It was a little before my time, but they still tell the story up in the Stink. If you're the same man, then you got that name when you robbed the garrison house up by the palace. Is it true that you climbed in through an arrow slit, fifty feet up the curtain wall?"

Loophole wheezed as he laughed. "Another time, I'll tell ye all, if you wish. Assuming you survive tonight."

Malden nodded. "I'd be honored. And you— 'Levenfingers—how'd you come by that name, if I might ask?"

"I was the king of the pickpockets in my day," the bald man said with obvious pride. "They used to say no man with ten fingers could be so dab at it, so I must have eleven." He held up his hands, which were gnarled and spotted with age but otherwise perfectly normal. "Just a nickname."

Malden smiled at the third man, expecting an explanation of his name. It was Loophole who gave it, however.

"Lockjaw? He holds his secrets well, that's why. Never gives anything away for free."

"Does he ever speak?"

"Not to the likes of you," Lockjaw grumbled, in a hollow voice like a floorboard creaking in an empty house. "Not yet."

"I see," Malden said. He was impressed despite himself. Thievery was a dangerous occupation. If you didn't die in some trap or under the spear of some overzealous guard, the law was always waiting. In the Free City of Ness, lifting even a copper penny from some fat merchant's purse was punishable by hanging. These three men, daring rogues in their day, notorious for grand exploits, had survived long enough to grow old without being caught. That must mean they were very, very good in their prime. Malden wondered what they could teach him. Of course, there was more pressing business at hand. "I was called here to meet with someone."

"Are you ready for your audience with our boss, then?"

"I suppose I'd better be," Malden said.

Lockjaw grunted out a noise that might have been a laugh. The three of them stood up in unison, then moved aside to let Malden have a better look at the box they'd been sitting on. It was a coffin made of plain wood, tapering in width at both ends. 'Levenfingers lifted its lid and Loophole gestured for Malden to get inside.

Malden had never thought himself squeamish or, worse, superstitious. Yet a cold dread gripped his vitals at the thought of lying down in the coffin. "Only a fool or a dead man would get in there happily," he said.

"If you don't get in," Loophole told him, "you're both, anyway."

Malden snuffed out the flame of his lantern, then placed it carefully on the ground. There would be no room for it. Then he clambered inside what, he assured himself, was truly no more fearful than a packing crate. The lid was closed and then nailed shut. He tried not to breathe too hard. He'd come this far, he told himself. He must see what would happen next.

# CHAPTER THREE

The darkness inside the box was a solid thing, as if the air had turned to obsidian all around him. All sounds that came through the wood were muffled and thick. Malden hoped very much he would be let out soon. The same moment the lid was hammered shut, he found that he had trouble breathing inside—perhaps it was just his mind playing tricks on him, but it seemed there was not enough air in the coffin to support his life. He began to panic, to lose control of his faculties. It took a true effort of will to calm down and resign himself to what was happening.

One fact alone sustained him, one thing he was relatively sure of. The master of this place had already had many chances to kill him. Which meant that, for whatever reason and however temporarily, he was expected to survive this.

That kept most of the panic at bay. The fear tarried longer.

The box was lifted—the three oldsters must be stronger than they looked, or they had help—and carried a short distance before it was lowered again, foot end first, into some variety of chute. For a moment Malden had the sense of rapid downward movement, and then the box struck a solid surface very hard, hard enough to push all the air out of his lungs. Not knowing what to expect, he forced himself not to inhale again.

His body protested and he started to gasp for air but he managed to hold his breath a moment longer. The only way to determine where he'd ended up was by listening to his surroundings. Though the sounds that came to him were distorted by the wooden box, he was able to make out a few things. He could hear voices, people laughing among themselves. A woman's giggle. So he was not alone.

Then there was a knock on the lid of the coffin, and he

sucked in air at last. "Anyone home?" someone asked, the voice thick with mockery.

"Let yourself in and have a look around the place," Malden replied.

The owner of the voice laughed wickedly but said no more.

It did not take Malden long to realize no one would come to release him from the coffin—that he would have to find his own way out. He was able to draw his bodkin easily enough, but then found it difficult to maneuver it within the coffin without stabbing himself. It was not much of a weapon, a triangular piece of iron that tapered to a sharp point. By law it was the largest knife he was allowed to own, the blade no longer than his hand from the ball of his thumb to the tip of his middle finger. It had no edge, just the point, and was only good for stabbing in a fight. But then, he wasn't a violent man by nature, and the bodkin was more than it appeared to be. He'd found many uses for it in the past, and killing had so far not been one of them. It served him well as he jabbed the point into the thin seam between box and lid. Without leverage it took some time to pry the lid upward, but when he did he was rewarded by a thin stream of light and—much more blessedly—a new breath of air.

The nails in the lid shrieked as he worked to free himself. Eventually he had the lid open enough to push it outward with his hands. Returning the knife to its sheath, he sat up and looked around.

The room was broad but low, its ceiling propped up on stout beams so it looked not unlike a mine shaft. The walls were bare, close-packed earth that glistened with condensation. The place was well lit by more than a dozen candles, some backed by reflectors of copper that added a rosy tint to the light. On a divan on one side of the room sat a man in a leather jerkin and particolored hose. He had the thick shoulders of a warrior, not a thief. Upon his lap was a red-headed girl with her bodice unlaced. She laughed prettily as he tickled her. Neither of them spared him a glance. In another corner of the room a group of men in colorless cloaks were throwing dice against a wall and cheering or groaning the result.

The final occupant of the room was a dwarf who might have been the epitome of his people. Dwarves were rare in Ness—rare anywhere in Skrae—but enough of them had come down from their northern kingdom, looking for work, that Malden was jaded to their presence. They were master craftsmen, brilliant artificers who could make better tools and finer wares than any human artisan. Dwarves alone knew the secret of making proper steel and thus were highly prized and given special rights wherever they turned up in human lands. Like all his folk, this one was skinny, perhaps four feet tall, and his flesh was as white as the belly of a fish. He had a wild mop of filthy black hair and a tangled beard. He was dressed only in leather breeches and was sewing pieces of metal into a silk glove. He glanced up briefly at Malden, then shook his head and went back to work.

Malden looked away and turned in a slow circle to make sure he'd seen all of the room. He did not want to miss some hidden threat, not now. Directly behind him, he saw the chute through which he had descended, a construction of thin hammered tin. It had been smeared with brown grease that glimmered dully in the candlelight. He could probably get back up that way, given enough time—and assuming no one tried to stop him.

The man on the couch had a sword at his hip, and Malden did not doubt that the others were armed as well. Someone, he figured, would try to stop him. After all, he'd been summoned here for a reason. If he tried to run away now he would be thwarting that purpose. Based on what the oldsters had said aboveground, he would not be allowed to escape in one piece.

A little stiffly, Malden climbed out of the coffin and regained his feet. He dusted himself off and strode over to the divan, intent on learning what he was expected to do next. The bravo on the divan looked up expectantly. "You must have made an impression on the three masters above," he said. Malden instantly recognized his voice as the one that had spoken to him when he was inside the coffin.

"Oh?" he asked.

"They let you keep your clothes and that knife at your belt. Sometimes the ones they send down here come naked."

"I'm quite personable when you get to know me," Malden said. "Now, if you'd be so kind as to direct me to your master? I'm told he wishes to speak with me."

The bravo's eyebrows drew together. "And what makes you think the master of this place is not here, right before you?"

Malden bowed in apology. "Organization like this, in such a secret place, leads me to believe only one man in the Free City might be master here. A man I know only by reputation, but that reputation leads me to believe certain things about him. I doubt he's one of these gamblers, who kneel and dice for pennies. I am relatively certain he is no dwarf, and she—well . . ." Malden searched his memory. "Her name is Rhona. She's one of Madam Herwig's girls, from the House of Sighs up on the Royal Ditch." The girl looked up at him with wide eyes, but he merely smiled at her in return. There were very few harlots in the city who Malden could not recognize on sight. "As for yourself, well, I do not think you are the chief here. While you cut a striking figure, sir, I will not believe you if you say your name is Cutbill."

At the sound of the name everyone in the room glanced over their shoulder. Even the bravo and his playmate frowned. Yet in a moment all concerns were forgotten again and the bravo laughed boisterously, which got the girl giggling as well. "You're smarter than we credited," he said.

"Yet not so arrogant in that wisdom, as to have avoided this summons in the first place," Malden said.

The bravo picked the girl up in his strong arms and put her back down on the divan as he rose and came bounding over to take Malden's hand. "I'm Bellard. I serve the one you named on those occasions when subtlety has failed."

"Well met. I'm called Malden."

Bellard laughed again. "Oh, I know your name all right. And you're correct, the master is waiting on your pleasure. He's just through there." Bellard made a sweeping gesture toward the far wall, where a stained curtain hung.

"So I just go through there, do I?" Malden asked.

The bravo smiled. "If you can, you're well on your way."

Malden bowed and headed to the curtain. Twitching it back, he found a wide door set into the wall, made of stout oak with massive iron hinges. A thick iron ring would open it. There was just one problem. A thick bar of iron passed through the ring and was anchored in either wall. It was held shut by the largest padlock he had ever seen.

# CHAPTER FOUR

Well. He knew what to do with locks.

Malden drew his bodkin and held it by the blade. The grip was formed of a very long piece of stout cord wrapped countless times around the hilt, ostensibly to create a more comfortable handle for the weapon. In fact the cord served far less obvious purposes. He picked at it until one end came free, then spooled it out with a practiced motion. Woven into the cord were his tools: picks, rakes, hooks, and a pair of tension wrenches. Two different skeleton keys for different size locks. These tiny pieces of steel were the most valuable things Malden owned, worth far more than their weight in gold. Worth his life if he were ever caught with them, for they had no legal use—their only function was to allow locks to be opened by someone who lacked the proper key.

He placed the tools carefully in order on the floor beside him, then knelt before the door to examine the lock more closely.

"Right there's a famous example of the locksmith's art," Bellard said from behind his shoulder. "Originally it secured the door of the seraglio of the northern chieftain Krölt. Imagine the exotic and untamed beauties it locked away, eh?"

Malden wondered if they had been half as comely as the lock itself. It was a thing of exquisite craftsmanship, no doubt—probably built by a dwarf, considering its complexity. The recurved case was wider than his two hands put together. It was made of bronze worked with copper, which sadly had grown furry with verdigris over the ages. The front was lined with rivets of brass sculpted to resemble handsome female faces. So profoundly intricate was the workmanship that each face had recognizably different features, and each was more lovely than the next.

The lock's shackle, also of brass, was cast in the shape of a maiden's braided hair. The massive keyhole was covered in a sliding plate to keep out dust and moisture that might foul the mechanism inside. When Malden drew the plate back he saw that the keyhole was big enough that he could reach inside with two fingers—if he dared. The key that opened this lock must have been the size of a shortsword.

The room's fitful light did not permit him to see much inside the lock mechanism, but picking a lock was a skill of the fingers, not of the eyes. He selected a saw rake from his tools and the larger of his tension wrenches. He hoped it would be large enough. He willed his hands not to tremble as he inserted the rake most carefully inside the keyhole and began feeling around for wards or tumblers.

When his rake made contact, the entire lock seemed to thrum as if a spring had been released inside. He just had time to see the rivets move before he jumped backward and caught himself with his hands on the floor. His picks went flying and clanged musically on the stones, but for the moment he forgot all about them.

"You're quicker than we credited, as well," Bellard said. He did not laugh this time.

The rivets shaped like the faces of women were not rivets at all, Malden saw. They were more similar to the dust plate covering the keyhole in that they could slide away from concealed holes in the face of the lock. From each of these holes now emerged a needle as big as a carpentry nail. Had he not jumped back in time, those nails would have scratched his hands in a dozen places. He looked closer and saw that the tip of each nail was coated in a straw-colored fluid.

"Poison, of course," he said.

"Old Krölt was a jealous cove, and he hated thieves. Of course, his poison dried up and flaked away centuries ago. The stuff we replaced it with isn't lethal, since the lock is meant for training new recruits. Which is not to say it's pleasant," Bellard said with a shrug. "It would leave you in a fever for three days, during which time you would suffer such agonies you would most devoutly wish we'd used hemlock instead."

Malden rubbed at the sweat rolling down into his eyes. Though he made his living at an occupation beset with certain risks, tonight he was being threatened with death and pain far too often for his liking.

And of course it wasn't over yet. If he failed to get through this door and keep his appointment with Cutbill, his life remained forfeit. He needed to pick the lock—but in such a way that he touched none of the needles. He would have to take great care.

He recovered his picks and then gripped them tightly by their free ends, to give them as much reach as possible. He had hoped it might be enough to let him pick the lock without touching any of the needles. Yet no matter how he tried, no matter how he strained or bent his hands into uncomfortable angles, the tools still didn't make it all the way inside the lock.

He sank back in frustration and anger and dropped his tools on the stone floor. What to do? What to do? He was not ready to give up. Sadu alone knew why he was being forced to this ordeal, to this series of gruesome tests, but there had to be some reason—he did not believe the master of this place would be such a sadist as to put him through so much just for grim amusement.

So there had to be some solution to the problem. Some simple, elegant answer that would lend itself to a man who knew how to think. Malden had always counted himself quite clever. He wasn't very strong—a bad diet had seen to that—nor was he accounted particularly handsome. He had the kind of face that no one remarked on, or remembered for very long. What he was, was smart. Quick, like Bellard had said. His best weapon now was his brain, his ability to think this through.

There would be a solution. It must be in this room, since he was not permitted to leave. And it had to be something he could discover if he would just open his eyes. He looked around, trying to see what he had missed before.

He glanced over at the dwarf. He hadn't paid the little creature much attention before. He had barely been aware of what the dwarf was doing. Now he gave the dwarf's piece-work his full attention.

The dwarf was sewing pieces of metal onto a pair of silk gloves.

Malden went over to him with his friendliest expression on his face. "My, those are rather fetching."

The dwarf sneered. "They might fetch a fair price," he said.

Malden could feel all eyes in the room turned on his back. He ignored them. "May I?" he asked. He picked up one of the gloves and studied it. The dwarf had sewn several dozen small tin plates onto the back and palm of the glove. They wouldn't work very well as armor in a fight, but they would be perfect for his current purpose. So perfect, in fact, that he could see no reason for their construction other than to help pick the poisoned lock. Malden opened his purse and took out a handful of farthings—copper coins cut into four pieces each. "I'm not sure how much you—"

"It'll do," the dwarf said, snatching them from his grasp. He counted them quickly, rolling the coins in his hand. "Miserly thieves. Half what they're fucking worth." He held out the gloves and Malden took them. "Now, that's just for hire," the dwarf informed him. "I take them back when I feel you've had 'em long enough."

"But of course," Malden said. He pulled on the gloves and hurried back to the lock. He had no doubt now they'd been made expressly for this purpose. The silk was quite delicate and would tear after even a little use, but it was also thin enough that it did not deaden the sensitivity in his fingers that was necessary for lock picking. The tin plates wouldn't protect the hands from any but the feeblest blows—but when he attempted to pick the lock again, he found they easily blocked the needles from scratching his skin.

Even with the gloves, though, opening the padlock wasn't easy. The lock was enormous and had dozens of pin tumblers inside. He had to tease each one into the proper position with his hooks, then hold it there with a rake while he applied just the right amount of torque with his wrench. It required perfectly still hands, but if he did not lapse in concentration even for a moment . . . yes . . . *there*. When the lock clicked again, he nearly jumped away a second time—but there was something different about this click. It was weightier, more solid, more final.

The needles retracted into their holes with a series of soft *thunks*. The shackle came loose and the lock hung swinging from the iron bar.

It was open.

Malden wound his picks back up into the hilt of his bodkin, then sheathed the weapon with a sigh. He removed the lock from the bar, though it was so heavy he could barely lift it, and set it down carefully on the floor. He stripped off the gloves, turning them inside out in case any of the poison had transferred to the tin plates. He tossed the gloves to the dwarf, who caught them easily. Then, going back to the door, he slid the bar out of the ring and pushed gently. The door opened with a creak.

He looked back at Bellard.

"He doesn't like to be kept waiting," the bravo said.

Malden nodded and stepped inside.

# CHAPTER FIVE

Beyond the locked door was a snug little office, heated by a charcoal brazier and kept insulated by heavy tapestries hanging on the walls. A massive desk faced the door, carved out of some expensive wood that had turned black over time, a very large and detailed map of the city posted behind the desk, a basin for washing one's face and hands, and a sideboard with a flagon of wine and several goblets. No one sat behind the desk, however. Instead, the room's sole occupant perched on a stool in the corner, scratching entries in a broad ledger held on a lectern before him.

He was a very thin man with long, mournful features and eyebrows that arched high onto his bare forehead. His black hair had receded well back onto his scalp and was shot through with two streaks of gray. His eyes were at once very dark and very bright—narrow, merciless eyes that did not look up at Malden as he came in.

Malden closed the door behind him and waited patiently for the man to finish his task. There were chairs, but he did not sit down, unsure what to expect inside this cozy room.

The man's quill pen scratched out a few more figures and then stopped.

"Your mother was a whore," he said, quite without inflection.

Malden's chest clenched but he understood what was happening. The man—who was certainly Cutbill, whether he looked like a mastermind of thievery or not—was testing him. Attempting to see if he would come at him in a fury or perhaps merely whine in offense.

There was no denying the truth of the statement, however. "She was. A good woman in a bad situation, who did her best to raise me with care and patience. She died of the sailor's pox when I was not yet a man."

Cutbill nodded, as if merely accepting this new bit of

information as something to enter into his account book. "Your father?"

"Half the men in this city might claim the title, yet none ever have."

"Sit down. You may be here awhile," Cutbill told him. Malden chose a chair near the door. "You lived in a bawdy house for most of your youth, performing small tasks and running errands for the madam. In that time you probably saw your fair share of illicit activity. I daresay you might have engaged in some yourself—rolling drunks, cheating paying clients—or at least tricking them into overpaying— procuring small quantities of various illegal drugs for the harlots. It wasn't until after your mother died that you began extending your activities to the larger sphere of the city, though."

"There wasn't much choice in the matter," Malden confirmed. "There's not much room in a brothel for a young man—not when there are so many unwanted boys around to clean the place and run errands. I was given a few coins but told to go forth and find my own fortune. I decided I'd see how honest folk lived. It turned out the city had little use for a whoreson with no estate. This place isn't kind to those who were born on the wrong side of the sheet."

If he'd been hoping to evince sympathy from Cutbill, he was disappointed. The clerkish man didn't even look up.

"I looked for work in various trades. I was too old already—no guild would take me on for prenticing at the advanced age of fifteen. I tried to find occupation as a bricklayer, as a carpenter, even as a stevedore down at the wharves. Each place turned me away—or demanded bribes. The gang bosses who organized such labor all wanted a cut of the pennies I would earn."

"And you were unwilling to pay such fees."

"How could I, and survive? It takes money to live in this world, money to eat, money for rent, money for taxes and tithes. The pay that work offered would have put me in debt the first week, and it would only have gotten worse. I'd seen this scheme before, and the ruin it caused."

"Oh?"

"It is exactly how the pimps keep their stables of women in line."

"Indeed," Cutbill said.

Malden fidgeted with the sleeve of his shirt. "There were no opportunities for one like me. None at all. Yet I needed money to survive. I could go out on the streets and become a beggar. Or I could turn to a life of crime. You know which I chose."

"And found you had a flair for it."

"You wish to know my life story entire?"

"I already know it. I'm simply confirming it. For the last five years you've been making a paltry living pilfering coppers from the unwary. Occasionally you've run a trick of confidence, but your real skills seem to lie in your fingers, not your voice. It was only recently you turned to burglary. For only a few months now you've been breaking into houses. Care to tell my why you changed your game?"

"People in this city know better than to carry much money when they go out. They know no purse is ever safe. The real money they leave behind, at home. It only seemed logical to follow the money, not the people."

The master of thieves made a small notation in his ledger. "You know who I am," Cutbill said. "You spoke my name outside."

Malden waved one hand in the air. "All of the Free City knows the exploits of great Cutbill, master of thieves, procurer extraordinaire, purveyor of unlawful euphoria, betrayer of confidences, extortionist to the high and mighty—"

"Spare me."

Malden sat back in his chair, a little dumbfounded. He had not expected the man to speak so plainly—or so abruptly. It was all he could do to keep up.

"You know that I run this city, or, at least, the clandestine commerce within it. That I have organized and consolidated the criminal class. That I have taken in hand the scattered gangs and crews that exist in any city of this size and made of them something more cohesive, something efficient." Cutbill put down his pen and sat up on his stool, lifting his chin in the air. "You know my reputation. I recounted your history to show I know yours as well."

Malden held his peace.

"I do not appreciate arse-licking, nor false modesty, nor unplain speaking. So I will say this simply: I have kept a close and admiring eye on you, ever since I became aware of your activities. I keep accounts of all who commit crimes in the Free City of Ness, whether they work for me or not. But you, Malden—you I've watched quite closely. You have the skills of a born thief: the lightness of step, the deftness of hands, the ability to keep a secret. And you learned these things all on your own. No mentor guided you, no school drilled you up in the ways of our profession. I find this quite impressive. Or I did so, until tonight.

"Tonight, you went in secret into the house of Guthrun Whiteclay, a master of the worthy guild of potters, and took from him a quantity of silver plate, some fancy cutlery, and a sack of silver coin he had hidden under his bed. Yet you failed to prepare for this jaunt properly."

Malden frowned. No one, he thought, could have been more prepared than he. "I cased the house for three days. Watched Whiteclay and his wife leave for a fete up at the moothall, saw him lock his front door but forget to latch a window at the side. I wrapped my shoes in cloth to deaden my footsteps. I studied the patrol patterns of the city watch and knew exactly how long I had to get in and out unseen. I even waited for a night when the fog would conceal the moon, and so darken the alley I used for my entrance and escape."

"Yes," Cutbill said, "but you forgot to ask anyone if Guthrun Whiteclay had *protection*. Do you even understand this concept? I have an arrangement with him. Nothing formal, nothing written down, of course. Yet I receive from him each month a certain sum of money. In exchange for this small payment, he is guaranteed against burglary, robbery, blackmail, and murder at the hands of his business rivals. You may think it easier to simply take all that is his and be done with it—but I assure you, over the years I have made many times as much money from this arrangement than you might ever see from reselling his household goods. Now you have cost me money, because I must send out my agents to recover the things you stole and have them returned to Whiteclay's house before he notices they are missing. Do you understand the magnitude of that task? Do you understand what it will cost me if I fail in it?"

"I see," Malden said, shifting in his chair. "So this is a shakedown. You wish me to return these things and to give you the silver I worked so hard to acquire. Well, I don't like it—but what choice have I? You can have your pet swordsman out there skewer me like a pig on a spit if I refuse."

Malden had the impression that Cutbill had never smiled in his life. One corner of his mouth did pucker, though, as if he were savoring some tasty morsel of knowledge that he had not chosen to share.

"Yes, yes, all of that. But more as well. I want you to join my operation."

Malden frowned. "I'm sorry?"

"I wish to offer you a job."

# CHAPTER SIX

Neither of them spoke for a while, as the meaning of Cutbill's words sank in. Malden had expected something quite different when he answered Cutbill's summons. Mostly, he'd expected to have to pay back the money he'd taken, and then receive a savage beating (if not worse) by way of a receipt.

"I've always worked alone," he said finally.

"And I cannot allow you to continue doing so. You are too good at this to be independent," Cutbill informed him.

"I don't like competition. I'd much rather have you in my stable. There are compensations you'll gain from accepting, of course. You know I have a considerable fraction of the city watch on my payroll, and more than one noble in the palace as well. Right now if you are caught stealing so much as one penny from a church collection box, you'll be hanged for your trouble. Under my wing, you will have some measure of safety from that fate. Furthermore you'll be allowed the services of my dwarf, Slag, who can provide tools of a fineness and quality you'll never gain from any human blacksmith. You can continue to pick your own jobs, though of course you must abstain from burgling any of my clients. And I have something else to offer you."

"Oh?"

"Your heart's desire. The thing you truly covet. I can offer you freedom."

"Every man in Ness is free. There are no slaves here," Malden pointed out. It was what made Ness a Free City. Outside of its walls most men and women were villeins, peasants, cotters—little more than slaves. They owned neither land nor livestock nor the clothes on their backs. They could not be married without the approval of their lord, nor could they move away from their farms unless they were sold to some other liege—and even then they could take nothing with them but their children.

But in Ness a man was his own. He could work to make a life for himself and his family, or he could laze about and eventually starve in the street. But it was his own choice. The city's charter guaranteed the right of a man to do either.

"I didn't say you were a slave. Rather, you're a prisoner. You have no family, no birthright. You dress like a common laborer and you have the accent of a peasant. If you tried to leave this city—if you stepped outside its walls—you would be scooped up by the first reeve who saw you. He would sell you to some petty baron and you'd spend the rest of your days tilling some field. Ness is a very large prison, Malden, and the door of your cell is wide open. But only because the powers that be know you'll never leave."

"If I had enough money—"

"But you don't, and living the life you do, you never will. If you keep operating independently you'll end up swinging from a rope or, if you're lucky, dying in poverty in some hovel. Come work for me and we'll change that. It will take time. You will work harder for me than you ever would for some shopkeeper. But your money will be your own. And with enough money, even the son of a whore can be a man of importance. He can go where he likes and live as he chooses. Freedom, Malden, is what I offer. True freedom."

Malden found his heart was racing. Cutbill did know him, heart and soul. How many times had he thought the same thing? How many times had he cursed fate for making him his mother's son?

"I will admit," he said, choosing his words carefully, "that is a strong incentive. May I ask what you get out of this arrangement?"

"I'll take a cut of everything you earn for my trouble. Let us say, nine parts of every ten."

Malden gaped in surprise. That deal was shameless robbery—worse than any demand a pander would make. But of course he must consider its author. There was in Cutbill's face a certain hardness of line that told Malden the numbers were non-negotiable. "And if I refuse your offer?"

"Then you are free to go, to walk out the door you came in by. Of course, in my disappointment I might forget to give Bellard the all-clear sign, and he may think you are trying to flee against my wishes."

"Of course," Malden said. "Well, in that case, I suppose my answer must be—"

Cutbill interrupted him. "You're probably thinking, right now, that you can rob me in some way. That you can short the money you turn over to me. Find some way to make my terms more agreeable. You've proved you're clever. Perhaps you think yourself more clever than me."

"Perish the thought," Malden said.

"I have no reason to believe you will play fair with me. So for a while, at least, you'll be under probation. You may eventually earn full position in my organization. I fancy our business here to be like unto one of the trade guilds.

Each new member must serve a period of apprenticeship, at the end of which he demonstrates his ability to perform the duties and the functions of the craft. For instance, one of Guthrun Whiteclay's apprentices might make an especially elegant and large drinking vessel—which would be called his masterpiece, because he made it to impress his master."

"I'm too old for prenticing," Malden insisted.

"Agreed. And I think we can consider your burglary tonight your masterpiece, because it certainly did impress me. So we'll start you off as if you were a journeyman, the next rank and title in our hypothetical guild. But there is another bar to entry at that level. One must pay one's guild dues, to be considered a member in good standing. So I'll expect a payment from you immediately, before you may enjoy any privilege of your new employment."

Malden clamped his mouth shut. What he wanted to say was this:

*Why, you loathsome double-dealing toothfish of a blasted cheat, is there no limit to the depths of your ignobility, your mendacity? You've held me here at threat of death, and bled me dry, and now you wish a gratuity for the service?*

What he actually said was this:

"How much?"

Cutbill flipped through the pages of his ledger. He consulted an entry near the beginning of the book, then looked up and for the first time directly into Malden's eyes. "I think one hundred and one golden royals should be enough. Or do you think that too little, after all the trouble you caused me tonight?"

"I . . ." Malden was briefly unable to speak. "I imagine . . . I think that I will laud your generosity to all I meet."

"Good. You can go now." Cutbill picked up his pen again and returned to writing in his book.

Malden rose from his chair. His legs shook. His hands had been steady when he picked the poisoned lock. He had not flinched when an arrow passed through his shadow. Yet now his body was rebellious to his commands. He turned toward the door. "You know, you never actually gave me the chance to say yes or no."

"I never do. In any business negotiation, if the outcome is not certain before you even begin, then you are fated to get the lesser hand. Remember that, Malden. Oh, and don't go through there."

Malden looked at the door. It was the only exit from the room that he could see. "But of course. You haven't given the all-clear signal."

"There is no such signal. If you walk through that door, Bellard will run you through, no matter what I do or say. I think that might sadden him—he seems to have a liking for you. So go through there instead." Cutbill flicked his pen toward one of the tapestries behind him. When Malden lifted it he found a very long corridor ending in a flight of stairs leading upward. Not looking back, he climbed until he found a trapdoor that opened on an alley in the Stink— the district of poor people's homes that lay just inside the city wall. The neighborhood of his own home, though he still had a long walk ahead of him.

He had only one thought as he headed there.

*One hundred and one royals.*

It was a fortune. It was a bondage—until he paid it, he would be Cutbill's slave, working for nothing but the payment of that blood price. It might take him a year to earn as much, even if he redoubled his efforts, even if he picked only the richest plums—plums, he was certain, that were already on Cutbill's list of protection.

One hundred and one! Royals! Coins so valuable the average journeyman in an honest guild might earn but one for a year's work. All of the plate and cutlery he'd taken from Guthrun Whiteclay, if sold to a very forgiving and generous fence, would earn him but two royals, perhaps three.

One hundred and one!

He reached his lodgings barely cognizant of the path he'd taken. He had a room above a waxchandler's shop, not much at all, but it was clean. He had a mattress full of straw which he went to as soon as he arrived. The plates and silver he had stashed underneath, below a loose floorboard. He was not surprised to find them gone. One of Cutbill's thieves must have broken in here to get them back. In their place was a bottle of cheap wine. A strip of paper was wound around its neck. When he unfolded the note he read:

*Welcome to the guild.*

It was signed, of course, with a crude drawing of a heart transfixed by a key.

# CHAPTER SEVEN

He drank the whole bottle and got rather drunk and lay in his bed with the world whirling around him, alternately cursing and blessing Cutbill's name. The guildmaster of thieves had held him to ransom—a ransom so large as to be absurd. Only a fool would take the offer, only an idiot would think he could make a hundred and one gold royals before he was stooped and old.

And yet . . . and yet . . . he kept coming back to what Cutbill had said. Freedom. Not a slave, but a prisoner. But he could break those shackles. Free himself, if he had the cash. Money meant everything in Ness, just as it meant everything the world around. A man with money was his own— he could buy fine clothes, buy a house of his own, buy, in short, respect. The good honest folk spat at him in the street now. With enough money they would tip their hats when he walked past. No, when he rode past, in a fine carriage, with a liveried servant driving the horses . . .

It was unimaginable. Impossible. And yes, alone, he could never do it. He could never be more than a petty thief, a second story man, fated to an ignominious death. But with Cutbill, with the power of the guild of thieves behind him . . .

His whole life could change. It could *mean* something, just like his mother had always wanted. Just like she'd dreamed of. Despaired of, on her deathbed.

All that was standing between him and that future was a stack of gold coins.

What could he do, then, but go back to work? But what kind of work, ah, there was the problem. His brain was seized by a fever of schemes and plans, but none of them paid off. At first he thought to burgle his way out of the debt, but that turned out to be . . . problematic. All the wealthiest citizens of the Free City were already on Cutbill's protection list. His options were therefore limited, and a couple days later he was back at the old routine, in the city's central Market Square. Right in the shadow of Castle Hill and its twenty foot wall.

No better place for the game he had planned.

"Forgive me, good sir, and the blessings of the Lady upon you!"

It was the oldest trick in the book, but that was how they got so old: they still worked. Malden had his right arm in a sling tied around his neck. Three mangled fingers and a fourth badly infected stump protruded beyond the edge of the cloth—a grotesque wound that would make most people look away rather than risk a closer inspection. With Market Square as crowded as it was that day, it was inevitable that the splinted arm would bump the occasional passerby. So far he had accidentally jostled a lady of quality with her hair in cauls at the sides of her head, the liveried servant of a noble house in black and green, and a fat merchant in a plumed hat wider than his shoulders.

"Pardon me, miss, it's this blasted arm," he would say, or "May the Lady save your grace, sir, I am sorry." They would turn to sneer and perhaps kick him away, but once they saw the arm they tended to murmur some words of empty forgiveness and then hurry off before he could start begging.

By then, of course, he already had their purses open. The broken arm was a fakery. Slag the dwarf had carved it from wood and then painted it to perfectly match Malden's skin tone. It was hollow inside and open at the bottom, so his real arm fit easily into the gap. In his actual right hand he had a tiny pair of sharpened shears and a square of damp felt. It was the work of a moment as his mark was turning away from him to cut open their fat purses and let the coins inside fall soundlessly into the cloth. Mostly he was securing pennies, groats, and farthings, nothing too worthy. At this rate, he calculated, he would pay off his debt to Cutbill in about twenty years.

Still, on a day like this, volume of business could make up for poor pickings. The Market Square was thronged from side to side, even though this was not a market day. The anonymity a big crowd offered made it easy, too.

Malden stopped for a while to take in the sights. It was impatient greed that carried more thieves up the gallows than any watchman or thief-taker. It was not wise to take too many purses even from so thick a crowd, lest someone raise the hue and cry and every man check their purse at once. Then it would be up to his feet and not his fingers to keep him alive. Anyway, even a working man like himself could enjoy the spectacle laid out for this day's entertainment.

Where the shadow of Castle Hill best cut the sunlight and the heat of the day, a wooden viewing platform had been set up, and there the mightiest men of the city sat with goblets of mulled wine, waiting on their entertainment. Men whom even Malden recognized. Ommen Tarness, the Burgrave himself, had come. The ultimate ruler of the city sat on a carved wooden throne, his simple coronet of gold polished and gleaming at his temples. He was dressed in cloth-of-gold and brocade, with an ornamental brass key hung around his neck. Despite the gaudy clothes, his face was that of a man used to command, the stern-eyed countenance of a ruler. There was little of mercy in that face, and much of resolution.

On his right hand, under a canopy, sat Murdlin, envoy of the Dwarf Kingdom. It was quite rare to see a dwarf by daylight—they were subterranean creatures by wont, and hated the sun. Murdlin had a wide-brimmed hat pulled low over his eyes but still he seemed agitated. His legs kicked at the air where they dangled from the seat of a human-sized chair. The dwarf's hair had been slicked down with bear fat for the occasion, and his beard had been braided in a hundred plaits, each set with a carnelian bead.

On the left of the Burgrave was the sorcerer Hazoth, his face veiled in black crape as befit one of his dread profession. There were stories about that man to chill the blood. It was said Hazoth had lived in Ness since ages past—no one knew exactly how old he was, but he had lived far past his allotted span. In the olden times supposedly he had summoned demons to save Skrae from the elves and then the dwarves in the endless wars that marked the kingdom's early years; that he had made the earth quake and the sky rain fire. Of course he didn't do things like that anymore. Summoning even a minor imp was enough to get a man burnt at the stake. Still, people drew back and turned their eyes aside wherever Hazoth went, and whispered stories that no one dared to disbelieve.

Behind these three stood the bailiff Anselm Vry and his reeves, the Burgrave's retainers, minor nobles, knights, ladies, and countless servants, enough so the wooden platform groaned with all their weight.

Below them, standing on the cobbles of the square, were the grand people of the Golden Slope, the district of the city inhabited by merchants, burgesses, guildmasters, and those of independent means. A colorful lot in their fitted hoods and gathered tunics, their checked and particolored hose, their snoods and wimples and wide baldrics. None so gaudy, of course, as their liveried servants, who wore hues bright enough that anyone could tell them apart at a distance. There were a scattering of drab cloaks and doublets as well, of course, for any such gathering could not help but attract beggars and the hawkers of sweetmeats and wine. Then there were the bravos and the hired guards, who favored black silk or leather dress, to show how serious was their profession. Yet even these made some concession to the gaiety of the crowd by draping garlands of flowers around the brims of their kettle helmets or tying the favors of their ladies to the hafts and hilts of their weapons. Today, by decree, everyone was to show some sign of pomp and excitement.

After all, it wasn't every day you got to see a public hanging.

# CHAPTER EIGHT

The accused was brought into the square on a hurdle, hoodwinked and bound. He wore nothing but a pair of breeches and a white nightshirt. His hair was blond and cut very short, and his chin had been shaved for his execution. Even with a filthy cloth tied around his eyes, Malden could see he had the face of a poet but the body of a warrior. Under the loose shirt the man's body rippled with muscle. More than one woman in the crowd turned to whisper excitedly to her neighbor as the cart trundled past on its voyage to the gibbet.

Malden hated the man instantly, just on principle.

Leaping down easily from the gallows, the masked hangman grabbed up the prisoner's bound hands behind his back and heaved. The bound man's back arched in pain and he grimaced (showing off perfect white teeth), but he refused to make a noise of agony. Struggling to stand up properly, he kicked out with his legs and found the first step of the gallows. Without hesitation he climbed to the top.

The crowd pressed close, murmuring with excitement. With barely checked glee. Up on the platform the criminal was on proud display, and the little chill of terror a hanging always evoked ran in waves ran through the people gathered to watch.

A list of charges was read out, but Malden didn't listen. He was far too busy at that moment lifting purses. The real trick to it wasn't deft fingers, really. It was choosing the perfect moment. You had to wait until your mark's attention was fully on something else, until he was totally unaware of the people all around him.

Then it was child's play. *Snip-snip* went the shears, and coins fell into Malden's hands. The fat merchant in front of him didn't even turn around to see who'd touched him.

Up on the gallows the show was just getting started, it seemed. Mouths fell open and eyes went wide as the condemned man lifted his chin and interrupted the reading of the charges. "May I not see my accuser, before I am put to death?" the prisoner asked in a voice as clear as a bell.

Over on the viewing stand the Burgrave rose from his throne. A sardonic smile twisted his lips. "I suppose you have that right, as a peer. Let him see me."

The executioner pulled off the prisoner's hoodwink, and for a moment the blond man simply blinked and squinted in the bright sunlight. Then he looked up and saw Ommen Tarness gazing silently in his direction.

"Ah," the prisoner said. "Greetings, milord."

"Exactly, Sir Croy," the Burgrave replied. "I am still your lord."

The crowd erupted in surprise. Apparently they had no idea that the man waiting to be hanged was, in fact, a knight of the realm. A man of property and good family—which made his execution that much juicier. Most interestingly, the dwarf envoy, Murdlin, jumped up on his seat at the news. The dwarf looked conflicted by varying emotions—in which state he mirrored the people who surrounded Malden on every side. A great chaos of voices and opinions raised itself, and it seemed no two citizens could agree on what this meant.

Tarness held up both hands for silence. "Croy, I warned you, when last we met, that I would not suffer you to return here. Yet you broke the letter of your banishment. I hope you have a very good reason."

"I do," the knight said, bowing his head. "I came for love."

The crowd erupted in noise. Some jeered, some expressed the utter disbelief that Malden felt on hearing this.

Others, many of them, cried out in sympathy. Tarness shook his head and sat down on his throne. "Enough of this nonsense. Proceed."

"Wait! Let me speak in my defense, I beseech you!" the knight shouted. "When you hear my tale, I am sure—"

Tarness made a gesture with one hand and the hangman struck Croy across the face. The Burgrave looked away in disgust and said, "Gag him so I don't have to listen to this. And then proceed."

Even Malden had to admit he found that a trifle unfair. The man was about to die—he ought to be allowed to prattle on if he liked. He gave in to his instinct to join the chorus of boos and hissing that welled up from the crowd.

Still, he had not come to see the knight's final distress, but only to do a little hard labor and reap a harvest of coin. He looked away from the scene on the gibbet and moved through the boisterous crowd, now looking for a final victim before he retired for the day. It would be easy to take a purse at the moment the hanged man dropped. At that moment every eye in the square would be turned to the same place. Few easy marks presented themselves, however, and suddenly Malden was in danger of being trampled. Some among the crowd had begun to shout for the prisoner's release, raising their fists in the air. They drew closer to the gallows, as if they might storm it and save the man themselves. The bailiff waved for the watch. The town's policing force, dressed alike in cloaks patterned with embroidered eyes, rushed into the throng and pushed back with their quarterstaffs until the crowd gave some way.

Knowing it would be folly to try to take another purse right under the noses of the city watch, Malden shrank back, away from the gallows, and stumbled backward directly into what felt like a wall of jangling iron.

He whirled about, a curse on his lips, but this he forestalled as he saw whom he'd tripped over. A man much broader and taller than himself who loitered at the back of the crowd, aloof from it as if immune to its bloodlust. He wore a hauberk of chain mail covered by a jerkin of black leather. His head was covered in a wild tangle of brown hair that didn't end until it wrapped around his chin in a full and glorious beard. The man peered down at him as if from a considerable height. A jagged scar crossed the bridge of his nose, nearly bisecting his face.

"Steady on there, boy," the big man said. "Are you hurt? Ah, but now I see you are. I'm a blasted pillock for not seeing you there."

Malden licked his lips. He'd been ready to call the man far worse than that until he saw the massive sword strapped to his back. So instead he kept his mouth shut, because he had a brain in his head. He never argued with a man wearing a sword. He held his peace for another reason as well. Under his sling, his long thin fingers had touched a fat purse on the swordsman's belt. By the way it hung low and heavy, it must contain something more precious than copper.

Up on the viewing platform the dwarf Murdlin was trying desperately to get the Burgrave's attention. Malden was barely aware that anyone else in the square existed. He was too busy running his fingertip across the milled edge of a coin inside the swordsman's purse. It must be silver, he thought, just based on how it felt.

It was folly to steal from a man so heavily armed, recklessness of a sort Malden never permitted himself. Yet the oaf had bruised him. Malden feigned unsteadiness and let the swordsman grasp his left arm. With his right hand he made a quick pass with his shears and felt the weight of the coins that dripped from the cut purse. They were heavy enough to be gold, even though he wouldn't know until later when he could examine them in private.

"The fault was mine, and I will beg your pardon, rather than insult you further," Malden said. He reached up and touched the cowl of his cloak in salute, then twisted away and pushed into the crowd before the swordsman could say another word.

Up on the gallows, the hangman draped the noose around the knight's neck, then pulled it fast. Better you than me, Malden thought. Best to get away now in the noise when the poor fool dropped. He took no more than a few steps into the comforting anonymity of the throng, however, before the swordsman behind him spoke the two words Malden dreaded most.

"Hold! Thief!" the man shouted.

From no more than five strides away, a watchman in an eye-covered cloak looked up and right into Malden's eyes. The watchman took a step toward him—but then something miraculous happened.

"Wait!" the dwarf envoy bellowed, up on the viewing platform. "I cannot let this go on. This man is beloved by the king of my people. Lord Burgrave, I demand you spare his life!"

It was enough to turn the square into a bedlam. The watchman had all he could do to hold the crowd back from tearing the gallows down with their own hands. Long before he and his fellows had the mob under control, Malden was off and away, his scrawny legs flashing under his cloak. It was the best chance he would get to make good his escape, and he planned on milking the opportunity for every drop of grace. Yet his luck was not unalloyed at that moment. As he fled he glanced behind him only once—and then only to confirm what he dreaded. The watch had lost sight of him, but the swordsman had not. The big man was right behind him.

# CHAPTER NINE

M alden pushed through the crowd, which tried to push back. He was a slippery fish, though, and ducked easily under raised arms or around fat bellies and even between skinny legs. His small size was an asset in a life spent always running away from something. He ducked around a party of student scholars too drunk to react as he whipped past them, then clambered on top of a cart full of fruit before the vendor could grab him. He plucked up a skinned melon, overripe and bursting with juice after being out in the hot sun all day, and waited for his moment.

"You there," the vendor began to shout, "come down and—"

Malden flipped the vendor a thruppence and the hawker turned away as if he'd never seen him. It was a dozen times what the melon was worth.

The bearded swordsman shoved his way through the students, knocking half of them down like ninepins. "Thief, hold, I only want to—"

Malden hurled the melon with pinpoint accuracy. It exploded across the swordsman's face and chest, the pulp forming great yellow clots in his beard and across his eyes. By the time he recovered from his shock and started scraping the mess off his face, Malden was off and running again.

Market Square was a central location from which one could reach anywhere in the Free City of Ness. Malden chose none of the half-dozen streets that led away from the square. He knew a better road, a kind of highway, where he could make much better speed: across the rooftops, where few could follow.

First, though, he had to get up above the crowd.

Along the south edge of the square there was a massive multitiered fountain, a gift from the third Burgrave to the people. It was in the shape of a series of bowls held by the handmaidens of the Lady, the Burgrave's favorite deity. Malden dashed for it and then leapt up one tier after another, his feet barely getting wet as he stepped on the stone rims of the bowls. Balanced precariously at the top, one foot on a handmaiden's cocked elbow, he looked back to see if his ascent was drawing the ire of the watch. He needn't have bothered. The people had mobbed the gallows en masse and were busy cutting down the imprisoned knight, while the Burgrave and the dwarf envoy bellowed conflicting orders at their various servants and retainers. Malden easily made the leap from the top of the fountain to a pitched roof beyond, dropping to all fours to get a better grip on the slick lead shingles. He had landed on the top of the civic armory, which normally bristled with guards, but they were busy rushing out to join the general melee in the square. He clambered over the roofline of the armory and up one of its many spires to leap over to another roof, this the top of the tax and customs house.

It wasn't the first time he'd climbed these heights. The district around Market Square was full of old temples, public buildings, and the palatial homes of guildmasters and minor nobility. It was called the Spires for its most common architectural detail—all of which were so heavily ornamented, carved, and perforated they were easier to climb than a spreading oak. Combined with how close the buildings pressed to one another, Malden could move through the Spires almost as easily as he could walk on flat cobbles.

Arms spread for balance, he hurried down the roofline of the customs house, one foot in front of the other like he was walking a tightrope. The sun glared on the pale shingles of the roof, made from slabs of stone cut thin as paper. At the end of the roof he slid down the steeply pitched shingles and sprang up onto a rain gutter, then launched himself across the narrow gap of the Needle's Eye, an alley that curled around the back of the university cloisters. The cloisters had a nearly flat rooftop running a hundred yards away from him, an easy place to gain some time in case he was still being pursued. Of course, that was impossible. There was no way a man wearing thirty pounds of chain mail on his back could—

"Oh, that's unfair," Malden breathed.

A puffing, roaring noise like the bellow of an exhausted bull chased him across the roof, and then the clanking noise of chain mail slapping on shingles. The swordsman clambered up on top of the customs house, dragging himself upward despite all the weight he carried. The bastard must be as strong as a warhorse, Malden thought.

"Just—want—to—talk," the swordsman grunted, hauling himself up onto the steeply peaked roof, staring at Malden across the alley between them. "Listen, thief," he said, "you needn't run—any further. I just—just want to talk."

"Is your tongue as sharp as your sword?" Malden asked. "Come no closer." Witty banter wasn't coming as easily as he'd hoped. Maybe he was too terrified to crack jokes. Well. Never mind. He drew his weapon. "This," he said, "is a bodkin."

"So it is," the swordsman replied, the way a tutor might speak to a student who had just mastered the first declension of a regular verb.

Malden sneered. "It may not look like much. But it's designed for one thing, and one alone. It has a wickedly sharp tip so it can punch right through chain mail and into an armored man's vitals." Of course, of the hundred odd uses Malden had come up with for his knife, that was the one he'd never actually tried. He imagined it would take a lot of strength to push it through the fine mesh of metal links. He would have to get his back into it. Assuming the swordsman hadn't cut his own spine in half before he had a chance to try. "If you attempt to follow me further—"

"I don't want to follow you over there. Bloodgod's armpits! That's the last thing I want to have to do today. I just want to talk to you. Truly."

Malden pointed the weapon directly toward the swordsman's midsection.

The swordsman responded by getting a running start and then leaping over the gap between the customs house and the roof of the university cloister. As the enormous man came flying toward him, Malden let out a yelp and broke into a run. Behind him the swordsman came down hard on the lead tiles of the cloister's roof and landed altogether wrong on his leading foot. He slipped and twisted around and fell with a great clanging noise that must have alarmed every student and scholar inside the cloister—unless they were all up in the square. The students of the university famously loved a good riot. The swordsman's legs and then his lower half slid over the edge and dangled in space, while his hands scrabbled at the roof tiles, looking for any kind of purchase. It was all the swordsman could do to keep from rolling over the edge and dropping into the Needle's Eye. From that height the impact would almost certainly break bones.

"Blast," the swordsman said. Then he shouted, "Cythera! Stop him!"

Malden was already running down the long lane of the cloister's rooftop. At its far end, he knew, was the Cornmarket Bridge, which was lined in allegorical statues. If he launched himself off the edge of the roof and angled it just right, he could easily snag the top of the Bounties of Harvest Time. That particular statue had wide hips and a cornucopia full of fruits and grains, which would give him plenty of handholds to climb down to safety on—

Malden had to stop short when a woman in a velvet cloak materialized out of thin air, directly in his path.

He gawped like a fish on a pier, from the shock of her appearance, of course, but also—also—from the nature of her appearance. His mind felt like it had slammed into a brick wall, and his eyes felt pinned to the spot. He could not look away from her.

The woman was astonishingly beautiful, though it was hard to tell. Dark, complicated, *disturbing* tattoos covered her cheeks and forehead and the bare arms she revealed as she swept the cloak back over her shoulders. Her eyes were very large, very blue, and altogether too heartbreakingly sorrowful to look at for more than a moment.

She smelled of some perfume Malden had never smelled before. Her hair looked softer than sable, and despite the circumstances, he took a moment to imagine what it would be like to bury his face in her curls.

It would be . . . very pleasant, he thought.

"Are you Cythera?" Malden asked, because he could think of nothing else to say to this bewitching woman. He knew he should be running, knew that the swordsman would be right behind him. Yet if he ran away now, that would mean tearing his eyes away from her exotic beauty.

She smiled. It was the single least mirthful smile Malden had ever seen. "I am." She took a step closer. That was when he realized what was so disturbing about her tattoos. They were moving. The complex patterns of interweaving tendrils, leaves, briars, thorns, flowers, and the like were slowly rearranging themselves on her face, seeking out new arrangements and complications, forming arabesques and elegant knots that resolved themselves while he watched into wholly new patterns, which . . . it was quite mesmerizing, really, just watching them. Just—

Malden tore his gaze away. He'd felt entranced, and well he should have. Something about the tattoos had dazzled him, clouding his mind. He never enjoyed being tricked— he was the one who was supposed to trick *other people.* He roared as he brought his bodkin around, the point angled toward her throat.

"That," she told him, "would be a singularly bad idea." It was not a threat. Somehow the tone of her voice conveyed the sense that she wanted nothing less than to see him hurt, that she really didn't wish him ill, but that he was playing with fire all the same. Or was that just another illusion? Perhaps she was some kind of witch and was quite happy about leading him to his doom.

Best, he thought, to break the spell and flee.

Slowly he lowered the bodkin. "I don't know what manner of creature you are," he told her, "but I really must be going."

"Oh no you don't," the swordsman said, coming upon Malden from behind. He grabbed Malden's head under one massive arm and squeezed. Apparently the swordsman had recovered from his stumbling fall. There was no way for Malden to break the hold: the oaf had the strength of a bear. He rather smelled like one, too. "You and I," the swordsman said, giving Malden's head another squeeze, "are going to have our talk now. All right? Promise me you won't," yet another squeeze, "run off?"

"I promise, of course, how could I have been so rash as to—as to—I promise! Just stop that! Your mail is digging into my neck."

"Very good," the swordsman said. He let Malden loose to stagger around on the roof, grasping at his throat. "My name, by the way, is Bikker. We weren't properly introduced before."

"I'm Malden." The thief bent over double for a moment. "Well met."

"Indeed. So. Malden?"

"Yes?" Malden said, lifting his head.

"This is for the melon," Bikker said, just before punching him right in the face with one massive mailed fist.

# CHAPTER TEN

Approximately three hundred yards to the northwest, Market Square had erupted into a melee as angered citizens brawled with the watch in their eye-patterned cloaks. It didn't take much to start a riot in a city of this size. The students of the university were deep in the thick of it, laying into the watch with bare fists, fueled by strong drink and the excitement of a day away from their dry and dusty studies. Most of the wealthier folk were attempting to flee the square, with varying degrees of luck.

To Sir Croy, up on the gibbet, it was like looking into the pit. He could not believe that all of these people were battling because of him. He had spent his whole life defending these people, keeping them safe, and now they were warring amongst themselves. That they were arguing over his fate was too much to bear.

"Friends! Please, I beg you, peace!" Sir Croy shouted. He wanted to wave his hands in the air to gain the attention of the throng, but of course could not, as his hands were bound. The noose around his neck didn't help either. The executioner beside him looked confused, uncertain as to whether he should release the trapdoor that would drop Croy to his fate.

Somehow Anselm Vry managed to climb up onto the gallows. The bailiff was the city's chief administrator and keeper of the peace, answerable only to the Burgrave. Sallow-skinned and lean of features, Vry looked like the kind of man who should spend his whole life with his nose in a book, but Croy had known him once and could see beyond the man's looks. Vry was an able administrator, a skilled organizer of men and matériel. He was above all a rational man. Croy couldn't resist beaming at someone whom he had once called his friend. The bailiff whispered in the executioner's ear, and at once the hooded man jumped down from the gallows and waded into the riot, aiding the watch.

"Anselm!" Croy called. "I knew you wouldn't let this— Oh."

Vry had taken up the executioner's post, his hand on the lever that would release the trapdoor.

"I see," Croy said. "You've come to see me off personally."

"Indeed," Vry said, shaking his head in disgust. "I hope you understand this was not my choosing. I pleaded with Tarness not to slay you, in fact."

"I'm much obliged."

Vry snorted. "I told him we could simply give you a commission and ship you off to fight barbarians in the eastern mountains. They would have killed you for us. But that wouldn't have worked, would it? You would have deserted your post and returned here in haste."

"Defy a commission of duty? Never!"

"Oh? Truly, you would have gone away and never returned?"

Sir Croy was not a man for deep thoughts or meditations on the future. He pondered this for a moment, then smiled. "I would have whipped the barbarians in six months. Then I could have come back here with a clear conscience."

Vry rubbed at his eyes with one hand. "Croy, please, for once in your life try to be realistic. Whatever quest is driving you this time won't let you stay away. Yet Tarness cannot allow you inside the city walls. You know things he wishes kept secret. I know you would never betray him, but there's always the chance someone would get the information out of you—if not by torture, then by wizardry. Banishing you the first time was an act of great mercy on his part, and it will not be repeated."

"I understand. Well, I forgive you old friend. We serve the same masters, you and I, and perhaps you are simply more loyal than me. That's hardly a quality to be condemned. Now, if you must—obey your orders." Croy lifted his chin and straightened his back. If he was going to die he would do so with proper posture.

"Noble as you ever were," Vry said, "and just as stupid." He started to pull the lever.

His hand was stayed, however, at the last possible moment. There was a flash of light that was instantly swallowed up by a thick cloud of yellow smoke. Croy's lungs filled and he was overwhelmed by a powerful reek of rotten eggs that made him gag and cough. He tried to stay upright and maintain his composure but the stench was just too great. He worried he might vomit—not exactly what the people would expect of a knight of the realm, not in public—

"Hold still, you freakishly large livestock copulator," someone hissed in the midst of the yellow cloud. The noose was lifted away from his throat, then a knife cut through the rope holding Croy's hands together. Small hands pushed him from behind. He went staggering forward and over the edge of the gallows platform. It was all he could do to land on his feet. Down at ground level the yellow smoke was rarefied and he could breathe again, but still he could see nothing.

Fortunately a figure with a cloth across its face was there to guide him. He was dimly aware that the figure was only about four feet tall. A child? Some magical sprite, with the appearance of a child?

"Stop standing there manipulating yourself in an erotic fashion. We don't have much time before the feces-smelling watch is upon us!"

Ah. No child. There was only one sort of creature in the world with such a vulgar tongue, yet such an academic grasp of human language. "Murdlin?" Croy asked. "Is that you?"

"It won't be either of us in a moment, if we're both dead as horse urine!"

They wasted no more time. Using the melee as cover, the man and the dwarf hurried out of the square. Once they were clear of the yellow smoke, Croy was able to understand why Murdlin had covered his face with cloth. It must have filtered out the worst of the stinking smoke and allowed the dwarf to breathe easy even in its midst. Was there no end to the cleverness of the diminutive folk?

"Murdlin, I am deep in your debt now," Croy said as he was led around a corner into Greenhall Street.

"Considering what you did for the dwarf king's daughter, the debt is crossed out," Murdlin told him.

"I only did my duty, as bid by my king," Croy pointed out. A year earlier the dwarf princess had been traveling to Helstrow, to be received at the royal court of Skrae. Along the way she'd been abducted by bandits who intended to hold her for ransom. Croy had spent six weeks tracking the bandits down and eventually rescued the princess. The dwarf king offered him anything he desired—steel, gold, even the princess in marriage—but Croy had never considered there might be a reward. A crime was committed, and someone had to put it right, that was all.

Clearly Murdlin felt some recompense was still owed.

"This way, most hurriedly, like a rabbit making love," Murdlin called.

Even as they dashed across the cobblestones, a wagon full of hay pulled up beside them. The driver was a dwarf with a hood pulled low across his face to keep out the sun. The wagon rolled to a stop as soon as it reached them.

"By the Lady, you work fast," Croy said.

"The moment I realized it was you on the gallows, I knew what course things must take. I sent one of my servants at once to fetch this conveyance. Now please, get into this body-odor stinking hay. It will hide you from view.

The wagon will take you outside the walls. By the time you arrive I'll have a horse waiting for you, so you may run off like a goblin that has fouled its own pants."

"You make escape sound less sweet that I would have thought it an hour ago," Croy admitted.

"It's only a figure of speech. A common expression in my first language," Murdlin told him. "I am taking a great risk doing this, Croy. Now, please! Into the hay that itches like pubic lice."

Croy rubbed at his chafed wrists. Then he started walking backward, away from the dwarf, almost breaking into a run. "You have my eternal thanks, envoy. But I've work to do yet, here in the Free City. My lady is still enslaved. What is freedom to me when she is in chains? Fare thee well!"

The dwarf cursed him and shook his small fists in the air, but Croy was already on his way, turning a corner into Brasenose Street and back into danger.

Just the way he liked it.

# CHAPTER ELEVEN

For a while Malden's world was only a terrible ringing, as if a bell were struck right next to his ear, and darkness, a kind of darkness that hurt. He could feel his body being moved about, but only from a distance, as if he were watching some other poor bastard being carted around. The pain he felt made no sense, really, and he kept probing at it with mental fingers, trying to remember what had happened.

Eventually he heard sounds over the ringing in his head. Gasps and shouts, and then the shriek of chairs being pulled back. His poor body was dumped without ceremony on a flat surface, and suddenly he rushed back into it, though that just made things hurt more. Gradually he managed to tease out voices from the noise all around him.

"—might have killed him with a punch like that. And we'd be back where we started. You really ought to learn some discipline."

"What? That little tap? I've hit flies harder than that. Look, he's already waking up. I couldn't possibly have done more than jiggled his brains a bit."

The voices were vaguely familiar. Malden couldn't quite place them, though. He was having a lot of trouble stringing thoughts together, even though the horrible ringing noise had faded away from his ears. He attempted to make a catalog of the things he knew for sure. He was certain, for instance, that he was lying on a very hard surface. Also, that his face hurt.

Suddenly his face hurt a very great deal.

"Oh," he moaned. "Oh, by the Bloodgod. Oh . . ."

"Open your eyes now, boy," Bikker said. "There's a good lad."

Malden looked around without sitting up. He was in a tavern, lit by smoking oil lamps. The few patrons present at that time of day were all staring at him. The alewife, a heavyset woman of middle age, was coming toward them with a tankard full of beer.

"Which one of you is paying for this?" she asked. "This isn't a sickhouse."

Slowly, Malden got his elbows under him and sat up. He had been laid out flat on a long table, a slab of oak that felt as hard as stone. It was patterned with old dark rings where tankards had overflowed, and was held together with strips of iron that dug into his back and legs.

Cythera—the tattooed woman—handed the alewife a farthing and passed the tankard to Malden. It was of the kind that had a lid on a hinge, to keep out flies, an earthenware vessel sealed at the bottom with pewter. An expensive bit of crockery. That told Malden roughly where he had to be—on the Golden Slope, the region of rich houses and expensive shops just downhill from the Spires. Had to be, as there were no taverns in the Spires, while if his two strange captors had carried him any farther downhill, the tankard would have been made of leather sealed with pitch. Knowing that was important. When he made his escape from this place, he would need to know where to run to first.

Wherever he was, though, he had to admit he was very thirsty. He lifted the lid and sipped carefully at the contents, thinking it must be some medicinal draught—but in fact it was only small beer. A drink fit for children.

"You like that, boy?" Bikker asked.

"I'm not an infant," Malden said, taking a long drink. "I'm almost twenty. Please stop calling me 'boy.'"

Bikker smiled broadly, showing off the gaps where some of his teeth used to be. "You going to try to run off again, boy, as soon as you can stand? Or are you going to talk to me now?"

Cythera glanced around the room. Whenever her blue eyes passed over one of the staring patrons, they flinched and looked away. "Bikker," she said, "we need more privacy than this. Where should we go?"

"I'm tired out after chasing this cur," Bikker told her. "I like this place just fine. You lot, out now. Barkeep, you can go, too."

"By Sadu's eight elbows, I will not," the barkeep told him. "Just run off like a scolded brat, and leave you here with my till and all my stock?" She snorted in derision.

Bikker shrugged hugely. Then he reached behind him and drew his sword.

It made a strange slick sound as it came out of its scabbard, and when revealed, was not the shiny length of steel Malden had expected. Instead it looked like a bar of iron, three feet long, with no real edge. The iron was pitted and rough, like something that had been left in a tomb for centuries before it was picked up again. It looked a little slick, too—and as Malden watched, bubbles formed on its surface, then congregated in thick clots until it looked like the sword was drooling. A drop of the clear fluid ran down the sword's edge and dripped on the dirt floor, where it hissed and smoked on the packed earth.

"You may wish to move aside," Bikker said to Malden, who jumped off the table quickly, ignoring the throbbing pain in his face and head. Bikker swung the sword around in a wide arc that brought it crashing down on the oak table. With an explosive hiss like a dozen angry snakes striking at once, the blade sank through the thick wood and through the other side. The table fell in two halves, split clean down the middle, against the grain of the wood. The wetness of the blade—it must be vitriol, Malden realized, of some very potent type—gave off foul vapors that stung his nose. For a moment he could do naught but look at the sundered table. It was still bubbling and dissolving wherever the acid sword had touched it. Then he looked up and saw that everyone—patrons and barkeep alike—had fled the room.

"There," Bikker said. "Privacy."

Cythera sighed deeply, though there was an affectation to the sound that made Malden think she was accustomed to being annoyed with Bikker's antics. "They'll be back soon enough. And they'll probably bring the watch."

Bikker shrugged. He sheathed his sword. Malden saw that the interior of the scabbard was lined with glass, no doubt to keep the acid from burning its way through. The big man said, then, "So let us speak quickly to the boy, and then we can all be on our way. Boy," Bikker called.

"Malden. At least use my name."

"Boy," Bikker said, walking over behind the bar and pouring himself a pitcher full of strong ale, "you are a thief, is that correct? This wasn't the first time you ever cut a purse. Judging by the way you scampered up those rooftops, I imagine you've done this sort of thing before."

"Listen," Malden said, "the silver I took from you, it's all—it's here somewhere." He reached down across his chest and realized that his sling and his fake arm had been removed. Looking up, he saw that Cythera held them—and his bodkin, too. "I'll give it back, right? And everything else I took today, you can have that as well. Just let me go."

"Bugger the silver! There's plenty more where it came from!" Bikker shouted. He lifted his pitcher and drank lustily from it until foam drenched his beard.

"We don't wish to punish you," Cythera said. "We wish to hire a skilled thief for . . . well, our purposes must remain unspoken, of course. We wish to hire a master thief for a certain job."

More where it came from, Malden thought. More silver. Enough the brute didn't even bother keeping hold of the pittance he'd had with him. More. "Are you?" he said. "Well, luck is with you, for I—"

"Can you recommend anyone like that?" Cythera asked.

"I—I can indeed," Malden said, and raised himself up to his full height. "I know a thief with no equal in the Free City. One more than up to whatever task you set him." He gave her his most dashing look.

"Yes?" she said patiently.

"Milady, I am at your service."

She frowned. "No, I mean, what is his name, this paragon of thieves?"

"It's—well, me."

Bikker laughed so hard he spilled his ale. Cythera's face didn't change, but her icy blue eyes looked Malden up and down and then flicked away.

"We don't want a pickpocket, boy! We want a *thief.* A . . . a burglar, a . . . second story man, a—"

"And I tell you, you've found him." Malden brushed past Cythera—she gave a short gasp as he nearly touched her— and over to stand before Bikker. He had to look up to meet the swordsman's gaze but he held it. "Why, just the other day, Cutbill, the master of thieves, expressed his deep admiration for my skills. He listened to the story of how I stole plate and silver from Guthrun Whiteclay's house and said he'd never heard of a finer scheme enacted so skillfully. And he should know."

"Cutbill." Bikker glanced across at Cythera. "You're one of his crew?"

"Indeed," Malden said.

"Only—we need this to stay between us. It can't get back to him, or the world will know our business. At least, it will if it has the coppers to buy the information."

"Discretion is my watchword. Though it does cost extra."

Bikker shook his head and quaffed more ale.

"You've seen how quick I am," Malden insisted.

"We did, at that," Cythera agreed. "He would have gotten away from *you*, Bikker, if I hadn't been there to distract him. And the man we need will have to know how to climb. He showed us that as well."

The swordsman hunched his shoulders. He was half convinced, Malden knew, and he already had Cythera on his side. Time to close the deal, before Bikker could reconsider.

"For this job I will require the sum of one hundred and one gold royals," Malden announced.

Bikker smiled. "You haven't yet heard what it entails. We might be getting a bargain for that price."

A bargain at one hundred and one royals? *More silver where that came from*, Bikker had said. How much more? "Of course, that does not include incidentals, the fees of the dwarf who makes my gear, bribe money, hazard bonuses, surcharges for quick resolution, gratuities—"

Bikker leaned back against the bar. "Don't get ahead of yourself, Malden."

# CHAPTER TWELVE

The sorcerer Aelbron Hazoth lived in an imposing four story edifice where the Lady's sacred parklands abutted the city wall, most of the way downhill from the palace, in the district called Parkwall.

It was not the safest district in town, though it had its recommending features. Like the Ashes, it had originally been a residential district for the poor until it burned down in the Seven Day Fire. Unlike that wasteland, Parkwall had been laboriously cleared, the remains of the old houses scraped away and the land allowed to go to seed. Now Parkwall was a zone of lush grass, a green common kept cropped by the sheep and goats of the people of the Stink, a spacious greensward in a city that had very little green space. The tall crowded houses of the Stink drew away on either side to let in the air. It was rumored to be the healthiest place in town—the plagues that swept through Ness every few winters often skipped Parkwall entirely—but its openness and lack of well-lighted streets had drawn footpads and thieves, and it was counted terribly dangerous by night. A few fine houses had been built in Parkwall to take advantage of the pleasantly rustic environs, but these were all surrounded by their own walls and wrought-iron fences to keep out the uninvited.

Such as Sir Croy, for instance.

The knight had found lodging at a nearby villa. After escaping from the gibbet, he thought he would be a hunted man, that no place would be safe for him, but in fact it did not take long before he had a place of refuge. He did not lack for friends in the Free City, some of whom were stalwart enough to hide him from the watch. A rich merchant had found him wandering in the Golden Slope and begged to bring him home. Croy accepted, though he had no money to pay the man. The merchant insisted none was required, and Croy had praised his good heart in all the words he knew. The merchant assured him that Croy would bring him great fame and social status, but Croy knew the man was just being kind. He gave Croy a suite of rooms all to himself and ordered his servants to see to his every wish.

This night he was laying spread out on a bench in a roof garden, pretending to take his ease. It was a likely enough occupation. This close to Ladymas and the hottest time of year, anyone with sense was up on a rooftop or in a garden, trying to catch a breeze. Anyone who saw him might think him yet another pampered noble attempting to stay cool. In truth, he had come up to the roof garden to watch Hazoth's house. Croy was a man of action, but this evening he had spent almost motionless on the bench, taking only a little wine and some nuts for sustenance. One thing only would bid him tarry so. For hours he had kept an eye on the place, watching who came and who went, hoping to spy a glimpse of Cythera.

After midnight he got his chance. She and Bikker came traipsing over the grassy common. The place had a reputation for being full of footpads after dark, but the two seemed to pay no special heed to their surroundings. Instead they were deep in conversation. Croy even got the sense they might be arguing.

He placed a salted almond between his lips and bit down hard. He longed—oh, how he desired it!—to call out, to wave, to get her attention somehow. He longed to jump down from his perch and run to her side, to catch her up in his strong arms (even knowing what a mistake that would be) and carry her off to his castle. Failing that, he would have been glad even for a moment's soft conversation, for a renewed exchange of promises and honeyed words.

But it would not happen tonight. Tonight he could only watch.

The guards at Hazoth's door challenged the pair, but Bikker reached for his sword's hilt and the armored sentries fell back. The two of them stopped just inside the sorcerer's gate, however, and waited for something Croy could not see. When it came, he felt it instead. There was a sudden change in air pressure, or perhaps merely the crickets in the grass all fell silent at once. It was like the night itself held its breath.

It lasted a bare moment. Then it was over, and Cythera and Bikker entered the villa's grounds and went their separate ways. He, toward a low shed at the side of the house that Croy knew served as barracks for the sorcerer's guards. She, into the house through the stables—like a common servant.

How he felt the need to rush down there and follow her, to reach—quite gently, of course—for her hand in the shadows, to breathe her name and see recognition in her eyes. But not tonight.

Not while the house was shielded so patently by some spell—a spell even she must wait to pass.

Not tonight. Not until he could get his weapons back.

It was time to find out what friends, if any, he had left in the palace.

# CHAPTER THIRTEEN

The next day Malden spent in preparation.

It was mad even to consider going through with this. The job he'd been hired for was, if not impossible, distinctly ill-advised. It was going to make of him a pigeon in the midst of a pack of dogs. If the plan failed in the slightest particular, it would mean a quick but nasty death, a spear through his lights, or an axe through his skull. Cutbill's influence could not protect him from that.

Yet if it worked—it couldn't, of course, it was the worst kind of folly, but—*if it worked*, he would be clear of his debt to the guildmaster of thieves before the sun rose tomorrow morning. He would be a full member of the guild, with all the rights and privileges thereunto pertaining. He would be a free man again. Better, by far, because he would be on his way to wealth. On his way to being a man of means.

In the Free City of Ness, that was the only thing that counted.

He made his way to the Ashes early, just as the sun was rising over the city's wall. The gang of children that guarded Cutbill's headquarters did not show themselves—they already knew he belonged there. Loophole, Lockjaw, and 'Levenfingers were inside the ruin already, though. As far as he knew, they were there all day, every day, sitting on the empty coffin. The old men greeted him warmly and asked him what schemes he had planned for the day. They asked every time he visited. "A little of the same," he told them. "Though to be honest, my heart's not in it."

"Be of good cheer, lad," Loophole told him. "Money comes to them that keep their eyes open."

"I'm sure you're right." Malden would gladly have spoken with the old men, for he'd learned they were a sure font of wisdom. If any of them knew how this job could be done, this fantastically impossible job, surely it was one of them. Yet he knew that anything he said to them—even to Lockjaw—would be reported to Cutbill at once. In addition, Bikker and Cythera were quite clear that his fee included a hefty sum to make sure Cutbill never learned of the plan. So he kept his peace and headed inside.

He had learned on his second visit, some days ago, that it was not necessary to travel by coffin every time you visited Cutbill's burrow. That was just for new arrivals, a kind of object lesson to remind them their lives were forfeit if they crossed Cutbill in any way. Actual employees had their own entrance through a trapdoor hidden in the debris of the fallen house. It led to a door below, hidden behind a curtain. There were many doors in Cutbill's domain, and all of them were hidden. Malden was certain he'd seen only a fraction of the guildhall in his visits.

In the main room, Bellard was throwing darts at a target on one wall. The permanent dice game was going on in the corner, but only two players had risen so early. There were others there, thieves like himself, pimps come to pay their tithe to the master, procurers dividing up their stash, and one fellow dressed in dusty traveling clothes that Malden did not recognize. There was something odd about the man, but in the dim light he couldn't get a good look.

The traveler was sleeping on the divan when Malden came in, but before he could take two steps into the room, the man bolted upright and reached inside his tunic, probably for a knife. His beady eyes twinkled in the candlelight as he shot them back and forth, and his lips pulled back in a sneer as if he expected Malden to attack him.

"Be at ease," Bellard said. The dust-covered man nodded, lay back down and immediately returned to sleep.

Malden glanced over at Bellard, who nodded and said, "That's Kemper. An unsavory character if there ever was one."

"He's a thief, like me?" Malden asked.

Bellard cocked his head to one side. "Hardly. Little more than a sharper—a card cheat. A vagabond by nature, never stays in any one place for long."

"What's he doing here? Is he one of Cutbill's?"

Bellard snorted in derision. "He's no member of this guild but he pays his respects when he passes through. We wouldn't abide his sort at all if we had a choice, as he's wanted by the reeves of every village within a hundred miles of here. He's called on an old tradition of sanctuary, though, so we must let him lie here until he thinks it's safe to head out again. Of course, the tradition doesn't preclude Cutbill from charging him rent."

Malden shrugged. Good to know such a tradition existed, he supposed—who knew when he might need it himself? Yet his business was with Slag, the dwarf, so he made his way quickly to the workbench and brazier at the far side of the room.

"Need somewhat?" the dwarf demanded, looking up as Malden approached. He was no less ugly in daytime, though of course the sun never shone down in Cutbill's hiding hole. "Or you just wanted a kiss?"

Malden smiled. "There's a job I'm casing right now," he said, "and it's going to be tricky. I need a few things to see it out."

"If I can't build it, you're not good enough to need it," Slag replied.

Malden listed his requirements and the dwarf nodded. He said he had everything in stock—the items Malden requested were not too exceptional—and would provide them for hire, for a price. The price was steep, but Malden could cover it with the coins in his purse, just barely. Good thing, too, as the dwarf expected payment in advance.

"That way, when your arse is killed on the job, I don't have to go down into the fucking Bloodgod's underworld to get what you owe me."

"Your confidence in me is inspiring," Malden said. He waited for the dwarf to go to his storeroom and fetch the things. It took quite a while, so he played at darts with Bellard to pass the time. He managed to lose another tuppence before the dwarf returned. Malden had deft hands, but Bellard had the keener eye.

The tools came wrapped in sailcloth that had been treated with tar to make it waterproof. It would keep the rust off. "Return 'em in the shape you found 'em, or there's an extra fee," Slag told him.

"And so I shall. Farewell, Bellard. Farewell, all." Bellard grunted a response but no one else even looked up as Malden headed back to the light of day. The three old masters were a bit more cordial, but he didn't spend long speaking to them.

He had some time to squander, so he walked all the way uphill to the old Chapterhouse of the Learned Brothers, which was said to be haunted, before heading south around the curve of the city wall, down through the warren of close-spaced houses that marked the eastern extent of the Stink, then farther south to the homes of the fishermen and sailors who took the goods of Ness to ports around the world. It was a very long and pointless route, but it kept him always in the broad streets where most honest people traveled, and away from dark alleys and sheltered closes.

It also led him past the King's Gate, so called because it opened on the road to the royal fortress of Helstrow, a hundred miles away. Malden paused a moment to muse that Helstrow might as well be on the far side of the moon. He had never traveled more than a mile in any given direction in his life. He could not, bound as he was by the city's walls.

The gate stood twenty feet high—tall enough for knights to ride through with their lances raised. It was made of the same bluish stone as the city wall, and on this side was fronted by a massive triumphal arch celebrating some military victory or other. Malden doubted anyone living in the Stink could have told him what battle it commemorated. He let his gaze wander briefly over the carved figures of soldiers fighting wicked elves, but what really drew his eye was the land beyond the gate.

It was green, for one thing. Green grass grew out there, catching the sun. It was so wide and open, and not a soul in sight. Malden took a few steps into the narrow tunnel of the gate and found the guards there didn't even look at him. No, of course not—they had no brief to keep people from leaving. The people of Ness were free to go outside if they pleased. They just weren't free to come back in.

The sun on the grass out there looked so warm and inviting. A summer breeze played with the blades of it, stirring them gently, then letting them fall back. Behind Malden, in the Stink, all was noise and grime and desperation. Out there it would be quiet, he thought. Quiet and peaceful and—

"Make way, you little fuck!" someone shouted, and suddenly a brown and black dog was snarling at him, its wet teeth snapping shut on his cloak. Malden looked up in startlement and just had time to jump back as a mounted man came thundering through the gate, heedless of where his horse's hooves fell. The owner of the dog, a footman wearing the same coat of arms as the rider, shoved Malden back against the wall of the gate with a cudgel. "There's people of importance trying to use this gate, and you're just standing here gawking?"

Malden tried to stammer out a reply. "I assure you, I was simply—"

The footman knocked him down with the cudgel, and probably would have beaten him senseless if he hadn't needed to run off then, to keep up with his master. Down in the dust Malden felt at his ear where the footman had struck him. He was glad his fingers didn't come away bloody.

"Oh, just get out of there," a guard said, grabbing his arm and pulling him away from the gate. "You're lucky I don't dump you outside and let the reeve take you."

Lucky indeed. The green grass out there might look inviting, but the second he trod on it he would have legally become a villein. A slave, in all but name.

But if he had a little money to his name—if he could purchase even a small plot of land in some cheap place . . .

the story would be different. And that was what Cutbill had promised him, wasn't it?

Cutbill had said he was a prisoner in Ness. Malden had never felt that way before—now he could think of himself in no other terms. A prisoner. And Cutbill had the means to set him free.

It could happen tonight, for the price of a little risk.

The rest of the morning he spent cutting purses down at the fish market by Eastpool. He needed to earn back all he'd spent or be penniless by nightfall. He supped on cockles at a little shack by the river gate and then rented a room in a doss-house frequented by sailors. He would gladly have gone back to his own rooms above the waxchandler's but he had to make sure none of Cutbill's people saw him when he met Cythera later.

Much of his movement during the day had been for this purpose. He knew that Cutbill would have spies watching him, especially if he seemed bent on some specific task. Then there would be the unaligned thieves, the pickpockets and grifters of too small account to join the guild. They tended to follow Cutbill's people around the way gulls will follow a galleon, hoping to pick up scraps left behind by the more established thieves. Malden knew he had to make sure none of either sort were aware of what he was doing, so he spent the day acting as if he had nothing planned at all. There had been no reason to rise early, and in fact he spent the afternoon asleep in his rented bed. It was just past midsummer, with the festival of Ladymas less than a fortnight away, and the sun would not set until well into the evening.

When he rose, he brushed the bed's freight of insects from his hair and clothes, then climbed out the window and up onto the roof of the doss-house. He was relatively certain no one was following him, but to be sure he crossed three streets by the rooftops, leaping silently from one building to another. When he dropped down to street level again he was at the very edge of the river Skrait. He traveled northward again, upriver, by moving from pier to dock to wharf—hundreds of them stuck out from the riverbank, as each house along the Skrait had its own. He ended up deep in the Smoke, the region of manufactories and workshops where tanners, papermakers and bookbinders, hatters, blacksmiths, brewers, and bakers all plied their trades. The shops stained the air with their fumes and turned the river black with their dumping, and the smell was intense—the region downwind of the Smoke was called the Stink for good reason. It was here that Malden was to meet Cythera.

He had time to consider what he was doing. He had time to wonder if he was mad, or if he truly expected to live through this. He had time to think of that green grass beyond the gate, and how good it would feel under his feet. Eventually the sun went down and he had no more time to think.

When she came for him, gliding out of the vapors in a tiny boat she rowed herself, she asked him if he was ready. He spoke no word, but simply dropped into the boat and grabbed a pair of oars.

# CHAPTER FOURTEEN

As they hauled away from the Smoke and up the river toward the Golden Slope and the Spires, the docks and piers that stuck out into the water grew fewer in number. The river narrowed and grew faster, so they had to row all the harder. The water turned clean again, with only the occasional floating bit of sewage or debris to mar its churning surface. The river Skrait had driven its channel right through the northern half of Castle Hill, creating a winding canyon through half the Free City. Conforming to the slope of the hill, the ground along the riverbanks grew higher until it had to be held back by retaining walls, so that eventually they traveled between two high and sloping walls of ancient brick, with moss slowly eating away its mortar. Here and there a tree had taken root directly into the bricks, and its branches swayed over them, its leaves making the moonlight flicker through the mist that hung over the water.

The river bent away from them, concealed by the rising wall. Malden saw a glimmer of light. "Hold, someone's coming," he whispered, and reached back to grab Cythera's arm. He was strangely hurt when she yanked her arm away before he could touch it.

What he saw took all his concentration and kept him from thinking why. A long boat came nosing around the corner—little more than a dugout, really, its sides well-patched. An old woman stood in the stern, poling the boat downriver, while half a dozen children leaned over the thwarts. They skimmed the water with long hooks, snatching at every piece of jetsam they passed. One held an oil lamp just above the surface, illuminating a milky patch of water.

"Move aside and let them go past," Malden said. Cythera steered her boat over toward the last of the docks on the southern side of the Skrait. One of the children raised his dripping hook in thanks.

"What are they looking for?" Cythera asked, her voice a tight whisper, no louder than the rustling of leaves.

"Anything they can sell. A cloak dropped into the water from the bank of the Royal Ditch. Waste leather from one of the tanneries in the Smoke." Malden shrugged. "A dead body that might still have a purse on its belt."

He heard Cythera gasp. "Truly? They might find such a gruesome haul? Those poor children!"

Malden frowned. He knew she had money to spare, but could she really be so sheltered by it that she didn't understand basic necessities? "They would cherish it. It would mean they could eat for a week."

The old woman waved cheerily at them as she pushed past. Malden waited until the boat of mudlarks was gone from view, then signaled to Cythera that they could move again.

"It's not well that they saw us," she suggested, but as if she hoped he would reassure her.

"Even if the city watch found them and asked what they saw this night," he said, "they'd never describe us. They know if we're abroad this late we're of their kind—of the great confraternity of desperate folk. They'd never betray us."

Behind him, he heard her sigh in relief. He wished he could assure himself so easily. But there was nothing for it—they couldn't turn back now. Pushing on, they made their way up the river until the walls surrounded them on either side.

There was no sound but the dripping and knocking of their oars. They saw no more boats, not at that late hour. Malden kept an eye on the tops of the retaining walls, making sure no one was looking down to follow their progress. He did not see anyone.

It was hard work, rowing upriver, and for a while they did it in silence. It was boring work, too, however, and eventually Malden started talking just to have something to do. He kept his voice very low, knowing that sound travels far over water, but she did not try to silence him.

"I'd pay good coin to know how you pulled that trick yesterday. When you just appeared like that on the roof of the university. It was magic, was it not?"

"If you could define what magic is, and what it is not, you would be wiser than the world's great sages," she told him. "It was simply what you called it. A trick."

"Hmm. And do you know many such?"

"Not many."

Malden saw that up ahead a zigzagging set of stairs had been carved through the wall, which at this point was nearly thirty feet high. The stairs ended at a solitary dock, but there were no boats at it. All the same, he held his tongue until they were well past.

"And the way you held my gaze? I could not look away, even with that great mountain of a man coming up behind me. Surely that was wizardry."

"What are you talking about?" she asked. There was no guile in her eyes.

"You charmed me," he said, looking over his shoulder, intending to take her to task for enchanting him. Yet she looked as puzzled as he. "You used some spell."

"You give me too much credit. I know no such incantation."

Yet of course it had to be a spell she'd cast on him. Didn't it? What else could have explained his sudden interest in her eyes, her hair? What explanation would satisfy the facts, other than that she had ensorcelled him?

Malden had grown up in the company of harlots, and knew well the ways of physical love. He'd often heard them talk of the other kind, of romance and true love. They'd even talked of the fabled love-at-first-sight, though most had considered it a myth. He himself had never considered he might feel that way about another human being, much less an enchantress covered in tattoos.

So it must have been magic. There was no other possibility. Was there?

He decided to talk of anything but, rather than continue in that line of thought.

"You intrigue me, Cythera. You seem a lady of quality, yet you associate with the likes of Bikker."

"He's not so bad. Honest, in his way."

"He's a ruffian. Cheerful, perhaps, but uncouth. I don't think you chose his company. You work with him because you were ordered to do so. I think you both work for someone else. Someone who wants my services, who—"

"Who shall remain nameless."

"Very well. Though the number of citizens who could afford your services must be small."

"Not every wage is paid in coin."

It was a funny kind of thing to say, and it birthed all manner of questions in Malden's mind. But it was clear it pained her to speak of it, so he let it go. He had another thing to ask her about anyway.

"Those tattoos on your face and your arms—"

"They are not tattoos." Her voice grew sharp when she said it.

"The designs, then. Did I really see them move?"

"Yes. They are never still."

"What artist paints them? What kind of pigment does he use?"

Cythera sighed. "No artist. No paints. They are a curse. Or rather, they were imposed on me as a gift by my mother. Or perhaps she meant to curse another."

"Your mother was a sorceress? I can believe that, for you certainly enchanted me." There it was again. That thought he couldn't explain.

She seemed unwilling to discuss it herself. "You'll hold that scoundrel tongue of yours, if you know what's good for you. My mother was never a sorceress. And she still lives. She *is* a witch."

"Naturally," Malden said.

Cythera sighed. "Must you always be so glib?"

"It's part of my charm."

"Oh, you have charm? I hadn't noticed." But she was smiling.

"You wound me to the heart," he said. "But it's all right. We'll find some way you can make it up to me. When this is over, what say you we both—"

"Stop," she said, interrupting his half-serious attempt at courting. "Ship your oars."

He did as she said. "Is this the place? Have we really come so far?"

"Conversation makes any night fly. Yes—look. There is the pipe I was told to seek out. This is exactly the right spot."

The pipe in question stuck directly out of the wall. Filthy water drained from its end in a constant trickle. It was big enough around for a man to climb through, if it hadn't been closed by an iron grating. Such a man would have been a fool, of course, for the pipe led nowhere but into the dungeons of the Burgrave.

Malden looked up—and up. The gentle cambered wall above him rose no less than one hundred and fifty feet into the air. Straight to the top of Castle Hill. Up there, far, far in the air, was the Burgrave's palace.

Malden knew one thing for certain. On Cutbill's secret

protection list, the Burgrave's name did not appear. The Burgrave, of course, had his own garrison of troops for protection and did not need the aid of the master of thieves.

Malden had never been given a reason why he could not break into the house of the ultimate ruler of the Free City of Ness and pilfer his most prized possession. Most likely this was because no one had ever thought him so stupid as to try it.

At least not until Bikker and Cythera had come along.

"When you reach the top, do not scamper over the parapets directly," Cythera whispered. "Remember—Bikker will create a diversion in the courtyard. The guards up there will rush to investigate. That is your only chance to get in unseen. Move quickly, though not so quickly you fall prey to a trap. Recover the . . . the item we asked for, then come back here as fast as you can. Do not take anything else. It is critical that you do not leave any evidence you were there, or create any suspicion that the thing is gone."

He was very aware she would not say aloud what it was she wanted, not now when they were so close to it. He filed that away under the myriad things about her he found curious and interesting.

"Start your climb now. I'll make sure Bikker knows when to do his part."

"How about a kiss for luck, before I go?" Malden asked.

Cythera laughed.

"From me, such a kiss would token anything but good luck. Quickly, now!"

Malden carefully stood up in the back of the boat. He waited for Cythera to brace herself, both her oars in the water to steady the tiny craft. Then he took a quick step and jumped at the wall, his hands out and fingers spread to find whatever purchase was there.

It was not difficult. The bricks were sturdy, but the mortar between them had crumbled away over time. His fingers fit easily between each row of bricks, so that it was like grabbing at the rungs of a ladder.

Once she saw him dangling from the wall like a lizard,

Cythera bent to her oars and got her boat moving away from the wall. Malden didn't waste time watching where she went. Instead he started to climb, hand over hand.

Straight up.

# CHAPTER FIFTEEN

M alden had learned to climb almost from the time he could walk.

He was not so unusual in that—every child in Ness learned to climb, since so much of the city was on a hillside. The streets were so winding and switch-backed that often the fastest way from one house to another was to go over the house in between rather than around. It was easy enough to move around up on the rooftops, in a city where the streets were so narrow and the second floors of houses almost came together over the alleys. There were places in Ness where if a woman left a pie cooling on a second-story windowsill, the man across the street could reach through his own window and help himself to it. Even small children could jump from one house to another with little danger of falling. A relatively nimble child could run from one end of the Stink to the other across the rooftops without having to do more than occasionally hop. There were few enough opportunities to play in the crowded streets, so children often headed upward to find space for their games.

Malden had shown a real talent for climbing at an early age. He'd had no fear of heights and a love of clean, fresh air, so the tops of the city proved his natural element. His few friends always dared him to climb to the top of a steeple or dance atop a high chimney. Later, when he turned to crime for his livelihood, he found that a man who could run across the rooftops was a man rarely caught by the watch. So he trained himself to climb faster and jump farther than anyone else.

This climb was like many he'd made before, he told himself. It didn't matter what was up top—hanging on and not looking down were all it would really take.

The wall of Castle Hill leaned away from him, so instead of a sheer surface it was like a very steep slope. Only a few of the bricks had crumbled with time, though many were cracked. It was not so hard a climb, or rather, it would not have been, if it weren't so long. Taking his time, choosing every handhold carefully, pausing now and again to rest, all kept Malden from falling, but nothing could keep the cramp out of his fingers forever. He looked always for features of the wall to aid him, and found a few. Here and there a dripping pipe emerged from the bricks. On occasion he passed a narrow window, wider than an arrow slit but never so big he could have fit through. These allowed him good spots to stand and massage his hands, to ready them for further climbing. Such spots were far apart and few in number, but they helped. They even gave him a chance to free his hands long enough to take a drink of wine from the flask he kept on his belt.

By the time he was sixty feet up in the air, however, his hands were pained claws. Another ten feet and he could no longer feel his fingertips. The whole front of his tunic was stained with brick dust, and sweat had begun to pour down the back of his neck.

At seventy-five feet up he had a new peril to worry about. Across the river's channel, the opposite wall gave out—the hill was lower over there, and topped with a strip of parkland thick with chestnut and oak trees called the Royal Ditch. Lanterns hung from some of the lower branches, tended by the proprietors of the gambling houses and expensive taverns that lined the Goshawk Road there. He could hear music playing and occasional bursts of raucous laughter carried across by the wind. Should anyone there chance to look over, toward Castle Hill, he would be quite visible—

and he had no doubt they would sound some alarm. The Free City of Ness was eight hundred years old and had never been properly sacked by invaders, but there was always a first time.

He had his cloak turned inside out, to show its paler side. It was like a hawthorn leaf in color, a deep forest green on one side, a lighter sage green on the other. The lighter hue would make him harder to spot against the wall, but still, when he moved he would certainly give himself away.

There was nothing for it, however. He would have to trust to luck that no one would chance to look across the water.

His luck was with him in that, at least.

Starting at eighty feet up the wall had been carved by ancient hands. A row of human figures was sculpted into the brick, each of them twelve feet tall so they could be seen easily from the Royal Ditch. Malden had seen them often from that not-so-distant vantage, but they looked smaller at the time. They represented the direct male descendants of Juring Tarness, the first Burgrave of the Free City of Ness. Each of them had been Burgrave in his turn. They were crude images at best, and the artists who carved them had made one foolish choice in their designs. The Burgraves were depicted each in full armor, their heads hooded with chain mail and square helmets mounted with the crown of the Burgravate. As a result it was almost impossible to tell them apart. One had a mustache, another a full beard—perhaps such facial hair had been fashionable in their day. Malden had never cared to learn their names or the dates of their respective reigns. He did not care to learn them now, though he was grateful to them for one simple reason: the carvings were even easier to climb than had been the bare bricks. He made a silent apology to the ancient Burgrave whose shoulder he trod upon, and made for the top without pausing.

One hundred feet up and his hands were frozen in the shape of hooks. He jammed them again and again into the cracks between bricks and continued hauling himself upward. One hundred twenty feet and he felt like all his toes were broken from repeatedly pushing them into gaps too small to admit them.

One hundred thirty feet—and he heard a voice from above. Instantly he froze in place, pressing himself as close as possible to the bricks. Not twenty feet over his up-stretched arms a guard was walking patrol along the wall of the palace grounds. If they should look over the crenellations, if they looked down—

"Tell me if anyone's coming," the voice said. Clearly the owner of the voice must be speaking to someone.

"No, no, it's clear," a second voice said, proving Malden's suspicion.

Then came a grunt, and a noise like chain mail rattling. And then something caught the moonlight as it fell past Malden at incredible speed.

He came very close to falling off the wall then and there. He was so desperately afraid of being hit by the jetsam from above that he pulled one hand free of the wall and swung away from his perch. A moment later he realized what was happening and cursed himself silently for his lack of for-bearance.

A stream of foul-smelling liquid was coming down from on high, a stream that spread out and turned to mist a few dozen feet below his position. The guard was pissing over the side.

Malden's lip curled in disgust. Was the man too lazy to find a privy? But there was nothing he could do but hold tight, and wait, and hope the wind didn't change. He spared a quick glance down to make sure Cythera was well clear. He couldn't see her little boat down there, though he was mightily impressed by how far down it was. He had no fear of heights, but it would take a man of far greater courage than himself to look down into that abyss and feel no vertigo.

When the guard had finished and moved on, Malden looked back up, toward the top of the wall. It was close now. One quick sprint and he would be on top. But his hands were so painfully cramped he knew he would arrive unable to use them for anything but climbing. He needed to rest a moment, to rub the blood back into his whitened fingers. He also needed to make sure he would not be seen when he reached the top. Looking around, he saw a window off to his left, no more than a dozen feet away. Moving carefully, as silently as a cat on a carpet, he shifted himself over in that direction. The window was broader than the others he'd seen, though it was also lined with iron bars. Still, it would make a great place to stand for a while. Just a few minutes, he promised himself. Just until he could feel something in the balls of his thumbs.

Yet as he approached the window he heard someone moving around inside. He had to freeze in place again and wait for the people there to go away. And that could have been when his luck ran out.

For exactly at that moment Bikker provided the promised distraction.

# CHAPTER SIXTEEN

C roy hated subterfuge, but sometimes the direct approach was just not appropriate. For instance, when one needs to recover one's property from a locked room inside the palace, and one is under an order of execution, it behooves one to act in a clandestine fashion.

So instead of marching up to the Burgrave's door and asking politely, he had come to this. Masquerading as the lover of a lady-in-waiting, and then sneaking into the most secure room in the city.

"I have the key here, somewhere on my person," Lady Hilde said, and placed a hand on the bodice of her gown. She seemed to be breathing very hard and her eyes were wide as she stared into Croy's face. "It wasn't easy to get, you know. I had to wait until the castellan fell asleep at his desk. Luckily for you he's so old and decrepit, he didn't wake up even when I took it from his belt. But now—where did I put it?"

He supposed she might be frightened. It was an understandable emotion. They were inside the Burgrave's counting house, a place no one of any rank was permitted to enter after it was locked up for the night. Even by day only the castellan and the bailiff had keys to the place. It was so secure that the castellan hadn't bothered posting guards out front—after all, anyone approaching it from the courtyard would have had to pass dozens of guards already.

Of course, if you had access to one of the Burgravine's ladies-in-waiting, and she was willing to do you a favor, there weren't a lot of places in Ness that were off-limits. Croy felt distinctly uneasy about what he was doing. This was very much counter to his moral code, and he was a man for whom ethics meant everything. Still, he was able to assuage his conscience a bit. He wasn't hear to steal—he was no thief. He had only come here to recover that which belonged to him. That which he was pledged to honor and uphold, in fact: the sword he counted as his soul.

The counting house was built into the wall that surrounded the palace grounds, and had to be the most secure structure in the Free City, because it was where the Burgrave kept his gold when he wasn't spending it. It was a vast trove, stuffed full of bags of coin, coffers overflowing with silver plate, great heaps of gems, and the jewelry of Ommen Tarness's wife, the Burgravine.

None of which was what Croy had come for. His swords had been taken from him when he was arrested, and brought here, placed with the most important relics and treasures of the Free City of Ness. Just behind the locked door he faced. Hilde had claimed she could get the key for him only if he brought her inside with him so she could see the treasures for herself. Lacking a better plan, he had agreed.

"I seem to be having trouble finding the key," she told him. "Perhaps you can help me look?"

He knelt with his lamp and looked around the floor at her feet.

"No, you foolish man," she said. "It's somewhere in my dress."

He opened his mouth to speak, and then found he could not close it again. Hilde was unlacing her corset. "Well? You were so handsome yesterday in Market Square, Croy. So dashing. It made my knees tremble. And other parts of me as well. Of course, it might just be that I haven't had a man all year. My mistress keeps me so busy. Maybe if the Burgrave could perform better his own husbandly duties, I could slip away more often. Oh, no, that's exactly where I want you," she said, as he began to rise to his feet. She giggled and put a finger on his shoulder, pressing him back down to a kneeling posture.

"Milady," he said, jumping up, "I fear I misheard you."

Hilde rolled her eyes. "Don't tell me you're one of those men who doesn't know what to do with a naked woman." She twitched her shoulders and her kirtle fell to the floor. Underneath it she was wearing nothing but a chemise and knee-length hose.

Croy blushed and averted his eyes. "Milady, I would never spurn, ah, true affection from your quarter, but . . . my heart belongs to another."

"You're . . . serious."

He bowed his head and tried to keep his thoughts pure. It was not easy with Hilde's underthings rustling so close to his face.

"Here," she said, and pressed a long iron key into his hand. "Do what you have to, while I put all this back on. I have no idea how I'm going to lace up this corset without a big, strong man to help, but—oh, never mind."

"Thank you," Croy said, and quickly opened the locked door. Beyond was a tiny room with a barred window. For a split second he thought he saw a shoe outside the bars, but that was quite impossible—outside that window would be a sheer drop to the river Skrait, more than a hundred feet down. He turned to look around the room, expecting to have to search high and low for his swords.

In fact, they were the only things present. Where were the religious relics the Burgrave was required to parade through the streets every Ladymas? Where the city's charter, for that matter? Perhaps they'd gone to the same place as the city's gold reserves. The swords lay perfectly alone on a shelf below the window, two long blades in shagreen scabbards. They were all he'd brought with him when he returned to the Free City. He hung them in their proper places on his baldric and stepped back out of the room.

Hilde waited for him near the door, tapping her foot with impatience. "Come along," she said. "I'll take you through the kitchens so no one sees you. Though it would probably do my reputation some good to be seen in connection with you."

"I'm a wanted criminal," he protested.

"You don't understand this city at all, do you?" she asked. "Surely you—"

A high-pitched scream of terror and pain split the darkness outside the door. Croy leaned over Hilde's shoulder to look out into the courtyard just in time to see a man of the city watch come staggering through the main palace gate. A dark stain spread across his cloak-of-eyes as he clutched at an arrow sticking in his side. Before he'd taken a dozen steps he collapsed face first onto the flagstones.

A second scream followed close, and a guard toppled from the battlements of the palace wall. An arrow had pierced him through the neck.

"Murder!" someone shouted. "Murder!" And then an alarm bell started to ring, high-pitched and wild.

# CHAPTER SEVENTEEN

Malden listened to the clamor beyond the wall for only a moment, then scurried up over the last twenty feet of bricks faster than a spider. He slipped over the crenellations at the top of the wall and found himself on a broad walkway. No guards were in sight. He crept to the far side of the wall and peered through an embrasure, down into the courtyard.

Castle Hill was the residence of the Burgrave and the seat of his administrative functions. It was also a fortress, a keep designed to forestall any invading horde. Within its walls stood the garrison where the Burgrave's personal retinue of soldiers lived, and the central Watch Hall from which the bailiff's civic guardians were dispatched. Both these structures were alive with light now as men in various states of uniform dress came pouring out of their gates to fill the broad courtyard and parade ground. There was a great deal of shouting and confusion, and knots of watchmen in their cloaks-of-eyes were gathered around two bodies that lay lifeless in the grass. A klaxon bell rang with a deafening strident tone. Meanwhile, a detachment of soldiers were storming up and around the walls and towers on the far side of the hill, over where it looked down on Market Square. They were thrusting torches into every shadow, stabbing their iron swords into troughs and haylofts, looking for whoever had shot the two men with arrows.

What, in the Bloodgod's name, had Bikker done? He'd killed two men in cold blood—just to create a moment of chaos.

Of course, Malden had to admit it made a most excellent diversion. Not a single soldier or watch man remained in the northern half of the courtyard. The counting house, the Burgrave's private chapel, and the kitchens were all deserted. So was the palace.

This last was a tall, el-shaped structure made of quarried stone elegantly carved and pierced on its lower level with many arches and broad windows of fine glass. It was airy and light and held up with slender flying buttresses, topped with gargoyles and peaked gables. Even the Ladychapel, the great church that stood across Market Square, was not so delicate in appearance nor more refined in ornament. The palace was a masterpiece of architectural skill. One determined barbarian with a sledgehammer could probably bring it crashing down. It was built around a much older and more sturdy structure that looked like a wart on the face of a princess.

Malden surmised that the tower at the end of the el shape probably supported most of the palace's weight. It stood five stories high and he guessed that its walls were five feet thick, pierced only by a few narrow arrow-slits. This was the original holdfast of Castle Hill's first inhabitants, where the first few settlers had fled whenever the elves came a-raiding. It had stood up against those bloodthirsty devils and the dwarves who came after them (back when the dwarves still had some fight in them), and even the human barbarians who scourged Skrae three hundred years ago, back before King Garwulf the Merciful had swept their tribes across the mountains far to the east. It stood as strong as it had ever been, and was still the highest structure in the Free City.

The tower was where he happened to be headed that night. He was going to break into it, when elves, dwarves, and barbarians had never been able to. Of course, back then the palace hadn't been there. It looked like an anemic toddler could break into that airy confection.

The palace stood about thirty feet clear of the wall, separated from Malden's perch by a wide patch of manicured garden. It was that gap he needed to cross.

He ran along the top of the wall to where he could stand directly opposite the palace roof. He took a moment to reverse his cloak so its darker side was outward, then took one of Slag's tools from his belt. It was a grappling hook made in two parts joined by a central hinge. Folded, it could lie flat on his hip, but when he opened its arms fully the two parts locked into place. The prongs were wrapped in padded leather so that when it connected with stone, the hook would not clang or rattle, but make no more sound than a dull thud.

Of course, with the alarm claxon sounding and the shouts of the men in the courtyard, Malden thought it unlikely that he would be heard if he were beating a drum. But it never hurt to be quiet.

He paid out a long double length of rope through the ring in the grapple's haft, then started to swing it back and forth. When he had the momentum right, he made his toss and watched it arc through the moonlight to kiss the palace roof. It slid for a while, then came to a stop.

Slowly, he drew it back to him by tugging on the doubled rope, twitching it now and again to try to get the hook to catch on a chimney pot or the leg of a gargoyle. The best purchase it found was in the join between two lead roof tiles. It wasn't as secure as he might have liked, but he thought it would hold his weight. Though he tugged and yanked at the rope to make sure, there was only one way to test the grapple's hold. He took the two ends of the rope and tied them tight around the nearest crenellation of the wall. Then he climbed out onto the rope—and hung from it like a monkey, crossing his legs around it and holding on with both hands so his back dangled toward the Burgrave's rose garden, twenty feet below.

The rope sagged a bit but held. Malden exhaled all the air in his lungs. He made his way across hand over hand, sliding his feet forward as he went. In short order he was able to clamber up onto the roof of the palace, where he waited a moment for his heart to stop racing. Then he recovered his grapple and his rope. By doubling the line and tying it off, he'd made a very long loop and was able to pull on one side of the rope until the knot came to his hands. It was a simple matter to untie the knot, then draw the whole rope toward him until he could coil it around his waist. He would have much preferred to leave it in place, and thus have a ready escape route, but couldn't dare leave it where it might be discovered. Looking down into the courtyard, he could see that the soldiers were already extending their search to the northern part of the fortress—it would not be long before they came to search the wall where he had just been.

The diversion had served its purpose well enough. Yet now it was having the opposite effect. Before Bikker started peppering the place with arrows, probably the bulk of the guards had been asleep or otherwise distracted. Now every man in the palace grounds was wide-awake and looking for a furtive trespasser. Malden knew that if they caught him, they would assume he was the phantom bowman—and would kill him before he could even speak in his defense. He cursed Bikker under his breath. Getting in had been easy enough: all told, simply a matter of the strength in his fingers and a little talent at throwing a hook. Getting out would be a great deal harder.

He might as well make it worth his while. Just below him, on the top floor of the palace, a balcony projected from the wall. He could see no lights down there, so he dropped easily to the railing, then pushed open the doors and darted inside.

# CHAPTER EIGHTEEN

Malden found himself in a small bedroom that looked like it belonged to a lady-in-waiting, with a canopied bed and a large clothing chest. Rushes were strewn on the floor and perfume had been sprinkled around liberally to hide any odors. There was no one inside, so he hurried to the door and pressed his ear against the keyhole. When he was sure no one was patrolling the corridor outside, he slipped out the door and down a hallway lit with oil lamps.

Cythera had told him that what he sought was in the

tower, on the same level as this top floor of the palace. "It is in a room that once served as the first Burgrave's bedchamber. It is placed there every night while the current Burgrave sleeps. Beware: it will be guarded well." One layer of its defense, at least, had been removed. Malden imagined that normally this hallway would have been full of soldiers, but Bikker's diversion had drawn them to the courtyard.

"They'll be away from their posts, but don't think that's the only way to guard a treasure. Men at arms are too easily overcome. Walls can be climbed, and locks picked. The Burgrave knows as much. So he'll have other defenses waiting for you."

He had paid close attention to her words. Now, he kept his eyelids stretched as he hurried down the corridor and around the el of the building, into the wing that led to the tower room. As he approached the door at its end he was already unraveling the grip of his bodkin and removing his picks and wrenches. A lock with a dead bolt had been built into the massive iron-bound door, but it gave him little trouble.

"Will there be spells on it, enchantments of protection?" he had asked.

"Unlikely. Magic is too unreliable under the best of circumstances. Not to mention expensive to maintain. No, it is not the handiwork of enchanters you need fear. It is the work of dwarves."

Beyond the door lay a corridor perhaps twenty-five feet long. Tall windows stood every ten feet or so down its length, and moonlight spilled in to form pools of silver on the wooden floor. Between each patch of light lay impenetrable shadows. It was as if the hall were one column of a game board with alternating spaces of light and dark.

"I cannot tell you what traps you may find," Cythera had said. "I can only tell you to beware any room that seems unused. The palace is a busy and a crowded place, so dust on a floor, or rooms that seem completely empty, are avoided for a reason."

There were no doors leading off the moonlit corridor, nor any furniture within it. At its far end he could just see the glint of something metallic. Malden stayed outside, beyond the door, and pondered what lay before him. No dust lay on the floor here, at least none he could see in the pale light. Yet there was a sense about the corridor, a feeling of distinct absence he couldn't quite explain. It didn't have the feel of a place that was used often. Ness was an old city, overcrowded even in its infancy. Every stone had been touched by a million hands over the years, every wall brushed by clothing until it was smooth and worn. This hallway, in contrast, looked as if it had been just constructed—by skilled and masterful hands.

Which of course was the hallmark of a dwarf's handiwork. Yes. This was the place.

Cythera had been quite clear. "There are more than three score dwarves living in this city. Their services are sought by all the wealthiest citizens, for they alone can build the cunning devices which are proof against thieves and murderers in the night. A human engineer might devise these fiendish pitfalls, but only a dwarf could build them. The Burgrave will have employed the services of the best among them, and the traps he has laid will be of unusual cunning and danger."

Well, he had a dwarf on his side, as well. Slag had raised an eyebrow when told what he required, but then, for the first time, Cutbill's dwarf had looked at him with something other than disdain. It wasn't exactly respect he had seen glowing in the dwarf's eyes, but it was at least an acceptance that he wasn't a complete fool.

Malden reached into a pouch at his belt and took out a lead ball wrapped in leather. It was as heavy as a cobblestone in his hand. With an underhand motion he rolled the ball down the hallway, then quickly took a step back from the doorway.

For a moment he felt quite foolish, like a boy playing games in an alley. The ball rolled merrily along through the first pool of moonlight, then disappeared into the darkness beyond.

Malden's heart pounded, however, when a moment later a portcullis gate crashed down from the ceiling, right where his leaden ball was rolling. Six long bars of iron crashed down and smashed into the floor.

He did not so much as breathe as he watched them slowly retract back into the ceiling. There was the ratcheting sound of a spring reloading itself, and then a click as the portcullis snapped back into place.

He peered through the half-dark hallway. The leaden ball he'd rolled was pierced right through its middle, nearly cleaved in two by one of the falling iron spears. Its end must have been razor sharp.

He took another ball from his pouch and threw it with a little more force this time, lofting it so it landed in the midst of the second pool of moonlight. It bounced once, without triggering anything, then rolled into another patch of shadow. A second portcullis identical to the first crashed down, jarring his senses.

"There will be a way through," Cythera had told him. "Every night the castellan must bring the treasure to the tower room, and every morning he must recover it. For his convenience, the route must not be impossible, nor even onerous. If you know the trick of it, it should be quite easy to make your way through the traps."

And now Malden thought he had the lay of the thing. The floor was rigged, designed to register any amount of weight that fell on it, but only in the dark sections. Those touched by moonlight would be safe. He got a good run-up, then jumped into the hallway, bounding from one pool of light to the next, careful to never let his feet touch any patch of shadow. One leap, two—he was feeling very pleased with himself for figuring it out—a third leap, directly to the final pool of moonlight at the corridor's end. And that was when he remembered something else Cythera had said.

"These traps are not made to be circumvented, they are made to kill thieves. The dwarf who designs them will know what you are thinking, and will find ways to confound your logic, to surprise you when you least expect it."

Despite heeding her advice in all other things, he was still not ready when his feet came down on the final pool of moonlight—and the floor gave way. A trapdoor there had been set to hinge open when any weight fell on it, and though Malden was slender and short of stature, he was more than heavy enough to trigger it.

# CHAPTER NINETEEN

Malden's feet kicked wildly at nothing as his body dropped like a stone into the pit. His blood sang in his ears and his heart galloped in his chest as he felt himself falling, plummeting. It was all he could do to keep a shriek from bursting out of him. His arms flailed out to his sides for balance and his fingers just barely grasped the edge of the pit. His body slammed forward into the wall of the pit, and that hurt so much it made him gasp and lose the grip of one hand.

But the other one held.

Gasping to refill his lungs, his face pressed up tight against the pit wall, he glanced down. There was a flickering light from below, not enough to see much but it showed him that it was a very, very long way down if he let go.

Carefully he reached up and grasped the lip of the pit with both hands. His fingers protested at taking all his weight. They were still sore and swollen from the long climb up the palace wall from the Skrait. He ignored their pain.

From below a distant sound came up, echoing in the shaft of the pit so it sounded distorted and hollow. Yet he could not mistake it: a scream of agony. It was followed by the noise of a great wheel turning, and then more sounds of pain. The pit must lead straight down to the dungeon, far below the palace. Should he fall now, he would be saving the Burgrave the trouble of having guards drag him thence.

He doubted very much there was a pile of soft straw at the bottom either.

Very, very slowly he pulled himself up and out of the pit. Once he had a shoulder above its edge it was much easier, and once he had a leg up and out of the shaft, he was able to just roll out and lie on the floor a moment. He was about to spread out his aching arms when he realized that would put his hand down in one of the shadowy zones of the hallway floor.

He was very fond of that hand. He did not wish to see it pierced by a razor-sharp iron spear. So he kept it by his side and just shook for a while, letting the fear drain out of him. He had expected danger on this job—any burglary was a risky proposition. He had never met such devious hazards before, though. Well, he supposed that should be expected, considering the value of the thing he'd come to steal.

Eventually he recovered his feet and stood up, at the end of the hall.

He must be very close to the tower room he sought. It must indeed lie beyond the very wall ahead of him. Yet he saw no door. Instead he found a niche that held a bronze statue of Sadu, the Bloodgod.

He searched the wall around the niche, looking for some hidden panel that would open to admit him to the tower. He could find none. He tapped the wall with the pommel of his bodkin, thinking to find any kind of hollow or thin place in the wall through which he might break through, but the wall seemed to be made of solid stone, of the same thickness throughout.

It was only after this exhaustive and pointless search that he chose to look at the floor, and noticed an obvious seam in the wood. The crack formed a semicircle five feet in diameter. He was standing within its bound, in fact. He tapped the floor in several places but found it as solid as the wall. Perhaps—yes, perhaps this was a door after all. If somehow the floor could be made to rotate, and the whole wall with it . . . but there must be some trigger, some way of activating the change.

The statue of the Bloodgod, of course.

The Burgrave was known to be a devout of the Lady of Abundance. Sadu was a much older god, one whose worship was not officially forbidden in the Free City but certainly frowned upon. The Bloodgod was the patron deity of the poor and the oppressed, a symbol of ultimate justice and even vindictive revenge. Sadu punished all men alike in the afterlife, and each according to his sins. He was hardly the sort of god a man like the Burgrave would ever want to meet.

The Bloodgod did have eight arms, though, and that leant itself to the obvious purpose of this particular idol.

The bronze statue depicted Sadu in the typical fashion, as he was worshipped in tiny shrines all over the city. The idol had seven arms on the left side of its body, each holding a different weapon: a sword, a falchion, a spear, a trident, a net, a flail, and an arrow. Different images of the Bloodgod always had different weapons in his hands, since Sadu was the master of them all. On the right side he had only one arm, holding an ornate crown, as it always did. Sadu's face was depicted as that of a snarling demon with massive tusklike teeth and wide, staring eyes. Malden had seen more terrifying versions, though this was a common depiction. Yet as he examined the statue quite carefully he noticed two things that were unique to this image in all his experience.

For one, the eyes were not just open—they had been hollowed out. Two sharp points of metal glinted from within their depths. Malden thought of the needles that sprang from Cutbill's lock. Perhaps these were the same—or worse, tiny darts that would fly through the air to poison him if they pierced his flesh. And of course this time the poison would be fatal.

The second thing he noticed was that all eight arms of the Bloodgod were attached to the body by stout hinges. One could move them, if one desired, independently from the rest of the statue.

Clearly he would have to push the correct arm to open the way to the tower room, while pushing any other would result in instant death.

He rejected the crown arm immediately. It was far too obvious.

Of the weapon arms, the net appealed to him first. It was the least deadly of the weapons, while the others could all kill you easily. The arrow was a bit confusing—it really should have been a bow Sadu held, should it not? But the arrow was also very similar to the darts hidden in the eyes.

Yet wouldn't that appeal to some dwarf artificer's twisted sense of irony? Perhaps you pushed the arrow arm to say you did not wish the darts to fire.

It was a gamble, but it seemed most likely. Malden stood well back of the statue, but still within the circular seam on the floor, and reached over to tap at the arm that held the arrow. Nothing happened. He applied more pressure, bending the arm backward.

There was a rumbling of massive gears, a shrieking of poorly oiled metal—and then the whole wall swung on its axis, propelling him directly into the tower room. The place where the Burgrave kept his crown when he wasn't wearing it.

# CHAPTER TWENTY

"You're—You're mad," Malden had said two days before, when Cythera finally revealed what she was after. "The crown of the Burgrave? What possible reason could you have to steal *that*? Why would anyone? If I'm caught with it, I'd be drawn and quartered!"

"You needn't be caught, if you stick to our plan," Cythera said. Though he could see in her eyes that she knew no plan was ever perfect, that events could always conspire to catch a thief. She was asking him to take an enormous risk.

"But—why? It's made of gold, to be sure, but it's only so big. Melted down, it isn't worth a tenth of what you're paying. And you would have to melt it down. No fence would ever touch it. If you so much as showed it to a fence, they would have no choice but to call in the watch."

"We have our reasons for wanting it. Intact," Cythera said.

"As soon as it goes missing, every watchman in the city will come looking for it." Malden shook his head. "They'll tear down the Stink looking for it, and for *me*. I don't—"

"No, they won't," Bikker said. He'd been standing by the fire, staring down into the flames. They danced in his eyes like light from the Bloodgod's pit. He came clanking over to where Malden sat and loomed over him, his face split by a grin. "That's the best part. As you say, there's not much to the crown on its own. A good goldsmith can make a replacement in a day. If the Burgrave appears in public without the crown even once, he'll look a fool. Everyone will ask where it is, and what will he say? That he just forgot to put it on that morning?"

Malden had to admit he had never seen the Burgrave without it.

"That's the heart of the plan," Bikker said, thumping the back of Malden's chair so he nearly fell out of it. "Do you see? He and his advisors will be too embarrassed by its absence to say a word. They won't call out the watch—they'll keep this a secret, from everyone they can. They will never let it be known, anywhere, that the crown was ever stolen. They won't even dare to come looking for it, because then they'd have to tell the watch what to look for. Do you really believe every watchman in the city would keep such a thing secret? No, the bailiff and the Burgrave will just pretend it was never stolen. They'll trot out a replacement, and that will be the end of it."

Bikker squatted down in front of Malden and cuffed him lightly on the shoulder. Just hard enough to leave marks. "So what do you say?" he asked, his eyes bright. "Are you the man for this job?"

# CHAPTER TWENTY-ONE

The crown—technically a coronet—was not a work of great art in itself. It was a plain circlet of gold, crenellated in the same pattern as the Free City's walls. No jewels adorned it, nor was it lined in fur, nor was anything engraved upon it. It was the crown of a leader of free men, not a king who ruled serfs, and so it was not meant to glorify unduly its wearer or set him apart from the common weal.

Honestly, to Malden it looked a little cheap. Even the head of the fuller's guild wore more ceremonial gold than was in the city's coronet.

But of course the crown had far more symbolic value. It could only be worn by a Burgrave. It was the symbol of his lordship, the image of his right to rule the city as he pleased. It was what separated him from the citizens, what imbued him with all of his power. The Burgrave wore it every time he went out in public—when he led civic processions, when he sat to watch a tourney, when he handed down judgments in the law courts. He'd worn it the day Malden saw him in Market Square, the day he'd condemned that blond fool to death. The crown *was* the Burgrave's power.

Malden was dimly aware in his untutored way that he lived in a kingdom called Skrae, that beyond the Free City's walls there was a grand feudal system of nobility with, at its head, a single monarch who had granted the city its charter and appointed the Burgrave's great-great-etcetera-grandfather to be the city's ultimate ruler. He had never paid taxes to that particular king, and had certainly never seen him. Even the portrait stamped on the larger denominations of money in the Free City was not that of the king, but of one of said king's distant ancestors. Inside the city's walls, the Burgrave was the only power that mattered, and Malden didn't care a jot for anything outside them.

The Burgrave ruled by the authority invested in the crown. A thief who could take the crown away would be sending a message: that the Burgrave's authority was not sacrosanct. That in Ness, in the so-called Free City, every man was vulnerable and no man was truly better—superior—to another.

Malden kind of liked that idea. He'd grown up the son of a whore, a man with no status whatsoever. A man who wasn't even respectable enough to clean the Burgrave's privy. That he could strike such a blow was a great triumph for the equality of men. It would be justice, of a sort. Of course, no one could ever know that he had achieved the theft, more's the pity.

As for the Burgrave, how much would he pay to keep its theft a secret? Surely that was the point of this ridiculous scheme. To extort the Burgrave for as much as his position was worth. It was certainly a dangerous plan, no matter what Bikker said, but still it seemed like it could be quite lucrative.

Malden was now close enough to the crown to reach out and grab it. The tower room was almost empty. Its walls were lined with old campaign banners and tattered flags. Its floor was strewn with sand that ground noisily under his feet. Of furniture, the room possessed a single piece, set exactly in its center: a simple stone pedestal, atop which sat a crystal bowl three feet in diameter.

The bowl was full to its brim with clear water. Inside the bowl, magnified strangely by its curvature, was the crown—and something else.

Cythera had given him one last piece of advice when they planned this theft together. "Such a treasure will always be guarded, of course. It cannot be left alone and unsupervised at any time. Yet I doubt you will find human guardians inside the chamber. Most likely it will be some variety of cursed beast or even a demon, bound to the defense of the crown. Such a creature will perhaps be the hardest obstacle you must overcome."

"Is this what you meant?" Malden asked now, whispering to himself as he watched the thing in the bowl squirm around in its tiny prison. It was a pulpy thing, with leprous skin and long boneless arms. It looked somewhat like an octopus, though it had no head that he could see, nor suckers on its tentacles. A particularly flexible starfish, perhaps.

Malden could easily have held it in his hand. As he watched, it writhed its way through the crown, wrapping one oozing arm around the golden band. He supposed, if he were feeling especially fearful (and he was, after his near brush with the pit in the corridor outside), that the beast might possess deadly venom. Or teeth—somewhere—sharp enough to take his finger at the joint, should he be so foolish as to reach into the bowl with a bare hand.

He had a better idea. He took the grappling hook from where it hung on his belt and paid out a few feet of rope. Then he dipped the hook into the bowl and fished for the crown. The spineless creature attacked the hook immediately, grasping at it with all of its legs at once, thrashing so hard at this intruder that it caused the bowl to rock back and forth on its pedestal. Malden tried to pull the hook free but the little monster's grip was strong as steel. Struggling against it merely aggravated the bowl's swaying motion.

"Release, you tiny bastard," he grunted, and yanked the hook free of its assailant. It came clear—but not without knocking the bowl completely off its perch. It fell from the far side of the pedestal and crashed upon the sandy floor with a noise so enormous that Malden was certain it must have alerted half the guards on Castle Hill.

He held his breath. He closed his eyes to try to hear better. No shout came to his ears, however, nor any sound of men rushing toward the tower. When he was certain it was safe, he opened his eyes and stepped around the pedestal to retrieve the crown.

The tentacle creature still had it, however, gripped in one unsolid arm. It flopped impotently on the floor in the wreckage of its bowl and a puddle of water that was already soaking into the sand. It was strange—but had the thing not looked smaller when it was in the bowl? Now it was larger than the crown it held, whereas before it had appeared smaller.

No matter. Malden drew his bodkin from its sheath. He did not wish to have it sting or bite him, so he supposed he would have to just kill it and take its prize by force. Not the way he normally chose to operate, but—

It was definitely bigger. Even as he watched, it seemed to swell. It was hard to say for certain with such an amorphous blob of a creature, but he was certain it was as big now as a dog. One of its flailing arms brushed across his shoe and he jumped back. It was like a sponge, which grows when full of water, Malden thought. With every squirming undulation of its being, it seemed to expand in size. Its arms were long enough to grasp the top of the pedestal, now. To grab Malden's belt if he wasn't careful.

He stepped quickly around it, looking for something to stab. It had no head, nor any eyes, nor even a body in the proper sense. It was more like a clutch of snakes all tied together in knots than a singular being. He took a swipe at one of its arms and connected but did it no injury—its flesh was rubbery and shied away from the point of his bodkin without so much as a scratch appearing on its mottled skin.

Not like a sponge placed in water, he realized, but the opposite. Water kept the foul thing in a manageable size, hence the crystal bowl. When it was exposed to air instead, it swelled—and the larger it got, the faster it seemed to grow.

It was as big as a horse suddenly. Much bigger than himself. Its arms smashed across his shoulder, his knee, his face. Battered and confused, Malden staggered backward, back against one wall.

The thing grabbed him around the waist and *squeezed*.

# CHAPTER TWENTY-TWO

Bile rushed up Malden's throat and his head swam. The breath exploded out of him and he nearly let go of his bodkin. The demon's arm throbbed around his midsection and constricted his guts until he thought for sure he would be pinched in half.

Then it picked him up off the floor and slammed him against the ceiling of the tower room. His vision went black for a moment and when he came to his ears were ringing like bells.

It had grown still larger, until it nearly filled the room. Its myriad arms waved limply in the air and slapped against the stone walls. One of its arms still held the crown, gripped carefully in a thin twist of flesh. It held the thing well clear of Malden's reach, even if he'd had the presence of mind to make a grab for it.

Malden stabbed wildly around him with the bodkin, but even when his knife struck true it merely sank into the pulpy flesh, then came out again without leaving so much as a mark on the creature's arms. The thing was sickeningly fluid, barely solid enough to keep a form, it seemed. Yet where it held him, its muscles were like ropes of steel. The thing was . . . unnatural. Unworldly.

Now Malden understood why the room was guarded by a statue of the Bloodgod. This was no natural beast. It must be a very demon, loosed from out of Sadu's pit of souls. It did not belong in the world of light and air. Whatever sorcerer had summoned it from its natural environment must have understood that. He or she must have known that it would grow, and continue to grow, when exposed to air. They had placed it in the crystal bowl of water to keep its size small. If he could submerge it again in water, perhaps it would shrink once more and—

It thrust him against the walls again and again, trying to

batter him to death. For a while he could not think or even see clearly as he was lashed against the flags and banners that lined the walls of the tower room. Pennons and standards crashed to the floor as his body knocked them free of their pegs. His left shoulder struck the stone wall hard and went instantly numb, and he could barely feel his legs.

*Water—there must be some water—somewhere—*

He could hardly think straight. He could hardly think at all. There had been water in the bowl, but it soaked into the sand that covered the floor. That must be what the sand was there for. The river was nearby, if he could somehow trick the beast into climbing over the wall and falling into the canyon beyond—but how he would manage that when he could not free himself from its grip was past his imagining.

*Water! He must have it! He—*

He had no water. But he had wine. The flask at his belt was still half full. Would it have the same effect on the creature? He could not be sure.

The beast had grown still larger. It filled the tower room entire now, and was crushing him against the walls with its bulk. As it waved its arms around, it smashed the stones to powder—its arms were as thick around as tree trunks now. Would it keep growing, would it grow so large it burst the walls of the tower? Would that be enough to kill it, when the upper stories of the tower collapsed upon it?

Malden doubted it. But he was certain of one thing—he, himself, would never survive such a collapse.

There was no more time for thinking. He reached around the tentacle at his waist and grabbed the flask of wine. It was leather sewn together with gut, the seams worked with wax to make them waterproof. It sloshed as he lifted it up to see it. When he bought the thing, he'd chosen shrewdly, picking a vessel that wouldn't leak, that would stand up to rough treatment. Now he cursed himself that he hadn't just bought some cheap skin he could burst with one hand. The damned flask was too sturdy. He brought his bodkin around and stabbed it. Wine squirted out of the hole he'd made and red drops ran down the back of his hand.

One drop fell onto the beast's skin. The arm that held

him pulsed wildly and he was thrown hither and yon, but the grip around his waist eased a trifle. Yes! The wine had some effect on the thing. He held the flask toward the tentacle and squeezed it as hard as he could, spraying wine all over its pulpy flesh.

Suddenly, blood rushed down into his legs and they burned with new sensation. His guts relaxed inside his abdomen and he belched as his stomach nearly loosed its contents. He squeezed the flask again and he was free, flying through the air as if the demon had thrown him like a ball.

The wall of the tower came toward him very fast, and he nearly crashed into it head first. He threw his arms up in front of him and managed to catch the wall with his sore fingers and then cling there like a spider before he fell back into the demon's arms.

Below him the beast thrashed like a mad thing, bashing against the walls convulsively. Stone crumbled and shattered and pulverized. A wide crack opened in the wall and then a whole section of the tower's stonework fell away, letting in a rush of cold night air.

The tentacles snapped at Malden's ankles and back, trying to get a grip, but they were slow and he was able to avoid being grabbed up once again. The main problem he faced was that the beast had grown so large there was precious little room in the tower it didn't fill, little enough that Malden had to press himself against the wall to keep from being crushed by its sheer bulk.

More of the wall fell away. The tower above began to groan as its timbers shifted, no longer able to support the weight. The tower that stood for so many centuries, that seemed eternal, now lurched and swayed like a ship in a gale. In a moment the room would collapse and he would be crushed. He had escaped one gruesome fate only to befall another, it seemed. And yet—perhaps—

Malden looked down and saw that he was very close to the statue of Sadu that was the secret lock to this room. The creature had enough respect for its creator, it seemed, not to smash the idol or even brush it with its tentacles. Malden waited until the tentacles were as far from him as possible, then dropped to his feet next to the image. He wasted no time pushing down on the arm-lever that controlled the door.

The pivoting section of floor and wall began to turn, and Malden readied himself to dash through it as it revealed the moonlit hallway beyond. Yet when the wall had swiveled only a few degrees through its arc, with only a sliver of moonlight coming through from the other side, the motion stopped.

The cause was immediately apparent. The tentacled beast's mass was pressing against the wall, keeping it from swinging open. Malden pushed at the wall, trying to force it to open, trying to squeeze his shoulders through the small gap, but to no avail. "No!" he screamed at it. "Get back, you infernal bastard! Let me go!"

The beast made no response but to redouble its thrashing motion. Malden laid into it with his bodkin, stabbing and thrusting wildly at its ever-moving arms. It was no use, though, because the thing was *still* growing, still expanding to fill more and ever more of the available space—

—and then the tower began to rumble, as if it were being shaken to pieces. Rock dust sifted down from the ceiling and the stone walls began to give way.

# CHAPTER TWENTY-THREE

A great crashing noise stopped Croy in his tracks. "That came from the palace," he whispered. "From the tower—did it not? And so soon after those two men were killed. Something's wrong here."

Hilde grasped his hand and dragged him farther into the

shadows beside the kitchens. "It's nothing to do with me or you. Come quickly. We can't let the guards see you here."

Croy held his ground, though, as another thunderous sound issued from the tower. The edifice began to shake and a block of stone fell from its top to crack the flagstones below. Then a fissure appeared in the side of the tower, about halfway up. The men of the watch who were out in force in the courtyard all turned to look as one, and there was a cry of surprise and alarm that could be heard even over the ear-shattering klaxon.

"It's going to collapse," he said, just before the tower's wall exploded outward, showering the courtyard with broken chunks of stone. The upper floors of the tower tottered over with a most horrible slowness, then all at once collapsed in a massive cloud of dust and debris. The watch were everywhere at once, shouting and calling for each other, for the guards, for anyone who was close enough to help.

"There might have been people in there," Croy said, turning toward the lady-in-waiting. "Hilde, you go seek shelter in the—" He didn't bother to finish, as she was already gone. She hadn't stopped to let him save her, but instead ran for dear life. Well, that was probably wise. He hoped she would find safety, and quickly. She might be a little confused, but she was a good woman at heart and he wished her luck.

The moral qualities of ladies-in-waiting was suddenly less important to Croy, though, than the groaning rumble that shook the very mass of Castle Hill and threatened to knock him off his feet, as the tower collapsed further and massive stones went bouncing and rolling across the courtyard.

Was it an earthquake? He'd never heard of such a thing in the Free City. Perhaps some sorcerer had attacked the palace? But Hazoth was the only sorcerer in a hundred miles who had the power for such a thing, and this hardly seemed like his handiwork. Croy drew the smaller of his two swords and made to run for the tower, either to rescue anyone inside the ruin or to slay whoever had knocked the tower down, he wasn't exactly sure which. He got no more than two steps, however, before a hand wrapped in chain mail grabbed his baldric. It threw him off balance and his sword went flying.

He rolled across the flagstones and got his elbows under him, bending his knees so he could leap back to his feet. Then an all-too-familiar face loomed out of the shadows and put a boot on his chest. The big swordsman pressed down hard enough that Croy could barely breathe.

Bikker.

Croy could hardly believe his eyes. He'd known, certainly, that the two of them would meet again. It was destiny. But here? At this time? It seemed fantastic.

"What in the name of Sadu's flaming arse are you doing here?" Bikker asked.

Croy could only stare up at the massive warrior. "I might ask you the same."

"I live here. This is my city," Bikker snarled.

"I meant—"

"I find myself in no position to answer your questions, Croy. But I will have answers to mine. I say again, what are you doing here? You were banished from Ness, never to return. I remember it well, since I was the one tasked with riding you out of the city gates on a rail."

Croy remembered that moment himself. The rail had been tied to the back of Bikker's horse at the time. He had been left bruised and abraded ten miles north of the city with nothing but his swords—even his clothes were ruined by the rough treatment.

"I returned for Cythera, of course," Croy said. "Once I have guaranteed her safety and her freedom, and once I take care of a few other standing engagements, I'll leave in peace. You have my word."

"Doubtful," Bikker said. "Oh, don't look so shocked. I know you're telling the truth. I also know that by 'standing engagements' you mean me. You mean my death. And since that's not likely to happen, well . . . Never mind. Tell me what you're doing here, tonight. Your presence is most inconvenient to my plans."

In the courtyard something crashed to the ground with a thud that shook Croy's teeth in his skull. He tried to rise and see what had happened but Bikker just pressed him down again.

He decided the best way to recover his feet was to answer Bikker. "I came to get my swords back. The Burgrave took them from me when he sentenced me to death. I imagine you were there at my hanging—surely you wouldn't have missed that."

"I had to leave early," Bikker said. He wasn't looking at Croy, but at the ruins of the tower. "I hear it didn't end well."

"Oh?" Croy asked.

"You got away. Croy, please do me a favor and keep reaching for the hilt of Ghostcutter. Please, please, try to draw your sword. It will give me the excuse I need to hack you to pieces right now."

Croy opened his hands wide and stretched them out at his sides. He had known Bikker for a long time. He was quite certain the man was willing to stab him where he lay on the ground, to take his life without the slightest shred of honor or dignity. And yet . . . he hadn't so far. He had every opportunity but still let him live. Was it just because Bikker wanted information? Or was it possible there was something still alive in Bikker, some shred of the honor he'd cast off like a stained tunic?

"Surely Hazoth didn't send you here to kill me," Croy said. "He could not have known I was here—unless he has been following my movements with a spell."

Bikker snorted in derision. "The wizard? I doubt he even remembers your name. He has no interest in you one way or another. He *has* ordered me to be discreet when I'm out in the city. Which is enough to save your life, at least for tonight. Blind me, what is that thing?"

Croy turned his head to look as best he was able at the fresh ruins. He gasped at what he saw. It was as if a nest of gigantic blind asps or equally large worms had been crammed inside one room of the tower and now they were writhing and striking at the air. Yet by the way they moved in concert, he could tell it was a single beast with many arms. Some of its numerous appendages grabbed at the fallen rocks in the courtyard and threw them at the guards that rushed toward it. Other sinuous limbs pushed against what remained of the tower as it tried to drag its enormous bulk out into the night. It made no sound other than a wet slithering.

"Fiend from the pit, do you think?" Bikker asked, with professional interest.

"Or a sorcerous abomination, at the very least," Croy confirmed. A thought occurred to him. Maybe he had a way of getting back on his feet. "Between Ghostcutter and Acidtongue, we'd stand a chance against it."

"Just like old times, hmm?" Bikker asked. "Is that what you're thinking?" He pulled at his beard, the way he always did when he was unable to make a decision. Croy understood, despite himself. The old times had never seemed older. Yet the two of them took an oath once, an oath on their souls. Such things died hard.

"That, and that we could save a number of innocent lives," Croy said.

"Bah," Bikker said, but Croy could tell his heart wasn't fully in the disdain.

The guards and the men of the watch were already peppering the demon with arrows. The missiles seemed without effect, so a detachment of guards were approaching it with halberds at the ready. As they watched, a tentacle lashed out and threw one poor guardsman half across the courtyard. The man landed in a crump of dented mail and broken bones from which he did not rise.

"Both you and I have good reason to flee this place before our faces are seen," Bikker said.

"And better reason to stay," Croy insisted. "When was the last time Acidtongue did what it was made for? A bloodied sword—"

"Is a sword that doesn't rust," Bikker finished. He looked disgusted for a moment. Disgusted, perhaps, with himself. Then he took his boot off Croy's chest and offered him a hand up.

# CHAPTER TWENTY-FOUR

It was all Malden could do to hold on. His strength was no match for the demon's, even with half its arms crushed under the fallen tower.

But he would not let go of the crown.

In the last moment before the tower collapsed, Malden's luck had returned in trumps. The doorway that had been jammed shut by the demon's bulk collapsed in front of him, its stones shattered by the creature's thrashing. Suddenly the way back to the moonlit corridor was open—and he was given a chance at survival.

He had nearly squandered it. Because even as the tower was collapsing over his head, when the stone was shrieking and roaring and smashing all around him, he heard a voice calling him. A voice of authority that demanded respect. A voice that could have commanded nations.

*Thief*, the voice had said. And that was all. It had not been his ears that heard the voice, of that he was certain. Though it sounded exactly like someone shouting just behind him, he knew the voice was inside his head.

He turned away from escape and safety to see who had spoken. It was not the demon—the thing had no voice, and even if it could speak, it would not have sounded like that. It was a human voice. Which meant, absurd as it might sound, that it was the crown that spoke. The simple golden coronet of the Burgrave.

Malden's childhood had been full of tales of statues that could speak, and of talking animals that were secretly men under the curses of dire sorcery. Those were simple tales, made to entertain. Yet magic was real enough. He was almost willing to accept that a crown could talk, even if he hadn't heard it himself.

When it spoke again, all doubts flew away.

*Thief, do not let me be entombed here.*

Malden reached out then, heedless of the demon's thrashing arms, and grabbed the crown out of the air. The fact that a slender tentacle was still wrapped around its other side did not matter. When that voice spoke, something inside Malden had no choice but to listen. He had grasped the crown, and then thrown himself clear of the collapsing tower, into the trapped palace corridor beyond. When the earth stopped shaking and the demon was crushed under a dozen tons of broken stone, Malden found himself lying on the floor dazed and bruised but with the fingers of one hand still clutching the crown.

He looked up to see the corridor transfixed. When the tower came down it must have shaken the entire palace like an earthquake. The vibrations had been enough to trigger every one of the traps in the corridor. The portcullises were all down, their spear points embedded in the floor. No matter how long he watched them, they did not retract—the delicate springs that controlled them must have snapped. He was trapped inside the corridor, between a massive pile of rock debris and a portcullis that looked uncomfortably like a set of prison bars.

He tried to rise carefully to his feet, intent on figuring out what to do next. "You wouldn't have any clever ideas, would you, crown?" he asked the thing in his hand. It did not answer—perhaps it only gave commands, and did not accept them. He started to dust himself off and consider his plight.

Which was when he was yanked off his feet again, to fall painfully to the floor. He looked in horror at the crown and saw that he was not the only one still holding onto it. The demon's slender tentacle was still wrapped around it in an unbreakable grip.

Slowly, with jerks and starts, the tentacle began to withdraw back into the pile of broken stone. The damned thing was still alive—and intent on keeping its treasure.

But so was Malden. He grabbed the crown with both hands and braced his feet against the pile of debris. He pulled with all his might, heedless if he bent the crown in the process. The muscles in his skinny arms bunched and tightened like lengths of rope, and he gritted his teeth as sweat broke out on his brow. It was certainly a losing battle. The demon was many times stronger than he was, he knew. As it tugged at the crown he felt the power in its gelatinous muscles straining against him. But Malden had heard that voice. The voice that could send men to their deaths, and make them believe they went only to glory.

He refused to let go.

# CHAPTER TWENTY-FIVE

Croy's blood thrummed with excitement, as if his veins were harp strings plucked by righteousness. As he and Bikker approached the fiend they were laughing. Each drew his sword, and the very air seemed to throb with potential.

The blades were made for one purpose alone. It had been a long time since they'd had a chance to perform that function.

Acidtongue seethed in Bikker's hand, its pitted metal slick with power. Ghostcutter leapt from Croy's sheath and shone in the moonlight like a torch of might. Croy's sword had no magic in it—instead, it had been made to cut *through* magic. Its blade was as long as Croy's arm, made of cold-forged iron as black as the pit. No man now alive—nor any dwarf—remembered the method of its manufacture: alone in the world, it possessed its special characteristics. One edge had been honed to razor sharpness, and had to be specially ground out when it dulled—no heat could be applied to the blade or the iron would lose its special properties. Silver had been fused along the other edge, carefully poured along the cutting surface to make a uniform coating. Trails and runnels of the silver streaked the central ridge and fuller like the drippings of candle wax. The iron edge did more damage to demons than the best steel ever could, while the silver could disrupt magic spells and curses, and, aye, even cut the ectoplasmic flesh of a ghost. It was a potent weapon, and it had served Croy well on more occasions than he could count. He knew its every peculiarity, had learned its balance and its heft so thoroughly that when he held it, Ghostcutter became an extension of his arm—an extension of his desire for justice and the right.

In many ways he thought of himself as an extension of Ghostcutter, instead of vice versa. The sword had a destiny, and a longer span of life than Croy ever would.

Now he waded straight into the arms of the demon, flourishing the sword above his head, totally without fear. He brought the iron edge down with a strong overhead swing that should have sliced one of the demon's tentacles in half.

Except that it didn't.

The rubbery tissue scorched where the iron blade touched it—the stench was overpowering—but it was like trying to cut water. The sword went through without resistance but the flesh simply flowed around it. Croy shouted his defiance and swung again, this time a low, sideways cut that could have cleaved a man in half at the waist. The tentacle before him split open—so it could be cut!—but oozed away from the stroke even before Croy had followed through.

He had failed to harm the demon much, but succeeded in one thing: he had gotten its attention. A tentacle lashed toward him even as he was recovering from his attack and wrapped itself around his neck like a living whipcord. There was no time to parry, much less dodge out of its way. In the Lady's sacred name the thing was fast.

The fleshy rope was dry and its skin was cracked, as if it had been exposed to the hot sun of the desert for days. It smelled of corruption and vileness, and had the consistency of a custard. At least, until it constricted. Then it felt like an iron chain lashed around Croy's throat.

A second tentacle wrapped around his thigh and staggered him. It yanked backward, and it was all Croy could do to keep his feet. The fiend would pull him down if he did not find some way to break its grasp. Croy struck at this second arm with his blade, but it held resolute, even as the cold-forged iron seared its skin.

The tentacle around his throat constricted until he felt his throat start to crush. Every breath became a hard-fought effort. He lost all interest in keeping his footing, as just staying alive became his main focus. His vision filled up with throbbing blood and his eyes bulged out of their sockets as the demon dragged him off his feet and toward its center. Was there a mouth in there, full of teeth to grind his bones? He could see none—perhaps it merely wanted to bring more of its arms to bear on crushing him into paste.

"Bik-k-k-k," he choked, ashamed to call on the scoundrel's aid but knowing he could not free himself.

"What's that, lad? You need to speak up," Bikker said. A tentacle tried to reach around Bikker's chest but the bearded swordsman punched it away with his free hand. Another lashed him across the side of the head, a glancing blow but strong enough to knock Bikker sideways. "Blast your eyes," Bikker said. "This is not what I expected of our reacquaintance." Bikker's sword whirled through the air, droplets of acid falling like rain on the beast so it recoiled in pain. The pitted blade sliced through the tentacle around Croy's throat as easy as it could cut paper. The stump of the cut arm waved desperately in the air, its wound cauterized by the hissing acid. Another swing and Croy's leg was free.

"My thanks," Croy called as he dodged away from another tentacle bent on snaring his sword arm.

"Save them. The damned thing is still growing. If we're going to kill it, it's best done soon. I'll clear you a path—go for its heart, if it has one!" Acidtongue swung around and around like a scythe mowing wheat. Bikker did not even bother with proper flourishes and cutting strokes, instead engaging the demon with a series of sweeping moulinet cuts. Though he barely touched the demon's arms, they were severed right and left, the tapered ends of the tentacles dropping all around them to writhe and die separately on the ground.

Acidtongue looked like a piece of rusted old iron, like a sword cast aside in a field, left out in the sun and rain for centuries. Yet when its wielder slogged into battle its true virtue made itself known. It secreted a concentrated vitriol more powerful than any alchemist's *aqua regia*, an acid that could cut through any substance known to man. The sword had to be kept in a special glass-lined scabbard just so it didn't eat its way through and burn the man who wore it at his belt. It was one of the most powerful weapons in the world, and Bikker was a master at its use.

Croy had to admit, not without a twinge of professional jealousy, that it made short work of the demon that had nearly overwhelmed him.

"Now," Bikker shouted, and Croy ducked under a flailing arm and into the gap Bikker made. A seeming wall of severed stumps lay before him. The demon had continued to grow even after the tower fell on it, and now it seemed as big as the palace. Severed arms beat at his head and shoulders, and smaller tentacles reached to grab his arms and legs, but Croy laughed as he brought Ghostcutter around with both hands wrapped about its hilt. He brought it up to his shoulder, then drove it down with all its might into the join between two tentacles. The blade met some resistance at first but then pierced the tough skin and sank deep into the demon's body, all the way up to its quillions.

That, it turned out, was enough to make the demon scream.

Its voice was high and chirping like a bird's, but loud enough to shatter glass windows in the palace. Its scream was wordless and atonal, a simple heart cry so pure and piteous that it could mean only the creature's death. It screamed with its mind, not with any audible voice, like many demons of Croy's experience. His brain was battered by a trillion small voices speaking gibberish, but pleading, begging, beseeching him to withdraw his sword. When Croy refused, the demon tried to pull back physically, to roll away from the sword, to thrash itself free. It redoubled its attacks, its arms wrapping around Croy's body so thick they covered him head to toe. But its strength was already ebbing and he only held fast, grunting in pain. By the time Bikker reached him and cut him free, the demon was already dead and its tentacles slithered off of him as if he'd been buried in a pile of so much rope.

Croy stumbled over its severed arms where they littered the courtyard and out into the moonlight, gasping for air. When he had a little breath back, he started to laugh. Bikker slapped him hard on the back and he nearly went down on one knee.

By the mercy of the Lady, that had felt good. To do the thing he was sworn to do, once more. Demons were so rare upon the land these days that he'd had to find other uses for Ghostcutter's puissance, and not always things he was proud of. He'd nearly forgotten the purity and the clear conscience that came from fighting demons.

Beside him, Bikker looked possessed of the same emotion. He was smiling from ear to ear, all malice gone from his eyes. Perhaps, just perhaps, there was something of the hero in the man yet. Perhaps the man who Croy had once know was not yet dead. He'd thought Bikker lost to the tide of cynicism and shifting morality that sullied this world, but perhaps . . .

The castellan came running from the palace, pulling a dressing robe around his withered frame. "Water!" the old man cried. "The Guardian must be doused in water, or it'll keep growing until it chokes the world! Fetch water from the well, bring more from the river! Water! Water!"

Eventually the castellan saw the corpse of the demon—his eyes had never been very good, and age had worsened them—and stopped his shouting. "Water," he said with a dejected air. "Water would have made it shrink."

"Cold iron and acid seem to work, too," Bikker said, taunting the old man. He laughed heartily. "Don't tell me, castellan, that you've been harboring a demon inside these walls. Don't tell me you made a pet of a pit fiend."

The three of them stared at the body as it began to smoke and dissolve. It was not a creature of this world, and lacking now its vital force, it had nothing to protect it from the abhorrence of nature. In moments its corpse would resolve to nothing but a stink of brimstone and a blackish residue on the stones.

"It's the Guardian of the—the—" The castellan's face turned dark with congested blood. It was a high crime for any man to summon a demon or to keep one hidden. For decades Croy and knights like him had been hunting down sorcerers capable of performing the necessary rituals. Now only a handful of them remained, and all of them closely watched. If it could be proved that, say, Hazoth had summoned this demon, he would be burnt at the stake. Even for one as powerful as the Burgrave, harboring a demon could be a hanging offense. Should Bikker or Croy bring news of this to the capital—

But then the castellan's face creased with shrewdness. He pointed one long and trembling finger at the two swordsmen.

"You are an escaped prisoner. And you have no right to be here," he said.

Croy looked at Bikker. "I'd hoped when we saved the palace from the demon, all might be forgiven."

Bikker grinned wickedly. "Did you expect justice in this life, lad? Have you learned so little of my teachings?"

"Guards!" the castellan shouted. "Take these two under arrest!"

Suddenly the walls of Castle Hill were crowded with archers, while men of the watch in their cloaks-of-eyes came streaming in through the Market Square gate.

"I had hoped to talk to you more. But we'll meet again," Croy said.

"You may be assured of it," Bikker agreed.

And then they split up, running in opposite directions as fast as their legs could carry them.

# CHAPTER TWENTY-SIX

"Curse you, leave off," Malden whimpered. His strength was nearly gone. The joints in his arms and shoulders burned, and his legs had cramped where he used them to brace himself against the pull of the demon. He would not let go of the crown, but inch by inch, inexorably, the tentacle was pulling it closer to the debris of the tower room. Sweat poured down into Malden's eyes but he didn't dare wipe it away. He heaved backward with every muscle in his body but still gained no ground.

And then—he did. He was able to straighten out a fraction, to pull the crown closer to his body. The tentacle throbbed and started to whip back and forth. Its grip loosened and then the crown slithered free of its embrace.

Malden fell back, panting like a dog. He stared at the tentacle, expecting it to renew its grasp, but it did not. In fact, it flopped across the floor and did not move at all. As if the demon had perished, unseen by him, and could fight no more. Even as he watched, the thing began to melt.

He could hardly believe it. He stared at the crown in his hands. It had not stretched or bent at all in the struggle, though it was made of gold, one of the softest of metals. Its crenellations had dug deep gouges in his palms and fingers, and his blood slicked its surface. He longed to put it down, to tend to his cuts, but he dared not let it out of his hands, even for a moment. He couldn't bear the thought.

Of course, he didn't have to put it down, if he just set it on his head . . .

*You have done well, thief,* the crown said.

"Say no more, I beg of you," Malden moaned. He thought how much he had risked for this prize. He could easily have been killed in that final moment before the tower fell—yet the voice had commanded him, and he obeyed. Now he knew it wanted more. It wanted him to put it on his own head.

Surely that was sacrilege. Wasn't it? He was no Burgrave. He couldn't legally wear it. If anyone saw him with it on, he would be arrested at once for impersonating a noble.

And yet . . . what sweet justice it would be, wouldn't it? It was almost maddening, it was so appealing. For a common thief, the son of a whore, to wear even for a moment the coronet of temporal power.

Malden began to raise it toward his head.

The thing was magic. Who knew what powers it might have? Maybe it would grant him wishes. Maybe it would turn him instantly into a man of estate, of power. Such things were told of in stories, sometimes, such things were . . .

. . . were . . .

. . . too good to be true.

Malden lowered the crown again. He didn't let it go. No, that would be too much to bear. But he forced down the urge to put it on.

He had a horrible presentiment—a certain hunch—that if he put the crown on his head, he would never willingly take it off again. And that would have presented more problems than it was likely to solve.

He felt the thing pulse in his hands, a little jolt of anger. He had thwarted its design and it wasn't happy. Malden had to fight with himself to contain his natural impulse, which was to do anything, anything at all, to make the crown happy again.

*If you will not wear me, then carry me to the castellan. He will see to my safety.*

"Be still!" Malden said, though he felt like a field mouse issuing orders to a lion. The strength in that voice, the resolute, firm quality of it, was hard to resist. "I'll do no such thing. I'm leaving now, and you shall accompany me."

*Find the castellan.*

"He would have me slain on the spot." Malden shook his head. He could feel the disdain radiating from the crown. It cared not a jot for his life or well-being. It only wanted its orders carried out. As far as the crown was concerned, he deserved whatever he got. Was he not, after all, a thief? And were not thieves hanged in this city?

An upright citizen, a more honest man, would never have disobeyed. Any such would have marched to their doom, just for the honor of serving the crown—or been seduced into putting it on, whatever horrors that might entail. Whatever intellect might inhabit it, it remained a symbol of ordained power, a representative of an iron-bound class system where every man knew his place. Even in the Free City of Ness men were born into a system of rank and from childhood had one lesson drummed into them: know your betters, and respect their wishes to the letter. Those who disobeyed faced beatings and upbraidings. Those who went along were left alone. Though the free citizens were proud people, they were not unlike the bondsmen outside the city walls in this regard—they knew better than to challenge power.

Yet Malden had never been a true citizen. He'd never been raised to be an honest man. His people were among the lowest of the low, and no one had ever cared to remind him of his rank because they assumed he would never rise above his station.

That expectation, or lack thereof, had given him ambition. And ambition bred will. Taking care, he removed one hand from the crown and flexed the fingers to get the blood flowing through them again. Then he placed the crown on the floor. Oh, that was hard, but once done, he felt so much better. He knew at once he'd made the right decision. He eased his other hand and wiped blood from his palm.

Then he began to consider, once again, how he was going to escape.

The hallway was blocked by the portcullis spears, and even if he could have fled through the palace, he would only arrive in the courtyard where doubtless every armed man on Castle Hill was waiting for him. The tower was collapsed and impassible. It seemed he had but one choice for egress, though he liked it not.

He could climb down the oubliette, the pit that nearly swallowed him before he reached the tower. He peered down into its inky depths now, and remembered what he had thought before—it could lead nowhere but into the Burgrave's dungeons, some hundred feet straight down.

It was the only way out.

Jumping into that pit would be folly, of course—he would never survive the fall. He could attempt to climb down, but from what he could see of the shaft, its walls looked slick and free of easy hand- and footholds to facilitate such a descent. Fortunately he still had the rope he'd used to gain entrance to the palace, and Slag's folding grapnel. The rope would be just long enough, if he could drop the last ten feet.

He wasted little time. No doubt guards were headed to the palace already, to check on the Burgrave and his retinue and make sure they had not been injured when the tower collapsed. At least some of those guards would be coming to check on the crown as well. The crown. Best to secure it now, so he wouldn't lose it. He picked it up again.

*Thief.*

"Be still!" Malden hissed. He would not let it control him again. He would let no man be his master, ever again.

Well. Save for Cutbill. And Cythera and Bikker, of course. He scowled at himself, but wasted no more time on that line of thought.

He threaded his belt through the crown—touching it gingerly, as if it were like to burn him—then fastened it again about his waist so he would not drop it in the shaft. Then he wrapped his grapnel around one leg of the statue of Sadu—it had been badly dented in the cataclysm, but was still sound enough to hold his weight—and lowered himself foot by foot down into the pit, with only the vaguest notion what he would find at its bottom.

# CHAPTER TWENTY-SEVEN

Warm gusts of air chased up the shaft and made Malden's hands sweat until he could barely hang onto the rope. The shaft was narrow enough that he could walk his way down, keeping his feet pressed against one wall while he climbed down hand over hand, but the walls were slick with condensation and gave little purchase to his soft shoes. For the first fifty feet or so of the descent he was in near total darkness, but as he passed the halfway point, the light from below grew strong enough that he could see the water forming thick, greasy droplets that held for a moment, then streaked down the walls around him.

From below he could hear the roaring of warm air as it rushed up the shaft. And something else—something he had dreaded as he came down the narrow chimney, something he had formed a fledgling hope he would not hear at all. A quiet moaning, the fatigued sighs of a prisoner. He had hoped that the clamor in the courtyard would have brought the gaolers of the dungeon running. That when he reached the dungeon, he would find it empty of guards. Judging by the continued sounds of torment issuing from below, that hope was forlorn. Getting down into the dungeon was going to be the easy part. Dealing with its occupants might be decidedly more difficult.

*One problem at a time,* he told himself, and kept descending.

The light was not enough to reveal the bottom of the shaft until he was almost upon it. When he reached the last few feet of his rope and peered down with great curiosity to see where he would land if he just let go, his heart flipped over his chest.

The floor at the bottom of the shaft was studded with spikes. Iron spikes mounted securely, three feet long and worked to nasty sharpness.

Reaching the end of the rope, he hung onto it by one hand with his feet stretched down as far as they could go. Seven feet of empty air still remained between him and those wicked points. If he just let go, the fall would not break his legs but he was like to be skewered.

He had no more rope to tie to the end, nor anything to extend his descent. Twenty feet of good stout cord were wrapped around the hilt of his bodkin, but it was not strong enough to hold his weight.

Malden ran one hand down the wall of the shaft next to him. It had been cut through solid rock with metal tools that left marks in its surface, no more than shallow dents—hardly enough to get his fingers or toes into. Yet perhaps if his strength had not completely left him . . .

He braced his feet against one wall as best he could, then pushed against the opposite wall with one hand. If he kept his legs bent and his arm straight, he could just about hold his weight up against the force of gravity. And if he used both hands, and if he was headed downward—it would not be a graceful descent. It would be more like a barely controlled fall. But that was better than an uncontrolled plummet.

It took a great deal of courage to let go of the rope. Malden might have been indolent, and not a valiant fighter, but when his life was in jeopardy, he rarely lacked for boldness. He let go of the rope and thrust both hands out against the wall at the same time, bracing himself in the shaft. The impact of his hands on the wall made a wet slapping sound that echoed up and down the walls, but he did not have time at that point to stop and listen to hear if anyone remarked on the sound. He was too busy rushing down toward the spikes, his feet and hands clutching at the tool marks on the walls for whatever small purchase they offered.

The rough wall tore and picked at his hands, already sore from the long climb up the wall of Castle Hill. The air rushing past him whispered of doom and folly and why there were so few old thieves. His teeth pulled back in a terrible rictus as he smashed his feet and hands again and again into the walls, trying anything, anything at all, to slow his descent.

The spikes hurtled toward him like javelins. If he didn't time this perfectly—

Just as his hands reached the bottom of the shaft and ran out of wall to grip, Malden ducked his head and kicked hard with his legs against the stone. He shot forward through the air, narrowly clearing the spikes, and curled himself into a ball as he made contact with the floor beyond them, to perform a perfect somersault and wind up sitting on the floor, his breath whooping in and out of his lungs.

"Wuzzat?" someone said. Someone nearby. Someone whose voice suggested to Malden that he would be quite a bit larger than himself. A slow shuffling step started toward him, drowning out the tired wails of the unseen prisoner.

Malden looked around him in a panic, searching for a place to hide. There was none whatsoever. He had dropped into a narrow room with a vaulted ceiling—a ceiling from which hung sundry articles of iron, many of them with sharp points, others made of heavy chain. The tools of a torturer. The shaft's opening was just a square of darkness on the ceiling, the spikes inconspicuous among so much hardware. Arches led away in four directions, with light coming from cressets set between each arch. Beyond one arch lay a flight of stairs heading up—surely the normal method for accessing this underground hell. The echoing footsteps came from another arch. He could have gone left or right and hoped the torturer was slow enough in chasing him—but he saw a better idea and took it. Jumping to his feet, he ran backward up the stairs until he reached the first landing, then walked back down them at a more leisurely rate.

As the torturer ducked through the arch, the man would only see him coming down the stairs as if he had just arrived.

"Who the blazes're you?" the torturer asked when they came face-to-face. He was an enormous man, though not overly tall, his body bloated and lumpy, his hair falling out in clumps. He looked half like an ogre and half like something that should not have been able to crawl out of its sickbed.

"The new kitchen boy," Malden said. "I was sent down to

fetch you. Fire's broken out above, and they need every man to help put it out. Hurry, you must get up there at once! Are there any others down here who can also help?"

"Just me." The torturer's mouth fell open and his eyes turned to slits. Malden had the impression he was squinting at him. The big man already had a massive wen over his left eye, so it was hard to tell. Other purplish growths adorned his chin and one side of his neck, like a grotesque beard half shaved. "Fire, you say? No great concern of mine, that. Naught to burn down here."

"Nor any other way out but these stairs," Malden insisted, hoping very much this was not true. "If the palace falls down on top of us—"

"Oh," the torturer said, his right eye opening wide. "Oh! Fire! I'd best get up there, see what I can do to help!"

He rushed past Malden on his way up the stairs, nearly knocking him down. Malden cheered him on as he thundered up the risers. Then he darted through the arch the torturer had just vacated, intent on finding another way out before the brutish man thought to wonder why a man of his age was working as a kitchen boy.

He had not gotten more than a dozen strides into the dungeon, however, before someone called out to him.

"You! Yes, you—ye're Cutbill's man, ain't you? Thank the Lady, ye've come to rescue me!"

Malden considered keeping on, ignoring the cry for aid. Had he truly been one of Cutbill's thieves, those honorless blackguards (whom he had been doing his level best lately to emulate), he would not have faltered in a single step. But he was, in some ways, still his mother's son. He turned aside from his path and went to look for the man who'd called him.

# CHAPTER TWENTY-EIGHT

Croy dashed into the shadows, keeping his head down as arrows buzzed past him left and right. If he could just get to where the archers couldn't see him— Yes. The wall of the kitchens proved exactly the cover he needed. Its shadow cut through the moonlight like a scythe. Of course, there was one problem. The kitchens abutted the defensive wall, so he had just trapped himself in a corner.

He turned around quickly and saw four men of the watch come hurtling toward him. Their cloaks billowed around them as they came, the eyes woven into the fabric seeming to blink as the cloth snapped back and forth. The four of them spread out as they approached, forming a half circle before him. That was smart. He could easily have taken them on one by one, but if he tried to attack any of them now, he would be leaving his left flank dangerously exposed.

The blades of their halberds flashed out and toward him, the weapons swinging in unison, just as their drill instructor had surely taught them. Croy had taught enough guards in his own time to recognize the technique. He couldn't see their faces under their hoods but he understood. These were men handpicked for duty on Castle Hill, trained well and ready for anything.

Croy reached over his shoulder. Ghostcutter he left in its scabbard—it was only for fighting demons and sorcery. Instead he drew his shorter, nameless blade. Nothing but honest steel to meet their iron.

"I don't want to hurt you," he said. "I know you're just doing your duty. However, I cannot allow you to arrest me tonight."

One of the watchmen snickered at that, an ugly sound. Another took a step forward and made a feint of cutting at his blade. Croy did not respond, drawing the sword back rather than let the halberd make contact.

"The Burgrave wants your head," the snickerer told him. "They say he'll pay good new-minted silver for it. There won't be any arresting."

Croy frowned. That did complicate things.

He knew exactly how much these guards earned. Once upon a time, when he'd lived on Castle Hill, he drew the same salary in the Burgrave's service. He knew they would be grateful for a chance to supplement their income.

Yet they must be good men at heart. They served a properly anointed lord and protected the Free City of Ness. So he couldn't just kill them. He knew Bikker would have—in fact, Bikker was probably doing that just now on his own way out of Castle Hill. Yet Croy prided himself on being made of different stuff. He would have to find another way out of this predicament.

"Last chance, gentlemen. I ask you, as honorable men, will you let me go in peace?"

A halberd spike came jabbing toward his face—and this time it was not a feint. He had received his answer. He smashed the point aside with the forte of his sword and then dropped low into a ducking sideways hop, moving like a crab as the four of them advanced as one. Two halberds clashed where his head, a moment before, had been, their wooden hafts thudding like drums. Another came low and nearly swept him off his feet. Croy jumped forward and smacked that watchman in the temple with the flat of his blade. It was a stunning blow, not a killing attack. The watchman staggered backward, nearly dropping his heavy weapon as he reached up to grab his ringing head.

Halberds were powerful weapons, half spear and half axe so they gave the user a wide range of effective fighting styles. They were slower than swords, however. By the time the next blow came toward him—this one a cutting swing aimed at the top of his skull—Croy had danced back and was able to lean away from the chop. As the weapon flashed past his face, he reached out with his free hand—his off hand—and grabbed the halberd right in its middle. Putting his back into it, he twisted the halberd sideways and out of the watchman's grip and then rushed forward, knocking down two of his opponents in a heap. He threw the halberd away from him and then sheathed his sword. He could kill all four of these men easily, but he had no stomach for it. They were honest defenders of the public weal—what good could possibly come from their deaths?

The last standing watchman ran at him, but Croy side-stepped the charge. Then he dashed to the side of the kitchen building and clambered up its wall. It was a half-timbered structure with protruding beams and nearly as easy to climb as a ladder. A halberd blade whistled past his feet as he made the roof, but it missed cleanly.

From the top of the kitchens it was simple to reach the parapet along the top of the defensive wall. Where he went from there was another question. He stood atop a length of curtain wall that lay between two watch towers. From both of them, men were pouring out of doors or jumping down from the tower tops to get at him. He seemed to be out of options.

Then he looked down and saw the river Krait, flowing briskly by a hundred and fifty feet below him. He tilted his head back and laughed heartily. The men of the watch would be on him in seconds, with orders to slaughter him where he stood. There must be a full company of them coming at him—far more than enough to take him down, fancy swords or no.

Jumping into the river from this height was utter folly. If he didn't hit the bottom hard enough to shatter his bones, there was a good chance he would drown. Of course, there was the slimmest of chances that he would survive.

He jumped, of course.

The air whistled past him as he fell, as fast as the pro-verbial stone. He could see nothing—it all flashed past him so quickly—and he could barely tell which direction was up. Somehow he managed to get his legs pointed downward with the toes extended so he hit the water like a knife blade.

Still, he hit it hard enough to jar every bone in his body. The shock of immersion in the cold river nearly stopped his heart. The breath exploded out of him in a torrent of silver bubbles. His brains reeled with the impact and his legs stung as if the skin had been flayed from them. Then he opened his mouth to inhale—he had no choice, his body was not accepting the commands of his will—and his lungs flooded with water. He flailed blindly, trying to swim up, unable to tell what direction he was facing, barely cognizant of the difference between right and left.

His head collided with something hard and wooden, adding injury to injury. His vision spun with blackness and he knew he was about to die. He nearly gave up then and there—if this was the time the Lady had appointed for his death, who was he to gainsay Her wish? Yet there was something in Croy that failed to stop even when lesser men could do naught but yield. He grasped at the wooden obstruction above him and pulled himself up and over it. His face hit the night air with a gasp and he sucked in breath— then turned his head sideways and coughed up a great gout of cold water. He shook his head to clear his eyes and finally looked at where he was and what he was holding onto. It was the rail of a tiny boat.

Sitting at its oars was Cythera.

The woman he'd risked all to find. The woman whose love he would defy even death to beseech.

Surely only one explanation could satisfy this great co-incidence. The Lady had smiled on him. Far from choosing this night to bring him to Her bosom, She had let him live, so that he could see Cythera once more. He nearly let go of the boat, wanting to raise his hands to the heavens in thankful prayer.

"You'd better get in, as we're going to be spotted any minute," Cythera said. "Stop playing around and— Hold. You're not Malden."

She made no attempt to help him. She did not reach for him. But then, it would be his death if she embraced him. Her curse made it so. She peered over the gunwale, searching his face with wide eyes.

"Croy?" she asked, looking horrified.

He pulled himself over the rail and into the boat. For a while he could do nothing but lie there gasping, looking up at the sky. At the top of the wall tiny faces were peering

down at him, tiny arms pointing with urgency at the little
boat.

"Row, Cyth. Row away from here," he panted. He
couldn't help but smile.

"I'm supposed to meet someone—"

A rock hit the river, not three feet from the boat, and sent
up a great column of water that splashed them both.

"I don't think they have boiling oil," Croy told Cythera.
"But I know they have plenty of archers."

"Let us away, then," she said, and bent to her oars.

## CHAPTER TWENTY-NINE

As a child growing up in a brothel, Malden had possessed few friends his own age or sex. Yet whenever
he chanced to find himself in the company of other boys,
one of the favorite topics of conversation had concerned this
very room—the torture chamber of the Burgrave. The boys
would name and describe all the instruments of torture they
could, and speculate wildly on their possible applications.
One frequent debate was held over which device one would
least like to be subjected to. It had all been in good fun, of
course, a gruesome contest of oneupmanship. He had never
considered the idea he would actually be in this room, or see
its true inventory.

"O'er here, lad, and sharpish! I can't take much more.
Oh, oh, I'll kiss the Bloodgod on the lips for this, when I
meet him," the prisoner announced.

As Malden headed through the arch to the torture chamber proper, he was more afraid than he had been facing
down the demon above, or when he first climbed into

Cutbill's coffin. On every side were the nightmares of his youth. The boot, and also its cruel if prosaically named cousin, the instep borer—which drove a screw through the fleshy part of a man's foot. The tramp chair, which didn't look so bad until you realized you would be locked inside it, unable to stand. The heretic's fork lay on an anvil where the torturer had been sharpening its prongs. Iron-rimmed breaking wheels lined the walls, while a selection of bone-breaking hammers hung by straps from the ceiling. Close by the arch, leaning up against one wall, was the scavenger's daughter (sometimes called the reversed rack). In pride of place stood the dread crocodile shears, which were only ever used on the slayers of nobility, for that which they took away could not be seen. At least not while the victim wore breeches. There were at least three sets of branks, or witch's bridles—specially designed headgear with an iron spur arranged in such a way that it projected into the mouth and placed a spike against the tongue. Any sorcerer who tried to speak a curse or cast a spell while wearing such a bridle would shred their tongue instead. A handy appliance to have, Malden thought, in a place like the Free City, where wizards vied with Burgraves and sent thieves to do their mischief.

"I heard yer voice, I know ye're still there. Come on, boy!"

But of all the things that could be done to a human body, all the bits of iron that could be plunged into soft parts, all the different ways to stretch sinews and ligaments until they burst, one device was always rated the worst. None could really say why—it did not seem half so horrible as the choke pear. Yet generations of boys had passed down the sure and certain knowledge that the paragon of suffering-inducing machines had to be the strap.

The prisoner's hands had been bound behind his back, then a hook inserted between his wrists. He had then been hauled up on a pulley until he dangled from the ceiling. His arms were twisted around behind him, and as a result his chest thrust forward at an awkward angle. To make this worse, a chain was wrapped around his feet, and from this chain depended a large, round stone. The weight pulled down on joints already strained by the strap that held the man aloft.

"Ah, and there ye are, ye clever son. There, over there—that knot!"

Malden stared with gaping mouth at the prisoner, and not only because of his state of distress. The man was naked, gaunt, and haggard of expression. He was also someone he recognized. It was the vagabond he'd seen in Cutbill's lair, the one who'd claimed right of sanctuary.

"You're the thief Kemper, are you not?" Malden asked.

"For the nonce. Sooner'n I'd like, I'll go by a different name," Kemper agreed.

"I'm . . . sorry?"

"They'll be calling me 'the late' thief Kemper, if'n you don't get me down."

Malden recovered his wits with a start. "Of course, at once," he said. He hurried to the wall where the other end of the strap was tied around an iron hook. He undid the knot with shaking fingers and lowered Kemper carefully to the floor.

For a while the vagabond merely rolled about on the flagstones, his face split by a piteous grin.

"Oh, I've never found such happiness at the bottom of a flagon, nor between a girl's legs," Kemper moaned. "Ye'll never know such ecstasy, lad, and ye should be thankful for that."

Malden had many questions for the man. "How did you come to be here? It was just this morning I saw you, at Cutbill's. You were safe enough there—how were you taken so soon after?"

Kemper grimaced. "A man can only abide so much stale bread and water. Cutbill gave me sanctuary, to be sure, but his hospitality was a mite lacking, if you catch me. Of all things, water to drink, ye'd think I was a horse! If I wanted real victuals, I decided I must go abroad. I snuck forth just afore dawn, made right for the Smoke, where I knew I could catch a game."

Kemper rolled over onto his side and moaned in pleasure.

"Found it easy enough. Didn't reckon one o' the players was a cloak-of-eyes on his off-shift. The bastard recognized me just fine and tried to haul me out o' there. Figured I was safe enough, as I've always been. Been caught more times'n you've kissed a girl, I figure, and always got free again before. Never thought they'd ken out me one weakness. Now, if ye please, me hands and ankles."

Malden went to free the vagabond's extremities and found they were bound by matching chains of bright metal, seemingly far too thin to hold up Kemper's weight. They tinkled merrily when he pulled them free.

"Keep'm as souvenirs, if ye like," Kemper told Malden, when he saw how the thief stared at the chains. "I've no desire to see'm again. Should be worth a mite, seein' they're solid silver."

"Silver?" He could make no sense of it. He knew nobles could demand that they be hanged with a silken rope, rather than the hempen cord commoners received. But why in the world would a petty thief be strapped with silver? It made no sense.

"Good 'gainst curses," Kemper said, as if that explained everything. "Mind, I'll need a cut on what ye sell'm for."

"But of course," Malden said. He pulled the chains free and stared at them in his hands. Why bind a man with silver? What had Kemper meant about curses? He lifted his eyes to ask the man directly, but in vain. Without a sound, without so much as a fare-thee-well, Kemper had disappeared.

# CHAPTER THIRTY

Malden rushed back through the arches, thinking Kemper must have slipped up the stairs while he wasn't looking. He sought only to warn his fellow thief that no good would come of heading that way. Yet as he reached the bottom of the stairs he thought better of chasing Kemper up the steps. No doubt the vagabond would be caught as soon as he made the surface. He would only be sacrificing his own freedom if he followed too close on the man's heels.

He had freed the prisoner from his chains. Surely, that was enough of a good turn, and he could be forgiven for thinking of himself next. He had to escape, with the crown, if he didn't want the night's fiasco to be in vain. And he thought he knew a way.

Malden cast about him, looking for something on the floor. He found it back in the torture chamber—a round iron grate that came up easily when he lifted it. It had to be the drain that led out to the river, via the outlet pipe he'd seen when coming in.

The problem with having a dungeon cut into the bosom of a hill was that it would flood every time it rained. The drain was there to alleviate such a shortcoming. It would also make a fine way of disposing of any victims who didn't survive their interrogations—or any parts of them they didn't need anymore.

Putting aside such grisly thoughts as best he was able, Malden dropped down into the drain, then pulled the grating back over his head, cutting off some of the light. The drain proved to be a pipe lined with bricks furred white with niter, about three feet wide, leading down at a steep grade. There was no light in the tunnel, of course, but part of the way down its length he saw a glimmering and started crawling toward it. Compared to some of the things he'd been through since he started working for Cythera and Bikker, the drain was an easy traverse. The worst thing about it was the smell.

It was foul at first. It quickly rose to a level of unbearability. The fetor of the drain made his eyes water, and even when he covered his mouth and nose with the hood of his cloak he could barely breathe. His body fought for clean air but there was none to be had. The source of the stench was no great mystery, Malden thought. The garderobes of the palace must empty directly into this same pipe—a clever enough alternative to having the Burgrave's ordure carted out every week. His guess as to the drain's purpose was confirmed when he reached a patch of light in the tunnel. It was coming down from above, through a shaft much like the one that led to the dungeon—though this time there were no spikes at the bottom. Looking up, he could just make out a circular opening, high, high above him, lit by flickering candlelight. The smell here was much stronger than elsewhere, and the condition of the shaft walls is certainly best left undescribed.

The smell made him want to retch, and the yielding texture of the floor he crawled over made him wince with each foot he covered. Nothing but the promise of freedom and safety kept him moving forward. Still, he supposed it could be worse. There was a fortune in gold waiting for him once he was out of this—no matter how briefly it would remain in his possession. Malden pitied the servant who must come down here and clean this drain every time it filled up, and was probably paid only in room and board.

There were more shafts intersecting the drain as it headed down toward the river. One of them was even in use. He waited patiently until the user was finished, then continued on his way.

At last he came to a point where they could see the outflow pipe. Moonlight streamed in through its grate, though its lower half was clogged with filth and detritus. Malden rushed forward and grabbed the iron bars with his much-abused fingers. He rattled them but they held.

He looked out through the bars, hoping to signal Cythera. Perhaps she had a way of bending iron bars he lacked.

But where in Sadu's name was she? The boat should be waiting for him—it was his agreed upon method of egress. If she wasn't there . . .

Then he would just have to swim for it, wouldn't he?

With a sigh, Malden drew his bodkin and began to work at the bars, trying to loosen them enough that he could make good his escape.

*Thief,* the crown at his belt said when he was quiet awhile. *Thief, go back.*

Malden growled at the thing, never slowing in his work.

# PART II

# An Unquiet Crown

# INTERLUDE

Bikker made his own exit from Castle Hill, though in a less dramatic fashion than Croy or Malden. In the confusion following the death of the demon, he merely stepped into some shadows by the wall, then through a doorway into a well-lit room near the main gate. Inside, a servant was waiting for him. The withered old man offered to take his cloak—Bikker declined—then offered him a cup of hot mulled wine. This he took, draining the goblet in a single gulp. "Is he here?" Bikker asked.

The servant nodded without looking up. He was busy mending a torn tunic, pulling his bone needle through the old fabric then plunging it down again. The old man was the castle's tailor, and he had a pile of clothes beside him, each item waiting his attention. "When things have calmed a bit, I'm to take you to the chapel. He'll meet you there."

Bikker eyed the tailor carefully. Was it possible this man was, in fact, his employer? He'd never seen the man who brought him into the cabal. It could be anyone in Ness, anyone with a compelling interest in bringing down the Burgrave. It wasn't an ideal situation for one of Bikker's talents, not knowing who he worked for. He was more accustomed to working for lords and merchants who insisted that he wear their personal livery. After all, what was the point in having a famous knight in your retinue if no one knew he was yours?

Still, Bikker supposed he could understand the need for secrecy. If anyone knew what the cabal was really meant to do, the jig would be up. The Burgrave would make short work of them all, probably hanging them in chains from the castle gates so everyone in Ness could see the wages of treason. Secrecy was paramount. Even Hazoth hadn't been filled in on all the details, and Bikker was certain there were elements of the scheme he didn't know about himself.

He shrugged and demanded another cup of wine. It didn't matter to him what happened to the city. What mattered was that he be far away when it happened. Far enough away not to smell the blood or hear the screams.

When enough time had passed, the tailor handed him a cloak-of-eyes, the traditional garb of the city watch. For the first time, Bikker realized why the castle's tailor would be a useful pawn of the cabal—uniforms and regalia of every kind came through the old man's hands. Any number of disguises would be at his disposal. Bikker threw the too-small cloak over his shoulders and let the tailor lead him through the dim corridors of the chancery, the unassuming building where the city's administrative work was carried out. They came through a dark refectory and then down a short passage that led to a chapel. A gilded cornucopia, symbol of the Lady, hung there above a modest altar. There were no pews, just a scattering of straw-filled cushions on the floor where supplicants could kneel. This was not a chapel for the use of the Burgrave and his family, but for the clerks and scribes of Anselm Vry's ministries—commoners, if well-paid commoners.

With a thin smile, the tailor bid Bikker to kneel. Perhaps he thought it would be amusing to see the knight in an attitude of prayer.

For Bikker it was anything but diverting. There had been a time when he stood vigil in far ruder churches. He'd been a sworn vassal of the king once. A champion of virtue. He took his place on his knees, the muscles of his back locking obediently into place. There was a certain method one learned to kneeling all night, a way of staying upright even when your body demanded sleep. He resisted the urge to place Acidtongue before him, his hands folded neatly on the pommel. He would not mock what he had once been, no matter what Croy might think of him now.

*Croy. Croy was here.* Bikker's skin itched at the thought. The foolish knight could cause all kinds of problems if he chose to poke his nose in where it wasn't wanted. Croy still considered himself one of the noble order of the Ancient Blades—which meant that whenever he discovered wrong-doing or malfeasance, he was honor-bound to root it out, uncover the criminals, and bring them to punishment. If Croy even guessed at the work of the cabal . . . but Bikker knew he could handle Sir Croy, if it came to that. He had trained Croy—had taught the younger knight everything he knew about holding a sword. But he hadn't taught Croy everything he knew himself. Bikker still had a few tricks up his sleeve that Croy had never seen.

"It's done," a voice behind Bikker said, startling him. "The crown has left Castle Hill. Good." Bikker did not turn to see who was speaking. His employer had been quite clear from the start that he did not wish his face to be seen. "Not as neatly as I'd hoped. But plenty of people saw the guardian demon before it was slain—that was to my liking. It will further humiliate Tarness."

"If you like, I can ride tonight for Helstrow. There I can inform the king that the Burgrave of Ness has been harboring demons," Bikker mused. He didn't relish the prospect—he was not well-loved in the royal fortress just now. But it would further their aims, and it would get him far from Ness before things went to perdition.

"Not just now. We'll hold that charge back as insurance. No, Ladymas is almost upon us. When Tarness appears in public without the crown, he'll be unable to explain himself. If we're lucky, the people will riot on their own, without further provocation. By manipulating their anger, we can inspire them to true revolt. The city will collapse under civil strife, and the king will have no choice but to intervene."

Bikker frowned. He stared up at the cornucopia as he asked, "That's the part I haven't fully grasped. The Burgrave will look a fool if he appears without his crown, true enough. But he's a man of formidable intellectual resources. Surely he'll find some excuse and the people will believe it. They love him, after all."

"They love *him*. They will not love what they see on Ladymas." The voice seemed to find this highly amusing.

"Trust me, Bikker. I've had years to plot this out. I know exactly what I'm doing."

"I'm sure," Bikker said. He wondered if he should tell his employer about Croy. But no. If the cabal thought Croy was a threat, they would take steps to slay the knight errant as a concerted front. Bikker didn't want that. He wanted Croy all to himself. So he held his tongue.

"Now. You know what you must do next? What your role is now?"

"Aye, I'll secure the crown. Get it to Hazoth's villa where it can be hidden."

"Exactly. Get the crown from the thief—pay him whatever he asks, it doesn't matter."

Bikker smiled. "Sure, since as soon as the crown is in my hands I can just kill the little fool and take the money back."

"What? No, you mustn't kill the thief. You're already a wanted criminal after tonight's endeavors. It's still against the law in this city to kill a man, and I don't want Anselm Vry's watchmen to pick you up for such a minor infraction. Not while I still need you. No, just pay the thief and let him be."

Bikker grunted in frustration. "This doesn't sit well with me. The thief knows too much, and he's hardly to be trusted. Leaving him alive is foolhardy."

"Yes, I'm aware of it. Which is why Hazoth is going to kill him. No need to get your hands dirty when we have one of the world's greatest sorcerers on our side."

"As you wish," Bikker said. Though it still rankled him. Not because he thought Hazoth wouldn't do it. Because he had intended to give Malden—whom he had actually come to respect, after a fashion—a clean death. He could only imagine the particulars, but he was sure that what Hazoth did to the thief would be downright gruesome in comparison.

# CHAPTER THIRTY-ONE

Croy and Cythera spent much of the night in furtive silence, as they wended their way from Castle Hill all the way down to Parkwall. The city watch was out in force and looking for them, and they had to take great pains to avoid capture.

Twice they came close to discovery. They had docked their little boat in the Smoke, in a place where two tanneries discharged the contents of their vats directly into the Skrait. Cythera thought the smell would keep the watch away and they could debark unseen. They nearly walked right into an armed guard who stood watching a pile of untanned hides that had just been delivered. The guard challenged them as they came up the riverside stairs, and they had to run as he chased them with a club. Croy could have made short work of the man, of course, but that would have just drawn more attention.

The second brush with the watch was more serious. They had arrived nearly at the edge of Ladypark Common, within sight of Hazoth's villa and the house where Croy was staying—only to find the grassy sward crawling with watchmen. The two of them retreated to a tavern a few streets away, where they were able to find out why the common was so heavily guarded. It transpired that a footpad had murdered the footman of a money-changer there earlier in the evening. It had been a particularly bloody killing, and the watch was called down in droves to find evidence and look for the assassin.

"They won't find him," Cythera said, when she and Croy could speak privately again. "That was Bikker's work."

"Are you sure?" Croy asked, looking as if he would grab his swords and run out into the night to find the big swordsman.

"No," she said. "I can't prove anything. But he was supposed to set a number of diversions, all the better to keep the watch away from Castle Hill. I didn't think he'd be so . . . expedient about it."

Croy settled down then. In his personal book of accounts, Bikker already had enough crimes under his name. One more didn't change how he felt.

They took a room at the tavern under assumed names and spent the night waiting for a knock on their door or the sound of hobnailed boots rushing down the hall. No one came to arrest them, though, or even to ask them difficult questions. When morning finally came it seemed they were safe. The patrols of the watch had diminished in size and frequency, and both of them began to breathe easier.

"I have to go back soon," Cythera said as she led Croy through the Ladypark Market, a winding street of shops and stalls just uphill from Hazoth's villa. Fishmongers wheeled their carts from door to door—this early, the day's catch had not yet begun to stink—as linkboys hurried home to bed, to wait out the day until their services were again required. Minutes before, the two of them had had the place virtually to themselves, but now the city's throngs closed around them. Bakers and brewers were already at their stations, of course, long before the dawn. With the sun, the market truly came to life, however, filling with women getting their daily shopping done.

Croy found himself strangely unwilling to give up the heightened emotion of their night outrunning the watch. As fraught as it had been with apprehension, he'd savored the time with his lady fair. He supposed, though, that every night, no matter its freight of sweetness or of terror, must end. The morning had broken crisp and clear while they were renewing their old acquaintance—he had longed for the sun to tarry beneath the horizon, but alas, every day must follow in its course.

"If I'm late," Cythera said, "Hazoth will want to know why. And he has a method of discerning falsehoods."

"One that works, even on you?" Croy asked. "I thought you were immune to sorcery. Is his too strong for your curse to bear?"

She smiled without mirth. "There is no sorcerer in this world who could break through my curse. But Hazoth, well . . . not every trick he pulls is by magic," she told him. "He's the cleverest man I've ever met."

"Cleverer than me?" Croy asked with a hurt look.

"By far," she said, and this time laughter creased the skin around her eyes. He was glad only that he could still bring her some small joy. There had been a time—a lifetime ago, it seemed—when he would cut capers and dance for her until she clapped her hand over her mouth to keep from guffawing like a fool. Now her aspect had changed for the morose.

"I didn't want to leave, back then," he said with sudden seriousness. "The Burgrave was my liege lord. When he ordered me away, I had no choice."

She did not reply. Instead she ducked inside a bakery and emerged again a moment later with a round loaf. When she cracked it open, steam burst from the spongy brown bread inside.

"When was the last time you ate?" she asked. "You were always so busy dashing hither and yon, you would forget to feed yourself. Don't pretend to me, now. I've learned some of my master's art and will see it in your eye."

"I suppose it's been no more than a day," he said, thinking of the almonds he'd eaten while he watched her go inside Hazoth's house the day before. He had to admit the bread was making his mouth water. "Not here, though. Let's break our fast properly."

They found an inn that had just opened its doors, and for a piece of silver they were given a private room. The hostler looked askance at the shifting tattoos on Cythera's face but said nothing, nor was he slow in bringing wine and a half wheel of cheese when they called for them.

"Sit. There," she said, and pointed at a bench by the room's sole table. Croy did as he was told. "Will you take a cup?" she asked, lifting the flagon.

"You don't need to serve me," Croy said, and took it from her hands. His fingers touched hers—only the lightest, gentlest of meetings, but enough to make her wince and nearly drop the wine. Croy made as if he hadn't seen her fearful gesture. "You're not my slave. Nor my wife. Yet."

"Oh, Croy, dreams are fine things, aren't they?" she said.

"Call it no dream. Say vision. Or prophecy." He cut the bread and the cheese with his belt knife and handed her a slice of the former. She took it very carefully. He studied her face while she ate. The painted vines that curled around her cheekbones sprouted new leaves—and new thorns—while he watched. Around her throat they were as thick as a tangle of briars, with shadows deep and black between them. Once, he saw a pair of bestial eyes glowing in that darkness, but they winked out before he could meet their gaze.

He knew perfectly well what those images meant. Cythera's mother—a woman of fierce demeanor and considerable power—had placed this enchantment on her, that Cythera would never be harmed by curse or spell. Such magic could never penetrate further than the top layer of her skin. Yet that arcane energy must go somewhere, and thus manifested itself as these fell images. The curses lingered on her skin until such time that any man tried to attack her physically—and then they would be released, like a shock jumping from an iron door latch to one's finger in the winter, only with far more lethal results.

It was rare that a woman of Cythera's character was the object of a truly vile curse, though. When Croy had met her—back when he was still employed as the Burgrave's bodyguard—there was only a single tendril of curling vine then, and that disappeared up her sleeve. She might have gone a lifetime without acquiring much more in the way of images, had she not needed money. Penniless, with no skills to earn her keep, nor the willingness to prostitute herself, she had found employment where she could.

Hazoth had taken her into his service when she was still a girl. He made an amulet out of a lock of her hair, which extended the protection of her enchantment to himself. And a sorcerer like Hazoth attracted his fair share of curses— cast by his enemies, of which he had many. He compelled service from the demons of the pit. Such creatures liked not making such bargains, and once they were free of his influence, sent magic to destroy him, or to pull him down into the pit with them where they could torment him forever. Now Cythera bore the brunt of those curses. Since entering Hazoth's service, her collection of tattoos had grown denser with each day.

Cythera's skin crawled with magic, far too much for her to safely contain. Magic never stood still—it was pure action, pure energy, and it hated being bound or constrained. Her skin could hold an enormous magical potential but it had its limit, and once that maximum had been reached, the magic constantly sought to be discharged. The slightest jar, the most well-meaning touch, could release that magic instantly. If Croy grasped her hand in a fit of passion, if he crushed her lips with his own—it would be his end.

He had to admit it was going to make the wedding night complicated. But perhaps they could find a way to release her from her magical burden.

"Come away with me," he said. "Tonight. Get away from the villa and meet me. We'll be on a ship, sailing for some pleasant southern beach before he even knows you've left him."

"You think it's that simple?"

"I think it can be, if we choose it."

She lowered her crust of bread to the table and looked at it very carefully, as if she could read the future there. Perhaps she could. "He would not allow it. I must be near him for our connection to work. He would grow wroth."

"Let him pout! What harm can he do us? He wouldn't dare hurt you."

"It's not myself I'm worried about," she told him. She looked up into his eyes. Her own were untouched by magic images. They were clear and very honest, and brooked no falsehoods. "He has my mother under his thumb. Should he desire it, he could extinguish her life with a wave of one hand." She reached toward his cheek but did not touch him, only mimed the gesture, her palm hovering a fraction of an inch above his skin. She'd had a long time to learn how not to touch other people. A very long time to live with no one touching her. "Oh, Croy. You should never have come back."

He stood up quickly from the table, scattering the crumbs of cheese he'd been toying with. "You said you needed to report in. That it would mean trouble if you were late."

"So I did," she told him. She rose from the table and wrapped her cloak tightly around herself, furling it over her arms so her hands were safely inside the garment. "You can't escort me any further, of course, or he'll see us together." She headed for the door, but turned before she slipped through it to take one last look at him. "Try to forget me. I'm lost, Croy."

"You're enslaved. Which is exactly what your mother was trying to protect against when she enchanted you. Hazoth is precisely the kind of enemy she wanted to forestall. Yet now he uses her against you. You've been captured by him as easily as if he *had* used sorcery to compel you." The words were harsher than he'd meant them to be. He had no right to speak to her like that, he thought, and shame burned in his cheeks.

"It's like I said," she told him. "Not every trick he pulls is by magic." And then she was gone.

# CHAPTER THIRTY-TWO

It took Malden the better part of the day to scrub the shit out of his clothes. He couldn't afford to hire a washerwoman, and he certainly didn't want to answer any questions she might have had, so he did it himself down by the river Skrait, rubbing his cloak against smooth rocks until its color was almost back to normal and it didn't stink. When the time came, he told himself—when he was in Cutbill's firm employ, and able to earn for himself—he would never have to wash his own clothes again.

Perhaps it would happen tonight.

He had been very worried after leaving Castle Hill that he might be arrested at any moment. The torturer got a good look at his face, after all, and could have reported his description to the watch. So he had spent the predawn hours slinking from one darkened part of the city to the next, spying on every cloak-of-eyes he could find, watching them to see if they were alerted and searching for a thief. And they had been—a woman, in a velvet cloak, in a little boat. Cythera. They were looking for Cythera.

Which perhaps explained why she had not been waiting for him when he left the pipe and unceremoniously fell into the filthy river. He supposed he could not blame her for fleeing once the guards spotted her. In the midst of the confusion in the palace above, they would be unlikely to listen to whatever story she spun for them. She could have ended up in the strap herself.

He would just have to make contact with her or with Bikker somehow, and make proper arrangements for handing over the crown. Which might be difficult if they were being sought by the watch—most likely they would have gone to ground. Still, he possessed ways to find them the authorities lacked. It would just take a little digging.

On his way back from the river he decided, though, that he could afford to rest and lie low for a day. He was exhausted from his nocturnal jaunt, and his hands ached and desperately needed to be idle for a while. He was also starving, as he hadn't eaten since the day before.

So he took his time heading home. Down in his part of the Stink, the river ran flat and wide through a district of fishermen's homes, all built on stilts to weather the annual springtime flood. He climbed up a bank thick with salt grass, where coracles and punts lay overturned, the tar between their timbers softening in the sun. The fishermen sat in their boats, to keep them from being stolen, waiting for the tide to turn. In the meantime they laughed and joked amongst themselves as they repaired their nets with thick, scarred fingers. They eyed him warily but without comment. Surely it wasn't the first time they'd seen a furtive figure, his clothes drenched with river water, come up the bank and slinking away in the early morning light. He hoped it happened often enough they wouldn't remember him when he was gone.

A short flight of stairs brought Malden up to the high street, where he bought a day-old loaf and three gulps of wine ladled out of a barrel. It was better fare than he often ate, but he was hungry enough to spend the extra coin. He picked apart the bread as he wended his way up the street, careful not to step in anything that might ruin his newly clean shoes. The houses here leaned over the roadway, their upper stories built out so far they were nearly touching. Even in the midday the shadows were thick under the eaves. He sat for a while on a horse trough to finish the meal, and watched the comings and goings of his neighbors.

The people of the Stink dressed plainly, and few among them had clean faces—in fact, most bore the pockmarks of long-healed disease, or other signs of bad diet and unsanitary living. None of them could read or write, and by the age of twenty-five even the most comely of girls looked old and stooped.

"'Ware below," someone shouted from above his head, and a cobbler's apprentice in the street had to dodge a cascade of garbage and filth poured out a second floor window. His leap sent him sprawling into a sawyer and they both went down in a heap, the woodchopper's load of firewood spilling out onto the cobbles. The man pulled the boy's ears for that, and demanded that he help pick up the wood, but the boy merely made a rude gesture and hurried on. Across the street a goodwife stepped out into her dooryard, her face flushed from the heat in her kitchen. She fanned herself with her apron for a moment, then hobbled back inside and back to her endless tasks. She had to work constantly to feed her family, and to have enough left over to sell so she and her husband could make the rent.

These people were miserable, and their lives meant nothing. Malden had never felt like one of them, even if he lived among them. And yet he wondered, as he often did, what his life could have been had he tried to be an honest man.

Not, of course, that he'd had much choice in the matter. The son of a whore—the bastard son of a whore—could never rise far. He had learned both letters and figures as a child, and kept the books for his mother's house, but such skills were useless to one of his station. No merchant would ever have trusted him to add up accounts. By the time he'd left the brothel, he was too old to apprentice in any lucrative trade. He could have given himself over to unskilled labor, and broken his back unloading ships or carrying goods to market for farmers too poor to own a cart. He thought he would not have lasted long at that business, though. He would have turned to drink, to soothe his sore muscles, and wasted that tiny pittance of money he earned.

He finished the last of his bread and got up again. He headed up a side street, a narrow, winding passage between two closes, piles of houses built around tiny, stinking courtyards full of livestock. He heard voices from all around him, snatches of conversation dripping from every window thrown open to catch a breath of air. Hundreds of people lived in the closes, pressed into a space the size of a rich man's parlor. Some of the houses were six stories high. Imagine, he thought, to every day go down to the river to fetch water and bring it back up all those stairs. He saw in his mind's eye an endless course of pails, sloshing and losing a bit of their contents with every step they climbed, a river of water moving up and down inside those tall houses every day. And every pail needed a poor blighter to carry it.

He shook his head and hurried up the street. His own room was in the next block over, above a waxchandler's shop. The shop turned out candles, whole barrels full of them every day made of beef tallow that stank when it burned or more expensive and reliable beeswax. His room stank always of paraffin, and the stairs leading to it were used to store extra spools of wicking and blocks of rancid tallow. Still, the room at the top of those stairs was warm all winter from the heat of the wax kettles underneath, and

he didn't have to share with anyone else. He headed up the
exterior stairs to his door and lifted the latch, thinking only
of his bed. It was a simple mattress stuffed with straw and
sagging in a frame of ropes. He wondered if he would care
enough to tighten them before he climbed inside. He wondered how long he would stay awake once his head touched
the scratchy sheets.

He hurried inside and closed the shutters. It wouldn't be
the first time he'd slept through an afternoon, wishing to be
rested for the night to come. Yes, just a few hours with his
head down and then—

*Thief. Hearken to me, thief.*

The damned crown!

When he first touched it, it had spoken to him. During
his escape from the dungeons it had mostly been quiet, but
only because there was enough noise to drown out its voice.
Now, when his room was still, when he was alone with his
thoughts and his exhaustion, he could hear it whisper to
him.

It never stopped.

*Thief, I can help you. I can save you from all dangers.
Simply listen to what I have to say. Thief! Listen to me!*

Malden stormed over to the middle of the room, where
he'd hidden the crown beneath the loose floorboards. He
stamped on the spot, hard enough he thought he might stave
in the boards and ruin his hiding place. Like a man pounding on the floor to tell his downstairs neighbors they are too
loud.

*I've seen what you desire, thief. And I can help you get it.
I ask only one thing. Place me upon your head.*

His stomping was of no use. The damned thing would be
quiet just long enough to let him crawl into his bed. Then,
before he could even close his eyes, it would speak again,
inside his head where he could not block it out.

*Thief, put me on. Place me on your head and I shall tell
you secrets. Thief, I can tell you where treasure is buried.
I can tell you how to make wealth out of thin air, how to
acquire all the riches you desire. Thief! I can make you
free!*

The thing had hardly stopped talking since he stole it.

And much worse—he was starting to believe the things it said.

All he had to do was put it on his head. All he had to do was wear it for just a moment and it would tell him anything he wanted to know. It would tell him why Bikker and Cythera wanted it so badly. It would teach him all the secrets of the Burgrave.

*And so much more, thief. I know the way to a woman's heart. The witch's daughter can be yours, thief. I can make her obey your every command. I can make her long for you until her body aches for your touch. Just put me on.*

The crown wouldn't let him get a wink of sleep. Long before dark he surrendered. Not to its suggestions, of course, but to the fact that he would go out again, as tired as he was, and find Bikker or Cythera immediately.

It couldn't wait another hour.

# CHAPTER THIRTY-THREE

Finding Bikker was easily enough done, for a man with the right connections.

Malden headed across the city again, this time taking the bridge that ran high over the Skrait to the Royal Ditch. He kept clear of the Goshawk Road there—that place was only for the sons of rich men, idle and carrying too much coin for their own good. They would have been an attraction for a man with his deft fingers if not so well-guarded. At every corner of the Goshawk Road armed men lounged, looking out for people like Malden. The guards, employed by the gambling houses and upscale brothels of the Road, would take him down an alley and beat him senseless without bothering to ask any questions first.

Besides, Malden's destination was in a far more humble part of the Royal Ditch. A part of the city he knew very well. He should, since after all it was where he'd grown up. As he headed down Pokekirtle Lane, a few haggard whores leaned out of doorways to shout propositions at him, but he ignored them. Too drunk to recognize him, they let him pass without impugning his manhood too severely.

Malden had to knock on the door of the Lemon Garden for ten minutes before he was answered—and then only from a window on the second story. Elody, the madam of the house, leaned out into the dusk, her shoulders barely covered by a frayed silk shawl. She clucked her tongue down at him. "Sorry, love, we're not open yet. Come back after dark."

"Afraid a customer will see the pox sores on your rump if they aren't hidden by darkness?" Malden asked.

Elody's painted face turned dark with anger—until he stepped back away from the door so she could see him. Then a wide grin split her face, showing her missing teeth. "Malden! It's been ages!"

It was true. It had been years since he'd returned to his childhood home.

Elody slammed the door shut, and he heard her racing down the stairs to get the door. She must have alerted the others inside to his presence, because half a dozen girls were squeezed in the portal when it opened, all of them giggling and simpering for him. He favored them with a warm smile, and a dozen soft hands pulled him inside and shut the door after him. The older "girls," some of whom had worked alongside his mother, tousled his hair and poked him in the ribs to see if he'd gained any weight. The younger doxies reached for other parts of him, only to have their hands slapped away by Elody.

"He isn't here for that," she scolded, "you spavined sluts. Malden's not a *customer*. He's *family*. He could have girls younger and more talented than you for the price of asking but he never does."

"Maybe he just hasn't tried someone his own size yet," a slender girl said.

"Or maybe he doesn't like seafood," one of the oldsters told her. "You might try washing it out after you use it all night."

"Maybe he doesn't like girls."

"You do like girls, don't you, Malden?"

"Don't you like me?"

"Learn some manners!" Elody shrieked. "Mirain, fetch him some wine. Gerta—you get some pillows together, make him a pile to lie on. The rest of you go finish putting your faces on, it's only an hour till we open. You don't get paid for fawning over our boy! Malden, Malden, it's good to clap eyes on you. How you've grown. Come in, come in!"

Elody was a madam who knew more of hospitality than any ostler. After all, she'd been entertaining men all her life. She let him take her plump arm and directed him into the courtyard garden that gave the house its name. A single withered lemon tree swayed there over piles of freshly strewn rushes. It was here the tupenny whores entertained their clients—the penny trulls (called penny uprights, sometimes) never bothered to lie down. In the rooms above, which had curtains instead of doors, wealthier clients might be entertained by girls who advertised themselves as virgins (unlikely) or by their varied specialties, which ranged a wide gamut.

Malden was led beneath the tree and provided with a bed of cushions and a cup of mulled wine. It wasn't very good, but he pretended to sip at it to appease his hostess. She smiled and saw to his every need and asked a million little questions about his life since leaving this place that had once been his mother's house. These questions he answered only vaguely, or with outright lies—Elody knew perfectly well how he earned his living, and wasn't asking for real information anyway.

He imagined he could have found this same reception in any brothel between the Golden Slope and the city walls. One of his jobs when his mother had still been alive was to run errands back and forth between the various houses of prostitution, and he learned early on that whores had three special talents other women lacked: one was the obvious, but another, less widely advertised, was that they took care of their own. They had to—even by the liberal standards of the Free City of Ness, a working woman was on the absolute bottom rung of the societal ladder. If they had problems, they turned to one another to solve them, because no decent citizen would ever stoop to aid a whore. The children of whores were treated like royalty among their number—because outside the walls of the brothel, they would be treated worse than livestock.

"It's been so long," Elody said, playing with a curl of her hair. The henna she used for dye left it thin and fragile, but she could never stop playing with it. "Why didn't you come back sooner?"

Malden smiled at her but made no answer. When he left, when he'd grown too old to be a baby of the house, when the previous madam of the place shoved him out in the streets, she'd not been unkind but was firm. There was no place for him there any longer. The house that had been his only home when he was a boy had suddenly seen him as a seed between its metaphorical teeth, and spat him out into the streets of Ness with as little ceremony. He could still remember the look on the faces of Elody and the other "girls" that day. They'd fought with themselves not to show him any pity. And they'd won.

For a while afterward, while Malden tried to find honest work—and then when he began his life of crime—he'd sworn to himself he would never return.

Now, seeing how Elody received him, he realized what a fool he'd been.

The madam patted his hand and let his silence go. She filled it with her own words instead. "So much has happened that I must tell you about. Wenna had her baby, she's a pretty little thing, and Gildie actually made good on all her promises, and bought out her contract, and is living with a wood-carver now, she's an honest woman at last. She who was the most scurrilous of commodities once, as you'll no doubt remember."

"Really? I thought she was all bluster, that one."

Elody laughed. "Nothing stands still for long these days. Even old baggages like me can change our ways when the wind blows—oh, and have you heard the latest? It's all the talk today. The Burgrave's tower fell down! It seems a wonder, even now when I've had time to grow accustomed to the notion. Eight hundred years it stood. They say it was lightning that done for it."

"I hadn't heard," Malden said.

"You must be the last." She squinted at him suddenly. Malden tensed, thinking she might guess he'd had some hand in the tower's collapse. She was a shrewd woman, Elody—one had to be to get to run a bawdy house in Ness. Could she see it written all over his face? "There's something different about you," she said finally.

"I'm the same as ever," he protested.

"No. What is it? What do I sense here?" Her face opened wide with a bright smile. "You've met a woman! You must tell me all, at once!"

Malden's shock could not be overestimated. "I—I—ah—yes," he finally said, simply glad to change the subject, not thinking overmuch on what he said. "But—how did you know?"

"You've combed your hair!" Elody said, exploding in laughter.

Malden reached up and touched his short hair. It was true he'd groomed himself before heading out that morning. He'd wanted to look presentable when he turned over the crown. It did not occur to him that he had done so thinking that he would see Cythera again, but—

"It's nothing," he protested. "She's a beauty, and far beyond what I might hope to attain. I've done nothing but make a fool of myself when I'm around her. Surely she's not interested."

"Some women like that," Elody told him. "But I can see your discomfort talking on this, so I'll let it be. For now. Tell me, Malden, why you've really come here," she said, a sparkle in her eye. He knew he hadn't heard the last of this. "I know you aren't here just for advice on love."

He set his cup on the ground and looked up at a shriveled lemon hanging from a branch above him. "I'm looking for someone. Either of two people, actually—a man and a woman."

"We've plenty of the latter, to meet all requirements," Elody japed.

He smiled and looked her in the eye. "How much of this place does Cutbill own?" he asked. He still wished to keep the master of thieves as far out of the job as he could manage, just as Cythera and Bikker had asked.

"That scrawny weevil? None," she insisted.

"In truth?"

Elody sighed. "You know we're not the finest house, nor the most lucrative. Truth be told, we've fallen on hard times, Malden. Cutbill could buy this place ten times over, doors, windows, coneys and all, and not feel the pinch. He never made so much as an offer. He steers clear of us because he doesn't want to absorb our debts."

Malden nodded understandingly. "I'm not sure if the people I'm looking for were ever clients of yours . . . or of any woman plying the trade. But perhaps you've heard tell of them." That was the third great talent of the harlots: they heard things. Men were famous for talking in moments of extreme relaxation. The working girls tended to share the juicier bits of gossip they acquired with each other. Had the Burgrave himself a dark secret to hide, if he whispered it into the ear of his favored concubine at midnight, for certain it would be the small talk of streetwalkers in the Stink by midday.

"Let's see what we can learn." Elody offered him a hand to help him rise from his cushions and led him up the stairs to the private rooms, where the girls were getting ready.

Once there, he described the shifting tattoos on Cythera's cheek to a girl who billed herself a Barbarian Princess (in truth, she was only tanned by the sun). While a trull twice his age coated her face with white lead to hide her wrinkles, he spoke of Bikker's acid-spitting sword. A girl of fifteen put powder of belladonna in her eyes while he elocuted on Cythera's ability to appear from thin air. When she was done, she looked as surprised as he'd been on the roof of the university, but she had no news to share with him.

It wasn't until he reached Big Bess's closet that he found what he was looking for. Bess was taller than Malden by a full head and broader through the shoulders. She wore a tight bodice that made her substantial bosom look as big as Castle Hill. Perversely enough, her specialty was for dwarves—the diminutive craftsmen liked their women sturdy, and far from home they would settle for Big Bess's powerful frame. It seemed they weren't the only ones.

"A bit wild, but a smooth talker, you say. Big sword over his shoulder, oh, aye." Bess grunted. "He leaves his chain mail on when he ruts." She rubbed red powder onto her cheeks to make them look permanently flushed, then smeared some between her breasts as well. "You say he's called Bikker? Milles is the name he uses, but of course it's not what they call him at home. He doesn't come often, but when he does I make him pay for the full night because I know I'll be bruised and no good for anyone else in the morning."

"I imagine we're speaking of the same man," Malden told her. "Bess, do you know where he lives? Or at least where I might find him?"

"Are you going to kill him?" the trollop asked while gluing on a set of horsehair eyelashes. "Because I won't have that on my conscience."

"No, no," Malden said. "Perish the thought. He owes me money."

"Ah!" Bess exclaimed. "In that case—"

# CHAPTER THIRTY-FOUR

When the Seven Day Fire finally burned itself out, leaving nearly half the Free City in smoldering ruin, a great wave of religious mania ran through the people. Both Sadu and the Lady were exalted for stopping the fire, and their adherents carried their icons through the streets in endless processions. Zealots of the two faiths came to blows in the streets, and thus began a civil war that might have finished what the fire began. The Burgrave stepped in then, crushing the leadership of the Bloodgod's mob with brutality and a lack of discrimination. When the bodies were cleared away, he declared the Lady the official tutelary of the city. In honor of this patron deity, he seized an entire neighborhood of houses where Sadu was the only god and had them pulled down. Every timber, every stick of furniture, was demolished and carted away. The people who had lived in those houses went to live with family members if they could, or to the streets if they must. The very ground where the houses had stood was cleared to bare soil, so no sign of the neighborhood would ever be found again.

Protests had been minimal. There were already plenty of martyrs with their heads on pikes up by Castle Hill, and even the most devout were loath to join their coreligionists there. Besides, the houses the Burgrave tore down had mostly been destroyed by the fire already. Yet the Burgrave's intention was clear—he had demonstrated that the faith of the Bloodgod was no longer an accepted religion in the city. If he allowed it to be practiced at all it was strictly at his pleasure, and he could clamp down on it whenever he saw fit. He needed a monument to that intention, and the cleared ground would be the place for it.

A stone wall ten feet high had been constructed around the six acres thus reduced. There were no gates in that wall, nor any way to enter the ground inside once it was completed. All sign of human habitation was removed from what came to be known as the Ladypark. Plants and wild animals were allowed to flourish there unchecked. Rumors persisted—and were reinforced by the roars and howls that plagued the district by night—that the Burgrave had introduced some large predatory creatures to the preserve before sealing it up. It was well known that anyone who climbed over that wall, perhaps looking to steal fruit from the many trees inside the park or to poach some of the holy game, would never climb back out in one piece.

It was a dangerous place, and a sacred one. Which meant that the watch never bothered to guard it. Perfect for Malden's needs.

The top of the wall surrounding the park made a narrow avenue winding through half of the Stink and all the way down to the common of Parkwall. Malden ran along its top, where an endless row of wrought-iron spearheads stuck up from the capstones. One slip and he'd be impaled, but Malden never slipped.

When he reached the end of the wall he squatted down and peered through the darkness. A sliver of moon lit the scene, while vapors of mist curled on the grass of the common where a few stray sheep slept on their feet. Beyond the Ladypark's south wall a hundred yards of open ground surrounded a grand villa. Parkwall was known for its enclosed houses, which belonged to those citizens rich enough to afford mansions yet willing to live so far away from the crowded merchant neighborhood of the Golden Slope. This house was the largest of them all: a massive three story pile of white stone, busy with gables and flying buttresses. Its walls were pierced in a hundred places by broad windows of clear, smooth glass—expensive—and in the front by a twenty-foot-wide rose window of stained glass, worked with cabalistic symbols—ruinously expensive. It would look very much like a cathedral, Malden thought, had it possessed any spires.

Smaller outbuildings clustered the forecourt, while in back of the house was a broad and meticulously tended garden of topiary and fountains. The whole was surrounded not by a wall, but by a simple fence of iron bars, pointed at the top to discourage anyone from climbing over. The fence looked imposing, but Malden might have laughed at the security it provided (had he not been trying to stay quiet as a mouse). A boy, or even just a very thin man, could slip between those bars by turning sideways.

He was not a fool, of course. He knew whose house this was, and that the fence would be the least of its defenses. It belonged to Hazoth, the only sorcerer of real power in the Free City of Ness. Malden knew of the man by reputation. Growing up in the city, unruly children were often threatened with a visit from the sorcerer, and even some adults used his name as an oath. Though Hazoth was accepted as a leading citizen (the only prerequisite of that status being gold), he was a reclusive figure who only came out of his home for grand public occasions. Such a character naturally attracted his share of attention and superstition—a reputation that was worth a dozen walls and moats and palisades. Whether Hazoth was truly as powerful as the legends made him out to be, no thief with natural survival instincts would risk drawing the man's attention.

Trespassing on the grounds of a sorcerer was reckoned a kind of self-slaughter. There was no telling what dread curse Hazoth might levy on a trespasser. He might turn your guts to water or make your eyes burst in their sockets with a simple wave of his hand. No doctor could heal that kind of injury, nor would any touch you for fear of suffering a like fate.

No, only a fool would bother Hazoth in his own home.

Even without the threat of magic, Malden had eyes in his head to see that there were armed guards patrolling the garden behind the house. They went with shining lanterns around the corners of the stables and the kitchens, looking for anyone who dared to slip through that fence.

Malden would never have approached the place in a hundred years—had he not had legitimate business there. His investigations told him this was where Bikker was to be found, and likely Cythera as well.

So he assumed that Hazoth had to be his ultimate employer. It must have been Hazoth's orders that sent Cythera and Bikker after the crown. What in the Bloodgod's name could a sorcerer want with it, though? Clearly it was enchanted—normal crowns didn't talk to people. Perhaps, Malden thought, the wizard merely wanted to study the magics imbued in the simple coronet of gold. Most likely he would never know the true answer. The motivations of Hazoth's kind would always be mysterious to the uninitiated.

The main result of Malden's discovery was to make him all the more eager to be quit of the thing. Hand it over, collect his pay, never think of it again. It seemed the only proper course.

Of course, it would have to be done with care. Hazoth had sought to escape scrutiny, hiding his complicity in the crown's theft behind a double layer of employees. He would not take kindly to even his own hired thief walking up to his gate with the crown in hand, not now.

Malden made his way along the wall until he was directly over the darkest part of the common. As he had expected, it was not completely deserted. A boy in a dark-colored cloak was crouched in some bushes just below the wall. He had a cudgel on the ground next to his right hand and a sloshing jug clutched close to his chest. He also had a scarf wrapped around the lower half of his face, which was a bit of a giveaway.

Malden drew his bodkin, then stepped carefully over a spearpoint until he was directly above the boy's head. The young footpad didn't even look up. He was too busy watching the common, looking for any poor shepherd who might have come late to collect his sheep. The take would be piss-poor, but for a certain class of desperate criminal no score was beneath plucking. Even shepherds had clothing, and there were places in the city where you could sell clothes in the middle of the night where no questions would be asked.

Without a sound Malden dropped down onto the footpad's back. The robber struggled and started to cry out, but he placed the point of his bodkin in the join between the boy's jaw and neck.

"If I wanted to slit your throat, I'd have done it already," Malden said. "Now, will you be quiet? I want a word."

The boy started to nod—and stopped when he realized that doing so would impale him on Malden's weapon. "Certainly, milord," he sputtered out. The alcohol on his breath was enough to make Malden's head spin. He supposed that lying-in-wait was thirsty work.

"You've a chance to earn some coppers tonight, lad," Malden said, and moved his knife a fraction of an inch away from the boy's jugular vein. "But first you must answer me a question true. Who do you work for?"

"My own self! That's all! I swear, your honor, I'm a good fellow, I say my prayers as often as I remember, and I've never done anything like this before, I—"

"You don't report back to Cutbill? He doesn't take a share?"

The boy squirmed violently. Perhaps the lad thought he'd been sent by Cutbill to kill him for unauthorized thieving.

"That answer's good enough," Malden said, easing up a little more. "Now let us converse like gentlemen of fortune."

# CHAPTER THIRTY-FIVE

The boy's face was freckled and his chin weak, when the scarf was removed. Malden held onto his cudgel and his jug while he conveyed the message. Walking like a man on the way to the headsman's block, the boy crossed the common and went right up to Hazoth's gate. He gave one last look over his shoulder—even though he couldn't possibly see Malden so far away in the dark—and then stepped inside the open gate.

The effect was immediate, and startling.

A crackling sound rustled through the grass, and then the boy lifted into the air, as if he'd been snatched up by some invisible hand. Inside the sorcerer's laughable fence all was suddenly action. Guards rushed out to see who the intruder was, and Malden heard dogs barking in their kennels and horses stamping in their stalls.

Slowly the boy sank back down to earth. There was a sudden flash, not of light but of darkness—like the pulsing of shadows after lightning strikes. Malden's eyes narrowed. He was glad he'd sent the boy in his place. Apparently the iron fence was only a symbol for a quite different kind of protection.

The guards circled the boy and drove him to his knees. The boy lifted his hands above his head as a spear was jabbed into the small of his back. Malden could hear him wailing out his message, the one Malden had made him rehearse several times to get every word right.

*You never told me it could talk*, the message ran. *Let us three meet at midnight, at the Godstone.*

It was a risk, sending this message. Someone might be listening—someone who belonged to the city watch or some other enemy. If they were, he had given them the time and place where they could seize him with ease. Hopefully the words were obscure enough to confuse anyone who didn't know all the particulars of what had happened.

The boy was released unharmed. The guards held him a bit roughly, perhaps, but they didn't break his bones for his impudence. Once he was beyond the gate again, the boy ran off toward the Stink, not even bothering to return to Malden for payment. Perhaps in his fear he had forgotten the thruppence promised him. Malden dug in the soft soil underneath the bush where he'd found the boy concealing himself. There, he buried the cudgel, the jug, and three pennies, wrapped up in the filthy scarf. If the boy was brave enough or bright enough to return for his things, he well deserved the money.

Then Malden fled back into the night, running the way he'd come, along the top of the Ladypark's enclosing wall. There was much to prepare.

The fact that his secret employer was a master of the arcane sciences worried him greatly, but not near so much as Bikker did. The big swordsman had killed two men just to create a diversion, and Malden had no doubt that Bikker would be willing to kill him as well. Either the swordsman would want to keep the gold for himself—or more likely, would want to keep him quiet, in the most expedient way possible. When he'd taken this job, Malden believed it was little more than a prank. The crown would be replaced with a duplicate, and no one would ever be the wiser—the Burgrave wouldn't even publicly acknowledge the theft, out of fear of embarrassment.

Now things had changed. The crown was enchanted, and thus far more important than just some well-wrought lump of gold. The Burgrave would want it back, and stop at little to secure its return. Bikker and his master would want to maintain total secrecy, and the only way they could assure that was to slit his throat and dump his body in the river.

Malden sighed as he ran atop the wall. No one had ever said his new life as a daring burglar was going to be easy. He came to a corner of the wall and slipped down to the street below, a shadowed lane running toward a row of houses in the Stink. The houses there closed in quickly, filling the available space around the common like a miser jealously throwing his arm around a pile of pennies. It felt good to be back on cobblestones, back in a district he knew well. He'd spent his life on these streets, and though he knew all too well their dangers, he knew how to manage them as well. He felt almost safe as he headed uphill, toward the eastern section of the Stink.

Not completely safe, of course. But he felt like he was the master of his destiny again. He felt like he could pull this off. If he was careful. There were still ways he could get his gold and keep his life, but it would take much planning and—

"Hold, if you please."

Malden's heart stopped beating, but only for a moment. He'd seen no one following him, had thought it impossible. Who could this be?

Whoever it was, he did not wish to meet him now.

He leapt back toward the wall of a half-timbered house. Its eaves cast a deep rich shadow on the street below that would hide him. He made no answer to the call. He did not so much as breathe. He considered closing his eyes so they would not glint in any stray beam of starlight. But no, he needed to see what was coming for him.

"It is not my design to hurt you," the voice said.

Light burst all around him. The other must have had a dark lantern and suddenly drawn back its shade. For a moment Malden could see nothing, and his eyes, adapted as they were to the darkness, burned with pain. Throwing his cloak across his face, he dashed to his left, intent on getting away from the spearing light—

—and near impaled himself on the point of a sword. He dropped his cloak just in time and drew up short as the tapering point bobbed in the air just inches from his throat. It was no blunt iron weapon either, but good, bright steel of the kind only a dwarf could forge. It would have run him through like a skewer through a sausage.

Squinting, Malden glanced over at the lantern. He could see now that it was sitting unattended on the cobblestones. If he had run toward it and kicked it over, he would be away into the shadows by now and free of this danger.

For the first time he looked down the blade of the sword at the man who held it. He was no watchman, at least. He was a blond man perhaps half again Malden's age, wearing a jerkin studded with iron and a fine samite cape. A man of some wealth, then, though his boots were muddy. He was smiling, but with warmth—not with the predatory grin of a cat pinning a starling with its claws.

It took a moment for Malden to recognize his accoster. When he did, he was only more confused than before.

"You're the fellow they were going to hang in Market Square," he whispered. "The knight. Sir—Sir—Sir Something. Well, it seems you have me at your service, Sir—"

"Croy."

Malden lifted a hand in salute. The knight knocked the hand away with the flat of his sword.

"I apologize for this rude meeting, but I saw no other way to gain your attention," Croy told him. Stranger by the minute, Malden thought. He was not used to armed men treating him with civility. "I wish to ask you but a single question. Will you answer?"

"Under the circumstances, I can hardly refuse," Malden replied.

"I saw you send a message to the villa of Hazoth. And I know someone fitting your description was on Castle Hill the night the tower fell. The night a certain boat was waiting in the river below."

Malden was especially glad then that this knight was no watchman. If Anselm Vry's men had put things together as neatly as this fellow, his neck would already be in a noose. "If you say so, milord."

"You don't deny it. The boat was there to collect you, wasn't it? Cythera's boat. I can see in your eyes it was so. So now I'll ask you—what business have you with Cythera?"

Malden's brow furrowed as he tried to understand what was happening. Was he about to be killed for reasons he would never know? Or would this fool let him go if he answered true?

For some reason, Malden thought he just might.

"I did some work for her, that's all. I'm arranging to receive my payment."

"In the middle of the night? Strange hours to take wages."

"I suppose," Malden said, "that depends on the labor."

Croy's face changed. The smile faded a bit and his eyes widened. "Tell me true, now. What job was it?"

Malden considered his reply carefully. "Sir Croy, I think your interest in milady Cythera is not of an, ah, adversarial nature. To be plain, I think you are her friend."

"More than that, I hope," Croy said.

Malden's heart sagged in his chest. Something he hadn't dared to actually hope for suddenly seemed out of his reach. But more than his feelings were bound to be hurt if he didn't speak quickly. "I will admit to caring for her myself. If this sentiment is one we share, then surely you will understand it would put her at risk if I answered that question? Especially out here, where someone might overhear?"

"I see," Croy said. He lowered his sword so it was no longer pointing at any vital part of Malden's body. "You're right, it's too dangerous to have this talk in public. In that case, let us—"

But Malden didn't hear the rest. He'd found the opening he had sought. As soon as the sword's point dipped, he twisted sideways and bolted for the dark, jogging to one side only far enough to kick the lantern as he went.

Sir Croy called hold again and gave chase, but not for long. Malden had a head start on him, and in the night that was all the advantage the thief required.

# CHAPTER THIRTY-SIX

Knightly interruptions notwithstanding, Malden's preparations were finished long before midnight. He scouted out Godstone Square—a modest plaza deep in the Stink, where the residents were unlikely to open their windows at night—and found the proper spot to lie in wait, then gathered together the tools he needed. This largely amounted to stealing some poor citizen's clothesline and digging an old but still sound basket out of a rubbish pile in an alley. Not the most sophisticated tools, but the simplicity of Malden's plan was its strength.

The Stink at that hour of night was all but deserted. Up on the Golden Slope, across the river in the Royal Ditch, the rich would be up and about, taking their night's entertainment in gambling houses or playing cards or listening to chamber music in their well-lighted apartments. They would be out in the streets in the murk of night, led along the wide avenues by the linkboys who ran through the streets carrying pitch torches. Down here, though, the poor could afford little light after the sun set. Candles were expensive, oil lamps doubly so. The people of the Stink kept out of their dark streets, sleeping early behind thick shutters and locked doors. Only thieves prospered after dark here. Thieves like Malden.

He took his place, then settled in to wait. His body drooped with the need for sleep and his belly was far from full but he'd learned a long time ago how to ignore his muscles and wait in silence for long periods of time.

It was no more than two hours later when Bikker and Cythera approached the square. They came silently, without lights, and walked directly up to the Godstone itself in the middle of the crossroads.

A monolith about fifteen feet tall, inscribed with dread runes that time had weathered to illegibility, it had been a center for the worship of the Bloodgod centuries ago. The first Burgrave had ritually defiled it, however, and the people stopped coming. Too big and too heavy to be carted away, it waited out the years and the rain in mute witness. Even the bloodstains that once washed its lower half had faded away to nothing, and now it served only as a landmark, an unloved boil on the face of an unloved district. Neither Cythera nor Bikker even looked at it as they approached. Their eyes studied the shadows, the corners, the recessed doorways of the houses around them.

They did not think to look up. Malden stirred himself carefully—his limbs were stiff with immobility—and cleared his throat.

His two employers did not flinch. As one they turned their faces upward and looked upon him where he crouched atop the stone. Bikker looked annoyed. Cythera looked merely like she wished to be somewhere else.

He could sympathize. "Did you bring the gold?" he asked.

Bikker's face softened. "You could at least have picked a less public meeting place."

"Certainly. A dark alley, perhaps? Or maybe we could have met at the top of a cliff above the Skrait, so you could just push me in."

"You don't trust us?" Cythera asked. There was no hurt in her tone.

"I don't trust *him*. He killed two just to draw attention." Malden rose to his feet and paced back and forth atop the stone. It was just barely two strides across. "As for you—I can imagine why you took your little boat away. I don't think any of us expected things to turn out this way."

"If you mean we didn't expect you to bungle the job," Bikker growled, "you're right, there."

Malden laughed—though not loudly. "We all survived. I have the thing you want. As long as you have my gold, I think we did just fine."

Cythera reached beneath her cloak and drew forth a bulging sack. It looked heavy in her slim hands, but she showed no sign of effort as she lifted it. "All the same, you'd do well to lie low after this. We drew more scrutiny than we would have liked. And they'll be looking for the object."

"Bah," Bikker said. "They probably think it's buried in the rubble. Come down here, boy, and give it to me. Then we'll leave your gold. Then we'll never see each other again, if you know what's good for you."

"I have a better notion." Malden kicked the basket over the side of the stone so it dropped to the cobbles at their feet. The clothesline tied to its handle had its other end in his hand. "Put the gold in there and I'll raise it up. *Then* I'll throw you your prize."

"Out of reach of my sword, up there," Bikker said. His face showed a kind of grudging admiration. "Of course, you can't stay up there forever. Eventually you'll have to come down, and I can wait a long time."

Malden favored him with a grim smile. If it came to that, he knew he could leap to the wall of the nearest house and be over its roof before the swordsman could climb the Godstone. He didn't say as much.

"Enough," Cythera said, and placed her sack in the basket. Malden hauled it up quickly, before Bikker could grab at it. It was as heavy as he expected—there must be ten pounds of gold in the sack. His heart lurched at the prospect. Opening the sack, he was relieved to see it was not full of stones or bars of lead. Quickly, he counted the money. One and a hundred golden royals! The exact amount he needed. He tied the sack to his back underneath his cloak.

"Many thanks," Malden said. "As for your prize—it's at the bottom of a horse trough two streets to the west. I would have brought it with me, but I couldn't bear its incessant babbling."

"You—You blasted fool," Bikker frothed. "What if some vagrant stumbled upon it and hawked it already to a pawner?"

Malden shifted his shoulders so the gold at his back clinked. "Not my problem anymore."

Bikker cursed and dashed out of the square, shouting for Cythera to stay and watch Malden. When he was gone, Malden slipped easily down the side of the Godstone, using the carved runes as handholds, and bowed deeply before her.

"It's not wise to anger him," she said with a sigh.

"I don't intend to meet him again." Malden turned on his heel to dash away. Something stopped him. He should have known better, especially after meeting Croy, but he couldn't help himself. What if there was a chance? "You, on the other hand—"

"Me? You'd wish to see me again?" she asked.

"I think I made that clear, when last we spoke. If you're amenable."

A strange look crossed her eyes. Her face was too opaque with tattoos for him to read it. "Then perhaps," she said, "I have something you might like to hear. There's another reward. From my master."

"Hazoth?" Malden said, confused. "I want nothing else from him."

"Then take it from me," she said, her voice soft and low. She stepped toward him and smiled. "A kiss. Just one. Don't you find me desirable?"

Malden laughed, but more from uncertainty than the

humor of it. "More than any woman I've known in a long time."

"Perhaps I find you handsome. Perhaps I merely want to show my proper thanks."

Malden's heart raced. The offer certainly held its attractions. Yet it seemed strange she should offer it as coming from Hazoth. What had she meant?

She was very beautiful. Especially by moonlight. White flowers were blooming in the ink just below her left eye. Exotic, and all the more comely for it.

She moved closer, close enough to embrace him.

Malden took a step back. Something was happening here, something he didn't understand. There was one thing he definitely needed to know. "Oh, milady, you've tempted me sore. But I'm not sure my new friend Sir Croy would approve," he said.

"Croy," she said, like a woman waking from troubled dreams. She blinked rapidly and straightened her posture. It was all Malden needed to hear. The offer of a kiss had not been given in good faith. Hazoth must have charmed her into making it—or maybe Sir Croy was testing him for some reason. "Did you say—"

Before she could finish her question, though, Malden was gone. He was really getting quite good at slipping away in the dark.

# CHAPTER THIRTY-SEVEN

An hour later Malden was fast, and finally, asleep.

He did not go home to his room above the waxchandler's, of course. That was for fear that he'd find Bikker

waiting there, his nasty sword dripping acid on the floorboards. Instead he took to sleeping rough, under the Cornmarket Bridge, just below Market Square. It was an odd and
exposed place to doss. The bridge passed not over a river,
but over the very houses of the Golden Slope. It had been
built to allow goods to be brought from the Smoke straight
to Market Square, without disturbing the wealthy citizens
in their mansions. Its span was like a ribbon of stone floating over the rooftops, and where Malden perched he had a
good view of a hundred chimney pots directly below, each
of them trailing a thin stream of smoke. It was like lying on
a cloud. It was a strangely exposed location, but its oddity
made it ideal—no one would think to look for him there. In
his rumpled, dusty cloak he looked the very picture of the
broken men who frequented the place. None challenged him
as he found a spot between two stone plinths and curled up,
his cowl pulled tight around his face for warmth.

Only once, during the night, was he disturbed. In his
sleep he felt rude fingers test the fabric of his cloak. His eyes
snapped open and he was instantly awake. Should someone
steal the gold now, it would be a foul jest, would it not?

His hand was already loosely closed on the hilt of his
bodkin. He rolled slightly onto his side and drew it from its
sheath as the hand grew more bold and insinuated itself into
his clothing. Then he spun about on his hip and brought the
knife up where it could be seen.

"Och, m'lud," the beggar who'd been trying to roll him
pleaded, filthy hands up and fingers spread wide, "there
ain't nothin' needful in that."

"Glad to hear it," Malden said. "Find elsewhere to bed
down, or someone less wary to plunder."

The beggar nodded heartily and scurried away. Malden
went back to sleep.

When he woke, before he opened his eyes, he reached
around behind him and touched the sack of gold at his back.
Still there.

He let himself smile broadly and luxuriate in the feeling.
A fortune, and though it would be gone shortly, by spending
it he would earn the right to replace it.

Today, he thought, will be the best of my life.

Then he opened his eyes. In the morning light the space under the bridge lost much of its charm. It was strewn with refuse and furry with gray, stunted weeds that never got enough sun. The penniless men who lived there lingered long in their slumber, brains still addled by the night's freight of cheap drink. All but one, who had a fire going—it looked like it was made of old table legs—and a pot made from a pikeman's rusty helmet. Whatever stew he was cooking up to break his fast smelled evil and looked worse, so when he offered to share it, Malden politely declined.

Exiting his erstwhile lair, he crawled out on one of the supports of the bridge and then clambered up and over its rail. A drover with a load of dressed stone bound for the palace gazed at him askance, but Malden had never yet been hurt by a nasty look. He fell in with the crowd of people heading down into the Golden Slope—servants and tradesmen and carters of sweetmeats and fuel, honest men up early to get to their work and earn another day's wage.

Malden did not sneer at them, for he pitied them some. They would slave and toil for decades until their backs gave out and their beards grew long, and it would profit them little. They would die as they had lived, beholden to masters who cared not a jot for their welfare. Whereas he himself, who had been spurned by their society as not good enough—well, he had only to drop off his earned fortune, to pour it out dramatically across Cutbill's desk—and then, and then!

And then he would be a full member of the guild. He would be a thief in good standing, with protection from arrest and a dwarf to make his tools for him. He would be, in certain circles, a gentleman of stature. He could begin to make money, real money, for himself. He would buy a fine new cloak, he thought, and rent better rooms. He would drink good wine from now on, instead of weak ale, and eat meat at least one meal a day. His standard of living—and concomitantly, his life expectancy—would improve by great measure, and all manner of things would improve.

And best of all—most important of all—he would be

truly free. A man with money could not be made a slave. He could travel where he liked and count himself safe. He could escape the tawdry past and make his own fortune. His own future.

*What a fine and clever fellow am I. What a wise and cunning scoundrel. My mother would be proud indeed.*

Such feelings put a bounce in his step and he made good time as he wended his way downhill, through the Smoke and the Stink, down to the Ashes. In the charred embers down by Westwall he even began to whistle a jaunty tune.

He saw no sign of the urchin army that guarded Cutbill's hiding hole. All to the good—they must recognize him now, he considered, and kept back out of respect. As well they should! Journeyman thief! Man of station!

He came around the corner of the ruined inn and merrily hailed the three old veteran thieves where they sat on their coffin . . . except they weren't there.

Odd.

Lockjaw, 'Levenfingers, and Loophole never budged from that spot, in his experience. Still, he supposed they must sleep sometime. And it was, by the standards of the larcenous crew, still very early. The sun wasn't even over Castle Hill as yet. Malden shrugged and found the trapdoor that led down into Cutbill's headquarters.

"Bellard? Anyone? It's Malden, and I'm coming down," he said in a forced whisper. He knew from previous visits the strange acoustics of the stairwell leading down, which widened as it descended and thus amplified all sounds that issued from its top. Malden thought it wise to announce his entry into that place, if the old trio could not do it for him.

Yet at the bottom no one waited for him, nor was he challenged by any sentry. The common room was, in fact, empty. Slag had deserted his workbench. No whores were sleeping it off on the divan, and for the very first time no gamblers were throwing dice upon the wall.

It took a moment for Malden to notice what else was different. First off he saw this: the divan was shoved out of its place, its legs having scuffed the stone floor. A booted foot stuck out from behind it. As Malden approached, with dread in his heart, he saw that it was Bellard back there. And Bellard was not down for drink, or white snuff, or even just a late night.

Blood frothed on the bravo's lips. His eyes stared at nothing at all.

"Bellard," Malden said, bending over the body. "Bellard, who did this?" He saw that Bellard was clutching at his stomach, and lifted the dead man's hand away. The wound beneath was a deep gouge that pierced his vitals. Clotted blood lay thick around the injury. It looked like someone had taken an axe to Bellard's middle.

Malden heard something—a door being drawn back, perhaps. A foot scraping on stone. He whirled about and saw, secondly, this: the ancient and historied lock that had always warded Cutbill's door was broken in pieces and lay scattered on the floor. And Cutbill's impregnable door stood slightly ajar.

Malden tried to run. He did not get far. The door slammed open and men with halberds wearing cloaks-of-eyes came boiling out. "Seize him," someone said, "whoever he is." And then a dozen hands were on him and they dragged him inside, into what had been Cutbill's private sanctum.

# CHAPTER THIRTY-EIGHT

The rough hands that dragged Malden inside the door threw him down to land on hands and knees. The butt of a halberd struck him in the back, and someone put a boot on his neck and pushed him down to the floor. His bodkin was wrenched from its sheath and his purse dragged out of his belt. A man of the watch found the sack of gold at his back and tore at it until it burst open and coins bounced and rolled across the rushes that strewed the floor.

"Lady's kneecaps, there's a treasure," someone swore. Malden could see little from where he lay save for boots and the bottom of Cutbill's desk. He could hear the voices of half a dozen men, however, and knew he was hopelessly outnumbered.

"Stolen, do you think?"

"Of course—where are we, but the citadel of crime?"

"Ought to seize it for the city coffers."

"Make an accounting of it, so we can split it later and—"

"Count it. All of it. And then place it here." When this last voice spoke, the watchmen around Malden all came to attention. "Let him up, so I may speak with him," the voice said. The boot on Malden's neck moved away and he scrambled backward to get to his feet. Finally he was able to see what was happening in the office.

The watch lined the walls of the room, the points of their halberds almost scraping the ceiling. In the center of the room Cutbill sat at his ledger, quill pen in his hand—just as Malden remembered him from their last meeting.

Standing next to him was Anselm Vry.

Malden recognized the bailiff of the Free City, as would any citizen of Ness. After the Burgrave, Vry was the human face of the city. As bailiff he not only led the watch but also saw to every administrative detail of city life—enforcing the Burgrave's edicts, seeing that weights and measures were kept scrupulously exact, overseeing the moots of the trade guilds. He was the second most powerful man in the city, and if he were here personally, it could mean only one thing. He knew the crown had been stolen, and he wanted to find it at any cost.

Malden had already seen the price that Bellard had paid.

"Is he one of yours?" Vry asked, staring at Malden.

The question was directed, however, at Cutbill. "One of my thieves? No, of course not," Cutbill answered. He made a notation in his ledger. "Look at the state of his clothing. My fellows can afford to dress themselves."

"And this money? This gold?" Vry demanded.

Cutbill did look up then. He glanced at the stacks of gold coins a watchman was placing on his desk. Then he turned his gaze on Malden and lifted one eyebrow. He was sending Malden a message, which was this: *be circumspect and do not gainsay me.* Malden was wise enough not to acknowledge that he had received the instructions.

Cutbill gestured dismissively with his pen. "The money is mine, yes. This boy is merely here to deliver it. Perhaps before we say anything else, he should be sent on his way."

Vry studied Malden with concentrated disdain. "Very well. Give him his knife back—he's no danger to anyone with that pig-cutter."

"Boy," Cutbill said, "if you leave by the door to my left, you'll find yourself well on your way back to the Stink."

Malden nodded and accepted his bodkin from the watchman holding it. He did not ask why Cutbill was sending him out through the door on the left, when it was the door directly behind Cutbill's desk that led back to the surface. He pushed back the tapestry that hid the specified door and stepped through. Beyond was a tiny room with no other exits—a closet, really, empty of furnishings or ornament.

It did have one defining feature, however. Just to one side of the door, at the height of a man's eyes, a very small hole had been drilled through the wall. Someone looking through that hole could see—and hear—anything that happened in Cutbill's office.

So this was a spy chamber. If Cutbill had sent him here, it was with good reason. Malden placed his eye against the hole and made himself silent.

Back in the office, the bailiff and the guildmaster of thieves were already in close consultation.

"If it was one of your thieves who stole the crown," the bailiff said, "I will hang every one of your crew. You I'll have drawn and dismembered, and your remains scattered across the kingdom. I'll have this place torn down, and your organization—"

"It was not one of mine. Of that I can assure you. Not one of my thieves would think the prize worth the effort. After all, how could they sell the crown once they had it?

No fence in the Free City would accept it, much less pay for it. That means its value for us is nil. You must look else-where, milord Vry."

"Perhaps someone else commissioned the theft. Some-one who would stand to gain by embarrassing the city."

"But why would one of my thieves take on such a job? Surely they would know how much trouble it would cause for my operation. I do not recruit dullards or fools."

In the closet, Malden winced.

"Enough of this nonsense," Vry fumed. "I can hardly trust you to speak the truth. You'll say anything to save your neck, won't you, Cutbill?"

"I've spoken plainly with you, and told all the truth I know."

"Luckily I need not take you at your word." Vry snapped his fingers and one of his watchmen hurried out of the room. He came back a moment later, leading a robed figure with a heavy wooden mask covering his face.

Malden gasped. Luckily no one heard him.

"A wizard, Vry? You'll put me to the question by magery? Surely not," Cutbill said as the magician was led over toward his lectern. "You'd never break one of your own precious laws."

Vry shrugged. "It's true. No man may be condemned in the law courts by sortilege or divination. Yet this is no law court. As for the point of ethics involved, well . . . needs must when the Bloodgod drives."

Cutbill pursed his lips and put down his quill. "Very well. And how should it be done, hmm?"

The magician brought something out from the folds of his robes. A slab of stone about the size and thickness of a book. One side of it had been ground and polished as smooth as glass. "It is a shewstone," its owner said in a burbling, un-natural voice. "It sees what is hidden, what is placed out of sight. I must unveil to use it properly."

The watchmen stirred uneasily at the thought. Neither Cutbill nor Vry reacted at all. "Do it," Vry said.

The magician reached up and pushed his mask up on top of his head.

Malden's cry of horror was swallowed up in the general chorus.

# CHAPTER THIRTY-NINE

Wizardry was not technically illegal in Skrae. It was not very widely practiced either. It could be highly lucrative. There were stringent laws about summoning demons, and the penalty for doing so was inalterable, swiftly meted out, and one hundred percent fatal. Yet other kinds of magic—divination, the infliction and relief of curses, the brewing of love potions and the like—were permitted, and there were plenty of customers for such a trade. The wealthy people of Ness were always looking for an edge, a way to maintain their station, and they would hardly turn their noses up at even the most disreputable worker of miracles. There were easily a thousand men at work in Ness that day who claimed to do magic, and of that number perhaps two or three dozen who could actually match their claims with results. They were all well compensated for the time they spent learning their art.

Yet they were never so numerous as to form a guild. For every child in the Free City learned one fact about thaumaturgy while still very young, and it was enough to keep most of them from pursuing the occult arts. It was this: *magic always has a price.*

Magicians drew their power from the pit and its infernal inhabitants. By making pacts with demons, they were able to work wonders and marvels beyond human reckoning. Yet in doing so they were exposed to the otherworldly energies of that place of torment, and it changed them.

Vry's diviner must have spent countless hours peering into his shewstone, looking for secrets. Whatever he found could not be worth what he'd paid for the knowledge. The skin of the left side of his face had thickened and callused until it resembled the bark of an oak, but it was as white as death. Even the bones of his skull must have changed, for his left eye had migrated downward until it stared, lidless, from where his cheekbone should have been. At his chin and along the left side of his neck, tendrils of pink flesh hung down like a ghastly beard. He could not close his mouth on that side—which explained his strange voice—and the teeth behind his altered lips were visible: they had become fused together in a pair of bony plates that didn't quite meet.

Had he been born like that, the magician would have been doomed to become a beggar, or perhaps a freak in a traveling fair. It was clear from the untouched right side of his face, however, that he had only come to this favor late in life. It must have happened gradually, over time. Malden wondered—when the man saw the first signs of what was to come, why had he not shattered his stone and given up magic altogether?

Perhaps for some the appeal of secrets was too great. The draw of the mysterious and strange. For some, perhaps, the price was not too steep.

When the watchmen stopped murmuring to one another and most had regained the color in their own faces, the magician looked to Vry with his good right eye. "Tell me what you wish to see. It will be revealed."

Cutbill left his pen lying on his lectern. Even he could not look away.

Anselm Vry turned aside. "Look again, as you did this morning, and see if you can find the crown. It may be in this very room—perhaps if you are closer to it you can see it better."

The magician nodded and bent over his stone. From the spy hole, Malden had a good view of its polished surface, but he saw no change there. Yet the very air of the office seemed to change, to grow thick as heavy fog. There was a whispering of invisible voices in the room and the flames of the oil lamps were stifled as by bad air.

The magician passed his hand over the stone a number of times, never quite touching the polished face, as if he were exhorting it to better seeing. Eventually, though, he shook his head and gave off. "All is as before. It exists, still, but its location is forbidden me. It is like trying to look for a coin at the bottom of a muddy lake. Occasionally a glimmer is perceived, but it wavers and is gone before I can grasp the image. Perhaps if I try again later in the day, when the etheric currents are less brisk and the stars take different stations in their wheels . . ."

Vry grunted in frustration. "Never mind. Do something useful this time, and look into that man's heart," he said, jabbing one finger toward Cutbill. "Find the lies he has recently spoken, and find the truth behind them."

Cutbill's lips compressed into a tight frown, but he did nothing to stop this.

The magician bent over the stone again. He made one quick pass with his hand, then closed his eyes and began to chant. He spoke no words but only moved his lips as alien and ugly sounds came bubbling up from his throat. Then his eyes snapped open and he looked to Vry.

"No lies," he said.

Vry thundered at the man, "What? He has never told a truth in his misbegotten life! Look again!"

"There is no need," the magician said. "I tell you, I saw his heart. He has been completely honest with you. He knows not where the crown is, or who might have it."

"Such a waste, to bend your principles for nothing," Cutbill said. "You should have listened to me, Vry. I have no reason to lie to you, and nothing to gain from doing so."

The magician passed his hand across his stone again. One of the oil lamps guttered out and left the room partly in shadow. "This also is the truth," the magician burbled.

Vry grabbed the stone out of the magician's hands and stared into it himself. "I see nothing here! This man's testimony is meaningless." He threw the stone back at the magician, who caught it as he might a falling baby.

"I say only what I see," the magician insisted. "Not what you want me to see."

"Useless! Get out of here. Go back to the palace and read the Burgravine's fortune for her. That's the only reason I let you live, you mountebank."

The magician hurried out of the room without further protest. One watchman went with him as an escort. Once he was gone the lights came back up and the air began to flow in the room once more.

"There," Cutbill said. "As you see—I am wholly innocent."

# CHAPTER FORTY

"I'm half of a mind to string you up anyway, just on principle. It might not get the crown back but it would make the city a better place."

Cutbill sighed and turned to the next page of his ledger. "That would be a foolish thing to do. I have long held a special arrangement with—"

"With the Burgrave. Not with me!"

"With the Burgrave," Cutbill agreed. "Who always saw me as a necessary evil. I am allowed to operate for the most part unmolested. In exchange I keep a tight rein on the crime in this city. The wealthier citizens are under my protection and the better districts safe at night. If you remove me and my influence, you'll have a hundred fat merchants to answer to."

Malden stifled a gasp. To think that the mastermind of crime was in league with the very authorities he flouted!

Not for the first time, his admiration for Cutbill's genius was enlarged.

Cutbill entered a figure in his ledger. "The commonest kind of thief will run wild in the streets, and while you'll catch them soon enough, there will always be more to take their place. The system works. You can't afford to kill me."

Anselm Vry grabbed the quill out of Cutbill's hand and snapped it in two. "You'll pay attention when I speak to you. I will find the thief who took the crown. And when I trace him back to you, Cutbill, I will be well justified in turning this place into a charnel pit. If your organization is needed, you can still be replaced!"

"Of course," Cutbill said. He closed his ledger, though he kept one finger between the pages as a way to mark his place. "No man is truly indispensable. Yet it would take time to find someone with my particular gifts, and more time to place him properly where he could be effective. And at this very moment you require my services. In fact, without them all hope is lost."

"How so?" Anselm Vry demanded.

"You need to find the crown. And soon. For the nonce you can say the Burgrave is ill, and that he cannot be seen in public. Yet in seven days he must appear. It will be Lady-mas then, and he must lead the procession. His position as head of the church demands it. He must also be wearing his crown when he does so."

"A replica can be made. No one will know the difference."

Exactly, Malden thought. That was what Bikker had suggested.

"Without being plain, which would be unwise just now as we are not alone," Cutbill said, referring to the watch-men still in the room, "you and I both know that would not work."

Vry scowled but said nothing.

In the spy hole, Malden pursed his lips. He wondered what that could possibly mean. A replica crown seemed a perfect solution—yet Cutbill and Vry both seemed to think it would not do. But why?

"I'm sure you have your watch scouring the city already, searching for the crown high and low. But I guarantee they will not find it. Whoever committed this crime is clearly intelligent enough to keep it out of sight."

"They'll go house-to-house then, looking for it."

"You don't have enough watchmen to carry out even a cursory search in that time. Whereas I—"

"Yes?" Vry demanded.

"—have a network of informants and observers who see everything that happens in this city. If I investigate with the fullness of my powers, I can find the crown, and return it, safely, to the Burgrave."

The bailiff glared at Cutbill with pensive rage.

Cutbill opened his ledger to the place he'd left off.

Then he stood up from his lectern, crossed over to his desk and took up a fresh quill.

With a sharp knife he trimmed the nib. Then he stirred it in his inkwell.

He sat back down at his lectern.

And began to make entries.

Anselm Vry was still staring at him.

Cutbill doesn't make an offer unless he knows what the answer will be, Malden remembered.

"No," Vry said.

Malden had not been expecting that.

The guildmaster of thieves did not react visibly.

"No. Too long, Cutbill, you have clutched this city like a hawk clutching a mouse in its talons. You have the temerity to think you are invulnerable. Well, I will show you better. I will find the crown myself, before Ladymas. I will find whoever is holding it, and I will torture them until they give me your name. And then I will return here, and I will finish you, and all your works. I will *eradicate* you."

Cutbill made another notation in his ledger.

"Did you hear me, you glorified cutpurse?" Vry demanded. A vein stuck out from his forehead. Even in the dim light streaming through the spy hole, Malden could see it pulsing.

"Quite clearly. It sounds as if our business is complete.

Now, if you'll excuse me, I need to get this place cleaned up before the day's receipts start coming in." Cutbill bent over his ledger as if the bailiff had already gone.

Vry fumed a while longer, but then signaled his men and they all trooped out of the office, out through the door to the common room.

# CHAPTER FORTY-ONE

And then Cutbill was alone. For quite a while he continued to make his notations. Then he sighed and pinched the bridge of his nose. "Malden," he said in a clear voice, "the main problem with skulduggery and subterfuge is that all the involved parties must actually know how it is done. For instance, they should know when it is safe to emerge from hiding without being told. Will you come out of there now? I have something to say to you."

Malden's heart fell inside his chest and crashed into his vitals. He opened the spy closet door and stepped out. Cutbill gestured for him to approach.

"I imagine you heard all that," Cutbill said, when Malden stood contrite and fidgety before him. "I imagine you followed most of it. Surely you grasped in just what desperate straits our esteemed bailiff finds himself. And you must have drawn the naturally following conclusion—that he will not be swept under the current alone. You understand, then, how much trouble has found its way to my doorstep."

"Yes," Malden confirmed.

"Someone, it seems, did a very rash thing. They stole the Burgrave's crown out of his tower. I can, of course, understand how a thief would covet it. It must be one of the most valuable things in the city. Yet it has never been stolen before, not in the eight hundred years since it was made. Do you have any idea why?"

"The . . . consequences that would follow from its theft."

"Indeed!" Cutbill said. He scratched another entry in his ledger. "It was my belief that you were a clever sort, and here I have proof. You follow me precisely. May I be certain, then, that you would never do something so foolish, so irretrievably stupid, as to bring down my entire organization? I'm afraid I can't be certain of that at all. I think you've done just such a thing, Malden. I think you've made a very bad blunder."

"I thought—"

"Here," Cutbill said, and tapped at an entry in his ledger, "is receipt of your dues payment. One and a hundred gold royals, paid in full. And here," he said, flipping forward a page, "is an expenditure of one groat." Cutbill dug a halfpenny out of his tunic and handed it to Malden.

"What's this for?" Malden asked in a small voice. He stared at the coin in his hand.

"It is the traditional severance fee. When a thief leaves my operation he receives that price."

"I see."

Cutbill made another entry. "It is to be placed in the thief's mouth. After his tongue has been cut out to make room. Then his throat is slit. Normally, Bellard does the honors, but he isn't . . . available today. Would you be so kind as to perform the necessary operations yourself, with that rather silly dagger you carry?"

Malden couldn't breathe. He tried to speak but no words would come. Unable to bear his own weight, he sat down on the edge of Cutbill's desk.

"In your own time, of course," Cutbill said without looking up.

Malden drew his bodkin and held it before him.

He could—he could kill Cutbill, now. He could strike the guildmaster down. There was no one in the common room to come to Cutbill's defense. He could kill the man, and then run—and run—and—

And yet, he didn't do it. Cutbill must have considered the possibility when he ordered him to self-slaughter. There must be good reason for Cutbill not to fear his blow. Perhaps . . . perhaps Cutbill had some defense that was not immediately apparent. A charm against blades. A spell up his sleeves. Or a cunningly hidden archer, ready to pierce him through with an arrow at the first sign of violence.

Yes, that was exactly the sort of thing Cutbill would have. Malden lowered his weapon.

"You," Cutbill said, "have achieved something Vry could never do. You have single-handedly destroyed my organization. All by making one phenomenally poor choice. You chose not to tell me what you were going to steal."

"I—I didn't wish to implicate you, or the guild," Malden protested. "Already that has paid dividends—the shewstone found no lies in your heart. And now Vry has no proof I was working on your behest."

"Proof? Proof is for the rich. When a man of property must be taken to court, and tried by his peers, then proof is required." Cutbill glanced up at Malden for the first time. "When the bailiff comes for me the next time, there will be no trial. He will have my name because he will torture enough people until one of them names me merely to make the pain stop. And then he will do as he promised."

"He only has seven days, though. He won't be able to find the crown in that time."

"Everyone knows that perfectly well. That will not stop Vry from destroying me."

"I know where it is," Malden said. "Right now. Or at least, who has it."

"That would be useful information. Too bad a dead man can't provide it."

"But you could simply tell Vry where it is, and—"

"That would change nothing. No." Cutbill laid down his pen and tilted his head back as if his neck was tired from stooping over the lectern for so long. "That would only speed the process. The only chance, the only possibility of a chance of resolving this in my favor, is if I could somehow recover the crown myself. If I could bring it to the Burgrave before Ladymas. He and I already have an understanding. He could chain Vry like the dog he is. But of course, I can't get the crown, now can I? It is in hands I dare not snatch at."

Malden shook his head. He knew exactly where this was going. Cutbill wanted him to come to the conclusion on his own, however. He, Malden, would have to regain what he had already sold. It would be his only chance to save his life. "Let me do it. Let me go to Ha—"

Cutbill clucked his tongue.

"—to the man who has it," Malden said, glancing at the corners of the room, knowing Cutbill did not wish to hear Hazoth's name spoken aloud, but unsure who might be listening. "I'll buy it back. Or trick him out of it."

"Quite unlikely," Cutbill said.

"Permit me to try," Malden pleaded. What choice did he have?

"Very well," Cutbill said. "Do what you can. Let us be clear, though. Should you fail, I will be killed."

"I know that," Malden said. "I heard—"

"I will be taken to the dungeon, and tortured, and then hanged. Perhaps drawn and quartered. That will take a few days. During that time, while I yet live, I will still be able to contact my remaining thieves. At least a few of them will remain loyal to me. They will ensure one thing: the moment I perish, your throat will be slit from ear to ear. If you fail, Malden, we will both die."

"And if I succeed—you must grant me a reward," Malden said.

"Oh? Must I? Tell me, what is your heart's desire?" Cutbill rejoined.

Malden swallowed the lump in his throat. "My life, of course. And reinstatement in your books."

"I suppose you can't have one without the other. Go, Malden. You don't have much time, so you'd better get started now."

"I promise you I will—"

"Leave me," Cutbill repeated.

Malden fled.

# CHAPTER FORTY-TWO

S ir Croy had been raised to be a knight, to be a champion on the battlefield, a slayer of demons, a devout and pious man. He had been trained from birth to command companies of men-at-arms and ride fiery-tempered warhorses.

That night he was called upon for quite a different kind of duty. His patron, the rich merchant who was hiding him from the law, insisted that he attend a dinner party as a guest of honor. He was to be put on display for the merchant's guests, a symbol to prove the merchant's largesse and power.

It was the only thing the merchant had asked for in way of payment for his kindness. Croy could not say no. Had a legion of demons erupted from a crack in the world at that particular moment, however, he would never have been happier to smell brimstone on the air.

"They say the Burgrave has taken ill—did you hear that, Croy? Mayhap he was hurt when the tower came down."

Croy turned to the woman on his left, who had addressed him. She wore a wimple and a ridiculous pointed hat, perhaps to draw attention away from the unfashionable roundness of her face. He could not remember her name. She was the wife of a rich merchant—a dealer in silks? Or maybe it was furs. He only knew that she had been trying to get his attention all night, and when she spoke to him she ran the toe of her slipper up his calf, under the table. Politeness demanded he ignore it. He saw that her cup was nearly empty and he refilled it from the flagon of good wine that sat before him on the table.

"I haven't been much for the news, of late," he apologized.

"The Burgrave didn't appear at the courts of law today," she went on, as if he'd said nothing. As a dish of roasted larks went past she speared one with her knife and dropped it on her plate. It was the seventh or eighth course—there were dozens more to come, small dishes brought out each as they finished cooking, as was the style at this sort of banquet. When the larks were offered to him next, Croy waved them away. He wasn't hungry. "I was there. There was a very interesting case waiting to be heard—a man had killed his wife. He said she had been inconstant, which normally would have been the end of it, but the witnesses said she was pregnant, which complicates things. I like to go to the courts of law some days. I like to look at all the men in the dock, they're so . . . desperate. So wild. I feel a little thrill whenever they gnash their teeth and demand their innocence."

As she prattled on he nodded politely. He'd been trained in how to attend such meals, and knew which salt cellar to use, and when it was permitted to belch, and how to keep his fingers from getting too greasy. One couldn't be a knight and not be versed in polite manners. He had never enjoyed any meal that took half the day, however, and his legs were falling asleep from sitting in one chair for so long.

And his thoughts, of course, were elsewhere. He kept seeing the face of that thief again, the one he'd followed from the Ladypark up into the Stink. Malden, his name was. Cythera had been waiting for him in her boat, Croy recalled, when he had jumped from the wall of Castle Hill. What possible business could that sort have with Cythera? He needed to find out.

"Sometimes I imagine I'm a magistrate, and as the condemned men kneel before me and ask for clemency, I— Oh. Oh, I do beg your pardon," the merchant's wife said. She had gone quite pale.

"Are you all right?" he asked, his attention dragged back to her at once.

"It's just—here I am going on and on about that man they're going to hang, and you . . . you were just on those gallows yourself. Even now you're a wanted man, in hiding from the watch. Why, at any moment they could come and— and—it's so exciting, I was quite overcome. But I've been tactless. You forgive me, don't you? Please tell me you do."

The doors at the far end of the chamber opened silently

and a face peered through. Croy's hand automatically started to reach for the swords at his back—though of course they were safely locked away up in his rooms. He was getting jumpy. Inaction and worry were making him a bundle of nerves.

"Of course," he said. "Will you take some of this sauce?"

"Mmm, please," she said, and stared deeply into his eyes. "You say you forgive me but I know I've been cruel. Perhaps there is some way to . . . earn your forgiveness?"

A footman in livery came into the room and scanned the table. Moving quietly so as not to disturb the banqueters, he moved around the table and over to where Croy sat. He hemmed and hawed for a while before bending down to whisper in Croy's ear. "Sir Knight, there is—there is a situation."

"Hmm?"

The footman licked his lips in apprehension. "Normally I shouldn't like to interrupt your meal, but—but there is a situation. An uninvited guest, er, that is to say—someone came to the door just now, I would have turned her away, but—"

"Speak freely, man. You're interrupting nothing of importance," Croy told him, keeping his voice low so the merchant's wife wouldn't hear.

"A woman, not a lady, but—but in some state of distress, has come to the door, and begged of me that I find you, and bring you to her. Just say the word, sir, and I'll give her a coin and send her on her way, but there was something about her look that made me think she was no beggar. In fact, I don't think I've ever seen a woman with tattoos on her face before—"

Croy didn't wait for the rest. He jumped up from the table and made a few perfunctory bows before hurrying through the door the footman had left open. He worried he was offending the merchant's wife, and perhaps even his host, but hopefully they would simply think he needed to use the chamber pot.

Cythera waited for him in the receiving hall. He saw at once she had been crying. He rushed toward her and barely remembered in time not to grab her arms as he begged her to tell him what was wrong.

"I didn't know where else to go," she told him. "I know this was a mistake, but—I couldn't stay in that house a moment longer. I had to get out. I've endangered you, now. I'm sure he was watching me when I left—and now he'll know where you are, Croy—I'm so sorry."

"I can take care of myself," he told her. "What happened?"

"I've been punished," she said. She clenched her eyes closed and sagged toward him. She did not touch him, but moved her face quite close to his. "I failed him."

"Hazoth?" Croy demanded.

She nodded.

Croy looked up at the gallery that overhung the hall but saw no eavesdroppers there. He pulled a chair away from the wall for her and she sank readily into it. Kneeling down next to her, he moved his hands over hers, wishing he could be of more comfort. "What do you mean, you failed him?" he asked.

She shook her head bitterly. "You'll think me wicked," she said. "Please . . . please don't think me wicked. Last night—you met a thief in the darkened streets, did you not? He was doing some work for Hazoth. Foul business. I was to meet him, with Bikker, and receive the goods he'd stolen."

"He seemed a good enough sort to me," Croy said. A twinge of something ignoble went through his heart, but he couldn't help himself. "A . . . friend of yours?"

Cythera shook her head. "Oh, he's just a cutpurse. Someone Bikker found—we needed a thief, and—well, that's a long tale. The point is this: Hazoth decided he must die. That he knew too many secrets, and that once we had our prize, we were to kill him. Bikker offered to do it, of course, but Hazoth seemed to find it more amusing if I was to be the instrument of destruction."

"You told him you wouldn't do it, of course."

Cythera turned her face away from him. "Croy, I had no choice. I must obey him. So when the business was complete, I—I asked the thief to kiss me."

Croy's entire body stiffened, but he said nothing.

"You understand, don't you? What that would do? Every curse I've stored up over the last five years would be released at once, into the poor thief's body. He would have been slaughtered in an instant. But he refused me. Lucky for him, he knew your name, and knew the effect it would have on me. He's really very clever for a pickpocket. And then he ran off, and I could not give chase. When I returned and told Hazoth that the thief had escaped, he was furious. He stormed about his library, making books jump off of their shelves, and his eyes glowed with magic. I thought he was going to turn on me and try to blast me with some spell. He has a terrible temper."

"Did he hurt you? You said he punished you—what did he do? Cythera, tell me!" Croy wanted to grab up her hands or pull her into an embrace. He didn't, of course. It would be his death.

"He cannot. His magic is no use against me. He can't even have his guards beat me. And that just made him angrier. So he did the thing I've dreaded for so long. He turned on my mother instead."

"The cur," Croy swore.

"He has her in one of his rooms, trapped inside a magic circle. She has languished there for so long at his pleasure, but never before has he actually taken advantage of her imprisonment. I thought . . . I believed that when this time came, he would use magic against her. That he would wrack her with a curse, or perhaps attack her mind with his mind. But he didn't."

Cythera covered her face with her hands.

"He had her whipped," she said. "With a plain leather bullwhip. Ten strokes across her back until the skin peeled away. And . . . he made me watch." She lowered her hands and stared into his face. "He made me keep count."

Croy stood up to his full height. "Wait here while I fetch my swords. I'll kill him. I swear it, Cythera. I will slay him, and free you and your mother from his bonds, and then—"

"Croy," she said, very softly, but it was enough to quiet him. "Croy, if you go there now, girded as for war, he will destroy you."

"If I die for honor, for love, for fellow feeling—"

"You'll still die. No matter how noble the principle, you can only die for it once. And then you'll be no help to anyone. I do not wish you to get yourself killed for my mother's sake, Croy."

"You can't ask me to listen to this story and do nothing," he insisted.

"No," she said. She straightened the hem of her dress. "No. That isn't why I came here. There is something you can do. Some action you can take that might help me."

"Finally," Croy said, with a sigh. "Tell me all."

# CHAPTER FORTY-THREE

Malden needed a plan, desperately. He needed some stratagem that would see him inside Hazoth's house, where he might find the crown and escape with it to safety. He needed to do a great deal of thinking and hone his wits to a razor's edge.

First, though, he needed to get drunk.

He could tell himself that he was looking for creativity in a cup, that the best plans were based on the kind of daring folly that came to one only when the mind was befuddled and the tongue loosed.

Mostly, though, he just needed to drink until he wasn't afraid.

"Ale," he said, and the barkeep obliged. Malden slid a wedge-shaped farthing across the bar and it disappeared. He did not have many left. He had chosen a particularly filthy tavern in one of the worst parts of the Stink, not for the ambience, but because it was cheap and his funds were small. The place had a few grimy windows made of the bottoms of old glass bottles stuck in plaster. Only a few beams of blue and green and brown light made their way inside. There was a bar made of an old door up on trestles, and behind that a stack of barrels with leaking bungs. There were a few tables but most of the patrons stood and drank from leather tankards and wiped the foam from their beards with their sleeves. A brawl had just been dying down when Malden entered, and one poor fool still lay knocked out on the floor. The serving wench stepped high over him every time she had to pass.

"More," Malden said when he was done with his cup. The barkeep waited until he took another farthing from his purse and laid it on the bar.

The fear of death was nothing new to Malden. At their first meeting Cutbill had threatened him casually enough, and he stood up to the promise of death without quaking in his boots. That had been different, however. The threat was meant as a spur, to make him take the action Cutbill desired. It was understood by all parties that he retained an option, that he had a chance to save himself. That had just been good faith negotiation. There were countless other times over the years he'd been in mortal danger, and every time he'd kept good cheer and found the way through. Even in the Burgrave's palace, when he faced instant death from the traps and the demon, he had known there was a way through if he was clever enough to find it.

Stealing from Hazoth, though, was another matter.

Bikker would slay him the moment he walked through that gate. There was an enchantment over the entire house— he had watched the footpad lifted into the air and held there like a starling impaled on the claws of a cat. There were armed guards all over Hazoth's estate, and no diversion to draw their attention.

Worst of all, should he succeed, and find some route into the sorcerer's inner sanctum—he would then be prey to magic.

No man was wise who flaunted wizardry. Magic was unpredictable at the best of times. Students of the arcane were more liable to blow themselves up—or drawn down bodily into the pit by angry demons—than to live long enough to ply their trade. Those who did succeed in their studies, however, became *powerful*. They gained access to abilities normal men could scarce imagine. And Hazoth was one of the greatest sorcerers of history.

Malden had begun to believe all the stories he'd heard about the sorcerer. There was the tale of how Hazoth drove the elves away from southern Skrae by making every tree for a hundred miles wither and die in a single night. Old men sometimes spoke of the day Hazoth wiped out an entire barbarian army almost single-handed, how a simple wave of his hand rooted the painted berserkers to where they stood so they could do nothing but rave and curse as the knights of Skrae cut them down at leisure. The stories of what Hazoth had done to men who crossed him were too gruesome for Malden to want to remember.

The sorcerer might place some dread curse on him that would make the rest of his life a living hell. Hezoth might make his skin turn inside out. He might boil his stomach inside his body, so he died shitting out parts of himself over a course of days. Or he might simply flay the flesh from his bones with a word and a wave of his hand.

"Another," Malden said, and slapped his money on the bar. He was starting to feel the liquor in his veins. It wasn't helping.

For distraction, he turned and studied the low-lifes in the barroom. Most of the patrons were honest enough folk— laborers in leather aprons, covered in flour or candle wax or soot from some forge. They talked loudly to each other and laughed lustily and stamped their feet when they made some jest or swore an oath. In the back of the room, near the hearth, a card game was in progress. The players looked like the kind of desperate bravos who would cut each others' throats over a mislaid wager. They were playing in earnest, though, and were almost silent as they took turns laying down their trumps. The game they were playing was unknown to Malden, so he wandered over to observe. One of the players, a mangy fellow with an unkempt beard and a smear of dirt on his forehead, looked up and growled, but the others insisted he play his hand, and he ignored Malden after that.

The game, it turned out, could not be simpler. The cards were thin pieces of paper with hand-drawn pips on one side and nothing on their backs. They were numbered from one to ten. Each player had a hand of five cards, drawn at random from the deck. He would throw coins into the center of the table based on how high his cards ran, and the others were required to match his wager or forfeit the hand. Then the player would lay down his cards to show the table what he had. If none of the others could beat it, he took all the money. Everyone who had played would draw a new card and the cycle would begin again with the betting.

One of the players had the king's share of the coins before him. Clearly the cards had been running his way. From the way the others glared at him, they must have been wondering how he got so lucky. He did not bother to look their way, instead pausing in his play only to drink from his cup. Bizarrely enough, he had a hollow reed stuck in his tankard, and when he wished to drink would place his lips around its end and suck up ale like water through a hosepipe.

"Are ye playing, lad, or gawkin'? 'Cause there's a tax for gawkin'," the lucky player said. The others guffawed, but Malden's mouth fell open. He had been paying attention to the cards and not the faces of the players, or he would have recognized the man sooner.

"Kemper?" he said. "What are you doing here?"

A ripple of anger went around the table as each player in turn stared wide-eyed at the lucky man.

"Kemper?" the gambler with the dirty face said, rising from his stool. "I've heard of a cove called Kemper. A cheat, they call him."

"Then they lie, don't they?" Kemper told him. "Now sit back down, ye piebald cur."

"I'll not sit at table with a card sharp!"

"Play, or leave, 'tis all the same to me."

"You've been taking my wages all day!" the gambler shouted. "Let me see those damned cards of yours. They must be marked!"

"Sit an' play," Kemper repeated.

Malden jumped back as the gambler grabbed up the table and hurled it aside. Coins and cards went flying as he rushed at Kemper, his belt knife suddenly in his hand. Kemper did not rise from his seat as the gambler thrust the knife again and again into his chest.

There were screams and shouts from every corner of the room, and the barkeep stormed out from his post with a hand spike, but it was already over. The gambler had gone milky white and stared at the knife in his hand. There was no blood on it. He staggered backward, and Malden saw that Kemper was unharmed, sitting with perfect composure on his stool, still holding his cards.

"Clean this up, then," Kemper said to the gambler, "and get back t'playin', a'ready."

The dirty-faced gambler ran gibbering from the barroom. The others eased away from Kemper as if they'd seen a demon jump up and save him from the knife. All but one of the cardsmen, anyway, who bent down to anxiously grab up coins from the floor.

"Leave 'em," Kemper insisted. "They's mine. For me trouble, like."

The greedy gamester nodded and hurried off.

"Ah, lad, yer timin' is not of the best. Yet I'm glad to see ye, I am," Kemper said, and finally rose from his stool. He pushed his cards in his pocket and stepped toward Malden.

"That knife—his aim was deadly serious," Malden said. He wondered if his face showed as much shock as he felt. "Yet there's no drop of blood on you."

Kemper laughed. "Here, shake me hand an' see why." He held out a callused and scarred hand, and Malden reached to take it.

It could not be done, however. Malden's hand passed right through Kemper's as though it weren't there. He felt nothing more than a cold clamminess, as if he'd tried to hold a wisp of fog. He gasped and grabbed at the man's arms and then his hair, unbelieving. He could not touch the man at all. He might as well try to grapple with his own reflection in a mirror.

"You're—a ghost," Malden said.

"A livin' ghost," Kemper agreed. "Which's the saddest contrary I ken."

# CHAPTER FORTY-FOUR

K emper drew too many stares after that to allow any comfort in the tavern. He gathered up his cards and his drinking reed—and of course the pile of coins scattered across the floor—and the two of them headed out into the streets, bound on a wild carouse. Perhaps just to spite those who glared, Kemper handed Malden his things and walked right through the closed door, which rose more than a few startled gasps. Malden bowed deeply to the astonished patrons and then walked right into the door himself, smacking his face on its wooden boards. Perhaps his three cups of ale had more of an effect than he thought.

Without looking back he opened the door and stepped out into the road. Kemper was waiting for him, whistling random notes that never quite added up to a song.

"It's good to see ye, son, it surely is. 'Tis always a pleasure t'have such company as one can speak plainly to, and not have t'worry 'bout keepin' secrets and bein' circumspect. I'll just have those," Kemper said, and took his things back. The reed and the coins went into his tunic, but he kept the cards in his hand and riffled them as he walked.

"How is it you can hold those cards, when you cannot hold a tankard?" Malden asked. He had already worked out that the reed was necessary as Kemper's hand would pass unheeding through any drinking vessel he tried to pick up.

"Well, now," Kemper said, coming to a stop and lifting his chin like an orator. "The curse on me's a strong 'un, yet a mite imperfect, if ye catch me meaning. If I concentrate hard 'nough on it somewhat, I can grip it. With long practice, I can hold just about anythin'. Like me reed, and me cards, which I've had since afore ye first soiled yer bedclothes in the night. I've mastered sittin' in a chair, and lyin' abed, an' food an' drink are available t'me. Seems the wizard what did this wanted me livin', and not allowed the peace o' death. I've not touched a woman, nor e'en changed me clothes, since the day 'twas done."

"It's a pitiable condition," Malden sympathized.

"Yet not without its consolations, y'know, for a gentleman of fortune like me an' yerself. It's a rare gaol that can hold me, an' I can carry coins, if they're silver. As ye see." He flashed a coin between his fingers and twirled it for Malden.

"Only silver?"

"None as is livin' can say why, I reckon. Yet silver's a metal no magic e'er touches, y'see?"

"I'm not sure I follow," Malden admitted.

The card sharp sighed. "Some virtue o' the metal, some property arcane, or mayhap a fault in the way magic's woven, who knows? Yet 'tis a fact. Silver'll cut through any spell, and no curse works 'gainst it. So even if I'm t'be punished for me sins, still I can clutch silver coins."

"Ah! Hence the silver chains—in the Burgrave's dungeon," Malden recalled. "I wondered why they would use such precious rope to tie you."

"Aye, lad. Only silver can hold me, and most places're too poor to afford so much as a silver bootlace. Ye can imagine the advantages this offers t' a man o' my profession."

"And when you disappeared—I thought you had run up the dungeon stairs, but instead you must have just walked out through the walls." Malden shook his head in wonder. "Yes, I can see how that would be advantageous."

"Yer a smart lad, I can see," Kemper said. "'Tweren't

easy, I don't mind tellin' ye. I had to walk through solid rock, aye, for what felt like leagues. Never really got a feelin' for that. Ye're blind as a bat the whole time, and wond'rin' whether ye'll come out sixty feet up over the Skrait." The card sharp reeled a bit as he walked—clearly he'd been drinking himself and wasn't quite sober. "Or, or, and this'd be worse, that ye'll just keep walkin', goin' deeper and deeper into the world till ye come out again in the pit itself, with ugly old Sadu starin' up at ye with them fiery eyes of his. I always figgered if'n that happened, I give him a proper salute, like, and walk right past like unto I owned the place. Confidence, confidence is key in our game. Hold up. Hold up, lad, I'm goin' to piss."

Malden stood at a corner and waited until the card sharp was finished. He had to admit a certain curiosity—would Kemper's water be as immaterial as his body? He thought it impolite to ask, though.

"How d'you like the look o' this place? Think they'd take kindly t'gamin' inside?"

Malden looked up and saw that they had come to the door of another tavern. Such were not infrequently found in the Stink. He knew this one by its sign, which depicted an ogre's severed head. "It's where the local priest of the Lady comes to drink," he said, shaking his head doubtfully. "Good honest folk come here."

"Me favorite kind," Kemper said with a smile. "Them's as honest themselves never cease to doubt the honesty o' their fellows. And if ye know a man don't trust ye, ye know how to gull him, right enough." He gestured for Malden to open the door for him.

There was much ale that followed, with Kemper graciously picking up the bill from his winnings. The night devolved from a continuous narrative into a series of isolated incidents, separated by muddy stretches Malden would not remember clearly in the morning. There was a lot of singing, he knew, and he was encouraged to add his own voice, which was untutored. There was a great deal of gambling, at which Kemper proved more than lucky.

Sometime during the night he confided in Malden his

great secret for winning. "Now y'see these cards, they're not marked at all, perish the thought," he whispered as they crossed the river Skrait by the Turnhill Bridge. "'Tis as I said—if a man doesn't trust ye, ye can take advantage. They expect me to cheat, y'see. They expect marked cards. I've seen marked cards afore, so cleverly done you'd think 'twould take a dwarf to find the spots. Yet always, always some clever fella's goin' to find 'em, for he's lookin' for 'em. 'Tis only a matter o' time afore he sees how it's done. An' then the jig is up, ain't it! Nay, me secret's simpler. Y'see how grimy they got, with greasy fingers holdin' 'em these many years, and general wear. I don't need 'em marked by now! Ha, lad, smell this."

Malden recoiled as the cursed card sharp shoved the ten of bells toward his face. He did have to admit it had a certain aroma of unwashed clothing.

"It's fouled," Malden said.

"Hardly! Smells like me armpit, aye, don't it? An' when any man holds that card, why, I can smell it 'cross the table. An' each of 'em's got their own partick-uler odor, don't it? Why, with me discriminatin' nostrils I can tell ye've got a high card, or a low. From long use and practice I know these cards a fair sight better than the back o' my hands, in troth."

"Brilliant, simply brilliant," Malden laughed, for by that point he'd reached the point where everything seemed admirable, the world was a lovely place, and death was never farther away.

The night provided all manner of diversions. At one point they were chased by the watch, but escaped easily—Malden by ducking into a shadowy alley that was mostly used as a privy, Kemper by simply walking through a wall.

They were ejected, sometimes by force, from any number of drinking establishments. On one such occasion it was because Kemper had grabbed at the buttocks of a passing serving wench. His hand went right through her skirt, of course, but she felt *something*. Her face had gone quite white and she dropped her tray and then whirled around in bitter anger to confront her molester—only to find Malden sitting alone on a bench, looking innocent. It was all he could do to stumble his way out of that place—only to find Kemper in the street outside, laughing boisterously. At the first sign of trouble, the card sharp had merely ducked backward through the wall and to safety, leaving Malden to bear the barmaid's wrath.

When he realized what Kemper had done, he could only laugh, and laugh, and laugh.

Then he was sick, over the side of a bridge. Afterward he felt weak and queasy, and Kemper assured him the best cure for what ailed him was more ale. Malden enthusiastically agreed.

The carouse ended only slightly before dawn—but on a sour note. They had wended their way down to the city walls without really meaning to, and Malden came up short when he saw the green common of Parkwall ahead of him. He was right back on Hazoth's doorstep.

"Kemper," Malden said. "Kemper."

"What?"

"The wizard who cursed you, who made you like unto—unto . . . The sorcerer who cursed you, was his name Hazoth?"

Kemper laughed until he wheezed. "Hazoth? Ye think 'twas him, the grandmaster of sorcerers, the auld bastard? Sadu's eight index fingers, save me skin from such a fate! Oh, laddie, nay. Nay, it was but some hedge wizard, in a blighted village a hunnerd miles from here."

"But this hedge—hedge wizard—must have been, you know. Very powerful. To do this to you."

Kemper shook his head violently. "Nay, in comparison, the bugger who got me—that is, compared to yer Hazoth— he was like hawkin' a gob o' spit next t'the ocean." He sat down hard on the grass. "Magic's strong stuff, it is. E'en a mild curse's no joke. Yet what Hazoth could do t' a body, I shudder t'think. Strip the flesh right off o' your bones and make it dance a jig, maybe. Or just crack th'earth open, right at yer feet, and drop ye into the pit like a pebble in a well."

"Oh," Malden said, and threw up again. Partly from strong drink. Mostly from fear.

"Izzat *his* place, then?" Kemper asked.

"This is the place," Malden said, pointing across the grass toward the sorcerer's villa. "The crown must be inside." Over the course of the night he'd told Kemper everything—including the fact that he had no choice but to break in there and steal the crown back. "It's not like he'll just give it to me," he said.

Kemper shuffled his cards with one hand, no mean feat considering how drunk he was. He seemed to think of something then. "Have ye asked?"

Malden blinked and tried to clear his head. He wasn't sure if what Kemper had just said was a stroke of genius or utter folly.

"Bikker would kill me the moment he saw me," he said finally, shaking his head.

"Then ye wait till Bikker's na' a' home," Kemper said. Then he started hiccupping and had to sit down for a while.

"It's too—too dangerous," Malden insisted. "No. I need to break in. But how? There's an invisible wall of magic around the place, not to mention guards and dogs, and—and Bikker, and Cyth—Cythera. I need to sit down, too."

He fell backward onto his fundament on the grass. He was not feeling at all well. He tried to lean on Kemper's shoulder and fell right through him, which made them both laugh so hard they couldn't breathe.

# CHAPTER FORTY-FIVE

It was not difficult to get into the Burgrave's palace, if you did so in the middle of the day and you appeared to have business there. The denizens of the palace consumed vast quantities of food, drink, firewood, and other commodities every day. Carts came in and out through the massive iron gates in the wall of Castle Hill almost constantly. Laborers carrying sacks of flour, rashers of bacon, or hogsheads of lamp oil passed into the palace proper through an entrance in the back, nearest to the kitchens. On this day they had to line up and each wait their turn, as the courtyard was full already with workmen, masons, architects, and stone-breakers overseeing the careful demolition of what remained of the tower. It was a great chaos of people dressed in every imaginable hue and style.

When Croy entered, walking alongside a cart full of grain, he was still stopped by a guard at the gate, but not because he'd been recognized. The harried guard did no more than to assure himself that Croy carried no weapons before sending him through. Though Croy was wanted for escaping the gallows, the guard didn't even glance at his face.

"You're growing complacent, Anselm," Croy chuckled as he headed across the courtyard toward the palace. There were no archers up on the castle walls, and what few watchmen he saw were arguing with the masons atop the ruins of the tower. The masons had set up a huge triangular crane that could lift away the chunks of broken stone, but the watchmen seemed to think they would damage the palace in the process. The masons argued they knew what they were doing and should be left to their work. Meanwhile their laborers stood around idle, leaning on picks and shovels or sharing a jug of wine. A group of apprentices, boys no older than ten, had started kicking a ball around the courtyard while they waited for the argument to finish so they could start work again. Croy took advantage of the chaos, slipped in through the back of the palace and walked right past the castellan. The old dotard was too busy counting bushel baskets full of candles to pay any mind.

Beyond the storerooms lay the servants' quarters, narrow little rooms smaller than the cell Croy had been given at the gaol. Because it was the middle of the day, these chambers were all deserted—the servants were at their work, of course. Croy climbed a spiral staircase at the end of the hall and came out on the second floor, near the Burgrave's chambers. Vry's office was nearby, in case the Burgrave should demand his presence on a moment's notice.

There was a guard at the top of the stairs. Croy was glad in a way to see that—he didn't like to think of such important people being so vulnerable. The guard was dressed in leather jack with iron plates on his shoulders and down his forearms, and he wore a wide-brimmed kettle helmet. Because it was a warm day—Ladymas always brought sunny weather—the guard had removed the padded hood he should have worn under such a helmet. He lowered his halberd across the exit from the stairs and bade Croy to hold. "What's your business?" he asked.

"I have a message for the bailiff," Croy said, trying to sound frightened. A real messenger would be staring at the blade of the halberd, he thought, so he turned his head as if he were looking at it. His eyes, though, never left sight of the guard's hands.

"Give it here, and I'll see he gets it."

"Oh, you want it?" Croy asked. "Very well." He brought out the sap he'd been hiding under his cloak and smacked the guard across the temple. The kettle helmet rang like a bell and the guard grimaced as his eyes fluttered closed. Croy barely managed to catch him before he collapsed to the floor.

Then Croy stopped perfectly still, crouched on the top riser of the stairs with the guard in his arms, and listened. The ringing helmet had made far more noise than he'd liked, and he needed to know if anyone had heard him.

He could hear the workmen outside grumbling about having to wait to offload their wares. He could hear horse hooves clopping on the flagstones of the courtyard. He could hear a guard atop the wall, hailing his fellow across the way, checking that all was well. He did not hear what he'd feared: no cry of alarm, no voice raised inside the palace to ask what that sound was. No one calling for the unconscious guard, to ask if something was the matter.

Very good. Getting the guard back down the stairs was not easy, but Croy had good muscle in his arms and a strong back. He shoved the guard into a verger's room, then stripped him of his armor and tied his hands together behind his back. With a gag in the guard's mouth, he thought he would be safe awhile. He threw his own cloak over the supine form of the guard for modesty's sake, then pulled on the leather jack and put the helmet on his own head. He found the padded hood on the man's belt and drew that on as well. It hid both his blond hair and his square chin.

Then he headed back to the second floor and straight to the door of Anselm Vry's office. He raised the knuckles of one hand to knock, intending to announce that there was a message from the moothall and a reply was expected. That would get Vry to open the door with no fuss.

Yet just before he knocked he stopped and listened a moment—and heard a conversation beyond the door that grasped his attention.

"You must put it on. People expect to see you wearing the robe." That was the voice of Anselm Vry, certainly.

Croy didn't recognize the other voice. It was that of a grown man, but there was a childlike petulance to it—and at the same time a sort of hollowness, as if the owner of the voice was gravely ill, or, for that matter, ghostly.

"You can't make me. You can't make me do anything. I'm free of it!"

"If you won't wear the robe," Vry said, sounding exasperated, "you can't appear in public at all. I'll have you locked up in your room. And then we'll see how free you are."

"I'm free. I'm free! Every night, when they took it away—every night I dreamed. I dreamed of this! And in the morning when they brought it to me again, I wept. You won't—you won't bring it back, will you? Promise!"

"I promise. Now put on the robe. And stop sniveling. It doesn't befit you. After Ladymas things will be different, just dream of that."

*Enough.* Croy had never been a keyhole-listener before. He did not relish gossip, or knowing other people's secrets. He knocked and announced himself firmly. "Message for you, your honor. From the moothall."

"Damnation—what do the shopkeepers want with me now?" Vry said behind the door. Croy heard footsteps approaching and he stepped back to allow the door to open. Vry poked his head out and extended one long-fingered hand. "Give it here, and be gone," he said.

Croy grabbed the hand and hauled the bailiff out into the hallway. Vry started to shout for his guards, but Croy was quick enough to get an arm around his throat and hold him still.

"You've come . . . to murder me, Croy? It doesn't . . . seem your style," Vry managed to gasp out as Croy put pressure on his windpipe.

"I saw no other way to gain audience with you, Anselm. No, I'm here for exactly the reason I said, to deliver a message—though not from the masters of the guilds. Will you listen to me if I release you? I have vital information you require."

"I'll listen," Vry choked. Croy let him go. "I'll listen, then I'll have you arrested. I don't know how you managed to get in here, and I can only wonder how you expect to get back out with your head attached to your neck. What message could be so important that you would risk your life for it?"

"The sorcerer Hazoth has the Burgrave's crown," Croy said.

"What? What are you talking about?"

Croy shook his head. "You needn't pretend. I know everything. And now so do you. The crown is safe, sealed in a leaden coffer in Hazoth's sanctum. What he wants with it I have no idea. Now, I must be going."

"You're right," Vry told him. "This is vital information. I don't suppose you'd tell me how you came by it."

"I'm bound to secrecy," Croy said.

"Of course, of course." Vry nodded in understanding. "Hazoth," he said. He tapped his upper lip. "Can you get the crown away from him, d'you think?"

"By myself? No. But you can marshal troops enough to wrest it from him, certainly?"

"I suppose I can. I owe you my thanks, Croy." Vry clapped him on the shoulder. "I only wish I could pay you back for this debt. But you know that the Burgrave's word is law, and he has ordered your death. What can I do for you, that will not counter his decision? It's not in my power to pardon you, much as I'd like to."

Croy clutched his friend by the forearm. "Just give me a head start. Don't call your guards for five minutes. That will be enough. Oh, and Anselm?"

"Yes?" the bailiff asked.

"You really should take better note of who comes and goes through your gates." Croy smiled broadly and gave the bailiff a deep bow. "I still serve the Burgrave," he said. "My duty was clear."

And yet—the words tasted wrong in Croy's mouth. For in truth it was not for the Burgrave he'd come to the palace. Cythera had told him all about the theft of the crown, and together they'd made this plan. She could not leave Hazoth's service as long as he held her mother prisoner—and while he lived, he would never release her. Croy knew he could not destroy the sorcerer on his own. No matter how strong his arm, no matter how puissant Ghostcutter's blade, he could not match Hazoth's magic.

Yet if it were to come to light that Hazoth was behind the plot to embarrass the Burgrave, well . . . perhaps the wheels of justice could turn in the right direction, just this one time. Anselm Vry would bring every guard and watchman in the city down on Hazoth's house, and they would see just how strong his magic was then.

# CHAPTER FORTY-SIX

It was not Anselm Vry who next approached Hazoth's villa, however.

It was Malden.

He had spent most of the day hiding in the bushes of the Parkwall Common, crouching like a footpad without even a jug of brandy to keep him company. The last thing he wanted after his night carousing with Kemper was more liquor.

It was easy enough to stay still. Every time he moved he felt like his brains sloshed back and forth in his skull. He felt weak and queasy. He was not sure if that was his hangover or only fear.

The gate of Hazoth's villa opened and Bikker came striding out. This was what Malden had been waiting for. The bearded swordsman clanked as he walked—Malden could hear him all the way across the common—and he scratched at one armpit as he headed toward Old Fish Street, the road that led to the wharves on the river Skrait. Malden had no way of knowing what his business there might be, but he didn't care. As long as Bikker did not return for an hour or more.

When Bikker was well out of sight, Malden rose painfully to a standing posture and then walked across the green common, in full view of Hazoth's house. He wanted very badly to turn around and run, or at least to approach in a less conspicuous manner—there were trees all along one edge of the common that would hide him well.

He did not turn away.

At the gate, Hazoth's guards were waiting for him. They stood well inside the fence, and Malden knew from watching them a long time that they would be inside the radius of the spell that protected the place. He offered them no threat and they made no move to challenge him. They leaned on their polearms and just watched him come closer, daring him with their eyes to step through the gate.

There were six of them visible. They wore chain mail and surcoats in the colors of Hazoth's livery: black and scarlet. One of them turned his head and spat as Malden stepped up to the gate.

There was no turning back once he was through.

He stepped over the threshold.

He could perhaps be forgiven for closing his eyes as he

took that fateful step. Yet nothing happened—at first. The forecourt of the villa was covered in crushed gravel, with here and there a dandelion or a sprig of clover poking up through the rocks. The gravel crunched under Malden's leather shoes. He took another step.

And that was when the spell took him. He felt as if he had run at full speed directly into a brick wall. His body tensed at the impact and his bones thrummed, though he could see no barrier before him. It felt like ghostly hands passed over his face and chest, and then something gripped him around the waist.

One of the guards laughed.

Malden did not cry out—he had no breath in his lungs—as the invisible force lifted him bodily off the ground. The grip around his waist and chest held him immobile as invisible fingers rifled through his purse and inside his tunic, as his cloak was lifted and checked for concealed weapons. He had been smart enough to leave his bodkin at home, but the buckle of his belt and the handful of copper coins in his purse grew searing hot for a moment, until he thought they would burn through his clothes. As quickly as it had come, however, that phantom heat dissipated.

The invisible hands lowered him to the ground again— but held him still.

"Good morrow to you," Malden managed to croak out. He caught the eye of one of the guards. "Will you let me speak?"

The guard came over and jabbed him in the chest with the butt of his pikestaff. Hard enough to rattle his sternum. "What business have you here, dog?"

Malden licked his lips. His mouth was still very dry from the night before. "I have a message for Hazoth. One he desperately needs to hear."

The guard smiled broadly. "Tell it to me, and perhaps we'll let you go."

Malden nodded agreeably. "Would that I could. I'm afraid it must be communicated directly to the sorcerer, however. It is information of a . . . delicate nature, and best not spoken aloud where unwanted listeners might hear."

The guard scowled. Yet he walked over to one of his fellows and conferred with him a while. Malden could do naught but wait—the invisible wall still held him pinned. He could not so much as scratch an itch.

The second guard ran into the house. He was gone quite a while. The others moved closer to the gate, weapons at the ready in case Malden had some charm that would free him from the invisible wall.

Not very clever of them, he thought. They should have been watching the fence, looking for some armed force approached from another direction. His own approach could have just been a diversion to hide the advance of a more dangerous force. The fact that he, who had no training in security, could see as much told him something. These were not soldiers, then, but only bravos hired to look menacing, not to effectively guard the villa. *Good to know.*

Not that he could make use of that information if the invisible guardian continued to hold him. It seemed he waited forever, exposed under the sun, unable to move. For a span nothing happened. Eventually, though, the guard returned from the house. He rushed over to his post as if nothing had happened, and Malden wondered if he should be left there, suspended in nothing, until he died of thirst.

But then Cythera stepped out of the doorway.

The hood of her velvet cloak was up, hiding her face in shadows. Her hands were bare, though, and seeing tattooed coils of ivy twisting around her fingers, Malden knew it was her.

She approached him directly, stopping five feet away. He supposed that spot must mark where the barrier ended on the inside—another useful thing to know.

"I am very glad to see you," he said, smiling down upon her. "I'd bow to you, as you deserve, but as you can see, I'm a bit indisposed. If you'd be kind enough to let me down I'd be most obliged."

"You're a fool," she said. "You'll die here."

"I'm desperate," he told her. "If not here, I'll die elsewhere, and just as certain."

She gave him a look of uncertainty. A questioning look.

As if she could not believe he had come here and risked so much. He smiled in return, hiding his true fear. A part of him was woefully glad to see her again, and not just because she was the only one who could get him out of the barrier.

"As you wish," Cythera said.

She lifted her hands in a complicated gesture, her fingers tucked in or stretched outward in weird contortions. She spoke a word that Malden could not hear clearly, even at so close a distance.

The air flexed with magic and he dropped to the ground, falling on his knees and scraping his hands on the gravel. The magic wall was gone. "I offered to bow, and now you see me kneel. You have my thanks, lady."

Cythera did not offer to help him up. Instead she turned on her heel and walked back toward the house. The guards weren't even looking at Malden. He staggered to his feet and then raced after her, through the massive stone doors and into the coolth of a dim portico.

# CHAPTER FORTY-SEVEN

When Malden's eyes adjusted he found himself in a broad marble hall held up by massive columns of braided stone. Light streamed in through tall windows at the far end of the room, which looked out over a garden maze. The glass alone in those windows would be worth ten times what a craftsman up in the Smoke might make in a year. Along the walls stood alabaster statues of ancient scholars and wizards, some of whom he recognized by the things they held or the way they were dressed. There was Antomach the Sage, who had proved the world was round.

He was identifiable by the compass he held before him, his other hand held high with a miniature planet floating above his upturned palm. Malden could not see how it was suspended—perhaps by magery. Another statue depicted the necromancer Vull, a figure of such antiquity no one living now remembered what land he'd hailed from. He was shown here in one of his favorite shapes, that of a massive bear with skeletal human hands. Other statues were draped in cunningly wrought shrouds of stone, or stood nude with wolves curling around their titanic legs.

At the center of the hall a double staircase of worked stone rose gracefully toward a gallery above. Standing next to the stairs on a stone plinth was something that shocked Malden as incongruous—a globe of iron, its surface pitted and mottled with rust. A fine sifting of red powder made a crimson shadow on the floor around it. It must have been fifteen feet across and was as ugly as the sharp end of a crossbow bolt. What it was doing in such elegant surroundings was a mystery.

Cythera's footsteps rang on the floor, which had been polished near unto a mirrored surface. "He's waiting for you through here," she said, and gestured toward a tall doorway in the wall to Malden's right. "Don't anger him by tarrying here while you gawk."

He nodded and let his gaze run over the hall's features one last time before following her.

"Surely you must realize you are unwelcome here," she whispered to him as she opened the door and ushered him inside. "I thought you were smarter than this."

"Think me not clever?" he asked, mocking hurt feelings. "I waited until Bikker went out, did I not? How soon do you expect him back, by the way?"

Her brow furrowed, though it was hard to tell from the tattooed creepers that grew upward from her eyelashes. "Bikker? He shan't be returning."

"Doesn't he live here?" Malden asked. "I thought he was a retainer of the sorcerer, like yourself."

She shook her head. "He's no servant of my master. And I am no retainer." She seemed unwilling to say more.

She brought him into a long hallway lined on one side with doors. More windows pierced the outside wall, their glare cut down by gauzy curtains that hung from the ceiling. Small tables and display cases stood between the windows, holding curios, some that Malden would very much have liked to stop and examine more closely, and others that made him flinch and look away. He saw one case that held a collection of severed human hands, while another was full of what appeared to be giant pearls. A stuffed and lifeless snake lay coiled on one table, holding a carved ball of white jade in its jaws. The purpose of such things—or if they even had a purpose beyond mere ornament—was lost on him.

At the far end of the corridor Cythera opened another door, which led into a library. Despite himself, Malden's jaw fell open once again.

It was a comfortable, snug space, though several times larger than the common room at Cutbill's lair. Sumptuous rugs covered the floor, and a fireplace filled half of one wall. Couches and chairs upholstered in leather stood here and there, where a visitor might choose to sit and read, and an enormous tapestry map of the continent hung from the ceiling showing all the cities, roads, and rivers of Skrae and the Northern Kingdoms in cunning detail. What really astounded Malden about the room, however, was the collection of books.

Books were expensive. They had to be inscribed by hand, then bound in costly hides. Illuminators and engravers were employed in their construction, and since very few people in the kingdom could read, there was a premium on their production. Even the Burgrave might have had only a single shelf of books in his palace, mostly devotional works praising the Lady.

Yet Hazoth had hundreds of books here—perhaps thousands. Far more than Malden could count. Thin folios and massive tomes, miniature librams that would fit in the palm of the hand, grimoires bound in carved wooden covers inlaid with gold and silver and bronze. Books adorned with gemstones, and others with leather covers tooled with a pattern of skulls and bones. Some shelves held loose papers in great sheaves, bound with string, or scrolls and palimpsests wound about ivory rods, or forms of printed matter Malden had never imagined—books built into miniature chests, or folded fans of paper, or books made of pentagonal signatures tied together with ribbon. Books that glowed with their own light, and books that looked like they had scuttled into the shadows at the back of deep shelves, as if afraid of the sun. Opened books sat on lecterns or scriptoria, written in languages and even alphabets he did not recognize. Ink pots of black and red and purple were arranged around one table, and quills from birds far more exotic than the typical goose or crow.

He had a chance to look at only a few of the titles inscribed on the spines of the books nearest to him, but they inflamed his imagination. *A Season Within the Pit, Marloff's Compendium of Diabolic Keys, The Book of The Names of The Dead, The Fraternity of Fame, Wand'ring Formes and Theyr Dispelment.*

"How could he read them all within one lifetime?" Malden breathed.

"He's older than you think," Cythera said.

"Older even than she knows," Hazoth replied.

Malden's feet left the floor in surprise. He whirled around to find the sorcerer taking his ease in one of the leather-bound chairs. He was dressed in a simple black robe and matching hose, with a black veil down over his face. Malden was certain he had not been sitting there a moment ago.

# CHAPTER FORTY-EIGHT

" So you can read, boy? I'm impressed."

Malden lowered his head in humility. "I have that gift," he said. "Milord Hazoth, I beg your pardon for my intrusion. I assure you I would not have come here had I not been in possession of certain information, which—"

"Cythera," Hazoth said, ignoring him, "perhaps things have changed since I was last abroad in the world. It is possible that manners have changed. Is it common these days for peasants to speak before they have been bidden?"

Malden looked up to see Cythera blush beneath the ink on her face. "Malden is no peasant. He is a free man, master. At least as long as he resides within the city's walls."

"Indeed?" Hazoth said, sounding surprised. "And that entitles him to come to my house and disturb my studies?" He rose from his chair and walked across the room to the tapestry map, as if trying to recall to himself where he was. "And if I were to, say, transport him instantaneously to—let us see—to here?" He pointed at a place close to the Western Reach, a region marked on the map as devoted to agriculture and possessing no towns large enough to merit inclusion at the map's scale. "If he were to find himself in the midst of a bean field, on some petty viscount's estate, with no way to return. What would become of him?"

Cythera glanced at Malden and shook her head a tiny fraction of an inch. He was not to speak now, that much was clear.

"He would be arrested for trespass by the reeve of that place," she replied. "Most likely he would be forced to accept an oathbond, and would spend the rest of his life toiling as a common farmhand."

"And then he would be required to pay proper respect when brought before his betters." Hazoth reached under his veil and stroked his chin. "It would require a certain ritual to send him thence, however, and such operations take time. Far quicker, I think, to simply ensure that he does not talk out of turn again." He brought his free hand up in the air and made a complex gesture.

Malden felt as if an iron pincer had gripped his throat. He tried to open his mouth and felt the invisible force constrict until he could barely breathe. It was much like the barrier outside that had held him aloft in the air, but worse—the barrier had been unpleasant, but this was actually painful. He had no doubt that if Hazoth so chose, he could cause the force to squeeze until his windpipe were crushed.

"There," Hazoth said, and moved back to his chair. "Much better. I hadn't finished speaking, boy. I had more to say, and now I can. I was going to say how impressed I was with you. Cythera has spoken quite highly of your abilities as a thief, but that is a subject I find uninteresting. I am far more admiring of your willingness to overcome your—quite natural—fear of anyone more powerful than you. Coming here today was an act of uncommon valor in a lowborn not-quite-peasant such as yourself. And valor is commendable, even in its cruder forms. Rudeness, however, is always unacceptable, and I will not have it in my house. Had you not impressed me so much, I would extinguish your life like that of a rodent I found in my larder, do you understand? But I have chosen to be merciful." He waved his hand. "You may now say, 'Thank you, Magus.'"

The hold on Malden's wind was gone, as if it had never been there.

"Thank you, Magus," he said.

"You are most welcome. There. Not so hard to be polite, is it? You may speak."

"I apologize," Malden said, his heart burning in his chest, "for my rudeness."

"Quite all right. I believe you had a message for me. Say it now."

Malden cleared his throat. "I've come to tell you that you are in danger. Anselm Vry, the bailiff of this city, is searching you out even now. He knows the crown has been stolen, and he intends to recover it regardless of who might be inconvenienced."

"That's all you came to say?"

Malden nodded. The sorcerer had not told him he could speak.

"Very good. It is ever so kind of you to come and tell me this. It shows good business sense as well. You were hired to perform a task and you were paid handsomely. I take it your coming here to offer me warning was all part of the service, hmm? You are acting out of pure altruism, and want nothing further as recompense. Surely you didn't think this would earn you some more coin. After all, the gold I gave you already should last a lifetime for one of such humble aspirations of yourself. That is, if you haven't already drank it all, or spent it on some shiny but worthless bauble. You may speak."

Malden chose his words carefully. "I admit, Magus, that my intentions were not unalloyed with self-interest. Vry intends to torture anyone connected with the theft until they provide the crown's location. I fear he has some way of discovering my involvement, and that he will put me to the ordeal. It had occurred to me that you might be able to offer me some protection from that fate. It would be in our mutual self-interest, as then I could not reveal—"

"You and I have no mutual interests of any sort," Hazoth told him. "Tell me something—you may answer me this— do you know why I wear this veil?"

Malden lowered his eyes. He thought of Anselm Vry's hedge wizard, and what came from peering into his shewstone. "It is my understanding that magic is never free. That power comes from the demons a magician treats with. So as his power grows, his body is twisted and deformed to resemble the creatures of the pit. I assume you wear the veil to hide some disfigurement." An eye out of place, a face turned the texture of tree bark, a beard of writhing flesh . . .

"Oh, very good! And yes, that is the reason for the tradition. I don't suppose your brain is capable of understanding what happens when one siphons power through the flaws in the underpinnings of our fractured cosmos, but you have the gist down pat. Perhaps you will brace yourself to take a look at what is beneath my veil."

Malden's stomach tightened as Hazoth reached up to lift the black crape away from his face. For a sorcerer as powerful as Hazoth, the price of magic must have been exceeding steep. Would the uncovering reveal skin as scaly and shiny as an asp's? Would there be pus, and open sores that never closed, or even wounds so deep the skull would be visible? Would the face look human at all?

Then the veil was rolled back and Malden saw Hazoth's face and he gasped in surprise. For the countenance thus exposed was perfect.

It was the face of a demigod. The cheekbones were high, the limpid blue eyes set perfectly far apart, the nose powerful without being over prominent. The skin was as clear as milk, with no blemish visible anywhere. It was a face of youth, of compassion, of inherent goodness and decency—except for the eyes, which were as hard as iron.

"I wear this veil," Hazoth told Malden, "because if I did not, no one would take me seriously. They would think my power slight, my magic untested. Whereas in fact the opposite is true. When one becomes powerful enough, one is able to shape one's appearance to fit one's fancy. And I am quite powerful indeed. Let Anselm Vry come to my door, as you did. I will welcome him inside, and if he troubles me, I will dispatch him like an obnoxious fly."

# CHAPTER FORTY-NINE

Hazoth rose from his chair and went over to one of his bookshelves. He ran his finger along a number of spines before selecting a slim volume and pulling it free. "It was good of you to come here and give me your warning, boy. However little it was needed. Do you have anything else to say before you leave? You may speak."

Malden bit his lip. Circumspection was everything now. "I can only plead with you then, Magus. Beg, if I must. I'm in a great deal of trouble, trouble I earned in your service. Does that not entitle me to some consideration? It would be a trifle for you to offer me some protection under your roof. If nothing else I could come work for you, in whatever capacity you saw fit."

"A job? You want a job? But you already had one, dear boy. If there were risks involved, you knew them when you took it. Or perhaps you will claim you didn't understand the magnitude of your crime. Well, considering your limited resources, I suppose that's understandable. Come here."

Malden's legs started walking toward the sorcerer before he thought to move them. He'd had every intention of doing as he was bid, but it seemed the sorcerer wanted to compel him anyway. When he was standing only a few feet away—inside knife range, he thought bitterly—his legs stopped and froze in place.

Hazoth gestured with the book he held in his hands. "If I needed a table boy, or someone to muck out my stables, I could have you with a thought. I could render you mindless and servile. Bind you to my service for the remainder of your life, and do it in such a way you would be unutterably happy, thrilled every morning to rise from your pile of straw and spend another day working for me until your fingers bled. If I wanted that, it would already have begun."

Malden swallowed carefully. His heart was racing.

"Such a waste that would be, though. You can read. Do you understand how rare that is? Reading is the difference, the mark, of a being capable of thinking beyond its own petty concerns. It is the one thing that truly separates humanity from the beasts. Somehow you have managed the art, and like a trained dog that can count with its paws, you amuse me. So no, I won't give you a job. Or my protection. But you may have this instead: the greatest treasure I can convey, or at least the greatest that you will be able to comprehend." Hazoth pressed the book into Malden's hands.

It was bound in calf's leather and was duodecimo in size. Gold characters were printed on the spine but in an alphabet Malden did not know.

"Read it at your leisure. I'm sure you'll find it most edifying." Hazoth smiled, revealing a double row of perfect white teeth. "You may thank me."

"Thank you, Magus," Malden said.

"It is nothing. Now. Cythera—perhaps you will see our little friend out. Take him the back way, so no one sees him leave. I have no doubt Vry is already watching this house and saw him enter. Or," Hazoth said, turning his frigid eyes on Malden, "did you not consider that when you came?"

Malden had not been told to speak, so he held his peace.

"Come," Cythera said, and headed toward a door at the far side of the library from which they'd entered. Malden glanced over his shoulder on the way out and saw that Hazoth was no longer in the room.

"A neat trick," he said as she led him down a side corridor. "This vanishing and appearing. You know it as well," he added, remembering how he'd first met her, when she appeared out of thin air on the roof of the university cloister.

"A simple one, once it's mastered. Mostly it is a matter of misdirection. Of moving when no one is looking." She pushed open a wide set of doors and brought him into the villa's dining room. Its walls were of carved oak, and the table could seat sixteen in spacious comfort. The chairs were pushed up against the walls—they were carved of some glossy wood in intricate patterns and looked far too delicate to support the weight of a human being. The table itself was a slab of marble three inches thick. Something about it demanded Malden's attention. When he looked closer, he saw it had no legs. The slab simply floated in the air, perfectly motionless. He couldn't resist the urge to push down on one edge, but the table easily resisted any force he put on it. Cythera sighed in frustration and pointed toward the door. "Leave that be, Malden. You must go now, and quickly, before he changes his mind. He is known to be capricious."

"Oh? You think he'll take his book back?" Malden asked.

"He has decided to let you live for today. I'm worried he'll rethink that choice."

At the back of the dining room was a small preparatory, where food brought in from the kitchens could be arranged on platters before going to table. The preparatory had a single high window that was open to catch the breeze. It didn't look like it could be locked.

"You're concerned for me," Malden said as she opened the doors to the garden. "I'm touched." He blinked in the sudden rush of sunlight when she led him out onto a gravel path.

She turned to face him, her face an impassive mask. "I don't like to see people hurt. It gives me no pleasure. In that way, I am different from him. But don't count on that fellow feeling for too much."

He sketched a simple bow as they hurried along, and made a show of stumbling so that his foot kicked a spray of gravel against the side of the villa with an annoying rattle. They were passing the kitchens, which were housed in their own outbuilding. That way if they caught fire they would not burn the main house.

"Do you find me handsome?" he asked, with a grin on his face.

"I find you brazen. If you think I'm going to swoon over your looks, or give you my kerchief to tie around your lance, you're fishing in the wrong pond."

"Ah—but you smile when you see me. You admire my courage. You like me, I can tell. Well, working for that sort, I can understand why you'd turn your affections toward gutter trash. We're easier on the heart."

She stopped in the middle of the path and turned to face him directly.

"After today, I will never see you again. So it really doesn't matter if I care for you or despise you, does it?"

Malden stretched his hands out at his sides. "Life is long, and the city is not so big. Only a fool says 'ever' or 'never.' "

"Then think me a fool." She moved her hands through the air, and it felt like a cloud passed through Malden's body and was gone. "There. The barrier is down. Go, and do not return."

She held out one arm and pointed toward the gate. But he didn't move. Not until she looked at him, as if to see what was the matter with him and why he didn't flee.

He caught her eye, though she tried to look away. She sighed and rolled her eyes, but he held her gaze until she stared back at him defiantly. Still he looked into her eyes, the only part of her he could see that was not covered in the images of sorcery. He held her gaze until something behind her eyes softened, if only for a moment. Softened, and looked back into his eyes, and did not flinch away.

"Just as I thought," he said. Then he touched his forehead in salute and left without awaiting a reply.

The back garden gate brought him out a hundred yards from the towering Parkwall, which cut off the sun and left him in deep shade. He hurried along the wall's length until the houses surrounding the common swallowed him up again, and only then did he allow himself to relax. As long as he had been in sight of the house he was certain he was still being observed. Once he was in the Stink proper, though, he headed toward a tavern several streets away and immediately headed into a private room in the back. A serving boy brought a flagon of small beer and some sausages when he called for them, then left him alone. Malden sat back in a chair to wait.

It was only a moment before Kemper walked through the wall and sat down next to him. "How went it, lad?"

"Like a charm," Malden told him. "They let me in with barely a question, and Cyth—that is, his servant—showed me half the house without meaning to. I even offered to come and work there, though I was rebuffed."

"A job! Y'asked fer a job!"

"Of course," Malden said. "Think on it—after a day inside those walls, I would have learned more than I can studying it from the outside for a month."

Kemper laughed heartily. "A bolder scalliwag I ne'er yet met. Ye've cased the premises, and him none the wiser, ha ha!"

"He even gave me a book," Malden said, and reached inside his tunic to bring it out. "I can't read the title, but it must be worth a fair handful of silver." He examined the small volume and admired the snug binding, the gilt lettering on the spine. He put a thumb inside the cover and started to open it, intending only to look and see if the contents were in the same alphabet as the title.

"He just gave it t'ye?" Kemper asked, his eyes suddenly suspicious.

"Well, yes," Malden said. "He was so impressed by— Blast!" He dropped the book to the table, where it fell open, facedown. A tiny droplet of blood welled up on his thumb. "I cut myself on the paper," he said. A second drop appeared on his flesh, and he stared at the wound. It didn't look like a paper cut. It looked like a rat bite.

"Lad," Kemper said, jumping away from the table. "Lad!"

The book was crawling across the table. It arched its back—its spine—and pushed itself along the scarred wood with its pages like a slug. It was headed for a sausage on a plate and left a trail of drool or slime behind it as it moved.

"He tried to kill me," Malden exclaimed, jumping out of his chair. "I went in there to give him a friendly warning, and he tried to kill me." He watched the book move for a moment, fascinated by its silent slithering. Then he drew his bodkin and brought the point down hard through the cover of the book. The thing flapped and shook for a moment, then a trickle of black ink ran out from underneath its dead pages.

Kemper stood as far from the table as he could get, and refused to come back.

"It's all right," Malden said. "I think it's dead now."

Kemper shook his head in distaste. "I'm glad I never larnt t'read," he said.

"I'll tell you one thing," Malden said as he cut a slice of the sausage and popped it in his mouth. He kept one eye on the predatory book, not unafraid it would rise again and come for him once more. "Before, I had nothing against the sorcerer. I was only going to break into his house because I had to."

"An' now?" Kemper asked.

"Now I'll be happy to take this bastard down a peg. Kemper, tell me—how did you make out? When the barrier spell came down, did you get inside?"

"Aye, son, aye," Kemper said. "An' none as saw me either. Let me tell ye what I found."

# CHAPTER FIFTY

Kemper had been reluctant to help Malden in his reconnaissance of Hazoth's villa, yet he admitted he owed Malden a significant debt. Had Malden not rescued him from the Burgrave's dungeon, he would have been tortured to death.

Besides—the plan had been half Kemper's idea, or at least it inspired by the card sharp's offhand comment the night of their carouse. Kemper had asked him why he didn't just go in and ask for the crown back. He had, of course, been joking. Yet when Malden sobered up he realized that he did in fact have the perfect cover story to get him inside the sorcerer's house. And casing the place was essential if he was to steal the crown back.

"I can see no other way to resolve my difficulties," he'd told Kemper. "Will you help me?"

"Aye," the intangible scoundrel had said at last. Together they formulated a scheme for it. Kemper could walk through normal walls like a ghost, but the wizardly wall surrounding Hazoth's villa would keep him out as well as if it had been made of solid silver. The wall had to be dropped, however, every time someone came in or out of the grounds.

When it was lowered for him, Kemper would have a chance to sneak in as well.

After the fact, Malden was deeply glad they had worked the thing so carefully. The wall didn't just immobilize those who tried to cross it. It searched him with invisible fingers, combing through his pockets and his clothes with studied precision. Had Kemper been caught in that wall even for a moment, the jig would certainly have been up—Hazoth would have known the game they were playing and would have destroyed them both in the time it took him to blink an eye. It had been a major risk anyway, since they had no way of knowing just how aware Hazoth was of who was in his house at a given time. They had proven, Malden decided, that it was possible to enter the house without immediately alerting Hazoth to one's presence, and that was a major step forward in the plot. Something to be grateful for anyway.

"I could tell, o' course, when it came down," Kemper said, leaning forward to suck drink through his reed. "I could feel it in me bones, smell it in the air. I knew I must be quick, so I dashed in through the garden, while the guards weren't payin' close watch. I think they was watching you up front, mostly, and I learned long ago how t'keep low and out o' sight. The door hard by the kitchens was closed, but 'twas no problem for the likes o' me. I slipped through neat as eel pie and found the stairs what servants use afore the wall was e'en up agin."

Malden had guessed beforehand—and been proven correct—that what he'd be allowed to see of the interior of the house would be restricted to the lower floor. In his experience, most rich men kept their offices on the ground floor of their homes, rather than force their guests to climb stairs. Thus he had tasked Kemper with exploring what he could of the upper two floors.

"The second story's about what ye'd expect, plenty o' bedrooms, a couple o' garderobes, storage fer linens, clothes, and whatnot. I didn't check much there, seein' I was bein' careful wi' the time. The third story's where things get int'restin', though. His own bedchamber's up there, and ooh, is it grand. Silken sheets and pillers, divans an' lookin' glasses ever'where. There's chains hangin' from the ceilin', too, with manacles on 'em, what felt like cold-forged iron. What you think he gets up t'wi' those, eh? Eh? Maybe human lasses is too normal for his lot. Maybe he's conjurin' up suck-you-bye from the pit t'have his way wi'. What you s'pose that's like, eh? Eh?"

Malden's eyes went wide just with imagining. In the House of Sighs, the most expensive of the city's whore-houses, there was a famous fresco of a succubus copulating with a sleeping man. He had run many errands to the House of Sighs as a boy, and that image had been impressed firmly in his youthful mind. He'd never before considered, though, that succubi might actually exist. Did they have wings, like in the painting? And horns, and— But enough. "What of the rest of the floor? Surely there's more than just the one bed-chamber. There must be. Did you see the crown?"

"Nay, lad, nay. But I think I mighta seen where it's hid. There's a study on that story, a mickle space for him to write letters and do his reckonin's. Then there's a workshop fit for a dwarf, wi' all manner o' tools and materials waitin' to be fashioned. There's a room full o' glassware, I ne'er seen its like, all manner and shape o' tubes and pots and bowls, some bubblin', some smokin', some full o' what looked like ghost-stuff. I didn't spend long in there for the smell, which were like rotten eggs. The biggest room up there's at the end of a hallway, ain't never used by the folk o' the house. There's dust on the rugs in there, and the doors is all locked up tight, and the lock's half rusted. I'm figurin' there's traps all over that corridor, set for any thief what dares to try for the big room."

"But what's in this big room?" Malden asked.

"That," Kemper said, "shall remain a mystery, I fear. I was bein' extra careful in that hall, in case there's such a trap as could kill a nosy ghost, mind. I was barely inside th' hall when I heard ye out in the garden, scuffin' up gravel and chattin' all frien'ly like wi' yer tattooed lady."

"I tried to make as much noise as I could, without caus-ing fuss, and stall as long as possible to give you time to make your escape," Malden promised. It had been their agreed upon signal that he would make some noise when he was being ejected from the house. Kemper had to exit the place at the same time he did or risk being stuck inside the magical wall when it was brought back up.

"Oh, aye, ye did marv'lous well. I fled down th' stairs and out th' side, where some trees grow right up t'th' fence. Now, trees or fence, it makes no diff'rence fer one o' my proclivities. I was out like a crossbow quarrel and away, e'er ye was finished makin' time. So who's yer leman, huh? Who's this bird, anyroad? Ye've taken a fancy to her?"

Malden blushed. He actually blushed at the thought. "She's fair enough to look at. Not fair as in light of complexion, of course. But underneath all that ink she's a beauty. But—this is silly talk. She's betrothed, I think. Or at least promised."

"Betrothed ain't the same as wed," Kemper said with a leer. He tried to jog Malden's ribs with his elbow, but of course it just went through Malden's flesh like air. He felt his breath turn to ice and coughed out a puff of vapor.

"Betrothed . . . to a fellow with a whacking great sword," Malden clarified. "I don't know that it would work out. She seems to like strapping men with chiseled features. I like women whose paramours can't cut my head off for looking upon them."

"No woman's perfect," Kemper admitted. "'Course, if'n you was diddlin' her, well, she'd be right useful t' a fella wanted t'break into her house, wouldn't she?" He sucked up a great sip of his drink. "What in the Bloodgod's hairy arse is this? Small beer?"

Malden shrugged. Small beer was what you served children, of course—milk being too useful for making butter and cheese, and water being nowhere in the city so clean you'd give it to any child you liked. "I figured after last night—well, my head's still pounding."

"And th' cure for that's this weak brew?" Kemper shook his head. "Nay, lad, ye've much I can teach ye yet. What we need now's brandy, and great lashings of it. Call the servin' wench. We've a great vict'ry today, let's celebrate it!"

Malden did as he was told, though in truth he didn't feel much like celebrating. He'd seen the inside of Hazoth's house, yes. But what he'd seen had told him his work was cut out for him. Stealing the crown had been hard.

Stealing it back would take a miracle.

# PART III

# The Crew

# INTERLUDE

Cythera prepared Hazoth's dinner that evening—a good haunch of venison and a plate of radishes soaked in milk—and laid it out on a silver tray. She started to walk from the preparatory to the dining room where he normally took his evening meal, alone at that enormous table. He had invisible footmen to serve him, but he didn't trust them to make his dinner—they lacked tongues or noses, and so had no idea how to properly spice meat, he said. Cythera suspected he had another reason for demanding that she cook for him. Perhaps it was yet another of the indignities he liked to heap on her, for—

Light sprang up around her, interrupting her thoughts. She felt her stomach slide sideways while the rest of her shot upward into the air, straight through the ceiling, and suddenly she was standing in Hazoth's inner sanctum, the tray still clutched in her hands.

She did her best not to gasp. It would cost her if she flinched or showed any weakness in his presence. Still, it was always surprising when he transported her like that.

Normally, magic did not affect her at all. The charm on her skin kept her safe from all enchantments and dweomers. Hazoth had explained, however, that the displacement spell he used to move her around his villa did not, in fact, work *on* her. It moved space around her instead, shifting the villa through various dimensions without ever touching her directly. It was one of his favorite tricks, probably because it disoriented her so.

She found herself standing before the rose window, red and blue light streaming across her face. The pattern of glass was a hex of considerable power—it was very good at shielding the sanctum from magical viewing. Cythera had

always found it beautiful in its own right, at least until recently.

She allowed herself a momentary glance to the side. She
moved only her eyes, and just enough to get a glimpse of
the wretched form in the magic circle. Her mother did not
lift her head. If Coruth was aware of her presence at all,
she made no outward sign. Cythera could only hope that the
witch had some other, more subtle sense that let her hear her
thoughts.

*Help is coming*, Cythera whispered in her mind. *Croy
will not fail us.*

She received no reply.

"Well, don't let it get cold, girl," Hazoth said, behind her.

Cythera turned and forced a smile. Hazoth liked her to
be cheerful when she served him. It was difficult to keep her
composure when she saw what he was doing, though. On a
long worktable he had the body of a minor demon pinned
down and cut open. It was little more than an imp, a long-
legged batrachian thing with eyes like fire opals. Hazoth
had his arms up to the elbows in its viscera. When the imp
turned its head to the side to look at her, she nearly dropped
the tray.

The demon made a horrible gurgling noise. Cythera
forced herself to ignore its obvious suffering.

"It screamed like a natural thing before I disconnected
its larynx," Hazoth assured her as she set the tray down on a
nearby table, pushing aside a number of arcane instruments
to make room. "This is going to take all night. I didn't wish
to be distracted by coming down to the dining room, so I
decided to sup here."

Cythera did not reply.

"Strange. There's no digestive apparatus at all," Hazoth
mused as he pulled his hands free of the vivisection. "They
devour their prey, everyone knows that, but they can't draw
sustenance from it. Unless they persist simply on the suffering and fear of their victims."

Cythera often wondered if the same could be said of her
master. She stood by, motionless, waiting to see if he required anything else.

Hazoth came over to the tray and stared down at it. Then he glanced at his hands, which were still coated in ichor. "Hmm," he said, "I really ought to wash. No time, though." Sneering at the slimy mess, he spoke a word that curdled in the air. Blue flames licked over his wrists and palms, consuming the gore that had coated them. Cythera did not even wince as she felt new vines and flowers blooming in the small of her back.

She watched in silence as Hazoth grabbed up the haunch and started chewing on it. She had a linen napkin tucked up the sleeve of her gown, and she removed it carefully in case he should require it.

"Oh, since you're here—there's something I'm sure you'll want to know. My little trick with the book failed. That rodentine thief of yours is still alive. You know, I'm almost glad. I admit I find him more amusing by the day. Maybe we'll have to bring him here and give him a job after all, hmm?"

It was not a question that required an answer. Cythera held her tongue.

"Of course, it's no great surprise he survived. We already knew he had an animal's uncanny sense for danger. After all, he knew better than to kiss you, didn't he? I really thought I had him there. What man could resist your charms, if he didn't know what the price would be? Perhaps you warned him, though. Perhaps you didn't try hard enough. Even though we both know you *wanted* to kiss him."

Cythera kept her eyes focused straight ahead. She did not allow her cheeks to flush, did not permit herself the slightest reaction. Hazoth only spoke to her like this when he was bored. It was a little game. An amusement. He would say something provocative—perhaps hint at some dark secret relating to her mother, or tell her a story of some perverse sexual encounter he'd had four hundred years ago. If she gasped or even so much as shuddered, he would crow and caper. And then he would punish her.

He had so many different ways to punish her.

"I could tell, when I saw the two of you together. I could hear your heart beating faster. The smell of your breath changed. You want him. You want the little thief to be your plaything, don't you, Cythera? Hmm? I asked you a question, girl."

"As you wish, master. If you wish for me to desire him, then I shall."

Hazoth laughed. "You can't hide it from me. I could taste it in the air, the change that came over you. You were *concerned* for him. *Afraid* of what I would do to him. Just ask me, girl, and I'll bring him here. I'll put a charm on him that will drag him straight to your bedchamber." He tore off a strip of venison with his teeth and chewed noisily. "I'll make him kneel before you. I'll make him burn for you. Just a word, and that can be yours. Of course, you'll destroy him the moment he paws at you with his coarse hands. One rough touch and he'll be torn to pieces. But maybe that would give you pleasure, hmm? Would that make you sigh? Would it make you moan?"

"I serve at your pleasure, master. Not my own."

Hazoth stared at her with his perfect, clear eyes. She knew he was trying to look into her heart, to winkle out her secrets. The charm on her skin made that impossible, but he still tried from time to time. He took an interest in her, certainly. After all, she was all that stood between him and a series of gruesome deaths.

"I think perhaps I'll summon your Sir Croy instead. That jumped-up man-at-arms needs to be taught a lesson one of these days. I think I'll bring him here right now. And then you'll tell him. You'll list all the things you dream of doing with the thief. Sir Croy will have to stand here and listen while you describe all your filthy longings. How does that sound? Do you think he loves you enough to listen to that and forget everything he's heard? Do you think he'd still love you as much after he heard those secrets?"

"If it would amuse you, master—"

He clucked his tongue in distaste. That was the worst part of the game. Even if she did maintain her composure, even if she swallowed her bile and kept her thoughts to herself, it simply angered him.

Sometimes that was worse.

"I could bring them both here, if you liked. I could bring them both to this room, right now, and make them fight over you. I could make them tear each other apart with their bare hands. Would you like that? Would it excite you, child, to see them struggle for your affections? Well? Would it?"

Cythera couldn't help herself. A small sound started deep in her throat, a tiny whimper. When it came out of her mouth it was so soft she thought it must be lost in the noise of Hazoth's chewing.

She was wrong.

"I've got you," he said, and dropped the haunch back on the platter. He wiped his fingers on his robe and came to stand behind her, his meaty breath hot on her ear. "I got through, at last," he whispered. "Both of them, no less! You care for them both!" He nearly giggled in his excitement. "Oh, Cythera, my dear, you'll stretch your heart too thin! I'll summon them both and make them both lust for you, shall I? Make them compete over who gets to deflower you first. Oh, I can see in your eyes how much you don't want that."

"I want nothing but—but—" she stammered.

He waved a greasy hand in dismissal. "Never you mind, Cythera. In point of fact, there's no need to do any of that. In a few days it will be Ladymas. In the confusion of that day, Bikker will hunt them both down and butcher them while the watch is preoccupied."

"Of course, master," she managed. She had regained her composure once she knew he wouldn't follow up on his threats. "May I go now?"

"I suppose," Hazoth said. "I should really return to my studies."

"Thank you, Magus," Cythera said. She waited for him to transport her back to the preparatory.

He began to make the necessary passes in the air with his hands—but then stopped without warning.

It seemed he had one more thing to say.

"I know you hate me, girl," he muttered. "I know you're plotting against me. I know you think Sir Croy is going to come here and save you and your mother. But it's hopeless,

Cythera. No one can help you now. You're mine, and always will be."

"I—I—"

"I think you need to be reminded of this simple fact."

In the end, there was never any way to avoid the punishments.


# CHAPTER FIFTY-ONE


There were many eyes watching Hazoth's villa the next day, when Anselm Vry sent his watchmen in to take the crown back. It was an overcast morning, with a light drizzle falling from time to time. For Malden and Kemper, who watched from the north end of the common, it was a miserable way to spend their hours. They had intended to spend the day studying what could be seen of the villa from afar. When the watchmen arrived, however, they hid themselves in the bushes hard by Ladypark and kept out of sight as best they could.

Kemper shuffled endlessly through his precious cards, reestablishing the bond he had with them that let him hold them when another deck would fall through his hands. Malden had nothing to do but sit and hold the collar of his cloak tight against his neck, trying to keep the chill rain from running down his back. Yet he would not have moved from the spot. Though he could not know for certain, he believed he knew exactly what the watchmen had come for. Somehow, it seemed, Vry had learned where the crown was—and that could be a very bad thing. If Vry found the crown now, if Hazoth allowed it to be taken, it would be the end of all his—and Cutbill's—schemes. It would mean death for both of them.

Meanwhile, Croy watched from the house of his wealthy friend, in comfort, with a flagon of wine and a loaf of bread for breakfast. This could be the day he finally freed Cythera from her bonds, he thought. If Vry was successful and found the crown, it would be the end of Hazoth. Cythera and her mother would be freed of Hazoth's enslavement and they could go anywhere they liked. Croy could take Cythera away from him, he could marry her and bring her to his castle. Everything could turn out right.

As for Cythera herself, she watched from inside the villa and perhaps had the best view. Certainly she had the most to gain from this. Hazoth's punishment of the night before had been cruel, and she ached for the sorcerer's comeuppance. She very dearly wished she could just watch and see it play out. However, she was forced to pay attention to her regular duties—seeing to the needs of the villa, arranging for foodstuffs to be delivered, sheets to be changed and washed, silver coins handed out to all Hazoth's retainers and servants, so she was often away from the windows. She did not know what to think, or what this raid could mean. She dared not hope for too much.

None of them would leave—or breathe easily—until it was done.

It seemed to take forever for the watchmen to gather at the southern end of the Ladypark. First came their serjeant, a big fellow in a cloak-of-eyes with a red hem. He brought two porters who set up a tent where he could sit in relatively dry comfort. Next his men arrived, four of them, carrying halberds and watching the sky with doubtful looks. There was a great deal of discussion between the four and their officer, none of it particularly heated.

Only four, Croy mused. Four against a sorcerer. What was Vry thinking?

When the time for discussion was done, the men each took a cup of ale. They leaned on the hafts of their weapons and drank their ration in silence. When the cups were empty, they left the tent and walked across the common. Their boots kicked up crystalline spray from the swampy grass as they marched toward the villa. The serjeant remained in his tent, where it was dry.

"Now ye'll see somewhat, lad," Kemper said with a wicked grin. "This oughta be a bloodbath, and no foolin'."

"You think Hazoth won't even let them in," Malden said.

"More fool if'n he does, eh?" Kemper laughed. "Ooh, it's gonna be good. After what they did t'me, strappin' me up in that donjon. I can still feel the silver bitin' into me wrists an' ankles. Let's see how them cloaks-of-eyes like it, bein' hoisted in the air. Ooh, it's lovely."

Malden could not share the card sharp's vindictive glee. He wasn't sure how this would play out, but he knew if Hazoth killed the watchmen, or even if he just refused them entry to his house, it would only mean more trouble. Vry couldn't leave it at that—he would have to send more watchmen, and more after that, until every armed man in the city was standing outside Hazoth's gate demanding to be let in. That could hardly end well for anyone involved, and it would make it impossible for him to get in and steal the crown back. He didn't know what he should hope for now. He could only watch, and pray for the best.

The four watchmen reached the gate of the villa just before noontime—though only Cythera was aware of the correct time. Hazoth had a mechanical clock on the second floor landing of the villa. Its persistent ticking had always soothed her before, the way it cut the day up into tiny portions, making her hours of bondage easier to digest. Now each tick and each tock were blows against her senses, as all her hopes depended on this next hour.

The watchmen stopped just outside the gate. One of them hallooed the guards and demanded entry in the name of the Burgrave. Cythera alone could hear the response—and alone was astonished by it.

"Well met, fellows. The Magus bids you enter and be welcome," the guard said. He turned and made a signal toward the rose window at the top of the house, and the magical barrier came down, the wet air itself seeming to sigh in relief.

The watchmen filed through the portico and into the great hall. Up on the gallery, Cythera was busy counting the silver—an important job in a sorcerer's house, since any spoon Hazoth ate with could be used against him by a rival wizard. She bent over the cutlery in case anyone (human or invisible) was watching, but listened close to what was said below her.

"I have an official message from the bailiff, which I must present to you, milord," one of the watchmen said. "Then we must ask to search your house."

Hazoth did not sound particularly worried. "Very good, let me hear it."

"It is as follows," the watchman said. He had not been carrying a scroll—most likely he'd memorized the message so he could recite it now.

"Greetings to our good friend Hazoth, much beloved of the Burgrave and of the king his liege. It is with heavy heart that I, Anselm Vry, must send you this deputation today. Certain evidence has been advanced concerning the theft of an item the Burgrave considers the most valuable of all his possessions. This evidence tends to suggest that the item in question may currently be found within the bounds of your property. Under common law I am empowering these men to search the house, outbuildings, and lands of your villa, with all care being taken to minimize the disturbance, and especially any damage, to said property. Your cooperation in this search, my dear Hazoth, will be most gratefully received. Should said item be found upon your land or property, or on your person, or in any way concealed or possessed by your esteemed self, this deputation shall have the power to remove it to safety, and at that time, but not before, criminal charges may be brought against you or any agent in your employ found to have any part in the theft, movement, or concealment of said item. Signed, your servant, Anselm Vry, Bailiff of the Free City of Ness."

The watchman cleared his throat. Apparently he had finished his message.

"I don't see nothin'," Kemper said, sounding annoyed as he peered out through the rain at the distant villa. "No flashes o' light, no hellish smoke boilin' from the windows. No fiery hands clutchin' at the watchmen or demons comin' up through cracks in the soil. You think maybe he just magicked 'em straight into the pit?"

Cythera stepped over to the railing of the gallery and looked down on the scene—watchers be damned.

Croy held his breath.

"Very well," Hazoth said. He lifted one hand and gestured toward the stairs. "Would you like to begin your search in my chambers, or down here in the public areas of the house? And may I offer you something to drink or eat?"

The watchmen looked embarrassed. "We're under orders, Magus, not to take aught from you, not even a cup of small beer, as it might be cursed. Not, uh, not that we would think you would do such a thing."

"Perish the thought," Hazoth said.

"If you'll just stand aside we'll get to things, and leave you in peace as quick as we can."

"Certainly," Hazoth said, and stepped away from the stairs.

The search took much of the afternoon. Cythera was required to assist the watchmen—she held the keys to all the locked rooms, and could open some of the magically sealed doors and cupboards for them. The watchmen seemed surprised by some of the house's more unusual furniture, but never said a word, even when a book in the library jumped off the shelf and fluttered like a fish out of water at their feet. It tried to follow the watchmen as they backed out of the library, as if begging them to take it with them and free it from Hazoth's villa. Cythera knew what the book contained and didn't blame it. Still, she bent to retrieve it, and running one calming thumb along its spine, slotted it back in its place on the shelf.

What's taking so long? Malden wondered as he toyed with the bodkin at his belt.

*They're being thorough, at least*, Croy told himself as he clutched his hands together and leaned forward in his chair.

The last part of the house to be searched was the third floor. The chains in the master bedroom drew the watchmen's attention, and they made a brave try at searching the laboratory, despite the noxious fumes. Other rooms barely drew their notice. By daylight most of the truly dangerous parts of the third floor were subdued and harmless, for which Cythera was glad—she would not have liked to explain some of the things the watchmen would have seen had they come after dark.

When they reached the sealed and locked hallway that led to Hazoth's inner sanctum, they didn't even glance at the door, just kept walking past.

"Here, I can open this for you, though you must be careful inside," Cythera told them. "I believe he disarmed all the traps, but still it would be well if you—"

"Milady?" a watchman said. "There's no door there."

Cythera frowned and pointed out the door again. "This one."

"Don't see nothin'," one of the others said. "Nothin' there."

She studied their faces—especially their eyes—looking for any sign that their minds had been clouded by magic. Hazoth must have enchanted them not to see the door, she thought—and she did not dare to try to break that spell. As for the watchmen, they just stared back at her, blinking occasionally, as if they were bored and wished to return to their work.


# CHAPTER FIFTY-TWO


An hour or so later the watchmen trooped down the stairs to the great hall again, where they apologized to Hazoth for any inconvenience and then took their leave. Hazoth headed back upstairs to return to his studies, telling Cythera along the way that she should return to her normal duties.

As the watchmen stepped back out onto the gravel forecourt of the villa—

—and Croy jumped up, his chair tumbling out behind him—

—and Kemper and Malden leaned forward to get a better view—

—and Cythera clutched a silver serving fork to her chest, bracing herself for she knew not what—

—absolutely nothing happened.

The watchmen were allowed to exit the villa without any further delay. They marched back to the tent, where they reported at some length to their serjeant. Then the porters returned to take down the tent, and all departed together, heading up the Cripplegate Road toward the Stink, and thence back toward Castle Hill.

And still nothing happened.

Hazoth returned to his studies. He did not leave his laboratory for the rest of the day. Cythera went about her duties. Normally she would have been glad for Hazoth's preoccupation. Any time to herself—any time when he wasn't demanding things of her, or torturing her for his amusement—was precious. Now, though, she was more frightened than ever. Hazoth might or might not realize her part in summoning the watchmen, but it didn't matter. When he finished with his day's labors he would want someone to blame for the interruption, someone on whom to take out his anger. What was coming would be terrible, even worse than the punishment of the night before. There was nothing for it, though. All she could do was keep at her work. If her head was slightly bowed, if her hands lingered on the familiar knives and spoons in the silver cabinet as if she were lost in gloomy thoughts, it didn't stop her from finishing the task.

Up by the trees, thoroughly sodden with rain, Malden clucked his tongue in disgust and looked over at Kemper. The intangible card sharp was dry as a bone—the raindrops had passed through him without stop. "I need to get dry,"

Malden announced. "Come, I have a spare cloak back at my rooms. We'll make a fire. And then we need to confer."

"I don't unnerstand it," Kemper said, trailing after Malden as he hurried up the street leading out of Parkwall. "He just let 'em in? Let 'em ransack his spread?"

"They didn't find the crown," Malden told his associate. "That much is certain. If they had they would have dragged Hazoth out of his hole and conveyed him forthwith to the palace dungeon. Or rather, they would have tried. He would not have gone easy."

"Now that, I would've paid t'witness," Kemper chortled.

Malden was thinking out loud. "Vry said he would search every house in the city for the crown. Yet I cannot believe that he would start here without some reason. I would think he would avoid Hazoth's wrath if at all possible. So he must know. He must have some sign that the crown is in there—and yet, his watchmen left without it, and without a fuss." He shook his head. "Perhaps he has another scheme in mind, and this was only a feint. Which only tightens our schedule. We must steal the crown back before he gets it— or all is lost." He shivered inside his wet tunic. "We need to sit somewhere and think hard on this."

"Aye, lad, and sure."

"Perhaps a brandy or two wouldn't hurt."

That seemed to cheer Kemper immensely.

The two thieves were around a corner and gone before they could see the one real consequence of Anselm Vry's raid. In the stables of a rich man's house just across the way from Hazoth's villa, voices were raised and a horse was starting.

"Just be reasonable, friend, it's your death out there!"

Croy turned on his host with flashing eyes. For a second he thought he might strike down the merchant who stood in his way. Then he gripped the man's forearms and leaned close to speak. "Forgive me. You've been so very kind, taking me in like this. I know I've put you in danger just by being here."

"Think nothing of it—but think of yourself now. If you go riding up there in this state of excitement they'll arrest you on the spot."

"Anselm Vry will listen to logic. When I show him I am his only hope, he will give me what I need to finish this," Croy said, and released the man. He grabbed up a saddle from a tack locker and threw it over the back of his host's most hot-blooded stallion. As his host pleaded with him, he cinched the girth tight. He reached back and checked both his swords, making sure they were tied down in their scabbards and wouldn't shake loose. Then he pulled a long felted cape over his back—the teased wool would keep out the rain, and protect his steel from rust. He grabbed the pommel and made to mount, but a hand on his arm stopped him.

"They won't just arrest you," the merchant said, shaking his head. "They'll cut you down like a dog. Once they see your blades, they will not show mercy."

"I will move their hearts with my plea." Croy hoisted himself up over the horse's back and dropped heavily into the saddle. He grabbed up the reins and jerked the stallion's head around so it faced the road.

"You say two different things. Is Vry a man of reason, or a man with a good heart? I've found them to be contraries not often reconciled in a single nature."

Croy shrugged. "One way or another I'll convince him. And if I don't—then maybe I'll die today. But I'll perish in the name of justice."

"Then do me one favor, before you die."

Croy grimaced at the delay, but he nodded. He never failed to pay his debts.

"When you reach the castle gates—dismount. Turn my horse around and give him a good whack on the hindquarters. He knows the way home. If I'm to lose a friend today, I can at least get my best palfrey back."

Croy laughed bitterly and dug in his spurs.

# CHAPTER FIFTY-THREE

Despite the cool day, the palfrey was panting and its flanks were dripping foam by the time Croy thundered up the Cornmarket Bridge and through Market Square. At the main gate to Castle Hill, a guard waved his pikestaff in the air to demand that Croy halt, but the man was wise enough to stand back rather than be trampled as Croy shot through the gate at full gallop and passed into the bailey. Workmen threw down their tools and jumped out of his way as he leapt the pile of broken stone before the tower. He didn't slow the horse until he was right before the main door of the palace, and then only long enough to jump down and send the horse wheeling away, headed back to its master as promised.

For a moment all was stillness in the courtyard. No one dared move, for they did not know why he'd come or what he wanted. If he had sprouted horns and bat wings in that moment, he doubted the watchmen and the guard would be more surprised by his appearance there.

He was thankful for their caution. It gave him a moment—the space of a few breaths—to make his demand.

"Anselm Vry!" he shouted, throwing back the hood of his cloak. He reached back and untied his swords, just in case.

He could hear the palace guards rushing into place behind him, their mail clanking and the butts of their weapons sounding on the flagstones. He did not turn to look at them. "Vry, come out, I would speak with you!"

There was much confusion and raised voices shouted at him, but he could barely hear them. The blood was pounding behind his eyes and the world was tinged with red. If Vry would not come out and speak, then he would go in—and the Lady help any man who stood before him.

But in the moment before he began to cut his way into the palace, Vry appeared, standing on a second floor balcony.

"Sir Croy, this is too much," he said. "I've tried to turn a blind eye, I've tried to earn you mercy with honeyed words, but—"

"Your men—they came and they went. Without—Without *it*!"

Vry looked around at the throng of people in the courtyard and then glared daggers at Croy. "Watch your tongue."

"They searched the right house. They were unopposed. How could they fail? There is only one way. Sorcery."

"The men of which you speak have not yet returned. I have not heard their report. There is no point to this chaos and nothing to discuss."

Vry looked peeved, but he made no order for the guards to attack. For the nonce they held their places, weapons ready. Perhaps none of them wanted to be the first to attack—they knew what Croy was capable of. Once the first of them moved, though, Croy knew the momentum would shift and they would all be upon him.

This was the moment, then. He would make his plea, and Vry must be convinced.

Croy drew Ghostcutter and heard the people around him gasp. Some screamed. He dropped to one knee and held the sword before him, point down to touch the flagstones. He bowed his head before it like a knight standing vigil in a chapel. Like the champion of the kingdom that he was. "Give me every man in the watch. Give me a company of them, at least. I'll tear that house down stone by stone. I'll carve it out of the magician's heart, if that's where he's hiding it."

"I can hardly do as you ask," Vry said.

"Don't take me lightly," Croy insisted.

"Believe me, I don't. If any man could do it, I believe it would be you. But don't you understand? My hands are tied by laws and customs. I'm not a field marshal to make war inside the city walls. I am bound to protect the citizens, not slaughter them based on unproven information and the fervor of *your* belief."

"A crime has been committed! Your city demands justice!"

"I'm afraid that's true," Vry said in icy tones.

Croy stared up at him without understanding.

"I've done all I can for you, Sir Knight. My duty requires this. Croy, you are under arrest. You have violated the terms of your banishment, and by remaining within the walls of the Free City of Ness you have invoked the punishment of death. Guards, take him—alive if you can, dead if you must."

And with that, Anselm Vry turned and went back into the palace.

Croy had failed.

"Drop that steel," someone said from just behind him.

"Get down on the flagstones with your arms spread out."

"Hold where you are or be cut down."

Three of them, then, of immediate concern. Doubtless there would be more behind them. Croy's heart, which had been burning with unquenchable fire a moment before, turned cold and froze over with ice. His brain quieted for the first time in weeks. Every instinct, every reflex he had spent years training and honing, came alive in him.

And he realized—even as he jumped up and spun around to face his foes—the horrible mistake he'd made.

The appeal he'd made would have brought tears to the eye of a general. But Anselm Vry was no warrior. He was a clerk. An administrator. For him the rules, the numbers of life, were everything. It didn't matter what was just or right. Only what was formally *allowed*.

Ghostcutter came around in a broad arc, Croy's hand loose on the hilt. He didn't need fine control for this stroke. The wooden haft of a halberd was cleaved in twain as the iron edge of the sword whistled through the air. A guardsmen's cloak was shortened by several inches. Even as the stroke came around, Croy reached behind him and drew his shorter sword. It fit his left hand just fine.

A halberd point jumped at his face. He parried with the shortsword and metal clanged off metal, not the ring of a hammer on an anvil but the nerve-wracking noise of blade grinding off blade. A pikestaff with a leaf-shaped point came jabbing in low, aimed at his groin. Croy side-stepped the attack, then tipped the pike up and away with Ghostcutter's foible.

The masters-at-arms who taught these guards had convinced them that polearms were superior to swords. That swords couldn't parry halberds and pikes because swords didn't have the reach.

That notion was based on the speed of an average swordsman. For an expert at blades like Croy, who spent every waking moment of his youth practicing ripostes and reprises, lunges and ballestras, the theory fell apart.

Which was not to say he was invulnerable. When a guardsman came up behind him and brought the axe blade of his halberd down toward Croy's unprotected skull, Croy didn't see the blow coming. He only heard it whistling through the air.

So he barely had time to lean back and let the blade slice down in front of him, while the haft of the weapon clouted him across the ear until his head buzzed and rang and his vision swam.

They would encircle him and bind him in a forest of wooden poles, he realized. He could only fight a few of them at a time. No matter how good he was, he couldn't hold off every guard in the castle. In time they would whittle him down, get him with near misses and grazing cuts. If he bled enough he would die, no matter how many men fell with him.

There was a part of him that thought it good. That dying like this, in Cythera's name, was worthy. Had he been a younger man, he might have given in to that death wish, that dream of honor and glory.

But he was older now. He knew what was truly important. If he died here, Cythera would remain a slave forever. As easily as that the bloodlust fled from his veins.

He waited until a polearm came down just before him, its blade cutting deep into one of the soft shale flagstones. Then he put one boot down hard on the polished wooden haft. Swinging Ghostcutter behind him to deflect an attack, he jumped forward and got his other foot on the shoulder of the guardsman before him. The man grunted in pain as Croy levered himself up and over the circle of attackers, jumping free of their ring of death. He came down hard on the pile of broken stone and rolled, tucking his swords in so they wouldn't fly loose from his hands.

Rolling to his feet, he looked around, breath heaving in and out of his lungs. He saw guardsmen everywhere—and more, watchmen streaming in through the gates to aid in the attack. Dozens of men, all of them armed, all wearing coats of mail beneath their tunics and cloaks. Croy had no armor at all.

Someone jabbed at him with the curved blade of a bill-hook. Croy deflected the blow easily with his shortsword with barely a glance. Guards were starting to scramble up the pile of stones to get at him, though. He needed to move.

## CHAPTER FIFTY-FOUR

Ahead of him, at the main gate leading down into Market Square, the guards were lowering the portcullis. The points were halfway to the ground already as they heaved at the winch. If he was going to live through this, he needed to get through there before it closed. Unfortunately there were half a dozen guards in the way.

Croy roared like a lion and charged forward, smacking one man in the face with the flat of Ghostcutter, knocking another off his feet by hitting him in the stomach with the shortsword's pommel. A spear came straight at him, point first, and would have skewered him had he not danced to the side and into the path of another man. The fellow looked terrified as he realized that Croy was inside his reach, his long polearm now a liability instead of an advantage. Croy headbutted him and ducked under the arm of yet another attacker. The point of a halberd dug into his back, but he barely felt it.

The portcullis was right before him then, with no man in the way. It was only a foot and a half from the ground. Croy threw himself forward and rolled underneath, the iron points tearing at his clothes. On the far side he climbed to his feet and stared back through the open grate. More men than he could count were racing toward him, shouting for the gate guards to raise the portcullis again so they could get at him.

He laughed, though not harshly. Then he sheathed his swords and turned to go.

And promptly slipped and fell on his own blood.

He reached behind him and felt the wound on his back. It had felt like nothing—but then, in the heat of battle a man's sense of pain was often skewed. Whether it was a mortal wound or not, he could not tell, but he could tell it was bad.

He had no time to stanch it, however. In a moment the gate would be reopened and all those men would be on his heels. He had to take what little advantage he had, and run while the going was good.

First, though, he had to stand up.

Croy sheathed his swords and got his hands underneath him. The muscles in his back quivered and a faint echo of pain cut through the numbness of battle. His body obeyed his commands, however, and he was able to get his feet beneath him. The oily blood on the cobblestones at his feet nearly made him slip again, but he slid forward and scraped the worst of it off his boots.

Behind him the portcullis groaned as it started to rise again. High above, atop the wall of Castle Hill, guards began to shout, raising the hue and cry. Theoretically that call would summon every able-bodied man into the streets, to help with apprehending Croy. He knew from past experience, however, that most citizens would simply shutter their windows and bar their doors. He had chased down his own share of criminals, in more civic-minded places than the Free City of Ness.

He bolted for Market Square just as archers appeared

atop the wall. As he dodged between a row of produce stalls, an arrow flashed past his cheek and buried itself in a side of beef. Croy ducked low around the front of the butcher's stall as more arrows peppered its tarred wooden roof.

Not even a trained swordsman like Croy could fight off a rain of arrows. Using the stalls as cover, he made a short line for the side of the square, where the custom house and a granary pressed close together. Between them a narrow alley ran down to Prosper Street, a broad avenue full of horses and carts. Squeezing out of the alley, he stared wildly down the street, hoping desperately it would be clear of watchmen. He saw none and dashed downhill. Men screamed and pressed up close to the shops on either side of the street when they saw his wound. It must be grisly indeed.

"Stop him!" someone shouted from behind Croy. He did not pause to look and see who it was. Just before him a cart full of boxes of fresh fish was headed down into the Golden Slope. Croy launched himself into the air and landed hard on his shoulder in a pile of smelts and sardines.

"Who—what . . . ?" The driver of the cart stared at Croy with wide eyes and gaping mouth. As Croy pulled himself up on the side of the cart and tried to think of what to say to the man, the driver shouted in fear and jumped off his bench and into the street. He hit the cobblestones wrong and went rolling away, even as the horses pulled their cart ever onward, leaving him far behind.

"Blast," Croy cursed. He got one leg onto the bench and tried to grab for the reins. The pair of horses must have smelled the blood on him, however, for they whinnied in fear and bolted downhill. He fell tumbling back into the fish, which were flying out the back of the cart and leaving a silver trail on the street behind.

The cart jumped and bounced—it had never been meant to travel at such speed. Croy found it barely possible to get to his feet and climb up onto the bench. The reins were dragging in the street, hanging down between the traces where he couldn't reach them. The horses' hooves were thundering on the cobbles, their iron shoes clanging so loud he could hardly hear himself think.

A boy—an apprentice in some trade, judging by his leather smock—barely jumped away in time before he was trampled. A wagon full of hay blocked half the road ahead, and Croy was certain he would smash against it, but the horses pulling the cart were not so made as to run headlong into that obstacle. They turned at the last possible moment, throwing the cart up on one wheel. Croy fell sideways as the seat under him shifted and nearly fell out of the cart, only holding on with one hand to its side, his feet bouncing and dragging on the cobblestones. He considered just letting go—he would hit the street hard and roll for a ways, but then at least he would be off the runaway vehicle.

But no—that he could not do. Without him on board, the cart would be totally out of control. The horses would run roughshod over anyone who stood in their way. He couldn't live with the notion of someone being hurt because he had to get away from the castle in a hurry. Fighting the pain of his wound and the red haze that filmed his eyes, Croy dragged himself back up onto the cart as both wheels crashed back onto the pavement. Heaving and grunting, he pulled himself into the seat, and looked forward to see where he was headed.

Ahead in the street men and women went racing in a panic to get out of the way of the runaway cart. Croy shouted out to warn them and waved his hands, but the only way he could avoid catastrophe was to get the cart back under control. Wounded as he was, that would take some doing.

Prosper Street ran down the length of the Golden Slope at a steep grade that only added to the horses' headlong speed. It traveled straight as an arrow's flight down into the Smoke, where it lost itself among a maze of byways. If he didn't slow the horses before they reached that district, the cart would surely crash. As the maddened beasts threw themselves downhill, Croy stepped out onto the tongue between them and then threw himself over the back of the left-hand horse, the leader of the team.

"Whoa, whoa, easy there," he said, trying to soothe the animal. He clutched to its mane and did his best not to be bucked off. The horse turned one wild eye to stare at him and bit at the air with its massive teeth. "All's well, be at ease," Croy crooned, but the horse merely redoubled its efforts to shake him free. This was no destrier, bred for war and trained by a horsemaster. It was a simple dray animal that had never known such excitement.

The horse on the right, the wheel horse, perhaps thinking its mate was under attack, nipped at Croy's shoulder. He pulled back to avoid it and nearly fell off.

Clearly the horses had no intention of obeying his commands. By giving them a common enemy to face he had slowed them a trifle, but there was still great danger of a crash. To save his own life he might leap off the horse's back—but at this speed he would hit the cobbles like a catapult stone.

He looked ahead and saw that the horses were only a few seconds from reaching the Smoke. The street there curved around a tanner's yard. It would be impossible for the cart to turn at speed and follow the road.

"You have my apologies, fishmonger," he said to the poor driver of the cart who was about to lose his livelihood. Then he drew his shortsword and sliced through all the traces that held the horses to the cart.

The effect was instantaneous. The wheel horse, riderless, broke for freedom and galloped down a side street. The leader, with Croy on its back, jogged out of harness and took the turn around the tanner's yard at speed. Just behind Croy the cart slammed into a fence of wooden palings and disintegrated, its cargo exploding into the air in a rain of silver mackerel and cod.

The noise only frightened Croy's horse more. It began to stand and balk, and it was more than Croy could do to hold on. His shortsword went clattering into the street and then his left leg got tangled in the harness. Trying to pull it free only unseated him and he was thrown to the ground, with barely enough time to tuck and roll so his neck wasn't broken. He somersaulted out of the way of the horse's flashing hooves and then fell back, beaten, bruised, and exhausted, and watched it run away from him, into the warren of convoluted streets that made up the Smoke.

# CHAPTER FIFTY-FIVE

There was nothing Croy wanted more than to just lie down on the cobbles and rest a moment. His body was wracked with pain and he was still bleeding from the wound in his back. Yet he knew it would be only moments before the watch found him there—he had hardly covered his tracks on the way. He rolled onto his side and put a hand down on the cobbles. His strength was faltering and he could barely sit up.

The wound in his back must be deep. He could not afford to lose any more blood. His shortsword lay in the street next to his outflung hand. He grabbed it up and used it to cut off a wide swath of his cloak. This he tied around his back, as tight as he could bear. It might help, a little. Then again, it might be too late. He had already lost a great deal of blood. He had rarely felt so close to death before. Never had its chill embrace seemed more welcoming, more to be desired.

Yet there was that within him that refused to give up. As tempting as it might be to close his eyes and let slumber take him, his work was not yet done. Cythera and her mother remained enslaved. Hazoth still had the Burgrave's crown. He had to get up. He had to move from this place. He could rest, he promised himself, but only once he found a safe place to lie down. Where that might be, he had little idea.

As long as he lived, though—as long as Cythera needed his help—he had to make the best of what strength he had. And that meant standing up.

He regained his feet. He did not know how he did it— the simple act of putting one foot under him, then the other, made his vision go black and his brain howl in protest until he could not think. His muscles were trained to keep going, though, no matter what occurred. They got him upright and walking.

He struggled with the remains of his tattered cloak, managing to pull it over the hilts of his swords so they didn't show. Down here, armed citizens were rare, and the swords would draw exactly the kind of attention he wanted to avoid. Not that he saw anyone about—or much of anything at all, really.

The air was thick with smoke and fumes, unhealthy vapors rising from the rendering vats in the tanner's yard. Down the street a great pillar of ash and sparks rose from an iron foundry. The Smoke was shrouded in a poisonous miasma at all times—on an overcast day like this its air was as thick as porridge. This foul air and its characteristic stench would flow downhill, into the district of poverty and crime called the Stink. It was the fumes that gave the Stink its name. He headed down a long street with no doors or windows, only blank walls like a great chute. At its end was an open yard where Croy saw two men in a ropewalk, walking backward as they braided together stout cords into rope. One made a joke and the other laughed boisterously. As he staggered past they turned to stare at him. One called out, but Croy couldn't understand what he said—the blood was pounding too loud in his ears.

He passed a cooperage where workers scorched the insides of barrels by swishing spirits of wine around inside them and then setting them alight. Red fireballs leapt from the mouth of each barrel as the lighter ducked down out of the way.

Next door was a brewery, the air around it thick with the smell of fermenting hops and steam off the great malting kettles. Croy started belching as he passed through a thick cloud of vapor. For a moment he could see nothing, the acrid cloud making his eyes water.

When he stumbled out of the cloud, someone put their arm around his shoulders.

"Careful now, friend! I mean you no harm," the stranger cooed as Croy reeled away and tried to draw his shortsword.

He let his hand fall back. "I know you—*urk*—not," Croy said.

"Ah, but I'm your best friend in the world, aren't I? A

fellow like you needs a good friend at a time like this. Here, lean against me, I'm solid enough."

The stranger was a fattish man in a tight jerkin and leather breeches. His eyes were set close together and he had very little in the way of a chin. He was certainly no watchman, nor a palace guard. He had a belt knife but no other visible weapons.

"Don't I have an honest face? Ha ha," the man laughed. "Come with me now, we'll see you safe and warm in a moment. I know a little place right around the corner."

He thinks me drunk, Croy thought. "What kind of place?"

"A sort of temple," the stranger told him. "A little shrine, for the right sort of devotee. Ha ha. It's just up here."

Had he been feeling stronger, Croy might have shaken the man off. He knew what game was being played out here. He lacked the strength to walk away, though. As it was, he had to lean hard on the stranger, but they managed to turn the corner. He had fully expected the man to lead him into an alleyway and there try to slit his throat, but it seemed this little temple was a real place: a tavern, where workers just coming off their shifts were spending the little pay they'd earned that day. It had an open storefront where an alewife poured ladles of watered wine for passersby. Behind her Croy could see a roaring fire and a crowded common room.

It would be good to get out of the mist and dry off, he thought. And perhaps a drink would bolster his flagging body. The laughing stranger hurried him inside and made a hand sign at the taverner, who leaned on a second bar inside. "Here, give me a coin, will you? An offering to the god of the house, call it. Ha ha."

Croy drew a coin from his purse and too late saw that it was silver. It was already in the stranger's hand. "Ooh, pretty, hark the way it shines, hmm? This'll do nicely, ha ha. Come, let us find a place to sit, oh, it's quite crowded out here, isn't it?"

"Private room," Croy rasped. "I need to—sit down."

"Sure you do. Long day's work for men like us, hmm? This way, this way, mind that fellow's feet, he's a real rough customer, wouldn't want to start anything, ha ha, here, here, no, over here, through the door, that's right. Here's a bench for you, and a little table. And, ah! Here comes the priest himself to perform the mass."

"Stow that nonsense, Tyron," the taverner said, backing through the door with a tray in his hands. He set an earthenware bottle of distilled spirit and two goblets on the table, but poured into only one of them. "He's probably so far gone he doesn't understand a word you're saying." He scratched his eyebrow with one filthy nail, then rubbed his thumb across his fingertips. The stranger—Tyron—nodded discreetly. So the taverner was in on the scheme, Croy realized.

Croy leaned forward on the edge of the table. Sitting down was helping, he thought. He hadn't realized how taxing just walking through bad air could be. A little strength trickled back into his arms.

"A bit of this will have you back on your feet, ha ha," Tyron said, and pushed the full goblet toward him. Croy made a show of reaching for it, then knocked it over clumsily so its contents spilled across the table. The liquor had the viscous consistency and milky color of blisswine. Even if it wasn't adulterated with some drug—and Croy was certain it was—it would have put him to sleep before he finished the generous portion. "Oh, clumsy, and that stuff's expensive, ha ha," Tyron japed, "lucky for me it's not my coin. Here, lean back, that's right. Get comfortable. There's no place for you to be, nothing needs doing. Let me loosen your cloak for you, it's catching at your neck." Nimble fingers undid the clasp and the cloak fell away from Croy's shoulders. "And here, this is too tight as well," Tyron said, reaching toward Croy's belt. Instead of opening the buckle, however, he began to pull at the strings of Croy's purse.

Croy lunged forward and knocked Tyron to the floor. The villain wasn't fast enough to dodge out of the way as Croy's shortsword sprang from its scabbard and came around in a weak swing—all he could manage—that left its point gently touching Tyron's throat.

"Thief," Croy said. "You thought I was drunk. You were going to—what's the word—roll me. Weren't you? Take my money and leave me unconscious in an alley."

"No, friend, you have me all wrong, ha ha," Tyron said, his eyes very bright.

"Don't lie," Croy said, and leaned forward a fraction of an inch. It brought the point of his shortsword that much closer to the man's jugular vein.

"Ha ha, now don't be so hasty, milord," Tyron said, his eyes roaming around the room. "There's plenty of fellows outside that door who know me. And none who know you from the Lady's archpriest, do they?"

"I can cut your throat before you can call for help," Croy pointed out. "Then I can—I can walk . . . walk out of here, and none the wiser."

"They know the score," Tyron said. He wasn't laughing now. "If you leave here without my arm around your shoulders, they'll know something's gone wrong. They'll stop you before you reach the street."

"That," Croy managed to growl, "will be of little comfort to you, as you'll be dead back here before I open the door."

"All right. All right. Take your ease," Tyron pleaded. "Tell me what you want of me, and I'll do it. I swear. Just take that cutter away from my throat."

A service. The man would perform a service, in exchange for his life. It was like the old stories. Like the tales of demons bound to grant wishes. But what did he wish for at this moment? What could possibly help him? He was lost in the Smoke, away from all friends and aid. Away from anyone who could ensure his safety. Nor could he count on his friends anymore. The rich friend who he had been staying with—the fellow who was kind enough to loan his horse—would surely turn his back on him now. Before, Croy had been a figure of fascination, a symbol of the man's generosity. Now he was a wanted criminal. No, even if his friend would take him in, Croy knew he would be doing him a great disservice by going back there. He thought of Murdlin, the dwarf envoy. Murdlin had saved him from the gallows once. But he'd also said their account was square, that he had repaid Croy in full. Dwarves never forgot a debt—but they never gave anything on credit either.

Perhaps, though—perhaps he could call not on a friend but on an acquaintance. Someone with whom he shared the slenderest of links, but a link nonetheless. There was one man in the Stink, one man who cared for Cythera, just as he did. One thief. Tyron might even know him—or at least how to reach him.

"You like silver, don't you? Don't you?" Croy demanded.

"Oh, aye, and who doesn't?" Tyron wheedled.

"Do me a service, and earn it, then. I have a message to send. And I think you might know how to deliver it."

## CHAPTER FIFTY-SIX

"It's just as I said, ha ha," Tyron told them. "Look, he's weak as a kitten. Three against one, those are fine odds. We cut his throat while he's sleeping, that makes even better sense. Then we take his silver and dump the body in the Skrait, yes? It'll be out in the ocean to be nibbled by the fishes before anyone even knows he's gone."

Malden shot a glance sideways at Kemper. The intangible sharper kept his face as still as stone, no doubt thinking exactly what he was thinking.

"Keep your voice down," Malden whispered. "If he wakes it'll take more than us to put him to sleep again."

"It don't take three men t'slit some sleepin' bugger's neckpipe," Kemper advised in even lower tones.

"You can't cut me out of this. I know too much, ha ha,"

Tyron said. "I've seen his face. A man of quality like that. A knight, or better, he is. But wounded like this, and so far from Castle Hill. There must be someone—ha ha—looking for him. But not someone, I wager, he wants to be found by. Else why would he have sent for the likes of you two? He's trouble, this one. You think the watch won't want to hear about this?"

On the floor, Sir Croy rolled over on his side with a moan. The hilts of his two swords stuck up at bad angles from his back. Sweat sheened his face and blood stained his clothes. He wasn't going to wake anytime soon.

"I didn't have to cut you in at all," Tyron went on. "I could have just waited till he slept, then taken everything for myself. We do this together, and then maybe you'll speak the right word in the right ear. Maybe I find myself in a new position, ha ha."

Malden knew what the man meant—his measure was already taken. Before agreeing to come with Tyron into the Smoke, he had learned the man's whole life story.

Tyron was not one of Cutbill's thieves. He was not really a thief at all, at least not all the time. Mostly he labored at a redsmith's, working brass into latten with a cloth-covered hammer. It was not pleasant work and it paid barely anything, so Tyron was always happy to supplement his income with a quick bit of thuggery. Rolling drunks, short change confidence games, picking pockets when he could get away with it—any quick and dirty scheme to make an extra bit of coin. He was smart enough to have an arrangement with the tavern's owner. That showed organizational skills—which had promise. He was just the sort of fellow Cutbill might take on as an apprentice, though it was unlikely he'd ever rise much higher. Tyron only knew he wanted the protection that Cutbill's guild could bring him, and that alone had made him actually carry out Croy's bidding.

When Croy had asked Tyron to fetch Malden, Tyron knew enough to contact one of Cutbill's agents. It might have gone no further, though, had Malden not been at Cutbill's lair at the time, conferring with Slag the dwarf. He and Kemper had come at once, with Tyron leading them. No more than two hours had passed since Croy tasked Tyron with his message.

Had it taken any longer, Croy might have been dead before they arrived.

Malden knelt down next to the knight, who was moaning softly now. The swordsman's face was fish-belly white. He must have lost a great deal of blood. It would be child's play to kill him now, but Malden had something else in mind. He carefully opened Croy's purse. He had a lighter touch that Tyron, though most likely it didn't matter. Croy was feeling nothing but pain.

"Here," Malden said, taking out a mixed handful of silver and copper coins. Not a farthing in the bunch. He picked out ninepence and tossed them to Tyron. "There's plenty more here, if you'll do one more errand. Find me a physick. A *discreet* physick. Bring him here and you can have half this purse. Then you're done—you leave and tell no one about this. There must be a dozen silver galleons here. Not bad for a half night's work, is it? Cross me, however, and I'll send my associate after you."

"Him?" Tyron said. "A beggarly card cheat? Why should I fear—"

Kemper lunged at the thug and drove both hands deep into Tyron's chest. Tyron opened his mouth to scream and a stream of icy vapor issued from his mouth.

"Are we agreed?" Malden asked.

They most certainly were.

Tyron returned shortly, leading a man in a robe and a long conical paper mask. Malden peered through the holes in the mask and saw bleary eyes staring back. He paid Tyron and sent him on his way, with a promise to speak well of him to Cutbill.

"You're a trained physick?" Malden asked when Tyron was gone and he could speak plainly with the healer.

"I am." The man removed his mask—meant to protect him from the disease-ridden vapors of the Smoke—and rubbed at his face. He wore a pomander at his belt and stank of flowers and garlic. "I'm a doctor of physick, if you would know. Trained up at the university, under doctors Jacinth and Detwiler, and—"

"Good enough," Kemper said. "But can ye keep yer mouth shut?"

The physick looked from Kemper back to Malden. "I'm usually employed by the workshops in this area. They pay me well to look after men hurt on the job. My employers prefer not to have suits of law brought against them—even in this place there are laws against negligence. So yes, I can be kept quiet. For the right price. Is this the man I'm to treat?" he asked, pointing at Croy.

"D'ye see anyone else who needs ye?" Kemper demanded.

"You might have moved him to a bed, if you cared about his health," the physick replied. "For all I know you're willing to let him die." He dragged Croy up to a sitting position, then pried the knight's mouth open to look at his tongue. He felt for Croy's pulses and put an ear to his chest to listen to his wind. "Has he moved his bowels since he came here? Or passed any water?"

"Ye want to see his piss?" Kemper asked. "What kind o' sick fella are ye?"

The physick clucked his tongue. "I don't expect that your sort knows *anything* of medicine, nor shall I explain myself in detail. But the urine of a man is a great treasury of secrets, to those who know how to read it. I might find traces of extravagant humors in it. There might be blood in it, which would be a very bad sign indeed."

"Tell ye what, buy me a coupla drinks, I'll give ye all the urine ye can stomach," Kemper said with a cackle.

The physick looked like he might jump up and leave on the moment. Malden rushed forward to put a hand on the man's arm. "Forgive him. He's little more than a peasant. Sure a man as worldly and learned as yourself can rise above such petty taunting?"

"I assure you, my interest in his urine is purely professional!"

"Of course it is," Malden said, "and professionals," he

added, taking coins from his purse, "are paid for their services."

It was enough to make the physick return to his labors.

While he worked, Malden stepped aside with Kemper
and spoke quietly. "You don't care for medicos, hmm?"

"Oh, was I rude?" Kemper said with mock shame. "Nah,
lad, I ne'er liked 'em, e'en back when I were reg'lar flesh.
'Specially not then. They're more like t'kill ye than heal ye,
if ye've anythin' worse'n a bruise on yer li'l finger."

Malden shrugged. "True, but if we do nothing, Croy will
die. I at least want a chance to talk to him before that. He
had something to say to me, and I can't afford not to hear
it right now. We only have five more days before . . . before
Ladymas. Croy is connected to what we're doing, somehow.
I'd like to know how."

"Aye," Kemper said, looking almost contrite. "Yer in the
right. Just don't let that butcher near me."

Eventually the physick straightened up and came over to
Malden. Leaning close enough that Malden could smell the
garlic on the man's breath, he said, "The wound is deep,
but it hasn't festered yet. I've bandaged it properly, which
is most of what I can do for now. He'll want an electuary of
borage root if he takes fever. Watch his stools for any sign
of flux. At the first such movement he'll need to be bled.
Do not tarry or the poison will take him in hours. If he's
hungry, give him foods that bolster the blood. Black pud-
ding, blood sausage, the like."

"Very good. Anything else?" Malden asked.

"You may want to offer a prayer to the Lady. If he does
survive through the night, it will be a marvel. If he's to
make it through tomorrow, his stars must be with him. If he
survives three days—well, I doubt that will happen. He will
almost certainly take to fever, convulsions, and black vomit.
Now. My fee."

He held out his hand and Malden poured the rest of
Croy's silver into it. Malden had never had a problem spending other people's money. "Is this enough to buy silence?"

"It is. Though let me warn you—I'm not the only one
who's going to recognize a knight of the realm when I see

him. Get him out of sight, and quickly. The bailiff has sent word down from Castle Hill that this man is a wanted outlaw." With that the physick left.

"Did you hear that, Croy? You're an outlaw," Malden said, nudging the knight's foot with his own. "Just like me now. And no better."

Croy moaned and fell over on his side with a crash.

# CHAPTER FIFTY-SEVEN

Croy didn't die in the night. He didn't wake up either.

By mid-morning, with time growing short, Malden resorted to desperate measures. He filled a basin with water and then dumped it over Croy's face. The knight sputtered and coughed and his eyes flicked open. One of his hands reached over his shoulder, looking for a sword that wasn't there.

The wounded man's face hardened. He looked around the room, even sat up a little. "You moved me," he said.

"You're safe. Or perhaps it's better to say—no one knows where you are," Malden told him. Croy was lying on Malden's own bed, in his room above the waxchandler's shop. "That's a good thing, because right now Anselm Vry has his watchmen searching for you in every district of the city. It could become a bad thing, because none of your friends know where to find you. It's up to you, Sir Knight, if you wish to leave this room again."

Croy nodded. He understood. "Who's he?" he asked, looking across the room at Kemper, who was paring his fingernails with the silver edge of Croy's unusual sword. He had trimmed his beard and his hair as well with the blade, for the first time since he'd been cursed. He'd never had access to a silver knife before.

"A friend. My friend," Malden said. "You needn't concern yourself with that right now. You sent a messenger to find me last night. Luckily for you he did. I had a physick look at your wound. He said it will most likely be your death. When he was finished treating you, I brought you here, to get you out of the public eye. So you owe me something, Croy. First off, you owe me an answer. Why did you send for me, of all people in the Free City?"

Croy pushed himself upright in the bed and put his feet down on the floor. Under Malden's thin blanket he was naked. "Is it still raining out?"

Malden sighed. He drew his bodkin and showed it to Croy.

"You can do better than that rat-skinner," the knight told him. "My shortsword should be around here somewhere. I assume you brought it when you moved me. It'll make a cleaner cut, and kill me quicker."

"Smart talk, for one's weak as a kitten just now," Kemper said. "Ye'd be wise to just answer the question, m'lud."

Croy nodded. "You're quite right, good sir. And I fully intend to do so, as soon as Malden stops threatening me with death. I have no fear of it now, so it's hardly useful as a spur. I just wished to make that clear."

Malden sat down on the windowsill and sheathed his knife. He'd seen the way Croy moved when the water hit his face. For a man with a life-threatening wound, he was still fairly quick. He'd heard, too, of what Croy had done up at the castle. A man that dangerous wouldn't go down easily. Perhaps it was time to stop threatening him and start getting actual information out of him, after all. "I'm sure there's something you're afraid of. If I need to, I'll find it. But for now, very well." He sketched a mock bow. "I won't kill you until I have a reason. Tell me first how you even know my name."

Croy scrubbed at his face with his hands. "Cythera told me, of course. She told me that you stole the Burgrave's crown and sold it to Hazoth. Ordinarily that would be a problem. I'm still technically the Burgrave's vassal."

"He banished you to the kingdom of the dwarves. Then when you returned he tried to have you hanged."

Croy lifted his hands in resignation. "He never discharged me from his service. I swore an oath to defend him until my last breath."

"And you still intend to keep it?" Malden asked.

The knight's brow furrowed. "Yes, of course. How could I break that troth and still live with myself? I would die a thousand deaths before I dishonored myself."

Malden stared at the knight. Then he looked to Kemper, who seemed as uncertain as he was. "So you came looking for me—why? To bring me to justice? Did you expect me to turn myself in, to show contrition now that the theft is done?"

"I thought you might know where Hazoth is keeping it. I thought you might know how I can recover it. If you stole something once, you might know how to steal it again."

Kemper started to speak, but Malden held up a hand for silence. He had no reason whatsoever to let Croy know that he was already bent on that very endeavor. "Do you have any idea how dangerous it would be to try? Can you think of any reason I would even consider the job you're talking about?"

"He's askin' how much yer payin'," Kemper suggested.

"I can't give you any money," Croy said. "But you would have the greatest of rewards—knowing you struck a blow for justice." Malden started to laugh, but Croy stopped him by speaking again. "Cythera is a prisoner of the sorcerer Hazoth. As long as he possesses that crown, she will never be free."

"And what, exactly, should that mean to me?"

Croy blinked. "Everything, of course. You've met her. You know she doesn't deserve that fate. When last we met, Malden, I got the sense you cared for her in some way. If I was wrong I've slit my own throat, clearly. But I don't think I was wrong."

"Let me get this straight," Malden said. "You found yourself in the Smoke, all but dead, hunted by the entire city watch. You knew your only way of surviving was to get the crown back from Hazoth. So you sent for me, the thief who stole it, thinking I would help you simply because there's a woman in peril who needs to be rescued."

"Yes," Croy said, as if very glad that Malden finally understood.

"What in the Bloodgod's name are you?" Malden asked finally.

"In the name of the Lady, I am an Ancient Blade," Croy answered.

As if that explained everything.

Well . . . it did answer a few questions. Malden knew the story of the Ancient Blades, seven legendary warriors so called because they wielded sacred swords. Those swords had been made by human hands in a time so long ago the Free City of Ness wasn't even a tower on a hill. The method of their creation was lost in time, but it was said even the dwarves could not create weapons of such power or with such keen edges.

Kemper looked down at the bicolored sword in his hands. Then he carefully set it down on the floor.

"That thing's one of the blades? It doesn't look like much," Malden insisted.

"None of them do. They weren't forged as parade weapons. They were made to do one thing. To fight demons."

# CHAPTER FIFTY-EIGHT

Kemper held the sword as far away from himself as possible.

Malden understood his reticence. Looking at the blade, a strange feeling passed over him. What had been a simple weapon before had taken on new dimensions, now that he understood what it was made for. He remembered the way he'd felt while holding the magicked crown. The voice in his head had the power of command, the ability to rouse men to deeds of foolish valor and great sacrifice. The sword had no such enchantment on it, yet he could almost feel the power contained in its length.

It was old, he knew. Older than he could imagine. It was a fragment of another time, a relic of when the old stories were all true. Malden disbelieved most of what he'd heard of Skrae's ancient history, of the war against the elves, of the forests full of giants and goblins that preyed on the first human settlers. He had discounted such stories as fit only for children and the feeble-minded. Yet here was a thing that had featured in its own share of those stories, and its reality could not be questioned. It was cold metal, and a kind of magic.

Suddenly all the stories seemed real. All those tales of brave knights wading into sorcerous peril, into the very maws of demons—they might actually be true. The seven blades, who stood alone against all the forces of the pit that would corrupt and defile the very world should they ever be set free.

"Demons are rarely seen now," Croy explained. "Thanks in no small part to the seven swords and the men who wielded them. We have almost wiped their kind from the face of the world—them, and the dread sorcerers who summon them here for nefarious purposes. There was a time, though, when they were thick upon the land. When they tore great swaths through Skrae, leaving destruction and madness in their wake. In that time the Blades were created, and without them I have no doubt humanity would have perished. They are that important.

"Any piece of iron," he went on, "is capable of killing a man, or a dwarf, or even an ogre. It just takes a strong arm to wield it. Demons, however, are different. They are native to the pit, where the laws of nature do not apply. Even dwarven steel is little use against them. To make matters worse, this quality that makes them so strong—that they are counter to nature—also makes them horribly dangerous. They were not created to breathe our air, to trod our earth. When they are dragged up out of the pit, they blight the land that receives them. Their evil is like a disease upon the very fabric of reality."

"Fabric o' what?" Kemper asked, but Malden hushed him.

"Some will turn milk sour inside a cow's udders if she so much as looks on them. Some wither crops wherever they pass. And some are capable of destroying our world, just by being here. The one that brought down the Burgrave's tower—"

"It was tiny," Malden said, nodding, "until it was exposed to the air. Then it began to grow, and did not stop."

Croy frowned. "Had it been permitted to continue, it would have grown until it crushed the entire city under its weight. Even then it would not have stopped, until its tentacles could wrap around the world and crush it to rubble."

Malden felt the blood rush out of his face. He had released the thing from its watery prison. If it had not been checked . . .

"Fortunately, Bikker and I were there to stop it."

Malden cried out. "That bastard's an Ancient Blade, too?" he demanded.

"Yes. He wields the sword called Acidtongue. Just as I wield Ghostcutter."

"Then you know him," Malden said.

"Oh, yes. Very well, in fact. He trained me." Croy rose carefully from the bed, walked over to the window and looked out at the rain, which had grown stronger overnight. "The swords are immortal, but the swordsmen are not. As each Ancient Blade ages and grows infirm, he finds a suitable heir to take the sword and the oath that comes with it. It's up to the others to teach this new blade how to fight. It is a sacred duty and not lightly conferred—but only twice has a blade failed to be passed on correctly. Two of the swords, Fangbreaker and Dawnbringer, were stolen from us by barbarians. Where they are now, no civilized man knows."

Croy stared into the middle distance, as if he could find

the lost swords in his own memory. Then he shook his head and continued with his tale.

"When I received Ghostcutter from its previous owner, there were five of us, gallant knights all. We were in service to the king, at his fortress at Helstrow. It was our duty to protect him from any demons his enemies summoned to attack him."

"Why aren't you there now?" Malden asked.

Croy lowered his head as if he were ashamed of the answer. "The king died. He was poisoned by one of his courtiers. His son, the new king, discharged us. He claimed we were bad bodyguards who had failed to protect our master. We tried to explain that our brief was not to protect against poison, but only demonkind. He didn't listen. Demons are rarely seen in this world nowadays. Our sacred work is rarely called for—as vital as it may be, it's difficult to explain to people how important we are when no one has seen a demon at large for nearly fifty years. The new king didn't understand why he should pay us to train endlessly for a threat that never came. He expected us to do other service to earn our keep. The five of us were forced to split up and go out into the world and find new occupation, wherever we could. Bikker brought me here, where we both swore allegiance to the Burgrave."

"That doesn't seem to be working so well," Malden pointed out.

Croy glared at him.

The thief shrugged off the knight's disdain. "I speak nothing but fact. Neither of you works for the Burgrave anymore. Bikker's working for the Burgrave's enemies now. And the Burgrave sentenced you to death."

"I haven't forgotten my oath, all the same. As for Bikker—something changed inside him. With nothing much to do, he grew bored here. There was not enough action to satisfy his bloodlust, and a man like Bikker must fight or he begins to die inside. Everything that was noble and valiant in him perished for lack of use. It was a great tragedy—but I cannot forgive him for what he has become. He broke his promise to the Burgrave and now he sells his services—and Acidtongue's—to the highest bidder. I called him faithless when he left the Burgrave's employ. I insulted his honor." Croy shook his head. "Now he seeks satisfaction for that slight. He will kill me if he catches me."

"What, because you called him a bad name?" Malden asked.

"Sure, son, an' only apologize, an' make it better, like," Kemper suggested.

"It was unforgivable, what I said. Don't you understand? Honor is everything to such as Bikker and myself. An insult like that is a mortal blow." Croy studied Malden and Kemper with a questioning eye. "You don't understand at all. Is it true what they say, then, that there is no honor among thieves?"

"Aye," Kemper said.

"Yes," Malden agreed.

Croy grunted in distaste.

Malden felt the need to explain. "If that's how you define honor, anyway. When you're poor you can't afford to take offense. If I had to kill every man who ever swore an oath in my presence . . . well, Ness wouldn't be so crowded anyway. But I suppose it's different for the nobility. When two men in the Stink come to blows in a tavern, it's assault, and they're both put in the stocks. When a baronet and an earl hack away at each other with their swords, that's a duel, and half the city comes out to cheer."

"I'm sorry you see it that way," Croy said.

And Malden believed him. Looking into the knight's eyes, he was convinced, utterly, that Croy's world really was that simple. That honor meant the difference between life and death. That there were more important things in the world than a full belly and a warm place to sleep.

And of course, in that world damsels in distress *had* to be rescued.

"Where does Cythera come into all this?" Malden asked.

Croy's eyes sparkled at the sound of her name. "It was while working for the Burgrave that I first met her. She and her mother lived in the Golden Slope then. Her mother is a witch, did you know that?"

"She mentioned it," Malden said.

Croy smiled. "Perhaps you think that I mean she is some toothless hag, selling powdered bat wings and working simple hexes on strayed lovers. Nothing could be further from the truth. Witchcraft is simpler than sorcery, but it's cleaner, too. Coruth—Cythera's mother—counted half the best families of Ness amongst her clients. She consulted with the Burgrave on matters magical . . . and once, when she came to the palace, she brought her daughter with her. Cythera. I was enchanted when I first laid eyes on her."

Malden looked away. He could understand only too well.

"We barely exchanged a half dozen words at that first meeting," Croy said. "Yet I knew when first we met that I would love her forever. I asked her to promise she would be mine someday. She wanted to say yes but she knew she was not her own mistress, not so long as Hazoth lays claim to her services. Anyway, she was too young then to make such a weighty decision. Now she has flowered into womanhood."

"Flowered is the right word," Malden said, thinking of her tattoos.

Croy didn't seem to get the joke.

"Never mind. Tell me more of Coruth. How did she end up in Hazoth's thrall?"

"For defying him. About ten years ago she decided to take Cythera away from here—she considered Hazoth to be an ill influence on Cythera's education. She knew Hazoth wouldn't like it. Should Cythera ever get more than a few miles away from him, the link between the two of them will cease to function and he'll be prey to every demon in the pit. Coruth knew he would do anything to keep that link in place. She tried to flee Ness with Cythera anyway. They made it as far as the city gates, but then—then Hazoth worked a spell on Coruth. He forced her to march back to his villa and submit herself to imprisonment in a magic circle. His power was just too great to resist. Cythera was immune to the spell, but for her mother's sake she could only watch in horror as Coruth struggled and writhed, fighting every step."

"Coruth has been locked away in the villa ever since?" Malden asked.

"Should she become free even for an instant, she could wreak a terrible revenge on Hazoth. He'll never let her go willingly, and as long as he has her, he has Cythera, too." Croy laughed. "That's where we come in. Together we'll fight our way into the villa, striking down every man who—"

"Sneak," Malden said.

"What?"

"We aren't going to fight our way in. We're going to steal in during the night and get the crown before Hazoth even knows we're there."

"And free Coruth in the process, yes?" Croy asked. He looked like he didn't like what he was hearing.

"If I can. For Cythera's sake," Malden said.

Croy seemed to take that as a yes. He clapped Malden on the shoulder. "You're a good man, even if you are a thief. For Cythera! You can keep the blasted crown. Once Cythera is free of Hazoth's bondage, she and I can marry. She will bear me a son, and if he is worthy, I will pass Ghostcutter to him when I am too old to lift it."

He strode over to Kemper and took the sword from the card sharp's hands. Kemper didn't try to stop him. The silver edge of the sword was one of the few weapons that could kill him, after all. Croy lifted the sword above his head and made a swooshing pass through the air with it, careful not to break any of Malden's simple possessions.

"In the past, I have been . . . confused. My duty to the Burgrave and my devotion to Cythera were at odds. Now I see, though, that destiny has led me to this pass. By freeing Cythera, I will recover the crown—and keep to both my oaths. My heart is clear."

He seemed lost in a reverie. Malden took the opportunity to whisper to Kemper, "What make you of this story?"

Kemper laughed. "Methinks we've a walkin' fairy tale in this 'un. Never once did I hear such piffle afore. Yet I heard he fought his way out o' Castle Hill 'gainst two dozen men or more. I wouldn't cross him, if'n I was you."

"I'm afraid you're right. Maybe we should have just cut his throat when we had the chance."

"O' course, mayhap there's a way to profit o' this anyway," Kemper pointed out. "There's liable to be some fightin', afore this is all through."

Malden looked over at the knight and the swords he was holding in his hands. "We could use a man who's good with a sword, it's true. This one's wounded, though. He wouldn't last five seconds against Hazoth's guards."

"Mayhap we don't need to tell the guards that he's hurt," Kemper said. "I bet they take one look at 'im and run off."

It was possible, Malden thought. Certainly, having the knight on their crew wouldn't hurt.

While they spoke, Croy pulled on his clothes and put both his swords back in their rightful scabbards. Any idea Malden had possessed of keeping the knight as his prisoner was forgotten. "I've listened to your story, Sir Croy," he said, "and I've decided to help you." Of course, he'd always meant to steal the crown back. Frankly, as he saw it things were the other way around—he would allow the knight to help him. But it didn't hurt if Croy saw it his own way. "Together we'll retrieve the crown, and together we'll save Cythera."

"You're a good man. I knew it when first we met," Croy said, bounding over to grasp Malden by the forearms. "I saw in your eyes that you were a friend of Cythera."

"A . . . friend. Yes," Malden said. "Of course, I will expect some sort of recompense for my trouble."

Croy's face darkened in mid-beam. "I told you, I can't offer you any money."

"No," Malden said, putting an arm around Croy's shoulders. "No, I don't suppose you can. But you do have one other thing that I want."

# CHAPTER FIFTY-NINE

Later that day, Malden climbed up on top of a house in the Stink near the cloth market. Below him lay Woolcomb Square—actually a triangular space where five roads came together—with merchants doing a bustling trade, hanging out bolts of fine loden and broadcloth on high wooden racks. The women who came there to buy grabbed up handfuls of the stuff and rubbed it against their cheeks to test its softness, or tugged hard at it to measure its strength.

In their midst a girl in a tattered kirtle sold ribbon from a tray around her neck, lengths of her wares hanging down like multicolored tongues. The ribbon covered her hands nicely, and Malden watched with professional appreciation as she went up to one goodwife after another and clutched at their skirts, begging them to buy a little something so her family wouldn't starve. When inevitably the female citizens clouted her across the ear to make her give off, she would cry and run away—straight to the dilapidated stall of a button seller who never seemed to make a sale. Her tiny hand would plunge deep into a barrel full of sequins and the button seller would nod in satisfaction. She was good, this urchin, and Malden chuckled because he never saw the coins she stole. She was just that fast.

Behind him Croy clambered up over a gutter and onto the roof. Malden gestured for him to get down, to lie prone on the scorching-hot shingles, just as he had.

"I beg your pardon for taking so long getting up here," Croy said. His face was white as milk. "I fear I'm not fully recovered yet."

"I'm less worried about your speed than your noise," Malden told him in a harsh whisper. "With all the metal you're carrying, you clang and rattle like a cutler's wagon. Do you really need to carry both those swords all the time?"

Croy frowned. "Well, yes. Ghostcutter has a special destiny, and should be saved for high combat, while simple bladework demands my shortsword, which—"

"Spare me," Malden said. He returned to studying the market below. "You're certain Cythera will come here today?"

"Once a month she ventures here from Hazoth's villa to replace worn or stained cloths," Croy told him. "Beyond her duties as a deflector of curses, she serves as the mistress of his household. All the necessities of life are her responsibility, as he cannot be bothered to see to his own arrangements. He spends every day in his laboratory or his sanctum, deeply absorbed in his studies."

"You've been watching his movements, too," Malden said. "Studying him with equal diligence."

"When I returned to the city I think I already knew that eventually I must face him. He will never let her go for any price. She's far too valuable to him—without her, he must suffer the rivalry of every demon in the pit, and be beset by the curses they send his way on a daily basis. No, I must force him to release her, one way or another."

"Well, that's what we're here for."

Croy frowned. "Are you truly sure we must involve her? She's pledged to his service. She might betray us if we let her know what we plan."

He had thought the same thing, of course. Yet he saw no other way. "If we're to have any chance at all," Malden said, "any hope, we need her on our side. If there's a way she can help us that doesn't put her in danger, I'll take it. But this is too important not to try to enlist her aid. Surely she'll want to help us, since we're her only chance, too."

"I pray you're right."

Malden watched with a frown as the ribbon girl's hand was seized by an especially wary shopper. Great sobbing tears and wails granted her no mercy, and the goodwife squeezed her hand until it opened. The ribbon girl held up her empty palm as emblem of her innocence, and the goodwife was forced to release her. The ribbon girl ran off as fast she could, pitching her ribbon tray on a pile of ordure in an alley. The ribbons had been worthless tat, Malden realized, valued only for the cover they gave her real occupation. Now that she was under suspicion it meant nothing to her. Ah, and it was too bad—a good scheme, but now the game was up. Doubtless she'd have another scheme cooked up by tomorrow, though. The button seller did not react at all to her desertion.

There was still no sign of Cythera. Malden shifted his position slightly to get more comfortable on the shingles. It might be a long wait.

"One thing I don't understand. What does Hazoth want with the crown? Does he simply wish to study its enchantment?" he asked.

Croy had no good answer. "It puzzles me as well. Hazoth was a good friend of the first Burgrave, Juring Tarness. They fought together against the elves that once held this place. Hazoth was instrumental to the founding of Ness. In the intervening years he's showed no sign of rebellion—Ness has always been a safe haven for him. He's been protected here, where sorcerers in other cities have been burned at the stake. In return for that protection he's always supported the Burgravate to the best of his powers. A less civic-minded sorcerer would have been run out of the Free City long since—he would have been burned at the stake. Such men rarely live long, and yet Hazoth has persisted through centuries."

"I imagine knowing all that magic helps," Malden pointed out.

"He is a powerful sorcerer. From the tales I've heard, though, he must have changed much over the centuries. In those days, before the Free City had its charter, Juring Tarness was a great general. He defended the kingdom against the elves and then against the dwarves, who had better weapons and impregnable fortresses all through this land. Hazoth turned the tide in that conflict, as the dwarves had no sorcerers of their own and could not resist his magic. Hazoth was hailed as a great hero, and Juring a protector of the realm."

"I saw the campaign banners hanging in his tower room,

when I took the crown," Malden said, thinking hard. "A great leader of men, was he?"

"Juring? Oh, yes. They say his voice had the power to compel. It was not magic, I think, but sheer force of character."

"So anyone he spoke to would be inspired to follow his orders. Interesting." Malden was beginning to put together a few facts, but so far he had no conclusions. He made a mental note to revisit the idea again.

Croy's voice had a note of the highest admiration as he said, "Juring was a born ruler, and yet he served his king faithfully. When he founded the city, he proved—as is not often the case—to be as good a statesman as he was a warrior. The king of that era asked him what reward he would choose for his service. Juring could have had anything— riches, a grand fief, a personal army. Instead he requested freedom for the people of Ness. They had supported him through a long and trying campaign, you see. A time of great suffering for his army. He used his reward to give them perpetual safety from taxes and bondservice. The freedom you now possess is only guaranteed by the charter he asked the king to sign. In fact—"

"Hold," Malden said.

Down in the market, Cythera had arrived. She was dressed in a fine purple velvet cloak and moved listlessly from stall to stall, barely fingering the cloth on display. She was followed by one of Hazoth's retainers, a sallow-faced man with a chain-mail shirt and an axe on his belt. He pushed a barrow to hold her purchases, but his eyes were watching the crowd, perhaps searching every face for sign of threat.

"I hoped she would come alone," Malden said. The plan had been to draw her into some secluded bystreet, and there converse with her in private. It was crucial she not be seen talking with either him or Croy, as word of such a meeting would doubtless get back to Hazoth. "All right," he said. "This will just take a bit of cunning. Follow me down."

The two of them climbed down a drainpipe on the side of the house, out of view of the crowded market. Croy had some trouble on the way down and nearly fell, but he caught himself in time. Malden led him around a corner and back into the market from a different direction. He did not approach Cythera directly, but made sure to cross her path so she saw the two of them.

When they were buried again in the throng of people, Malden whispered to Croy, "Did you note her face when we passed?" He had been careful not to look at her, but he knew Croy would not have been able to resist.

"She saw me," Croy said, but he sounded crestfallen. "Her eyes—they went cold, and she looked away. Malden, she did not even smile at me."

Nor at me, Malden thought, and then chastised himself. Any hope he'd had of catching Cythera's favor—and it had been a forlorn hope, at best—was gone now that Croy was in the picture again. He'd heard the way Croy talked about Cythera, about how they had pledged to marry. Surely he had no chance of competing with a knight of the realm. A man who owned a bloody castle, for Sadu's sake. No, it was for the best if he put those feelings away. Let them die a natural death.

Still. It hurt.

He waved one hand in the air as if to dispel a miasmic vapor. "That's because she's wise enough to be discreet, nothing more. Come. I have a notion of our next move."

# CHAPTER SIXTY

The button seller looked up with a broad smile as Malden approached his stall. "Well met, sir, come, come, take a look here, finest horn—and not just ox horn, no sir, this is made of shavings from a unicorn's famed weaponry. Proof against poison, sir, you'll never need fear bad drink or food again."

Malden frowned. He met the button seller's eye with a meaningful look and then placed his hand on a barrel of sequins. He pushed his fingers through the thin bits of metal, as if he would root around in the bottom of the barrel. The ribbon girl's takings were at its bottom, he was sure. The button seller stared at him with suspicion in his eyes, but only a moment. Next, Malden stepped over to a barrel full of assorted buttons. Many of them were broken and all were worn and discolored.

"You want none of that dross, I assure you," the merchant told him. "Come, look at these. Genuine pearl, from the shells of clams as big as carts. They grow in only one sheltered cove in the far and mysterious Northern Kingdom called the Rifnlatt, and cost a pretty penny to import, but for you sir, well, I like your look, so—"

Malden took a coin from his purse—a tuppence—and dragged it across the surface of the buttons, digging a narrow furrow through them. With two more sweeping curves and a couple more lines he sketched a simple drawing of a heart transfixed with a key.

The button seller stopped talking at once. He reached for the coin and took it from Malden's hand, in the process smoothing out the buttons and obliterating Malden's handiwork. "I'm up to date on my payments," the merchant insisted. "Move on before someone sees us together."

"He—you know of whom I speak—calls on your aid. You'll be rewarded."

The button seller cast a suspicious glance at Croy, who was standing a ways off, trying to look inconspicuous and failing, utterly.

Malden sighed. "He's a mark," he said, a half lie. "I'm running a game on him. But to pull it off I need a distraction. Did you see a woman come through here, wearing a velvet cloak, followed by a bravo with a barrow? If you saw her face you'll remember her, for it was painted from chin to hairline in vines and flowers."

"Aye," the button seller agreed. "I saw her."

"I need the bravo out of the way so I can speak with that woman. The guard doesn't need to be distracted . . . permanently, just for a few minutes. Do you think you can help me?"

"For—For him," the merchant said, meaning Cutbill, "I can."

"My thanks. And his." Malden wandered away from the stall, one hand reaching for a bolt of patterned damask hanging from the next stall over. Croy came running over to join him, and Malden cursed the knight silently. If he didn't need Croy to gain Cythera's favor he would never have come out with him like this.

"It's done," Malden said, and no more.

"When? Where shall it occur?"

"Keep your eyes open," Malden told him.

They moved through the crowd drawing as little attention as possible. Malden stopped at several stalls and even haggled for a moment with a seller of thread, though he had no intention of buying anything. Croy kept staring at the faces passing by, but there was no help for that. Malden made sure they stayed close to wherever Cythera went, but not too close. When the diversion came he was no more than ten yards away.

"Sir, please sir, my sister, she's gone mad with fever, and she's locked me out of our house. Sir, please, I need your help, I need your axe, milord, please, I need you to chop down our door." It was the ribbon girl, though Malden barely recognized her. She had tucked her hair up inside a snood and turned her ragged kirtle inside out to show a different color. Such talent—Malden hoped Cutbill knew what a marvel he had in his employ, and what she was worth. "Sir, please, your help is most needed!"

Hazoth's retainer snarled and kicked at the girl but she was fast enough to avoid being struck. The tale she spun was obviously something she'd come up with on the spot, but the details didn't matter. The retainer shouted for her to leave off, and suddenly every eye in the market was turned in his direction.

It wasn't so much that the marketers were astounded that a grown man would shout at a girl like that, or threaten her with a naked blade. It was hardly likely they'd been moved by her impromptu tale of woe. But entertainment was where you found it in the Free City of Ness—and this looked like it could be diverting indeed.

Not for the first time Malden gave thanks for the prurience of his fellow citizens. Now that they were all distracted, he could move where he liked through the crowd, and no one would see him go. Better yet, they wouldn't see Croy. The big knight was simply impossible to make inconspicuous—unless people had something else to look at.

Most importantly of all, no one was looking at Cythera. She slipped between the shoulders of two burly men who were laughing at the sight of a toughened bravo beset by a street urchin. Instantly Cythera was swallowed up by the crowd.

"There," Malden said, and pointed to a dark alley closest to where Cythera had disappeared. "Go. Now," he said, and clouted Croy on the arm. The knight headed straight for the alley, and Malden worked his way through the crowd in the same direction, though not by such a direct route.

At the mouth of the alley he stopped and looked into its shadows. Cythera and Croy were already there, deep in conversation. Malden took one last look out at the market. The ribbon girl had managed to pull a length of poplin from a bolt and was weaving it through the bravo's legs. She did it so deftly it looked like she'd pulled the cloth by accident, caught it with her flailing hands. Anyone lacking Malden's trained eye would have no idea what she was doing or what fruit it was about to bear.

Hazoth's retainer lifted one mailed hand to swat the girl away but she was already gone—along with his purse. He must have realized that as soon as he returned his hand to his belt, because he cried out that he'd been robbed. He tried to give chase but was tangled in the poplin and fell flat on his face. The owner of the bolt of poplin came storming out of his booth to berate the fallen retainer, and the crowd laughed riotously at this spontaneous farce.

Perfect. Malden reminded himself to ask for the girl's name. She was born to the game, he could tell.

"—solve all our problems with one stroke," Croy was saying, his voice rising in volume. Malden came rushing toward the knight to shut him up. "And it will only cost—"

Cythera did Malden's work for him by interrupting.

"Last night he had her arm broken," she said, speaking over Croy's words. Her voice was ice hanging in the air.

The effect on Croy could not have been more profound if she'd slapped him across the face. "What? I don't understand," he said. He looked like a whipped dog.

"Did you think Hazoth would not hear of your antic at the palace?" Cythera demanded. "Calling on Vry to storm his home. Such a fool! I cannot believe I ever pinned hopes on your star, Croy." She turned away from the knight in disgust. "Hazoth knows about our connection, of course. He believes I set you to this reckless end. I could not convince him otherwise, and when I refused to confess, he sent two of his men with a bar and a piece of rope. They tied her arm double, and then twisted the rope with the bar until I heard the bone snap."

A tear ran down the garden of painted lilies that decorated Cythera's cheek.

"I meant only to—"

"I know what you meant to do! How much do good intentions mean in your world, Croy? In this storybook place you inhabit, where brave knights ride to the rescue of poor helpless women, is there glory in merely wanting to do good? Because in my world—and his," she said, jabbing a finger toward Malden, "what's in your heart means *nothing*. Not when all your best hopes and desires only make things worse."

Malden watched the two of them closely. Croy was like one thunderstruck, unable to speak or move. Cythera was so wracked with care that her skin was ashen under the vines and flowers on her face.

There was no time for this.

"Milady," he said, "we have moments only before your watchdog comes sniffing for you. Think me not heartless."

"No, Malden, I know you care," she said. She took a cloth from her sleeve and dabbed at the tears on her face, though with such gentle and hesitant motions she barely mopped up any of them. "What say you?"

"I am taking an enormous risk by trusting you. I have no way of knowing you will not repeat to Hazoth everything I say. Yet I have no choice but to ask your help. I seek to get the crown back. Once it is in my hands, Anselm Vry will have no choice but to arrest Hazoth, and likely execute him. Your mother will be freed, and you with her. Croy will be so beloved by the Burgrave that his banishment will be lifted, and with it the noose that belongs around his neck."

"And you, Malden? What will you gain? Can I afford your services?"

"I get my heart's desire," he said. He lowered his eyes. "But you need not pay that price. Meet with us tonight if you can. I have a room in the Stink." He described the street where he lived and how to reach it from Parkwall.

"Very well," she said. "At midnight, Hazoth will retire to his bedchamber and be occupied there until dawn. I'll come then."

"My thanks," Malden said. He watched her head back into the square, never once looking back. "Croy—we have to go now. There is no more time."

The knight didn't move. "Her arm?" he asked, his voice very small.

"Come! Or be damned," Malden hissed. "I only needed you to make contact with her. Get yourself killed now, if that's how you'll find your glory. But if you would aid me— if you would aid Cythera further—come. Now."

Eventually, Croy followed where Malden led.

# CHAPTER SIXTY-ONE

Malden spent the day drawing crude maps of the villa, showing all of its entrances and exits that he knew of, and the location of each room he and Kemper had seen. He studied them over and over with a feverish intensity. Endlessly he made corrections to them as he remembered something, as some detail that had previously seemed trivial suddenly offered new possibilities—or new hazards. His hands grew black with charcoal as he drew the maps again and again, then tore them up and made new drafts.

As confounded as he might seem to an outside observer, Malden was in his element. This was what he had been born for, he now knew. There were two kinds of thieves in the world, in his experience. There were those who turned to crime because they wanted money and they didn't want to work for it. Those were the kind of thieves who ended up very quickly swinging from a rope. The other kind were the sort for whom a perfectly planned burglary was a labor of love—a work, in fact, of art. The planning, the considering of angles, the second-guessing of one's own abilities and of one's opponents' motivations, the sudden inspirations that made the impossible seem, at least in theory, possible—these were what drew Malden to his profession, and in a way, he was quite happy poring over his maps.

Then again, perhaps he was just glad that for all of a day no one tried to kill him, or chase him across the rooftops, or threaten him with baneful sorcery. It was a nice change of pace.

The day fled, and night came all too soon. For hours he'd been thinking through every angle of his plan without bothering to rest or even eat. Now he took a pickled fish from a pot and chewed on its cold flesh without even tasting it. "Tomorrow morning," he said, "we'll have four days until Ladymas. I'd like to get this done as quickly as possible. We

don't know what will come in the next few days. Anselm
Vry might have tricks up his sleeve still. Hazoth might be
aware already of our scheming, and be taking steps to forestall us. So it behooves us to get it done soon, rather than
later."

"Agreed, lad, yet ye mustn't rush," Kemper said. He had
his deck of cards in his hands and he was rubbing each one
with his thumb, which he said always brought him good
luck. "That's been the endin' o' more thieves. This'll be
hard enough."

"I know," Malden said. He scratched his head and
thumped the table with his fist. "All right, let's go through
it one more time." He pulled the map of the villa's ground
floor and the garden toward him. "The magic barrier comes
this far, very close to the fence. I'll be here, and you'll be
. . . here," he said, pointing out a spot with his finger. "You
can hide in these bushes. The guards relieve each other at
midnight." It had taken some dedicated spying to learn that
much, but it seemed to happen the same time every night.
Hazoth didn't seem to rely overmuch on his retainers, and
hadn't trained them with military discipline. Malden had
even seen one fall asleep at his post one night. It was too
much to hope that they would all fall asleep at once, though.
"When the night's sentries come out from the barracks,
here, the relieved guards head inside, ready to fall into their
bunks and sleep. It will take some minutes for the fresh
batch to reach their stations. While they're all in front of the
villa, we'll get Cythera to lower the barrier. It will be down
only for a moment, just long enough for us to run up here, to
the preparatory door."

Kemper nodded. "And where'll yer titled friend yonder
be, then?"

Malden looked over at Croy, who was lying on the bed,
staring at the ceiling. He had barely moved from the spot all
day, and then only to pass water. "Him? I'm not counting
on him at all. When we brought him in on this I thought
he'd be useful, but I've seen now he'll never be one of us.
He's wounded and can hardly run, and anyway, he makes
too much noise even when he's trying to be quiet. He did his

part by helping us contact Cythera. Now that's done. Forget him."

"Just the twain o' us, then," Kemper said, sounding doubtful. "'Tis much work for two, in the time we got."

"I know. We'll just have to be fast. Once we're inside, you'll head to the front hall. There's likely to be a guard inside—I'm counting on it, in fact. You'll make yourself seen and he'll sound the alarm, drawing the rest of the guards inside."

"I must say I like this bit not," Kemper grumbled.

"You have nothing to fear. None of the guards has so much as a silver boot knife that we've seen—and even if they do have some way to hurt you, you can just slip through the wall and be gone before they catch you."

"Mayhap Hazoth's got some charm 'gainst spectral folk," Kemper said, shaking his head. "Some spell or other t'trap me."

"Probably," Malden admitted. "But if he's locked up in his laboratory, or better yet, in his bedchamber—remember those cold-forged iron chains—then he's not likely to come out just because one of the guards thought he saw a ghost. They know nothing of you, remember. It's my face they've all memorized."

"So be it," Kemper said finally. Malden could tell the card sharp was not satisfied, but Kemper owed him—if he hadn't freed Kemper from the Burgrave's dungeon he would be dead now. Besides, Kemper stood to benefit from this caper in more tangible terms. Hazoth had a full set of silver plate and cutlery, which Kemper could carry out of the villa and keep for himself. Malden wanted nothing of the treasures the house contained. He would be satisfied with the reward Croy had promised him. His efforts in the villa would be all about getting the crown back.

Which led to the far more difficult phase of the plan. "It's up to me to reach the third floor undetected. The crown is in the sanctum, at the end of this hall—Cythera told Croy as much. The hallway, we know, is full of traps. I'll have to overcome them somehow." Without knowing what they might be, that was a lot to presuppose. But there was no way around it. "Then I can get into the sanctum, grab the crown, and beat a very hasty retreat. The guards will all be inside looking for you, so when we exit through the garden there'll be none there to stop us. Cythera will lower the barrier once more and we escape, both of us unscathed, me with the crown, you with all the silver you can carry. After that we split up. I'll go to Cutbill and you'll leave the city by means I don't want to know about."

"Aye," Kemper said, and shuffled his cards distractedly. The simple motion of his hands seemed to soothe him. It made Malden want to reach over and grab them away from him, throw them across the room, even tear them up and throw the pieces out the window.

He was under a bit of strain.

There were too many variables. Too many things he couldn't plan for. What if Hazoth took the night off from his studies? What if Cythera betrayed them? What if Anselm Vry was watching them right now, waiting for them to make a move—just so Vry could seize the crown as soon as he brought it out of the house, so that Cutbill couldn't claim to have recovered it?

"This plan will work," he said, trying to convince himself.

"Aye," Kemper replied.

"It's the best plan we've had so far."

"Aye."

"With a little luck—"

He stopped because Cythera was sitting on the sill of his open window.

"With a great deal of luck," she said, "that plan will see you both killed very quickly. That way Hazoth won't be able to torture you. He's very good at that."

It was midnight.

Four days left.

# CHAPTER SIXTY-TWO

"Milady," Malden said, bowing low. "I thank you from the bottom of my heart for coming, as—"

"Obsequiousness does not suit you, Malden," Cythera said. She climbed down from the window and came over to the table where the maps lay. Malden noted that she didn't even glance at Croy. "This plan doesn't either. You've badly underestimated the villa's defenses."

Malden stepped back from the table and let her peruse the maps. After a moment she went to the unlit brazier in the corner (Malden used it only in the wintertime), took out a piece of charcoal and began to sketch in parts of the map that neither Malden nor Kemper had been able to draw.

"I take it you've decided to help us," Malden said when she seemed to be done.

"What choice do I have? If I betray you now, for the sake of peace, I will only be delaying the inevitable. He'll find some excuse to torture my mother regardless of what I do. No, her only hope is your foolish scheme. Which still won't work."

Malden looked down at the additions she'd made to the map. Mostly she had drawn in the rooms on the second floor, which did not concern him overmuch, but she'd added two walls on the third floor he had not known were there—and which would have caused him significant problems when he got inside.

"And . . . how is your mother, if I might ask?" Malden said. "Is she at least safe, for the nonce?"

"You could say that," Cythera told him without looking up. "She turned herself into a tree."

"A what, lass?" Kemper asked.

Cythera looked up then. She had never seen the intangible scoundrel before. Yet she did not demand to know who he was. "A tree. A rowan, of course."

"Of . . . course," Malden said.

"The rowan is sacred to witches and magicians. Its wood is the only proper material for magic wands, and its berries are a potent charm against sorcery. Coruth has not fruited yet, though. She is still a sapling, for she lacks the strength to increase her size through magic. At first I thought she had a cunning plan—that she would grow, as a tree, and eventually her branches would break through the roof of Hazoth's house. In that way she might free herself in, say, fifty or one hundred years from now."

"She expects to be prisoned that long?" Malden asked in surprise.

"She expects," Cythera said, "to be held there forever. Hazoth does not age. As long as she is trapped in a magic circle, neither will she. He will never release her, of course—he draws power from holding her captive, for one thing. The demons he commands delight in her agonies, and make gifts of their magic to him in exchange. For another thing he knows that if she ever does free herself, her first order of business will be to annihilate him utterly."

"Fer revenge," Kemper said, nodding agreeably.

"For justice, call it." Cythera turned to Malden. "It was just an hour ago that I realized another reason why she chose to make herself a tree. That was when I decided I would come here and aid you all I can."

"Oh?" Malden asked.

"Cruel boys break the branches of trees all the time, but trees do not feel pain."

"Ah."

"Hark," Cythera said, "I don't have much time. Hazoth is closeted in his bedchamber but he will emerge before the third hour of the morning. I was able to confuse the guards enough they did not see me go, but I must be back before he calls for me. He always does after consorting with demons. He knows the smell of brimstone nauseates me, you see. He is most subtle in his tortures, is Hazoth."

"You must hate him," Malden said.

Cythera stared at him with burning eyes. As if he could

not comprehend what she felt for the man. He supposed in many ways he couldn't, so he looked away.

"One thing I don't understand," he said. "Forgive me, but—you have so much power bound up in your painted skin. Couldn't you simply . . . I don't know. Strike him? Grab him forcefully. Wouldn't that be enough to destroy him? Surely that would satisfy justice." And save me a great deal of trouble, too, Malden thought.

It was Cythera's turn to avert her gaze. "Not all of his protections are magical," she said, her voice almost a whisper. "But there is a simpler reason. The magical link he has with me would make such a gesture futile. I could release the curses I have stored up against him, yes. But the link would simply send them back to me." She shook her head. "There's no answer there. You must find another way."

"I've been working on a plan," he told her, and showed her the papers on the table. "You heard the gist of it, and said it would fail."

"Yes. Look. Here," she said, and pointed to the map. Her finger was aimed at the great hall on the first floor.

Malden knew exactly what she was pointing out. "The great iron sphere there, by the stairs. I wondered about it, but knew not what it might be."

"It's another power source for Hazoth's wizardry. He has many, and I do not know them all."

"But what is it? It's made of iron. Doesn't iron discomfit demons? I would hardly think they would put their power into such an object."

"Cold-forged iron is their bane," Cythera said. "Iron forged in great heat actually strengthens them. It is why normal iron weapons, and even more so, dwarven steel, don't hurt them. This iron was formed in the heat of the pit itself. But it is not the iron that is magical. It is the pit-thing inside the iron."

"There's a demon in there?" Malden asked.

"Sure, an' it's like a magic circle, which'll hold a fiend, aye, only this 'un's in three d'mensions 'stead o' two," Kemper insisted.

Malden and Cythera both stared at him.

"D'you think me a simpleton?" Kemper asked, looking hurt. "Or mayhap you think me unversed in magics? D'you think one o' my affliction wouldn't learn a thing or two?"

"That's Kemper. He's cursed," Malden explained to Cythera.

"And largely correct," she said, shrugging off her surprise. "Yes, the iron is there to contain the demon. But not because Hazoth fears it getting loose. You see, the demon inside the iron sphere is an embryo, still. It has yet to be born. The iron sphere is not its prison, but its egg."

"It's like a babe in the womb?" Malden asked.

"Yes. But do not be fooled into thinking it weak or helpless. Demons are born fully formed and are quite dangerous the moment they are hatched. Otherwise they would never survive in the pit. Demons have no bonds of affection for one another, not like humans do. Even a mother's love for a child is unknown among them. A she-demon will devour her own brood with glee if she gets the chance."

"That's horrible," Malden said.

"It's just how things are done there. The demons see it as natural. As a result, those demons born weak and mewling like human infants don't live long. The ones that do survive are the ones born already strong. This demon is a perfect example. I've seen full-grown examples of its kind, and they are unstoppable slaughterers. The moment this one emerges from that egg it will be ready to hunt. Even before its proper time it will be a terrible thing to behold. I don't know how close it is to being born, but I know it will be hungry, and it will be ready to kill. Hazoth can release it any time he chooses. If he detects you inside his house, even for an instant, he can force the creature to hatch—and to give chase. It will follow you to the ends of the earth, if it must, and devour you. Do you understand?"

"I think I do," Malden said. His hands were suddenly very cold—his blood had turned to ice.

"You won't be able to fight it. Its claws will be sharper than any steel you bring to bear. Its teeth will rend through solid stone. Even with an Ancient Blade in your posses-

sion—and I doubt Croy will just loan you Ghostcutter—
you would never stand a chance against it in single combat,
Malden. You won't be able to hide from it either. It will be
born blind, but with an exceptionally keen sense of smell.
You could try to douse yourself in perfumes, or cross running water, or any of the stratagems that might drive a dog
from your trail. None of them will work with this creature.
Once it has your scent it will find you. And kill you."

Malden went to the bed and sat down on its edge, careful
not to disturb Croy. "What infernal pact did Hazoth make to
contract such service?" he asked, because asking questions
was much easier than contemplating what a newborn demon
would do to his tender flesh once it had him. "Did he get this
thing from torturing your mother?"

"No. He earned its service the oldest way. By siring it."

"Hold, now," Kemper said.

For the first time Croy sat up in the bed and spoke. "You
can't be saying that—"

Cythera looked down at the maps and met no one's gaze.
"You saw the chains in his bedchamber. I see you've even
drawn them in here on your diagram. That is how he enter-
tains his succubi. The demon in the egg was the fruit of one
such union. It is his child. It is not his first."

# CHAPTER SIXTY-THREE

"But . . . why?" Malden asked. He thought of the mural
of the succubus in the House of Sighs, and he supposed
he could see why a man would find that attractive. Yet he
was reasonably certain that mural had not been painted
from life. And even if it was, it seemed Hazoth's intent was

not to take pleasure from his succubi, but a wholly different end. "Why would anyone . . . want to . . . Why?"

"You wonder what would make a man desire a demon child. You wonder why any human being could compass such a thing. You forget that Hazoth does not think of himself as a human being. He does not consider himself bound by conventional ethics."

"I got that when I met him," Malden agreed.

"A sorcerer like Hazoth lives only for power. He cares not for gold, or love, or any of the things that entice normal men. He wants to expand the scope of his knowledge, and to possess power that others cannot match. He's already capable of things beyond your imagining. Yet for a very long time he's felt like a prisoner."

"Truly? But who could possibly compel him?"

"The Burgrave. And the king. There is a law against what Hazoth does, Malden. There is a penalty, if he's caught, and it's burning at the stake. Everything he does in the average day is probably illegal according to the laws of this land." She looked over into the corner of the room, where Ghost-cutter leaned against one wall. "The Ancient Blades exist to enforce that law."

"Croy told me Hazoth lives in Ness because the Burgrave's ancestor granted him a sort of safe haven here," Malden pointed out.

"Exactly. Now he's trapped here. If Hazoth left Ness he would be under constant suspicion. Croy and his brother knights keep a constant watch on any sorcerer who looks powerful enough to draw a demon up from the pit. They are never allowed a moment's rest until they prove they are faithful to the law. Hazoth couldn't live under that kind of watchful gaze. Eventually he would be caught summoning a demon or doing something else so infernal he would be arrested for it. He would be given a trial, but his sort are never very good at defending themselves in a court of law. He would be found guilty and sentenced to death. After so many centuries of life, to be caught by petty reeves and burned at the stake by peasants would seem utter injustice to him."

"Yet why would he want to travel abroad when here, in

Ness, he could live forever and be unmolested?" Malden asked.

"Can you imagine what it is like, to be called a free man, but only if you agree never to leave a certain place? Can you imagine the irony in that freedom, which requires you to remain always inside what must feel like a prison cell?"

Malden pursed his lips. He could imagine that exactly. He remembered when Cutbill had described his own situation in just the same terms. He had never wanted to feel sympathy for Hazoth. Nor did he now—at least not much— but he had to admit he could see Hazoth's motivations.

"Once his demon child is born, it will protect him from such a fate. He can go where he pleases—do what mischief he pleases—and none can stop him."

Malden stroked his chin. "Croy told me something else as well. About demons. How they're unnatural, and how they distort reality around them. How their power will eventually wreck the world if they're not stopped. There was one in the Burgrave's tower that would have choked the world if it wasn't checked."

"This one is much the same, though its dangers are less obvious," Cythera agreed. "Hazoth knows the risk he's running. He just doesn't care."

"That is troubling," Malden said.

"I meant it to be."

"For right now, though . . . it's also immaterial. You say that once the demon is born it will hound me to my death. Well, that just adds one step to my plan. I'll have to make sure Hazoth never becomes aware of my presence in his house—so he can't birth the demon."

"That'll be a nice bit o' work," Kemper said, "if'n ye can pull it off."

Malden shrugged. He hadn't expected this to be easy. He honestly did not expect to survive the job. Yet that thought was unworthy of being dwelt upon. He had a chance, a beggar's chance, to make this work. That was all he would allow himself to think. "It's better that way, at any rate. Even without the demon Hazoth is perfectly capable of destroying me. This changes nothing."

"There are other concerns as well," Cythera said. She stared deeply into Malden's eyes. For a moment neither of them spoke. What was she looking for? he wondered. For conviction, for self-confidence?

Eventually she closed her eyes. The downward-drooping petals of painted cyclamen blooms made her eyelids white as paper. The flowers began to wilt before she opened her eyes again. "There are the traps, in this hallway."

Malden looked down at the map. "Kemper discovered them, though he couldn't discern their nature. We were hoping you might tell us what they were, and thus allow me to take measures to circumvent them."

"That hope is forlorn," she said. "I have lived in that house most my life, but never have I walked down that hallway. Hazoth doesn't use it himself. When he goes to his sanctum—and on those occasions when he takes me there—he transports himself directly without passing through the intervening space. The hallway is a ruse, meant to confound thieves. The traps, I know, are very real, and quite deadly. They can be disarmed by a simple mechanism inside the sanctum. There is a candle always burning there. To deactivate the traps it must be snuffed. But of course, you need to be inside the sanctum to do so. As I have no access to that room, I cannot do that for you."

Malden nodded. "I expected to have to weather the traps myself. I have proven already—in the palace—that I can master such."

"Indeed. Well, that leaves only two layers of defense we have not discussed. There is the magical barrier that surrounds the house and prevents anyone from entering until they have been passed by the sentries."

"But that's where you come in," Malden said. "You'll lower it for us, when the time comes."

Cythera shook her head. "Had you come to me two days ago that might have been possible. Before Croy made a public spectacle of his desire to slay Hazoth."

On the bed, the knight turned his head away.

"Hazoth," Cythera told Malden, "knows I am connected to Croy. When he heard what happened up on Castle Hill, and what Croy said to Anselm Vry, he took the natural step of ensuring I could no longer lower the barrier. It is done with a certain hand gesture. The gesture can be anything—a sign drawn in the air with one finger, a clap of the hands, it doesn't matter. But you must know it to pass the invisible wall. Hazoth changed the signal and didn't tell me what the new pass sign is."

Malden's heart sunk. "But you escaped tonight."

"The captain of the guards knows the new sign. I was able to convince him to perform it for me—but only when I was not looking. I had to lie to him to get him to do it. I told him that Hazoth required some special incense for a ritual, and that it could not wait until morning. Such a thing has happened before, and the captain believed me. It is not an excuse I can use twice, however. The next time I try, he will become suspicious, and he will ask Hazoth if what I say is true. That would defeat your purpose, I think."

"It would."

Cythera scratched very delicately at one eyebrow. "You will need to give them a reason to lower the barrier."

"I'll find one. Is that all, or have you more bad news for me?"

Cythera smiled without humor. "Only one more item. As I mentioned, Hazoth expects Croy to attack him. He does not fear Croy overmuch—he knows that Croy is more full of bluster than bravado."

The knight cringed on the bed but said nothing.

Cythera glanced his way, then went on. "However, he is taking no chances. If one Ancient Blade is opposed to him, he will align himself with another. Tomorrow I am ordered to go out and find Bikker, and bring him to an audience with Hazoth."

Malden cursed under his breath. "I thought you said Bikker doesn't work for Hazoth."

"He doesn't. I don't know who Bikker's master is, actually. I only know Bikker will definitely come when I call him."

"I don't understand," Malden said.

"Stealing the crown in the first place was Bikker's idea.

Or rather, it was the notion of he who pays Bikker's wage. Bikker first came to the villa a month ago. He said he represented a wealthy patron who wished to contract for Hazoth's services. Hazoth cannot be bought with coin, but there are things in this world he covets. One is his privacy. The king would have him burnt at the stake should he ever learn the experiments Hazoth performs in his sanctum. So when Bikker proposed this scheme, Hazoth listened, for Bikker's employer promised him no one would ever learn what he was about. Whomever it may be—I have never met the man, nor learned anything of him—he convinced Hazoth he could offer his protection in exchange for Hazoth's part in the plot. It was Bikker's employer who decided a thief would be found to steal the crown—you know that much, of course—and then Hazoth would be employed to keep it in hiding. There really is no safer place for it in the Free City. The spells on the house prevent any spy from seeing it, and also any diviner from locating it with magic."

Malden thought of Anselm Vry's hedge wizard, and his shewstone. It had, as she said, not been able to locate the crown.

"It would take a small army to besiege the house, and a more powerful sorcerer than Hazoth—if any exist—to breach the barrier. If you wanted something of exceptional value to be kept safe, Hazoth's sanctum is exactly what you'd need."

"Interesting. I thought Hazoth wanted the crown to study it. Now I learn he is only an agent for some other player, who remains unknown. But what, exactly, do they hope to achieve? Bikker said no one would come looking for the crown. That the Burgrave would simply have a replica made, and forget the theft ever happened. We know that was not the case." And Cutbill had told Anselm Vry that a replica crown would not suffice—but why not? There were so many questions Malden had no answers for, and imagined he never might. "What do they want to happen?"

"I am unclear on the specifics," Cythera admitted. "I do know what they think will happen. The Burgrave will appear in public on Ladymas, without his crown. Somehow that will cause the people to riot. Bikker and his employer intend to turn that riot into a full-scale revolt. They mean to whip the people into a frenzy and cause them to overthrow the Burgrave."

"But that would be madness!" Malden said. "The king would revoke the city's charter on the instant. He'd have to, just to restore order. And then every man in Ness would lose his freedom."

"There are many who would benefit from that," Cythera pointed out.

Malden scratched at his chin. His whole skin had begun to itch. He chafed under the yoke of his low birth already. Without the freedom granted by the city's charter, he would be no more master of his own destiny than a farmhand out in the countryside.

He would rather have been confined in the pit, tormented by demons night and day.

"The point of all this," Cythera said, "is that Bikker's employer will not wish the crown to be stolen back. So Bikker will be there when you try. He will be leading Hazoth's guards."

"That's a major problem," Malden admitted. "My plan depended on the guards being sloppy and undisciplined."

"Bikker won't allow that luxury. He'll command them personally."

"And if he should discover me inside the house—"

"I don't know if you should be more afraid of the demon, of Hazoth himself, or of Bikker. Not one of them will let you live."

# CHAPTER SIXTY-FOUR

"I'm afraid I've been of little help, save to make you think this hopeless," Cythera said, straightening the maps on Malden's table. "And now I must go. I do wish you luck—for my mother's sake, at the very least."

"Not for my own?" Malden said. "Don't answer that. Get back safely. If Hazoth realizes what you've done, I can imagine you'll suffer, one way or another."

"Yes," she said. She frowned and looked over at the bed. She sighed deeply, but clearly there was something she had to say to her betrothed before she went. "Croy," she said softly. "Croy, we must—"

The knight jumped to his feet and came over to stand quite close to her. "Cythera, how can I gain your forgiveness? I've caused you nothing but trouble. How can I make this up to you?"

"You owe me nothing, Croy. You made a promise—well, we both made promises, didn't we? But sometimes life gets in the way of promises." She looked away from him. Malden could see how upset she was, but he didn't dare intrude.

Then something odd happened. She met Malden's eye. She looked into his eyes and for a second he thought she was pleading with him to say something. To jump in and save her from the hard thing she was contemplating.

As he had no idea what that might be, he could say nothing.

She sighed again and turned to face Croy.

"I don't want you to get killed," she said to the knight. "And right now, if you try to fight Bikker, that is exactly what will happen. So I want you to tell me that you won't try. That you'll let Malden handle this alone."

Alone? Malden thought. So it's all right if Bikker kills *me*?

"Milady," Croy said, dropping to his knees so hard the

floorboards creaked. "I would die a thousand times in your service—"

"But why? Why would I want that? It would accomplish nothing!"

"But I took a vow to save you and your mother—"

"You and I will have to talk when this is over. If any of us are still alive," she said. "Oh, Croy, don't look at me like that."

The knight dropped his gaze.

"Be of good cheer," she told him. "I don't like seeing you like this. Anyway, perhaps things will work out. Maybe a thief can succeed where a knight failed."

Malden glanced over at Kemper, and they both shook their heads. As much as Malden wished his own troubles gone, he would not have traded places with Croy at that moment.

"I didn't mean that to be cruel," Cythera insisted. She tried to meet Croy's eye but he wouldn't look up at her. "I have not forgotten all you've done for me," she told him. "But you must realize—my mother's safety, and my freedom, mean everything to me."

"And to me," Croy said.

"Then you must free me," she said.

"But that's exactly what I—that is, what Malden and I are trying to do," Croy pointed out.

"An' me, son, don't forget I'm riskin' my neck, too," Kemper insisted.

"And Kemper, too, of course. We're all trying to free you," Croy said.

"No, not from that . . . you infuriating man!" Cythera moved toward the door. "Croy—please. Let me go."

He did look up at her then, with utter confusion on his face. "I would never dream of delaying you."

"Then forgive me already and let me be at peace," she said.

"Forgive you . . . but for what?" Croy asked.

Cythera's face creased in grief. "You don't understand. I can't make you understand. Just tell me you forgive me. Even if you don't know why."

"Of course, then, I forgive you. I forgive you all—there is never anything you could do I would not forgive and forget, on the instant . . ." The knight's voice trailed off. Maybe he was starting to get the point after all.

"I go," Cythera said. "Goodbye. Malden, I'll try and come to see you again the day you make your move. If anything changes before then I'll make sure you know it. I'll have to come to you during the day, when I do my marketing."

"I'll be ready," Malden told her.

Cythera left then. The three men watched her head up the lane toward Turnhill Bridge, which would eventually lead her down to Parkwall. When she was out of sight Croy walked over to the table and slammed it with his fist.

"What did she mean by that? Why would she ask for my forgiveness? What has she ever done to harm me?"

Malden bit his lip and went to sit on the bed. It was late and he just wanted to go to sleep.

"Lad," Kemper said to Croy, sounding sympathetic, "ye've not much experience with women, have ye? I don't mean with yer mother or sisters either. Ye don't seem the type fer whorin', but have ye e'er swived one?" He took his cards from inside his tunic and started shuffling them, rubbing each one with his thumb.

"I've spent most of my life learning how to swing a sword properly. She's not the only woman I've ever . . . cared for, if that's what you mean. There was the dwarf king's daughter. I was her protector, and saved her from a fate worse than death. In reward, she allowed me a single kiss."

Malden couldn't resist asking the question he knew was probably foremost in Kemper's mind as well. "Did she have a beard?"

Croy's face went dark. "No. No, she did not. A bit of a mustache, perhaps. But no more than you'll see on many a human woman's face. And I'll have you know," he insisted, when he saw the two thieves were laughing behind their hands, "she would have given me her body, had I asked. But I had my oath to Cythera to consider."

"Methinks that's not a concern now," Kemper said. He

riffled his cards absentmindedly. "Mayhap ye should go back to yer dwarven princess."

"Speak plainly, damn you," Croy shouted. He was bright red.

"He's saying that Cythera was asking your forgiveness for breaking off her betrothal to you," Malden said.

"She . . . she . . ."

"She didn't want to say it in so many words, because she was afraid of your reaction. She was hoping you would just understand." Malden stared at Kemper. Why did the card sharp have to spell it out for Croy? Now the fool knight would probably spend another day lying abed and staring at the ceiling. Malden supposed if you were rich enough you could afford to be moody. "Enough," he said. "Enough. I'm going to bed. Tomorrow morning I'll need to make a whole new plan. And you," he said, rushing over to Kemper, "quit shuffling those damned cards."

"Here now, boy—"

Malden grabbed the cards out of Kemper's intangible hands and shoved them in his own tunic. "I can't think when you're doing that. Now, to bed, all of us."

He doused the lamp and pulled off his tunic, then got into bed and pulled the blanket up to his chin. He did not, however, get to sleep much that night. Croy made too great a racket with his sobbing tears, and Kemper kept grumbling about his cards.

Enough, enough, enough, Malden thought to himself. Kemper was largely safe from harm, no matter what came. And Croy would be nowhere near the villa when he broke into it. The knight would be useless in any scheme he could imagine.

It was up to him to get the crown back. He could put together a crew but he couldn't truly count on them. He would have to pass the barrier, get through the hallway of traps, and retrieve the crown, all without being detected. He would then need to do that which might be harder, which was to escape with his skin intact.

Even then his troubles might only begin anew. Anselm Vry might be watching him at that very moment, waiting until he recovered the crown before swooping in and taking all credit for himself. Cutbill might have him killed regardless of what happened, just for causing so much trouble in the first place.

And Hazoth would still have his demon, and Bikker would still have his acid-drooling sword. And both of them would have reason to want him dead.

The problems seemed insoluble.

Well, they always had. He had to keep going.

He had to think of something.

Eventually Malden did sleep, despite the companions of his bedchamber. He sank deep and came back only when the first rays of dawn burst in through the gap between the shutters and the window. He opened his eyes, checked that his bodkin was under his pillow where he left it, and only then sat up.

"Good morning," Croy said, smiling down at him.

The knight had never looked happier.

"Hmm," Malden said. He rose and pulled on his tunic, slipped his bodkin into its sheath. Kemper was lying curled in one corner, snoring and farting, dead to the world. Croy, however, was fully dressed and looked like he'd just taken a bath. He had his shortsword out and was polishing it with a cloth.

Malden wondered if the man had gone mad during the night. Maybe Croy was going to kill himself. It was not something he wanted to witness. "You seem recovered from your cares," he said cautiously.

"Oh, yes. Everything is better now," Croy said.

"It is?"

"I had a dream, Malden." He put the sword down and rose to his feet. "No. I tell a lie. It was a vision. I saw Cythera in her bridal veil. I saw myself standing before her, with flowers woven in my hair. And when I woke, I understood. Nothing is broken between us that cannot be repaired. She is merely testing me."

"Is she, now?"

"Indeed. All the stories of knights and dragons and fair maidens go like this. The maiden refuses to accept the knight's troth until he slays the beast. He must prove himself, in combat, before she can truly love him."

"In the stories, you say," Malden went on.

"Yes. So my path is clear. I will earn her love. I will do this by killing Hazoth. A sorcerer is in many ways like a dragon, is he not? I will slay him. And maybe Bikker as well. And anyone else who opposes me."

"Even though she asked you not to," Malden pointed out.

"That," Croy said, with a gleam of insight in his eye, "is the crux of the test. I will free Coruth. And only then will Cythera look on me with favor once more. What do you think?"

"I suppose," Malden said, "that anything is possible."

# CHAPTER SIXTY-FIVE

Malden sent Kemper to keep an eye on Hazoth's villa—discreetly—while he went over to the Ashes to see Cutbill's dwarf, Slag. Croy insisted on coming along. "I must do all in my power to assist you. And when the time comes, it must be my swords that cut the sorcerer down," he said.

"Fine. But for today, you leave them behind," Malden told him.

The knight errant looked at the thief as if he were mad, but Malden stood firm. Eventually Croy did as he was told, unbuckling the swords from his baldric and stashing them beneath the loose floorboards of Malden's room.

"Now," Malden said, "walk from here to the bed and back."

"This is folly," Croy said, but he did it.

Malden listened to the man clank his way across the room as if he were a walking thunder crash. "Are you wearing a mail shirt under your jerkin?" he asked.

"No," Croy said. "What is the point of this?"

Malden studied the man's dress, then made him take off the baldric. The heavy leather sash was covered in buckles and hooks that clinked together when he moved. With the baldric off, Croy made far less noise than he had before—but somehow his swagger still made the floorboards creak and the room shake.

"You are the noisiest man I've ever met," Malden told him. "You'll never make it as a thief."

"But—why in the Lady's name should I want to be one?"

Malden stared at him. "You're trying to steal a crown from a wizard's house. By definition, methinks, that makes you a thief. Or a would-be thief."

"Ah, I see the problem," Croy said, smiling. "No, no, we are not common thieves if we take the crown back from Hazoth. We are liberators. Heroes!"

Malden doubted very much that Hazoth would see it that way. He also wasn't sure how he felt about being called a "common" thief. But he had better things to do than argue. "Walk back this way," he said, and listened closely. "Maybe it's your boots?"

Whatever the source of the clamor, there was no more to be done for it. Together they went out into the street and crossed the Stink, keeping well clear of areas regularly patrolled by the city watch. Should a cloak-of-eyes spot Croy, they would give chase on the instant. Not for the first time, Malden thought of turning the knight over to the authorities just to get him out of the way.

When they reached the Ashes he raised one hand in warning. "Don't jump when you see them. Don't make any quick move. Just stay calm."

"See who?" Croy asked, but he didn't have to wait long to find out.

A boy of no more than eight was standing in the road before them. His face was smeared with ash and he was holding a long shard of broken glass in one hand. He did not speak, of course.

Croy dropped to one knee in the soot. "Why, hello there," he said, and held his hand out toward the boy. There was a piece of crystallized ginger in it.

Where in the Bloodgod's name had he gotten a bit of candy? Malden wondered. Perhaps Croy carried sweets around just in case he ever met a child.

He doubted Croy had ever met a child like this. The boy did not take the ginger. He just stood there watching them, his face impassive. Waiting to see whether he should give the signal that would bring a hundred armed children down on the two of them with murderous intent.

"You know me," Malden told the boy. The boy nodded. "I have business here, with *him*." He tapped his chest above his heart. The boy knew what he meant. "This one," he said, gesturing at Croy, "should not follow me." He mused for a moment. "But I want him in one piece when I return."

The boy shrugged. That was up to Croy and how stupidly the knight acted while he was gone. It was the best answer Malden would get.

"Fair enough." He turned to Croy, who was smiling broadly at the boy and even crossing his eyes to try to make the child laugh. "Croy, he'd rather cut your throat than let you tousle his hair. Just mind yourself while I'm gone. I won't tarry."

He jogged around a corner and into the ruin above Cutbill's lair, where he was quite pleased to see the three oldsters sitting once more on their coffin. "I feared you were driven off by unwelcome visitors, or worse," he said, and clasped Loophole's hand.

"Nay, son, we just scarpered at the first sign of trouble," the old man replied. "That's one of those things you learn how to do if you want to get to be an old thief. I'm glad to see you alive, though. We weren't far away, and when we saw you coming in, we wanted to warn you but there was just no way, not without giving away our own position."

"I understand. It was a close thing but I survived my encounter with the law. Did, ah, did Cutbill tell you anything of what it was about?"

Loophole frowned. "And why would he think to do that? His business is his own. And we don't ask questions, the answers to which might get us in trouble."

"Another sound policy," Malden suggested. Some strange intuition gripped him then—a preternatural sensation that something was deeply wrong. He shot a hand down at his side and grabbed a scrawny arm. 'Levenfingers was trying to lift his purse. Malden laughed with glee. "In this mutable world I am glad to see some things don't change."

"It's good to see you as well, Malden," 'Levenfingers said. Lockjaw just scowled.

"So, have anything big planned?" Loophole asked.

His face was the picture of innocence. Malden shot him a shrewd look, but the oldster simply blinked as if he didn't know anything.

Which told Malden what he needed to know. Cutbill might not have told them what had happened, but Malden knew perfectly well that they had asked the dangerous questions—they had just asked them very discreetly. How much they knew would remain a mystery, but it was next to impossible to keep a secret from these three. "Well, as a matter of fact . . . there's a certain house on the Lady-park Common, a very special house—do you know the one I mean? I shouldn't make it any more plain."

"Then there's only one you *can* mean," 'Levenfingers said with a shiver. "Ooh, I wouldn't want to be in that place in the dark. But good luck to you. No one's ever tumbled that place and lived to tell the tale."

"Even I wouldn't try it," Loophole agreed. "And I'd steal pearls off the queen's throat, were she here now."

Lockjaw mumbled something and then spat into the charred ruins.

Malden and the other two oldsters turned to stare at him.

"I said, 'ware the eye, and that's all I'm saying," Lockjaw snarled. "Now get inside, before someone sees you out here."

"My thanks," Malden told him. Then he headed down

into the lair and was pleased to find that things had returned to a kind of normalcy. Bellard wasn't there, of course, but the dice game in the corner was back in swing. More importantly to Malden, Slag was working at his bench, putting together some kind of collapsible fishing pole.

"It's for taking hats," Slag said, hefting the pole. "You know the arch under the Royal Ditch bridge? Aye? Windy fucking place. You crouch up in the supports, in the shadows, and you pluck the hats off the wealthy shits as pass underneath, and they think the wind took them."

"Brilliant," Malden said.

"It'll fucking do. What do you want now?"

Malden described his needs while the dwarf scowled at him.

"The climbing gear I have in stock, no problem. This other thing, though—it'll take a week, maybe more," Slag told him.

"I can give you no more than three days," Malden told the dwarf. Even that was pushing things—it meant he would not be ready until the eve of Ladymas.

"Fine. Now pay me. Gilding metal's not bloody cheap, if you want it to look right."

"Ah," Malden said. "Well, perhaps I can owe you."

It was commonly believed that dwarves never laughed. This was perhaps because most people were not so foolish as to ask them for credit. Slag did laugh at the idea, though the sound was not like a human laugh. It sounded more like a squeaky wheel coming free of a rusted axle.

"It really is important," Malden said. "Perhaps there is some way we—"

"Sod off," Slag said, turning back to his fishing pole.

It seemed to be a day for marvels. Lockjaw had given away a secret (or part of one), a dwarf had laughed—and now the door to Cutbill's office swung open and the guildmaster of thieves leaned out.

"I'll pay for the work," Cutbill said.

Malden bowed low toward his master.

"Of course, Malden, you'll pay me back," Cutbill said.

"Of course."

Cutbill shook his head. "At a rather ruinous level of interest."

Malden bowed lower. "Of course," he said again.

His business in the lair done, he headed back to the surface. Perhaps Croy had been filleted by the beggar children, he thought. Or maybe they'd just doused him with lamp oil and set him on fire.

One could hope.

Yet when he returned to where he'd left the knight, he stopped in his tracks and just stared. A score of the vile little children had emerged from their hiding places and gathered around Croy. They sat in the dust, staring up at him with rapt faces.

While Croy told them a story.

". . . the dragon came swooping down," Croy was saying as Malden approached, "with fire in his jaw, ready to roast the king's men in their armor. It was fifty feet from wingtip to wingtip, and its eyes blazed red in the dark as its tail swung out behind it like a pennon flapping in the breeze. And then—"

"It breathed fire and they all died. The end," Malden said.

The children scattered like crows when a boy throws a rock among them. They hurried back into the ruins, worming their way through gaps and crevices too small for an adult to pass through and were gone.

"We have work to do," Malden said. "Come with me."

Croy rose and brushed soot from his breeches. He followed along as Malden headed back into the Stink.

# CHAPTER SIXTY-SIX

"Where are we going?" Croy asked as they headed up Midden Lane, where the city's refuse was gathered and sorted and gleaned for anything of value. The smell was horrible, but Malden knew the watch never came down that road.

"A tavern I know." He stepped in something foul and scraped his leather shoe against the cobblestones. Not that it helped much—in this district the cobbles barely protruded through a thick layer of scum that had hardened into a kind of paving. "There we'll find bravos willing to sign on for coin. I need men who are good with weapons to fight Hazoth's retainers—and Bikker, for that matter."

"I'm going to fight Bikker," Croy pointed out.

"Not on your own—not wounded as you are. Even Cythera could see you had no chance to take him."

"And you think a band of common street toughs can? They won't last a moment against Acidtongue."

"Well, that's what they get paid for. To die for some pointless cause. The place is just up here." Malden lifted his chin and pointed. "They only have to live long enough," he explained, "to convince the guards to lower the magical barrier. If they die once I'm inside, they'll have served their purpose. The coin I give them can go to their mothers, or widows, or orphans, what have you."

Croy shook his head. "No, hold, Malden. I'm quite serious. If you're going to engage Bikker you need more than brave young men with stilettos. I can't allow you to throw away lives just for a diversion."

"It's all I can afford!" Malden turned on the knight. "You need to understand something, Croy. I know you've never wanted for anything in your life. You've never had to want for anything since you were a babe. Any problem that might arise could always be met with a sword stroke or a purse of gold, and so you never had to learn about survival. Down here in the Stink that's all we know. Those children back in the Ashes—they already know more than you ever will. They know when to hold their tongues. And when to cut someone's throat. They know how to stay alive, and they don't count the cost too dear."

"You make them sound like bloodthirsty savages."

"Yes! Because that is what they are. They are perfectly suited to the life they've been handed. I admit it's an ugly life, but it's theirs."

"They just need a little compassion shown them. I always find that's worth more than coin."

"Do you really think a few sweets and a stirring tale of brave hearts will change their plight?" Malden demanded. "They're among the very few people in this city with less of a chance at life than I have. They'll never be anything but beggars. Or thieves if they're lucky. All because their parents died before their time. Tell me where the justice is, there. Tell me why they shouldn't become savages, if that helps them survive."

Croy looked confused for a moment. Then he nodded as if he'd thought up the perfect answer. "There's nothing ignoble about begging," he pointed out, "if that's the station the Lady assigns to you."

"The Lady—" Malden caught himself before he could tell Croy exactly what the Lady could go and do. Knowing Croy, he'd probably take that as blasphemy and burn him at the next convenient stake. "Tell me, Croy," he said instead. "Did the Lady choose me for a thief?"

The look of confusion passed over Croy's face again. "Well, no. Since thievery's a sin in Her eyes. Instead, you should have chosen to enter an honest trade."

"Had I known it was so easy, I would have become a goldsmith," Malden sneered. "You think I didn't try?"

"Not hard enough, apparently."

Malden's blood rushed into his face. How dare this hoddypeak of a knight say such a thing to him. What could Croy possibly know of what had driven him to a life of crime? How dare Croy judge him?

But of course, he knew the answer. In Croy's world the poor were simple, honest folk, too crude in their sensibilities to know anything but how to toil and farm. Knights and lords were there to care for them like kindly parents. To make decisions for them since they were incapable of doing so for themselves.

In Malden's world—the world he'd been seeing ever since Cutbill opened his eyes—people like himself were prisoners, caught inside bars of poverty. And people like Croy were the gaolers who made sure they never got out. The Lady, the goddess Croy worshipped so fervently, was the warden who assigned each inmate to his given cell—and made sure they could never, ever escape.

He wanted to slap the knight across the face, or perhaps just call him names. That, of course, could have been dangerous. Yet he couldn't just let his anger go. Croy had been quietly disapproving of his life ever since they had met. It was time to show Croy what the real world was like. "Come. I wish to show you something."

He didn't have time for this, not really. But the knight had rubbed his nerves raw, and he wanted to rub reality in the fool's face for once. He took him down to the bottom of Midden Lane, where the gleaners labored.

A city the size of Ness generates a mountain of dross every day. Though the citizens never threw out anything that could be cleaned out and reused, still they created junk by the wagonload—after all, wood eventually rots, iron rusts, and eggshells and fish bones are only good for so much. The city's moldy vegetables, broken bottles, and the unusable parts of pig and cow carcasses were collected once a week and piled up in great mounds in Hunnicart Yard. It was a great rotting tower of filth, a palace of decomposition, and the smell rivaled anything the tanner's yards up in the Smoke could generate. The heap of it glistened in the sun, the ugly rainbow sheen of rancid grease.

And on top of it whole families were employed.

The work of the gleaners there was never done. Old men in smocks, matronly women with forearms like pestles, even their scrawny children, all worked the mounds, up to their thighs in ordure, flies thick on their backs as freckles. They dug through the middens with their bare hands, searching for any bit of bone that could be carved into a spoon, any torn and soiled rag that could be shredded for its fibers and used to make paper. There were legends of the gleaners, of the ones who found gold coins in the trash, of the gleaner who pulled a magic spear from the bottom of the pile where it had laid for a thousand years, and used it to slay a giant who threatened the city. If the teller of the tale were leaning over a fire for effect, and trying for maximum realism, he would tell of human bodies found at the bottom of the heaps, still moving feebly and begging for help, and what the gleaners did to make sure the watch never came around asking questions.

A wooden palisade ringed the middens, a high fence hammered together from scrap lumber useful for no other purpose. Dogs barked just inside, ready to attack any intruder, and a guard with a cudgel stood at its gate, overseeing the carts that came down the lane laden with garbage. The guard eyed the thief and the knight warily, as if he expected them to break in and steal all the trash in broad daylight. Probably because sometimes thieves tried just that.

"These people are among the hardest workers in the city," Malden said as Croy stared in horror. "They toil in shifts to make sure nothing is missed. Their bodies are riddled with plague and disease, they eat nothing but thin pottage, and they die years younger than their fellows, because they breathe nothing but foul vapors. They toil in the heat of summer, and when winter comes they shovel the snow off those heaps and sort through the offal wearing fingerless gloves. They don't do this for glory, or honor, or love or justice. They do it so they can eat for one more day."

"That's terrible, Malden," Croy said. "I never knew. Are they slaves that do this work? I thought there were no slaves in Ness."

"There aren't. No one compels them to this life. In fact— the gleaners have a patent from the Burgrave that gives them sole right to do this. If you or I were to wade in there and start looking for treasures in the trash, they would drive us off with clubs and thrown stones. They kill anyone who tries to encroach on their livelihood. Generations of men have worked these heaps—when a father dies, he passes down his writ of patent to his sons, who are glad to have it, for they know they'll be able to feed their children."

"So they have pride in their work," Croy said, lifting his chin. "I find that admirable."

Malden shook his head. "Don't you understand what I'm trying to tell you? There is competition for this. There are people willing to risk their lives to sneak in here in the middle of the night and sort through rusted nails and the guts of slaughtered chickens. Because their own lives are *that much worse.*"

Croy was silent for a moment. Then he said, "The Lady gives each of us our lot in life, and her abundance sustains us all. This I believe, and this I live."

Was he quoting from some missal? Malden had never listened to the blandishments of the Lady's priests. Not since he'd realized that Her teachings gave an excuse why rich men should always be rich, and the poor shouldn't try to rise above their stations. Like most in the Stink, whatever religious feeling he possessed was directed toward the Blood-god, who promised equal justice for all, if only after death.

"You'll never understand, will you? I can't make you see it. Enough. Let us find our bravos and be done. Perhaps you can be of some little use by pointing out which of them are likely to last the longest against Bikker's sword."

Malden hurried away—the prospect of the middens never gave him any joy, nor did he wish to linger in that disease-haunted place.

"Hold," Croy said. "If it's strong arms you need, perhaps I have a better idea."

# CHAPTER SIXTY-SEVEN

The river Skrait was the Free City's lifeblood. It flowed through every district of Ness and was used by every citizen. Where it entered the city in Swampwall it flowed clean and pure, and its water went right into cookpots or horse troughs. As it flowed east it became a dumping ground for refuse too liquid for even the gleaners to cart away. After it bent around Castle Hill it supplied the great manufactories of the Smoke, and then washed away the poisons and the waste products of those workshops. Finally, where it widened out at Eastpool a whole flotilla of fishing boats rode its current out to the sea, some miles off, and then rode it back in the evening, rowing against its flow. Ness owed half its prosperity to the mighty river Skrait, and it had always been counted one of the city's best assets.

Yet for one Burgrave in the city's youth, it must have seemed the city's greatest weakness as well. Where it entered the city on its western end it was open to the world outside. An invading army could send war galleys up the Skrait to attack Castle Hill, or fireships to set the city ablaze. To plug that gap, said erstwhile Burgrave had extended the city wall across the course of the river and forced the Skrait through a pipe no more than ten feet across.

He had not consulted with any dwarven engineers before embarking on this great public work. Had he, they might have told him that narrowing the Skrait where it entered the wall would cause it to flood its banks once it came inside. A wide swath of the lowest section of the city was deluged in the weeks following the pipe's construction, and no one had been able to drain it since.

No man or woman lived in Swampwall anymore. Ferns and tall grasses and willow shrubs had taken over the streets, and only the weathered foundations and a few walls of the old houses remained, sticking up through the shimmering plant life. Here and there a bit of old architecture could be discerned—a listing chimney toppling in slow motion toward a pond, a horse rail sticking up from a pool of mud. As Malden—at Croy's behest—picked his way down the muddy slope into the swamp, he followed the remains of a cobblestone street, the old stones worn as smooth as glass under three inches of stagnant water. There was plenty there to be dragged away and refurbished, yet Swampwall had been left alone far more than the Ashes had. Malden could see why. "This place breathes with fever," he said, sneering as his shoe was sucked down into black goo. "And the flies—Bloodgod take these flies!"

"It's farther down than I thought," Croy said, frowning at the expanse of fen before them. "The last time I was down here I came on horseback. Still, it's just over there."

"What is just over there?" Malden demanded. Croy was pointing to a low point in the swamp, where reeds as tall as houses shimmered in the sun.

"You'll see."

Otters plunked down under the water and crabs scuttled away from their feet as the two men clambered into the muck. It never got past Malden's ankles but clung to him like the hands of dead men in a haunted graveyard. He sloshed noisily through the water and pushed at the reeds with his hands, trying to make a path.

"This is your revenge, isn't it?" he demanded. "You don't like the way I talk to you, as if we were equals. So you bring me down here to remind me I'm the lowest of the low."

"Hardly! I only think—" Croy stopped speaking to pull his boot out of the mud. He had to bend down and get his back into it, and he winced at the pain as his wound grieved him. "I only think that if I told you what we were looking for, you would insist that we run away."

"Ah. So you think I lack courage," Malden said. He drew his bodkin and tried to slash at the reeds but they just bent away from the sharp point. For the first time all day he wished he'd let Croy bring his swords.

"No," Croy said. "No, I've seen you be brave. It's just—well." He pushed a stand of reeds down so Malden could see their destination. "Here we are."

They had arrived at the pipe itself. Its entrance was flush with the Swampwall, which rose up before them toward the sky, its face hidden by generations of creepers. The pipe's bottom was buried in the murk, but it made an arch taller than a man. Sunlight streamed inside its length but only penetrated a few dozen feet before it was lost in perfect gloom.

Malden leaned into the pipe and smelled foul air. Water dripped from the curved ceiling and echoed like drumbeats as it fell into the turbid water below. The bricks that formed the side of the pipe were rotten to the touch and thick with niter.

"In there?" he asked.

"Yes," Croy said. "If he's at home."

"I've heard . . . stories. I think maybe we should run away after all."

Croy strode into the pipe, the sloshing of his steps like thunder crashes. "I thought you might. Come—if you dare."

Malden followed, not wanting to be thought a coward. He was ready to dash back out of the pipe at the first sign of danger, though. Children in the Free City of Ness knew what was inside that pipe, even if the adults claimed it was just a tale. Growing up, he had learned not to believe. Now he wasn't so sure.

Before coming down to Swampwall, Croy had stopped in a chandler's shop and bought a pair of candles still strung together by their wicks. Now he cut them apart with his belt knife and lit one with his tinderbox. The flickering light did little to alleviate the pipe's gloom, but it gave Malden something to follow.

Underfoot, the water was moving at a steady rate, pushing Malden's feet backward as he tried to slog forward. It was hard work just to stand up. If anything, the current grew stronger the farther in they went.

Ahead, the pipe curved to the left and Croy followed, putting one hand against the bricks to steady himself. Malden hauled himself along with both hands and kept up as best he could. Around the curve they saw that bars had been embedded in the pipe's walls, forming a natural fence against anyone so foolish as to try to come into the city from the river beyond. Detritus and bones—animal bones—had built up into a thick scurf at the base of the grating, so the water crested as it flowed over and around the debris. It plashed as it came and made it impossible to hear anything, and it took a while for Malden to realize that Croy was talking to him.

"—not here, I'm afraid," the knight repeated. "Have to—back later—"

Malden nodded in agreement and turned to rush out of the pipe, glad to have an excuse to leave. He hurried around the curve, the current pushing him along faster than he could run on his own—and then tripped and fell to all fours in the water.

His heart thudded painfully in his chest and he couldn't breathe.

At the exit from the pipe, not more than fifty feet ahead, a massive figure was silhouetted against the incoming sunlight. Malden could make out few details but he was sure it was far too big to be human.

# CHAPTER SIXTY-EIGHT

Malden looked to right and left, but there was nowhere to go. The grating behind him blocked that route of escape, and the monstrous thing at the mouth of the tunnel would surely catch him if he tried to run past it. He reached for his bodkin but didn't dare draw it—what use would it be against this massive beast?

At his side, Croy peered ahead toward the light, shielding

his eyes with one hand. He said something, but in the roar of the water Malden couldn't hear him at all. The knight lowered his hand, then shouted some kind of strangled war cry—

"Gurrh!"

—and dashed forward, right at the beast, which lifted its arms as if to crush him in a vicious embrace. For the first time Malden saw it was holding something huge, like a tree branch or a stone club.

Pressing himself up against the mineral-stained wall of the tunnel, he closed his eyes, dreading the inevitable crunch as Croy's bones were shattered inside his body. The fool didn't even have his swords.

But the sound he heard next, amplified and distorted by the weird acoustics of the tunnel, was a joyful one. It was the sound of booming laughter and astonishment, the noise of old fellows well met.

Malden opened his eyes and saw the most surprising thing he would encounter that day. Croy and the beast were clasping hands and japing with each other.

"Malden," Croy said, "come out already. Come and meet my old friend, Gurrh."

Malden staggered forward, pushed by the current, and stepped out into the light beyond the pipe's mouth. He got his first good look at the monster and nearly soiled his breeches, even if it was a friend of Croy's.

It stood eight feet tall and had the same general shape as a man, though it was far broader and its muscles were as big as those of a horse. It was covered from crown to sole in coarse black fur, matted with grease, and stinking of death. Only a small patch of skin, from nose to forehead, was exposed, and that was as white as the corpse of a dwarf. Its eyes, while merry, were the size of saucers, and its nose was crooked and bent to one side. On its forehead and around its eyes were inscribed some ancient runes.

The thing it held, which Malden had thought was a club, was in fact the carcass of a river otter missing its head. From the look of the stump, the beast had already gnawed the head off, perhaps by way of breaking its fast.

"Thou," the creature said, with a deep, rasping voice, "art a friend of Sir Croy?" It stuck out its free hand. "Then in the Lady's name thou art well come into my home, gentle. I am called Gurrh; a common sort of calling amongst my clan."

The clan of ogres, Malden thought. This creature, with its honeyed words, was an ogre. There could be no doubt. Tentatively he placed his own hand inside the palm of the giant. The ogre took it carefully and shook it gently.

"But . . . how?" Malden asked.

He might not know many of the details of Skrae's history, but he had the broad outlines down pat. He knew that when his ancestors came over from the Old Empire they found this continent already occupied by the elves and the dwarves. Centuries of warfare had been necessary to clear the land for human habitation—bitter centuries, when the likes of Hazoth scorched whole mountains from the face of the world and dug out broad valleys with their magic, when the seven Ancient Blades were forged to fight the demons that roamed the night. At the end of that hellish time, the elves had found themselves unable to resist the onrushing wave of human might. They made pacts with their own ancestral enemies for aid—the goblins, the trolls, and, most fearsome of all, the ogres. The hairy giants were unstoppable in battle, it was said, their tough hides proof against iron blades and axes. They were able to catch arrows out of the air and throw them back at the archers, or to simply pick up human warriors and pull them to pieces with their bare hands.

He had believed that ogres were gone from the world. They had fought tirelessly, but the elves who commanded them were driven from existence, betrayed by the dwarves they'd once considered their allies. The dwarves had always been practical folk, and knew when to make a treaty with humankind and call it a day. The ogres had been too disorganized to keep fighting on their own. The wizards of that time slaughtered them remorselessly, hunting them down wherever they hid, until none were left. Oh, there were stories of survivals, of individual monsters still roaming the wild parts of the woods, but those were just stories. No one believed them.

"I thought the ogres were as dead as the elves," he said.

"Wherefore hath I survived, when all others like unto this favor hath vanished, as smoke into the air?" Gurrh asked. "When at last the killing was done, when the age of man had come, some few of us did still live. The merciful king Theobalt—may the Lady hold him to her ever-abundant bosom—came unto that wretched scattering and bade us bow at his feet. Many there were who refused, and rose up, and were slaughtered in their turn. Yet not all."

"He swore an oath of loyalty to the crown," Croy explained. "He was given a pardon for all past crimes, under the condition that he would serve the king whenever he was called upon. He took the Lady into his heart and was given a place to live. Here."

"And the Burgrave knows he's here? And hasn't sent pikemen and priests to roust him?" Malden asked. "No offense meant, Sir Ogre," he added, looking up into the giant's face. The ogre smiled, showing a double row of huge peg-shaped teeth.

Croy clapped Malden on the back. "He had a royal pardon. The Burgrave had to respect that. Nor would he evict Gurrh if he could. My friend here does a great service to the city, by keeping the pipe clean and making sure the Skrait flows unchecked into the city. Should any spy or sapper try to come in through the pipe, Gurrh would be here to stop them. He keeps to himself down here in the swamp, living on the wildlife, and shuns human society. Every month or so an envoy is sent down from the palace to check up on him and make sure he has what he needs."

"It must . . ." Malden rethought his words. He had been about to say that it must be difficult, being hated and feared by the people you guarded. He didn't know, however, if the ogre was aware that children told stories of the monster in the pipe and dared each other to see how close they could get before running away. If the ogre didn't know about his own legend already, it would be cruel to enlighten him. "It must be very lonely down here," he said instead.

The ogre shrugged. "I hath the birds to singeth me lullabies, and the trees to whisper their orisons o'er me at night."

Ah, Malden thought. So he has gone mad with the solitude.

"Tell me," Croy said to the thief, "would Gurrh be a useful addition to your crew?"

Malden thought it over. Ogres were notoriously difficult to slay, at least according to the stories. They could shrug off the blows of iron weapons, and only steel had proven capable of piercing their thick hides back in the old days—back when steel was rare as gold was now, before the dwarves started selling it to anyone with enough coin. And Malden had to admit that even Bikker would flinch when facing a rampaging ogre coming toward him with claws a-snatching and teeth a-gnashing.

He looked at Croy and nodded shrewdly.

"Gurrh," Croy said, "the Burgrave has need of you once again."

"Hath he? Certes, an' that pleaseth me, Croy. I serve at his pleasure," Gurrh said, and made a deep bow.

Malden frowned. "You don't want to hear what we're paying?" he asked.

"Thou speak of gold? When milord hath need of me? My arm's his, for the asking, and always shall be. Service hath its own reward."

Definitely crazy, Malden thought. But perhaps—usefully so.

# CHAPTER SIXTY-NINE

A new and much improved plan had begun to come together in Malden's mind. He ran through it time and again, arguing over the finer points with Kemper and looking always for the places where it could go dreadfully wrong. There were far too many of those for his liking, of course. He still did not know who had originally paid to have the crown stolen—Bikker's employer remained mysterious. The plan depended far too much on Hazoth being preoccupied and taking no interest in what happened within his house. And at any time various players—Anselm Vry, the Burgrave, even Cutbill—could decide to move in and put an end to things in whatever way they chose.

Still—if everything went exactly right, and he made no mistakes . . . maybe it could be done.

At all hours he had either Croy or Kemper watching Hazoth's villa, looking for any sign that things had changed inside. From time to time they reported something interesting. Cythera was seen going out to market and carrying on with her usual business, which meant she had not betrayed him to Hazoth (willingly or no). Bikker showed up one afternoon with a haversack over his shoulder and took up residence in the guard barracks. Hazoth never left the house—more's the pity—but at night, ofttimes, strange lights could be seen illuminating the rose window at the front of the villa.

"Like unholy fires blaze in there," Croy said. "They dance and tremble and then are extinguished. None of the guards pay any mind."

Malden knew not what to make of that. Hazoth could be summoning demons until his halls were stuffed with them, for all he knew. Or he could simply be engaged in some esoteric study Malden could never comprehend. He tried not to think of it overmuch, and focused on those things he could control.

The special gear he had tasked Slag with constructing would not be ready until the very day before Ladymas. The job would have to take place that night, which was cutting things very fine. Again, there was nothing he could do about that.

It left him with far too much time to think, however. He spent as many hours as he could going over the plan again and again, rehearsing bits of it with Kemper or taking his own turns watching the villa. But eventually he needed a rest, just a pause to refresh his mind. He headed for one of the few places in the city where he still felt at home: the Lemon Garden, up in the Royal Ditch.

Elody took him in without a word. Perhaps she could see in his eyes how haunted he was by what he was about to do. She led him to her own private rooms and gave him wine to drink and a plate of fresh fruit. "Your generosity is welcome, but I know you can't afford this," he pointed out as he stabbed an apple with his bodkin and brought it to his mouth. "I'll pay you back, I swear."

"Oh, Malden, just having you around is payment enough. You get the girls all excited when you turn up. That makes them frisky and they earn more, so in the end I have a net gain." Elody laughed. "You can have any of them you like, on the house. You just have to ask."

Malden shook his head. "The woman I want isn't here," he said, even though he knew what that would elicit. Elody's face lit up and her eyes glowed as she descended on him, demanding gossip, wanting to know all about this new sweetheart.

"She's not mine," Malden said, a bit glumly. He had come here to cheer himself up but suddenly he was in a foul mood. "Most like she never will be. She was betrothed to a knight, of all things."

"Was?" Elody asked. "But she isn't now?"

"I don't think so—it's all so confusing. I think she might have been trying to tell me something the last time I saw her, but . . . I just don't know. How can I compete with a man like that? He has a *castle*, Elody. A castle."

"Not every woman is so mercenary with her favors as the ladies who raised you," Elody replied. "Some, I hear, would rather have love than money." She looked almost wistful when she said it. "You need to give her what he can't. Is he handsome? Does he have strong arms and golden hair and a noble bearing?"

"Yes, all of those," Malden agreed. "He is a bit dim," he added, though, because he couldn't help himself.

"Then try being clever. It shouldn't be so hard for the likes of you," Elody told him.

"When I'm around her I feel an utter fool. I feel as if I'll never be clever again," Malden confessed.

"Then it must be true love," Elody said, and they laughed together.

She kept him there late that night and plied him with wine. He told her everything—of Cythera's cursed skin, of Croy's pledges and vows. She gave him what advice she could, then sent him home very drunk and a little less fearful. He fell into bed thinking he almost had a chance.

In the morning the early light convinced him otherwise. It was the day before Ladymas. His head was pounding, and he had work to do.

When Slag's things were ready, he went immediately to Cutbill's lair and took possession of them. He tied them up in a bundle and went straight back to his room above the waxchandler's. It was almost noon by the time he arrived. Coming up the stairs he heard voices inside where only Kemper should be, and he opened the door warily, ready to run at the first sign of trouble.

When he saw Cythera inside, sitting at his table, his breath caught in his throat. He nearly *did* run away.

"Kemper, go relieve Croy at his watch," Malden said when he'd divested himself of his gear.

"Lad, it's dull as ditchwater down there. Nothing's like t'happen afore ye get in place."

"Then you shouldn't have any trouble," Malden told him.

Kemper muttered something under his breath. "At least gimme cards back. I miss me little friends."

"Your cards." Malden still had them in his tunic, where they'd laid against his skin for days. "You can have them back when we've got the crown." Their eyes met for one last time, and Malden saw that Kemper was ready. It was important that Cythera didn't know the real reason why Malden had been holding onto the cards. "I don't want to hear you cut off your watch early to find a quick game," he said.

"I ain't stupid, lad," Kemper replied, his chin nodding almost imperceptibly. "I know ye'd have me hide if I did."

Malden nodded and watched his companion leave. When

he was alone with Cythera, he closed the shutter of the window, even though it was a hot day.

"Bikker has the guards complaining," she told him. "He's put them through harsh discipline and punished them severely for any slight change of routine." She shook her head. "He doesn't know what's coming, though. Neither does Hazoth. How are things on your end?"

"Everything's ready and in place," he told her. "As much as it can be. I have completely changed my plans, thanks to your information. We start by sending in our pet ogre to—"

She shook her head. "Don't tell me. If Hazoth questions me, he can make me give up your secrets. Unless I don't have them."

"Very well," Malden said, appreciating her wisdom. "Then let me say only: your mother may be free by morning."

Her eyes flashed with hope. She crossed the room to him, her velvet cloak swishing around her feet. "Malden—thank you," she said. "I know you have your own reasons for doing this. But thank you."

He started to bow but then thought better of it. Instead he held out his hand.

She smiled and held her own just above his palm, a fraction of an inch from touching him. Painted clematis and brier rose twisted around her knuckles. "No—don't," she warned when he leaned over her hand to kiss her fingers. "Please, Malden, for your own sake—"

His lips touched her skin with the gentlest of pressures. Had he only breathed upon her hand she would have felt it more.

"Oh, what are you doing?" she asked, her eyes wide. "Kissing me! Malden, once I tried to kill you with a kiss."

"I've faced less sweet dooms since," he told her. "I'd rather die on your lips than on the point of Bikker's sword."

"You . . . you speak words of love to me."

Malden shrugged. "Are you surprised? I've felt something for you, Cythera, since the first time I met you. Tell me that was just a spell. Some charm your mother cast on you, to make you irresistible to men."

"No," Cythera said.

"Then what I feel is real," he said.

For a moment they only watched each other, like duelists preparing to begin. He knew she felt something as well. She must! Yes, it was complicated. Yes, it was dangerous. But he'd been leading up to this for a very long time.

She took a step back. "One rough kiss would be all it takes to release the magic in my painted skin. It would destroy you."

"I'm not afraid of the curses you've stored up," he said. "A rough kiss would set them off, you say. Yet a gentle kiss is harmless, as we've seen."

She laughed, delighted. "You are quite nimble, aren't you?"

"I could show you just how deft I am," he told her. "If you have an hour before you must return."

"Malden, you dare much."

"Do I offend? Then slap me across the cheek," he told her, daring more.

He touched her wrist with one finger and traced a tattooed creeper that ran up toward her elbow. He kept his fingertip barely in contact with her skin, but enough so. He had lived among whores long enough to gain some basic knowledge of the erotic arts. For instance, he knew that a feather-soft touch on sensitive skin could be more maddening and arousing than a rough caress.

"Croy—" Cythera said, but then closed her mouth as a shudder ran through her body. "Croy—"

"Is not here," he told her. He placed a soft kiss on the inside of her wrist. "How long has it been, Cythera, since you were touched like this?"

"Too long," she said.

"But you remember how it feels, don't you?" It was a careful way of asking an important question.

"Yes," she said. "Before I met Croy, there were . . . others. They were brutes, for the most part. Too quick to take what they wanted, or they were cruel and wanted what I did not wish to part with."

"But what do you want?" Malden asked her. He reached

up and unpinned her hair, letting it fall down across her cheeks.

She sighed. "I don't think any man has ever asked me that question."

"Would you like to sit down? My bed is just over here."

She laughed again, as if she didn't know how to react. "If Croy knew what you were doing, his heart would crack like a badly forged bell."

"Is there any reason why you would tell him?" Malden asked. "I'm no brute, Cythera. Nor am I cruel. You can stop this with a word. But if you remain silent . . . well. The choice is yours."

# CHAPTER SEVENTY

When Croy came in, an hour later, Malden and Cythera were sitting on opposite sides of the room, trying to work out between them who Bikker's mysterious employer might be. There were plenty of likely suspects.

"The king wants the charter revoked," Cythera pointed out. "So he can tax Ness. He must lose thousands of royals every year because of a promise his distant ancestor made to the distant ancestor of our Burgrave."

"He has the motive, I'll grant it," Malden said, "but my money's on Bikker himself."

"What do you mean?"

"I think Bikker invented this phantom employer. I think he knew Hazoth would never take him seriously, or maybe he wanted a scapegoat if everything went wrong. When the city riots, I think he'll present himself as its new ruler. A man with an Ancient Blade could rally the people to his standard—and end the violence. He'd be a hero, and a sure bet to be named as Tarness's successor."

"Is a magic sword all it takes to lead men? Why, then, Croy might be our hidden enemy," Cythera pointed out. She and Malden both stared at Croy as if they'd discovered a dire secret.

Croy stared back as if they'd both gone mad. When they laughed at their little joke, he turned bright red and went to Malden's washstand. "Does it even matter?" Croy asked. He poured water over his hands in the basin and scrubbed at his face. "It's too late to make use of such information. It's almost time to begin. The plan can't be changed now."

"I must go," Cythera said. "You know I cannot aid you once things are in motion," she said, glancing at Malden.

He nodded. "You must act as surprised as anyone. But you'll know it has begun when the ogre appears on your doorstep."

"An ogre," she said. "You mentioned it before. Where in the world did you find one of those?"

"It was Croy's doing, actually," Malden said. "His contribution to the scheme. You should see this creature in calmer times, Cythera. It has the voice of a poet and a soul devoted to the Lady, but it looks a fright—twice as big as a man, covered in dark fur, its face engraved with ancient and baleful runes." He laughed. "It should give the guards a good scare."

"Yes, but maybe not much else," she said, looking concerned. She glanced over at Croy, who didn't meet her gaze. "Malden," she said, "these runes. Do you remember what they looked like?" She took a piece of charcoal and drew on one of his maps. "Were they like this, do you think?"

"Yes, exactly." Malden smiled. "I'm sure they say something menacing, like, 'I am your death' or 'Face me at peril.'"

"Not exactly. It's a curse your ogre wears on his face, but not for his enemies. It's for himself. One of the simpler curses, actually, and very effective. Translated, the words you see here would read: 'An you harm any, thou shalt perish.'"

Malden's eyes went wide. "What's the nature of this curse?"

"It's commonly used on paroled prisoners or creatures who have killed men in the past. If your ogre hurts a human being—even in self-defense—the runes will grow hotter and hotter until they burn right through his skull." She wiped her fingers quite carefully on the hem of her cloak. "I don't know your plan. I don't want to know your plan. But if you were counting on this ogre to fight the guards or Bikker, I only hope you have a contingency up your sleeve."

"Thank you, Cythera," Malden said, between lips pressed together to stifle a shout. She nodded and left his room, headed back toward the villa before she was missed. When she was well gone, Malden slowly turned to face Croy.

"You knew all this, of course," he said, quite carefully.

Croy didn't answer directly. Instead he went to kneel above the loose floorboards where his swords were still hidden.

Malden was faster. He drew his bodkin and had its point at the small of Croy's back before the knight could reach for his weapons.

"The success of my scheme depended on that ogre," Malden said. "There's no time now to find a replacement. Have you betrayed me, Croy?"

"Are you calling me faithless?"

Malden almost concurred. Then he remembered that it was the same word Croy had used to describe Bikker—the word that started a blood feud between the two of them. "I'm asking a question. Did you make some deal with Hazoth, to foil my plans? Or perhaps you work for the same master as Bikker."

"Never," Croy said.

"Then why, exactly, did you not tell me that your ogre was hobbled?"

He watched the muscles in Croy's neck tighten. "I am not a liar, by inclination or by practice," the knight said. "But I was left with no choice."

"Speak plainly!"

Croy sighed. "Don't you understand? If I'm to recover

Cythera's trust, I must earn it. I must be the one who frees her and her mother."

"I've been generous enough to let you play a part, but that's all," Malden pointed out.

"The role you've set for me in your scheme is meaningless. I am to stand as a lookout, and nothing more. How can that show Cythera the depth of my devotion to her? It should be *me* fighting for her freedom. It should be my arm, my sword, that strikes the telling blow. And no other man has a right to fell Bikker. That is my duty, and I will perform it."

"You're wounded," Malden said. He did not allow the point of his bodkin to shift even a fraction of an inch. "Even at the fullness of your strength, you're no match for Bikker. He would have bested you up at the palace if the demon there hadn't diverted his attention. He would have killed you then. Are you so hot to die at his hand now?"

"Love will strengthen my arm," Croy said. "Justice will be my shield."

Malden chuckled, and the point of his knife bobbed up and down, just a hairbreadth. Apparently it was enough.

Croy shifted under Malden too fast to follow. One of his legs kicked out and knocked Malden's feet from under him, and the thief fell backward against the bed. It was all he could do to stop his fall with his free hand, while keeping the bodkin pointed in Croy's direction.

Before he had recovered himself, Croy was looming over him with his shortsword in his hand, the point just under his chin. The blade shone so bright Malden could see his own shocked expression in its surface.

"I may be wounded. I'm still an Ancient Blade. You can mock my ideals all you want, thief. You can't deny my skill."

"I suppose not," Malden said. "Very well. Who am I to deny you your own destruction? You fool. Maybe you've cost us everything by this deception." He wanted to spit in disgust.

"I can slay Bikker. I must!"

"As you wish it. Take the ogre's place. Die, if that's what you want. As long as you survive a minute against the retainers, that's all I need."

"You'll find that even if I'm not as strong as Gurrh, when it comes to swordplay I am matchless. Anyway, you have no choice." Croy lowered his sword. "It's almost time to begin," he said. "There's no time to find a replacement. Not even a band of bravos."

Malden nodded. He was still looking into the sword's blade, meeting his own eyes in reflection. "Yes," he said. "Strong. He's still very strong, even if he can't fight." It was like the sun had just come up in his mind. He saw it now, a way to make this work. "Croy, I've just had an idea that might save both our lives. Can you get word to the ogre and give him new instructions? He may have his uses yet."

# PART IV

# The Job

# INTERLUDE

Slag the dwarf climbed up into one of Cutbill's chairs and puffed out his cheeks. "That boy Malden doesn't have a fucking chance, does he?"

Cutbill had a great deal of respect for his dwarf. The diminutive craftsmen had a foul mouth, it was true, and a fouler disposition, but his work was immaculate and it allowed Cutbill's thieves to do things that should have been impossible. So he showed the dwarf the signal honor of putting down his pen before he looked up and said, "Probably not."

Slag nodded and scratched at his wild beard. "I just heard from Loophole. He thinks you don't know that he's been asking around, which is just fucking stupid. But he says Anselm Vry is turning half the city arse over eyebrows looking for the—"

Cutbill arched one eyebrow. His office was one of the most secure places in the city, and there should have been no chance of any unwanted ears listening at his doors, but in a world where the bailiff had a wizard with a shewstone at his disposal, no conversation was truly safe.

Slag nodded and held up his hands in apology. "—for the thing," he concluded. "Vry's watchmen are tearing open every damned door in the Stink, as if some poor bastard of a cobbler is hiding it in his privy. You think his wits are buggered? Seems like he's lost his mind with terror."

"Oh, no," Cutbill said. "What he does makes perfect sense. He will fail to find it, of course, but then he can at least show the Burgrave that he made an honest effort. He's looking in the Stink rather than the Golden Slope for the same reason he made no real attempt to recover it from its current location—because he's afraid of the occupants. The rich citizens in their mansions up by Castle Hill would never put up with such outrages. The poor folk living under the Smoke can't afford to be as particular."

"So he won't find it in time, and Malden doesn't stand a chance either."

"I wouldn't say that. I'd say his chances are quite grim. But I picked Malden for a reason, Slag. It wasn't because he showed such ability when he robbed Guthrun Whiteclay. It's because he has a brain in his head. One sees that so rarely in the men who come through my door. If anyone can pull this job off, it's Malden."

"That why you're sitting here, still scratching fucking notes in your fucking book?" Slag asked, gesturing at Cutbill's ledger. "Like any other day. You might be dead tomorrow morning. Shouldn't you be out whoring or drinking yourself sick?"

"I imagine if I am to have my throat cut on the morrow, a bad hangover or a case of the crotch rot would not, in point of fact, improve the experience. But no, I am not working so late because I expect Malden to succeed. I am working in case he does not. This ledger is more than just a record of accounts. It is my life's work. It can never really be done, but I am attempting to make it as complete as possible. It includes a number of instructions that are to be carried out if I do meet my creator in the morning. I called you in here specifically because I need your help with that. Later tonight I want you to vacate the premises well before Anselm Vry and his soldiers arrive. And I want you to take this book with you. There are a number of people who should see it: the Pirate Queen of the Maw Archipelago will be most interested, for one. The Great Chieftain of the barbarians, Mörg the Wise, absolutely must be allowed to read page three hundred and nine if we are to avoid a war with his people."

"Such desperate fuckers as them need to see the guild's records of payments and income?" Slag asked. The gleam in his eye was one of distinct curiosity. Few things could break a dwarf out of his dark moods, but a juicy mystery was near the top of the list. "What's really in there, then?"

"You're free to read it and find out," Cutbill said. He turned the ledger around so it faced Slag. The dwarf made his way across the room and climbed up on Cutbill's desk to see better. Reading along upside down, Cutbill watched as Slag's eye ran down the endless columns of numbers to the spidery glyphs that appeared in the margins of each page. Slag stabbed the coded symbols with one delicate finger.

"Huh. Fucking clever. It's in cipher."

Cutbill favored Slag with a thin smile. "One I'm sure you could break, given enough time."

"That's not why you want me to take the book, though."

Cutbill shook his head. "No. I've chosen you for this task for a very simple reason. When Anselm Vry comes here tomorrow, he will kill every member of the guild he can get his hands on—with one exception. The law will not allow him to kill you." It was true. Any man who turned his hand against a dwarf, so much as to slap him in anger, would forfeit his own life. It was the treaty humanity had made with the dwarves when they allied against the elves at the end of the long-past wars. It was a treaty never broken or ignored, simply because only dwarves knew the secret of making steel, and that made them more valuable to the king than his own subjects. "Furthermore, you are allowed to travel anywhere in the continent you please, and no one can stop you. You are, my friend, the *only* one I can trust with this duty."

"Sure. That's what they always say about the shit jobs." Slag squinted at Cutbill as if the guildmaster of thieves were either an exquisite gem or a worthless piece of paste and he wanted to decide which. "I never had a blasted clue before tonight. But there's more to you than people think, ain't there?"

"On the contrary. I am exactly what I appear to be."

"Oh?"

"I am a man who has very good reason to keep his secrets safe." Cutbill smiled once more. "Now I'll ask you to leave me, if you'll be so kind. I have a great deal to get down before they come for me. Oh, one last thing: if, despite the obvious odds, Malden does succeed somehow—I must ask you to never mention this conversation to him, or anyone else."

"Sure. If that happens, I'll be so surprised I'll probably bust a vein in my skull and forget all about it anyway."

"I do so admire the optimism of your people," Cutbill said.

The dwarf headed for the door. He had work to do of his own. "Ah, sod off, you bigoted bastard," he replied.

# CHAPTER SEVENTY-ONE

It was the night before Ladymas, one of the most important fair days of the year. Though dark had come and the streets were unsafe as ever, still the Free City of Ness bustled with activity. There was much to prepare and make ready before dawn.

In the Ladychapel up in the Spires, the junior priests brought out the giant gold cornucopia that would be the centerpiece of the morning's procession. They polished it with soft cloths until it shone like the sun, even in the light of a single candle. Others started loading it with the hundreds of small cakes and pieces of fruit that would be thrown to the poor as it was carried along. The lesser icons—the rudder, the globe, and the wheel—were touched up with gold paint to hide the chips and scratches where the wood beneath showed through. The senior priests kept vigil at the altar, intoning plainsong prayers and staying on their knees all night before Her sacred image.

In Market Square, vendors fought over the best places to set up their stalls. Most of the disputations were only squalls of words, with the occasional brandishing of a piece of paper as one or another claimed the right to a certain favorable spot. These pieces of paper were of limited utility, however, since most of them had been written by one of Cutbill's expert forgers. The few authentic ones sold for ten times the price, but in the presence of so many counterfeits, they could not be honored either. Occasionally a fistfight broke out, which the few watchmen on hand had trouble breaking up. There was real money to be made at a fair day, after all.

On the Golden Slope, where most houses were already deserted, the last few wealthy citizens supervised their servants as they packed chests full of clothes and food for the next two days. Anyone who could afford to, fled the city during fair days and locked their houses up tight, because it was commonly believed that crowds spread plague. Some of Cutbill's best agents were on the rooftops, making notes.

Down in the Smoke the giant furnaces were banked, a laborious process that was only performed twice a year. The fires that smelted and shaped the Free City's iron had to be throttled down slowly and precisely, lest the forges cool off too rapidly and crack under the stress. Normally the furnaces were kept roaring all through the day and night. The law required that all fires be put out during fair days, however. During the festivities the population of Ness would triple, and should any house catch fire there would be no way to check the conflagration before it spread across town.

In the Stink every shrine of the Bloodgod was holding late services, accepting the small sacrifices of fish and meat the people brought. They lined up for blocks just to leave their scraps and make the proper signs. The poor couldn't afford to displease either god or goddess, and so made a point of placating both in quick succession. At dawn they'd be on their knees in the little chapels of the Lady that dotted their neighborhoods, trying hard to stay awake through the morning prayers.

The watchmen took full advantage of the piety of the poor to break into more of their homes and rummage through their meager belongings. No crown was discovered in these searches, but plenty of copper coins and pieces of cheap jewelry were. It was a holiday for the watch as much as for everyone else.

At every inn the house was full, and travelers were forced to bed down in the stables, or sleep six to a bed in the house, and there was no wine to be had, only new ale and strong beer.

At the Lemon Garden, Elody opened her doors and hung a brass cornucopia over her door, advertising the special rate she gave to pilgrims far from home. She'd brought in extra girls for the increased foot traffic—honest women every other day of the year who wore masks tonight to make a little extra cash, since they could find cheap expiation in the morning for any sins they committed this night.

On the Goshawk Road opposite the northern wall of Castle Hill, the gambling houses closed their doors—but not their tables. The devoted card players and dicers inside kept their voices low in case the watch was listening, but that just drove the stakes higher. Fights broke out there just as in Market Square, but these ended much more quickly. Either the proprietors of the gaming houses ejected the brawlers with due dispatch (if they were of the more common sort), or (in the case of the gentry) helped the combatants make assignations for future duels. To be held only after Lady-mas, of course. No nobleman would be so uncouth as to shed blood on the Lady's sacred day.

In the Ashes the beggar children who watched over Cut-bill's lair gathered in a burned-down chapel and worshipped their own image of the Lady. It was only a charred piece of an old tavern sign that showed a less-than-divine woman holding a giant ale tankard, but the faith in the children's eyes burned no less bright for it. If anyone needed to court fortune and abundance, it was these urchins.

In the Ladypark a yale bleated as it was brought to bay by a pack of feral dogs. It turned to face them with its wicked swinging horns, but it was severely outmatched. If the yale knew it was sacred to the goddess, it didn't know how to call upon her aid.

In a rarely used chapel on Castle Hill, a certain figure

sat with a bottle of wine and a good book. He would not be sleeping that night—at least until he heard from his fellow cabal members, Bikker and Hazoth. When he was certain the ungrateful thief was dead and Ghostcutter was ready to be passed on to a new owner, then he might relax—but only for a moment, before the real work of the conspiracy began.

All across the city hymns were sung. They could be heard through every window and on every street corner.

Everywhere people made merry, or atoned for sins, or simply enjoyed the warm summer's night.

And on Parkwall Common an ogre walked sedately across the grass and up unto the gates of Hazoth's villa. The guards there challenged him and shouted for him to leave, but he ignored them, and all else. As if he'd found a pleasant place to spend the evening, the ogre sat down on the grass just beyond the gate, and watched the house with his massive, staring eyes. After a while he folded his hands in his lap. He made no attempt to enter, nor gave any sign of violence. Yet a lightning stroke touching the rose window would have elicited less surprise.

# CHAPTER SEVENTY-TWO

A t the side of the house, Malden crouched with Kemper beneath a willow bush. He peered through the dark trying to see what was happening. There were torches guttering at the gate, and he could make out the ogre plain enough, but he needed to see how the guards reacted to Gurrh's presence.

"Ye'll know when it's time, lad," Kemper soothed.

"We need to be ready to move at a moment's notice,"

Malden insisted. "Are you prepared? You know what you must do?"

"Aye. Now quit yer jawin'. Look, there. Is yon bastard this Bikker ye're so afeared of?"

"It is," Malden said, grinding his teeth together. The big swordsman was leaning against the side of the villa, scratching at his beard. He did not look well pleased, which was comforting. He kept craning his head around the side of the house to see what the ogre was up to. Which was nothing.

Malden had foreseen this. It was quite possible that Bikker would see through this phase of the plan. The ogre couldn't get through the barrier any more than Malden could. The guards were completely safe inside—and of course, they would be perfectly safe even if the barrier were lowered. Bikker might know the meaning of the runes on the ogre's face and realize he had nothing to fear from the monster.

Yet it would take a man with ice water in his veins not to worry when such a brute showed up on his doorstep for reasons unknown. Bikker was smart, he was disciplined, but Malden was counting on the fact that he had hot blood in him. If Bikker wouldn't respond to the ogre's presence, Gurrh had been told to make him react.

"Now, Gurrh," Malden said, as if the ogre could hear him.

Perhaps he could—who knew what the hearing of an ogre was like? Without apparent provocation, Gurrh rose to his feet and went over to the fence that ringed the villa. He grasped one of the wrought-iron uprights and tore it loose from the crossbeams with a noise like a demon being dragged out of the pit—a groaning, shrieking sound that set Malden's hair on end. The upright came loose with a clang, and suddenly Gurrh was holding what looked very much like a wicked spear.

The ogre, smiling broadly, swept it through the air and brought it clanging along the other uprights of the fence. The noise was rhythmic and intense and impossible to ignore. A guard shouted for the ogre to stop but his voice was lost in the clamor.

It was enough, perhaps. The guards rushed backward, away from the fence, caterwauling in their fear. Just as Malden had hoped, at the side of the house Bikker pushed himself away from the wall and came striding out toward the gate.

"You there," the hairy knight called. "You—beastie. What in the name of all that's perverse do you think you're doing?"

Gurrh shrugged and brought his spear around for another pass. The clanging, banging noise was even louder this time. It was enough to hurt Malden's ears, even so far away. Gurrh seemed to pay no attention to Bikker's demand—he looked for all the world like some mindless brute who had just taken a fancy to making that dreadful racket for his own reasons.

The fact that he was obviously there for some distinct purpose must, Malden hoped, be driving Bikker mad. Bikker might be a ruffian, but he was also a trained soldier, and Malden had learned from Croy that the one thing soldiers hate more in the world is an enemy doing something they don't understand.

"The master of this house doesn't want to be disturbed," Bikker announced. "I don't know your game—though I can guess your owner, I think. Leave now or I'll set my dogs on you."

Gurrh made a third racket, and suddenly Bikker was moving, taking long strides toward the barrier. "Lower this damned thing," he shouted, and the captain of the guard came running forward to salute. "You three—and you, boy, drive this thing off."

The four guards he'd chosen balked at the task, but it didn't take more than a few clouts to get them moving. Bikker must have really put a fear into them, Malden thought. They waited for the captain to make the necessary gesture to lower the barrier, then dashed out through the gates brandishing their polearms. They jabbed and thrusted at the ogre the way a swain pokes at a pig to scare it into motion, but the ogre easily fended off their blows with his spear. One glaive blade got past his defense and scored a hit on his hairy stomach, but Gurrh just laughed. The blade bent and then snapped off its pole.

"Sadu's blood an' balls," Kemper said, astonished.

"All the old stories say how hard it is to slay an ogre, that no normal weapon can cut their furry pelts. Come—this is our time to act. We must be quick."

The thief and the card sharp ran across the grass toward the fence. Malden slipped through between two uprights while Kemper just walked through them. The two of them kept very low as they hurried across the garden. Malden was terrified that Bikker would turn around and see them, but his attention seemed absorbed by the ogre.

This was exactly according to plan. Thanks to Croy's recklessness, Hazoth had come to expect an attack on the house—a direct, frontal attack of the kind a knight would make against a fortress. The ogre appeared to be providing exactly that.

Which was not to say this was going to be easy.

Malden and Kemper slipped around the back of the house. Only one guard remained in the garden, and he was doing his best to see what was happening at the front while not technically deserting his post. Bikker had trained and disciplined these guards into a formidable fighting force, but he'd only had a few days to do it. He could not have completely broken all their bad habits in that time.

The back door of the house, which led into the preparatory room behind the dining chamber, was in deep shadow. There were no torches or other lights back there—they would have served no purpose but to ruin the night vision of the guard. Even better, Malden saw that the high window above the preparatory door was open to catch the night air, as it had been a quite warm day. Perfect.

Kemper walked through the door and disappeared. Malden took a length of rope from around his waist and uncoiled it. It was not very thick, nor even particularly strong, but Slag had dipped one end of it in molten silver—at Cutbill's expense. The silver gave that end some extra weight, so that Malden could toss the end up and through the preparatory window. He let the rope play out, then grasped it tight when he felt it go taut. The other reason for the silver was to allow Kemper to hold it. He braced Malden from inside while the thief climbed up to the preparatory window and through. He clambered down in the darkness and dropped a few feet to the floor. There was just enough light to see Kemper's teeth glinting in the gloom.

Malden pulled the rope through the window and tied it once more around his waist. No point leaving it there where the guard might notice it—he didn't intend to leave the house by this same window.

He felt a clammy coolth pass through his elbow—that was Kemper's touch—and reached inside his tunic to take out Kemper's cards. They were a bit damp with Malden's sweat. He handed them to Kemper, who took them without a word.

Together they made their way through the dining chamber and into a corridor that ran from one end of the villa to the other. Windows along one wall shed enough moonlight to show a hall furnished with small tables, a chest of silver plate, and thick carpets on the floor that would soak up the sound of footfalls.

Kemper gave Malden a silent salute, then started off down the corridor. He paused at one of the tables and on its top laid a card, the two of hearts. Next he stopped at the chest. Its lid creaked as it opened. Malden tensed and prepared himself to run, but a mouse might make as much noise. Kemper slipped the seven of acorns inside the chest and closed it again, this time without a sound.

All correct. Malden parted ways with Kemper then, heading back through the dining room and into a servant's closet. A narrow flight of wooden stairs led up to the second floor from there.

A window pierced the wall by the stairwell, and through it Malden could hear the ogre laughing and Bikker shouting terse orders.

Perfect.

# CHAPTER SEVENTY-THREE

The second floor of the villa was as silent as a tomb. Malden reached the top of the stairs and stepped into a hallway with a single candle burning at its far end. There was just enough light to see the doors on either side. Framed pictures hung on the walls here, and he stole a glance at one, but it made his head hurt so he looked away quickly. It didn't seem possible that the woman in the picture would be able to accommodate the giant insect she'd taken as a lover. He did not intend to waste time resolving how it was done.

Kemper had explored this floor and found little of interest—bedrooms, a garderobe or two, linen closets. Malden made his way down the carpeted hall as noiselessly as possible, ignoring the doors until he saw one begin to open. Instantly he pressed himself against the wall and pulled his hood down over his eyes so they would not shine in the candlelight.

He heard a woman's sigh as the door opened fully, letting pale light out into the hall. The woman's shadow was projected on the wall opposite, and he could see from the silhouette that it was Cythera.

He would gladly have made himself known and spoken with her. She could provide valuable information that would aid him in his skulduggery. On the other hand he had far better reason not to let her see him. If he startled her, she might cry out. At the very least, if she spoke to him, someone else might hear them. He could not afford to take that chance.

So before she stepped out into the hall, he took the great risk of opening the door nearest to him and slipping inside. He did it quickly but without making any noise at all. Luckily it seemed the room he'd entered was empty—an unused bedroom, with the furniture all shoved up against one wall and covered in cloths. He pressed his ear against the keyhole of the door and listened as Cythera stepped out into the hall and walked away. He counted to one hundred in his head before he considered leaving the empty bedroom again.

When he was certain it was safe, he tried the door's latch—and found that it had locked behind him. He wanted to curse but didn't risk the sound. What kind of door locked automatically from the inside? It made very little sense to him. Whoever stayed in this room would be trapped until someone came along and let them out.

He turned and looked again at the furniture against the wall. There was a bed, a clothes press, a basin on a stand, a low stool—all common enough fixtures. Something about the bed looked odd to him, though, and he twitched the cloth back to have a closer look. It was then he saw the manacles bolted to the headboard, and the bloodstains on the straw-filled mattress. He let the cloth go in disgust. Curiosity got the better of him, though, and he lifted the lid of the clothes press.

Inside, instead of the garments he'd expected, he saw trays full of rusted steel implements. He recognized only a few of them—a saw, a hammer, a variety of shears and pincers in various gauges. A great many knives. There was one tool with a watertight leather bulb at one end and a long tube on the other, and something else that resembled a meat hook stretched out long and thin.

He could hardly guess at their purpose, but then something occurred to him. He looked to his left and saw it again as if for the first time. There was one piece of furniture in the room he definitely recognized, from his childhood. The stool. A low three-legged stool about twelve inches high. It was the kind of stool midwives used.

When Malden realized what that meant and where he was, he wanted to close his eyes and just make this all go away. He wanted to jump in the Skrait and drown, because at least then he could die clean.

He was wasting time. He closed the press and pulled the cloth back over the bed exactly as it had been, then went to the door and unwrapped the lock picks hidden in the hilt of his bodkin. The lock on the door was a simple mechanism, easily defeated, and soon he had the door open. Yet as he was stepping back into the hall and closing the door behind him, again a sensation, unbidden and very much unwanted, came to his mind.

Malden had the distinct impression someone was coming up behind him. Was it Cythera, returning from some errand? Or a less welcome intruder? He flattened himself against the wall, knowing his only chance was to hide in the semidarkness of the hall. It was a forlorn hope. The light from the candle was plenty to see by—but his reflexes were such he couldn't help but try to hide.

It turned out not to matter.

The thing coming up behind him wasn't human. It was only roughly man-shaped in outline, and seemed to be made of living smoke. It left misty footprints of condensation on the floor where it walked, but it passed Malden without even turning its head—assuming that lump at its top was some kind of head. It walked right past him and into the stairs and then was gone.

He had no idea what that thing had been. A demon of some manner? A ghost? A spirit of the upper air?

More to the point, had it seen him? Could it see at all? Would it warn Hazoth as to his presence? He couldn't know. He could only hope that by keeping still and not touching the thing, he'd somehow escaped notice.

If that was incorrect, he was sure he would find out very soon.

With a shudder, he stole down the hallway, toward the gallery at its far end.

On that gallery he chanced a quick look down at the enormous sphere of iron by the grand staircase. The egg of the demon. It remained motionless and seemingly quite inert— a thin stream of powdered rust fell from one of its sides, but otherwise it could have been dead inside. That was a good sign, of course—it suggested Hazoth was as of yet unaware of his presence in the house—but he couldn't help but associate it with what he'd seen in the locked bedroom. What he might call the birthing room.

Enough. He was frightened enough without adding to his

load of troubles. A flight of stairs led up from the gallery to the third floor, and his destination. He crept up the risers, keeping close to the banister, where the steps were least likely to creak.

He didn't have much time left, perhaps less than an hour. When Croy and the ogre were both dead, slain by Bikker if no one else (as he was certain they would be), the barrier would be closed again and he'd be trapped. It was crucial that he find the crown and escape before that happened.

## CHAPTER SEVENTY-FOUR

Gurrh made no attempt to fight the guards, but they couldn't harm him either. He fended off most of their attacks with ease, and when one of them did manage to strike him, he either shrugged off the blade or just laughed as if he was being tickled. From his hiding place, Croy watched Bikker get more and more red in the face.

"All of you, get out there," Bikker ordered. The guards rushed forth as the barrier was lowered once more, all except the captain.

"But sir, why aren't you leading the men?" the captain demanded. "Surely your sword would make short work of that thing."

"I can't very well abandon the house, now can I? Did it occur to you that this might be a trick? Do as you're told."

"Yes, sir," the captain said, and hurried out to join his men.

Gurrh grabbed a halberd that came whistling toward his nose and snapped its haft like a twig. He buried the blade end in the grass by his feet. Its owner tried to smash at the ogre's eyes with the broken length of wood in his hands, but to no avail.

Two of the guards got around behind the ogre to attack from the rear, but Gurrh didn't even turn to engage them. One of them sunk a military fork into the thick matted hair near Gurrh's spine, but the ogre only rolled his shoulders as if he were having his back scratched. The other aimed his pikestaff at Gurrh's left kidney, and this time Gurrh did respond, but only by shifting slightly to one side so the guard staggered past him with the momentum of his charge.

The flanking maneuver was not without result, however. As Gurrh sidestepped, a guard with a glaive saw his opportunity and jabbed upward, right past the metal fencepost Gurrh was using to parry. The long curved blade of the glaive slipped through Gurrh's defense and caromed off the giant's cheek. A dark line of blood appeared on Gurrh's preternaturally white skin.

Croy gasped. He'd been convinced that the ogre was invulnerable. He'd never have suggested Gurrh for this job if he'd thought there was a chance the gentle creature could be hurt. It was all he could do not to run out of hiding and rescue Gurrh from his attackers.

Not that the ogre really needed the help. Gurrh grabbed the glaive away from the retainer and threw it into the dark grass behind him. Its owner raced after it. The giant blocked two more attacks, then reached up with his free hand and patted at the wound on his face.

"Thou hast bloodied me," the ogre said. He seemed more surprised than angered. He brought his iron spear around and put a deep notch in the wooden haft of a billhook that might have touched his chest if its wielder had been faster. "I thought it not possible."

Croy bit his lip. The ogre's face was his one weak spot—the one part of his body not covered by the thick protective hair. This fact was not lost on the retainers. They might be sell-swords, cheaply come by and poorly trained—but some of them, at least, were not fools.

Suddenly every attack was aimed at Gurrh's eyes or nose or mouth. The severed end of a polearm (Gurrh had already broken off the iron blade) slammed into the ogre's lower lip, and more blood leaked from the white flesh there. A guard with a bow started firing arrows toward Gurrh's eyes, releasing and notching a new arrow as fast as he could. Glaive and halberd blades were jabbed and swung at Gurrh's face with great rapidity, and it was all the ogre could do to keep them from slicing his features to ribbons.

It was time. Croy could wait no longer. He would defend his friend with his own blades. There was no curse stopping him from fighting. Malden's original plan had required him to stay behind as a lookout while Gurrh took on Bikker and his men, but Croy refused to accept that role.

He would show Cythera what he was capable of. That she could trust him—that he could save her, and her mother, if he was just given a chance. Enough skulduggery! Enough thievery! This was work for a real knight.

Croy slipped his shortsword out of its sheath and brought it to a low ready position. He stood up from the bush where he'd been crouching like a footpad. Enough, he thought. Enough skulking, enough lurking.

It was time to fight.

# CHAPTER SEVENTY-FIVE

Croy's wound throbbed as he strode across the grass. It did not pain him, but only sought to remind him that he was not at the full extent of his powers.

He ignored it.

The ogre was beset now, with guards on every side trying to bring him down. They focused their attacks on his vulnerable face, and it was all the ogre could do to protect his eyes. Already he was bleeding from a dozen cuts on his cheeks and forehead.

"Enough," Croy said, loud enough to be heard over the clamor of battle.

His announcement did not have the effect he'd hoped for.

One of the guards looked over and saw him, but the rest maintained their attack on Gurrh. Apparently the guards still thought the ogre was the main danger, even with the presence of an Ancient Blade on the field. Well, Croy thought, he had taught plenty of men to respect the sword he carried and the office it represented. He snarled and lifted the round oak shield he'd strapped across his left forearm. Normally he fought with two swords and no protection, but his left arm wasn't strong enough yet to hold a sword properly so he'd chosen the shield instead. It had an iron boss in its center and a strip of steel around its rim. He'd trained with every manner of shield made by man or dwarf, and he knew exactly what to do with them. Just now, he clanged his shortsword against the boss, making a noise as loud as a ringing bell. "Over here," he shouted.

That got a few more of the guards looking at him. One split off from the group attacking the ogre and jogged over to confront him. He was a big man carrying a military fork, its two long tines sharpened only at their points. A weapon usually meant for bringing down horses on the battlefield or for punching through heavy armor.

Of course, it would pierce Croy's vitals just fine, should he allow its owner an opening.

"Who are you, and what in the Bloodgod's foulest name do you want?" the guard challenged. He brought his fork down and shifted his hands backward on the haft. That put his points close to Croy's chest and kept the guard well outside of sword range.

The knight smiled. "I am Sir Croy, and I serve the Burgrave, the king, and the Lady. I want you to drop that thing and run away. But I don't think you will."

"I think you're right. Get out of here, knight—we have our hands full already."

Croy shook his head. "I can't do that. I want you to know

that I'm sorry about this. But you serve an evil master, and I have much work to do tonight. So I can't offer you any quarter."

The guard's lips curled back and he started to laugh wickedly.

Gurrh screamed then. It was not a pretty noise—it sounded like a lion being brought down by archers. The guard looked over his shoulder to see what was happening.

Croy took the advantage. It wasn't the most honorable thing he'd ever done, but he was hard-pressed. He jammed his shield forward onto the tines of the military fork, hard enough to embed them deep in the oak. Before the guard could respond and pull them free, Croy twisted his left arm around—it hurt, but he had the strength to do it—and wrested the haft of the polearm right out of the guard's hands. Then he hurled himself forward, leading with his right shoulder, and let the shortsword whistle through the air.

Swords *wanted* to cut. They *wanted* to draw blood—it was what they were made to do. Like a horse that when given its head will follow a track rather than traipsing off into brambles and rough ground, the sword cut through the air with very little help from Croy's strength. It connected with the guard's shoulder and bit deep into the meat of his arm. The guard howled and dropped to his knees as blood darkened his sleeve.

It wasn't a killing blow. The guard would heal in time and feel no lasting effects. But it was a painful wound, and it would render him unable to fight with a polearm for the rest of the night.

Croy had promised himself that he would kill these men if he had to. He had steeled himself against the necessity. But this man had barely been paying attention. A killing stroke would have just been unsporting.

A good shake of his left arm—which was starting to pain him—loosened the military fork from his shield. Croy let it clatter on the ground and then lifted his blooded sword high. "Who among you shall be next?" he shouted.

Suddenly all the guards were staring at him.

# CHAPTER SEVENTY-SIX

Malden crept down a hallway that ran the length of the third floor, looking for the locked door that would lead to Hazoth's sanctum. He could afford to be a little noisier now, since the hallway itself was far from silent.

Visitors to the house would never be allowed up here, he knew. Because this was where the villa got *strange*. The floating dining room table, the living books, the man of smoke he'd seen downstairs had all been miraculous, even wonderful. But up here was where Hazoth's real magic was done.

The door to the laboratory was open, and Malden could hear foul ichors and mysterious fluids bubbling and oozing inside. A greenish light leaked out of that room, and the air before its door shimmered as if something inside were enormously hot—though when Malden passed it, he felt a chill and unwholesome breeze. The next room down the corridor concealed a kind of bestiary, judging from the mournful howling and frightened whimpering he heard. What manner of beasts were trapped within, whether ordinary animals to be experimented upon or exotic creatures kept as curiosities, he could not guess. He was not so foolish as to open the door just to find out.

A third door seemed to breathe in as he passed it, then exhale as he watched. As if the door itself was alive. He could see a dim, shimmering light coming from the crack between the bottom of the door and the floorboards. The light was the dark red of pitfire. Malden couldn't help himself. He reached for the doorknob, thinking to throw open the door and see what lay beyond.

Just then, however, the door exhaled again—and filled the air before him with the stench of brimstone. He withdrew his hand quickly.

It couldn't be, could it? This must be some kind of sorcerous joke. There was no way even a man like Hazoth would have a door in his house that led directly to the pit itself. What if someone opened that door by mistake?

But then—no one who was allowed up here would ever make that mistake. Not unless Hazoth wanted them to.

Malden kept moving. He passed another door and heard a very different kind of sound—no less plaintive—coming from within. Someone was weeping in there, though not someone human. The sounds were unnatural and unnerving, rising now and then to a crescendo of wailing that never came from any human throat. Lower, and harder to hear, was a rhythmic grunting that did sound human. It would seem Hazoth was . . . entertaining in there.

An urge to throw open the bedchamber door and see what a succubus really looked like gripped Malden, but he was able to fight it back down. It would be his doom, for one thing—to surprise Hazoth like that would be the very definition of folly. For another, judging by the sounds she made, he was willing to guess the succubus looked nothing like the toothsome painting on the wall of the House of Sighs.

A few steps farther and he came to a quite ordinary door that proved to be locked when he tried its latch. This must be the door Kemper had described for him, he decided. The door that opened on the trapped corridor. Beyond lay the sorcerer's unholy sanctum—and the crown.

To this point Malden's trespassing had gone without significant setbacks. Beyond this door the real game would begin, he knew. He wished for the thousandth time he could guess what lay beyond. Kemper hadn't dared risk it, and Cythera had been unable to tell him anything. He would be wholly reliant on his own wits.

Glancing up and down the corridor to make sure Cythera wasn't about to walk up behind him, he knelt on a rug before the door. He unwrapped his tools from the hilt of his bodkin and laid them out carefully beside him. Then he took a small dark lantern from his belt, and carefully lit the tiny candle inside. The tin lantern let no light at all escape until he slid open a hatch on its side. The beam thus released was just wide enough to shine into a keyhole. He needed that light to determine which of his rakes and picks would open the lock.

Yet when he looked into the lock, he recoiled in fright.

There were teeth in there.

Not metal spikes filed to points. Not the teeth of cog wheels. These teeth were the color of ivory and they glistened with saliva. Malden had no doubt that if he placed a finger inside the keyhole, those teeth would strip his flesh to the bone.

There was no tongue in there that he could see. He did not think the mouth in the keyhole would scream if he tried to pick the lock. He inserted a long thin hook to test this hypothesis—he was ready to run and find some other way to the crown if it made any sound at all—but the only result was that the teeth bit down hard on his hook, and snapped it off an inch from where Malden's fingers clutched it.

Blast. That hook had not come cheap. Yet it could be replaced. He selected a much stronger tool, a torsion wrench, and slipped it into the lock. The teeth bit at it but Malden jerked it away in time—then shoved it in past the teeth when they opened up again. They closed on the iron tool and worried at it, but lacked the strength to chew right through it.

Good enough. He fitted a stout rake inside the lock and felt for tumblers. They were there, just beyond the teeth, but they felt wrong. Less like the precisely crafted cylinders he was used to, and more like the ribbed flesh on the roof of a dog's mouth. Malden pushed down his squeamishness and tickled the pins until they started to slide back. He put some tension on the wrench and it started to turn.

Instantly the teeth began to gnash and chew at his tools with great fervor. A thin trickle of drool leaked from the lock and spilled down the outer surface of the door. Malden grimaced and rubbed the rake back and forth across the tumblers. It was no time for delicate work. One by one the tumblers slid back and the wrench turned all the way around. The dead bolt slammed open and the door creaked slightly as it opened an inch or two. Malden felt the pressure on his wrench and rake slacken, and he chanced another captain approached, he breathed deeply and readied himself to move.

"Your beast is strong," the captain said, "but he has no belly for a fight. He hasn't so much as scratched one of us. I think you may have picked the wrong partner."

Croy nodded at the man in way of salute. "He's served his purpose. Half your men are disarmed, or carrying pieces of kindling that used to be weapons."

"But half of them are not. And we have plenty of spare weapons inside the fence. You look like you're ready to take us all on by yourself, Sir Croy. I'd know why, before I order your death."

The wound in Croy's back pulsed angrily. His body didn't like being held so immobile. "I've come for the Burgrave's crown. Thieves hid it here. If your master will give it up, I will leave you in peace. I'm not here to kill anyone, if I don't have to."

"I'd prefer to avoid it myself. The city watch will be here soon, I have no doubt. Half the city must have heard us fighting down here. When they do arrive, I don't want to have to explain what a dead ogre—and a dead knight—are doing on my lawn. I don't know anything about a crown. But if you leave right now, I'll let you take your pet away with you. This can just . . . stop." The captain stared in frustration at Croy. He knew very well it wouldn't end that way. "Surely, Sir Croy, this is the best you can hope for!"

"I won't leave without the crown," Croy insisted.

The captain raised his hands in disgust. Then he turned on his heel and threw a hand gesture toward the archer.

The bowstring twanged, and the arrow shot through the air too quickly for human eyes to follow. It was headed straight at Gurrh's uninjured eye. Simultaneously, the four guards around Croy stepped forward in perfectly drilled unison and lunged with their halberds and glaives.

Gurrh snatched the arrow out of the air a split fraction of a second before it pierced his eye. He snapped it in half between his fingers.

Even Croy's senses, heightened by the thrill of combat and the onrushing specter of his own demise, could not

look into the lock. There were no teeth in there anymo
just a simple mechanical lock, something any dwarf c
make in an afternoon.

Yet when he inspected his tools, he saw dents
scratches all over them. The teeth had been real. Now
were not. He wrapped his tools back up and stepped int
hall of traps beyond, having no time to consider the na
of magic or the dubious humor of those who practiced i

# CHAPTER SEVENTY-SEVEN

Gurrh dropped to one knee. The iron fencepost he'd t
wielding clanged on the ground as he clutched at
left eye with both furry hands. The captain of the gua
shouted an order and his troops moved back, giving
archer room to draw a perfect bead on the ogre's face.

The archer held his arrow and did not fire.

Four of the guards rushed to take position around C
boxing him neatly. They made no immediate move
attack, but kept their weapons up and ready. As soon as
captain gave the order they could lunge forward in conc
and skewer Croy as neatly as a bird on a spit.

It seemed the captain wanted to parley first.

In some ways that was a bad sign. It meant the captain
or more likely Bikker—knew of Croy's reputation, a
that he'd survived against far greater odds up at the pala
Of course, then he'd had the option of running away. T
wasn't possible here.

Croy stood to his position, his shortsword pointed at
ground but held away from his body so if he needed to bri
it up he would be ready to sweep it in a broad arc. As t

follow everything that happened next. Luckily, he didn't need to see or hear everything. He had run through this exact scenario a thousand times, back when he was training to become an Ancient Blade. His fencing master—Bikker—had known this day would come, when he was trapped in an unwinnable contest. He had trained Croy to be ready for it.

In such a situation there was only one course of action that could be countenanced. You defended against every attack that time allowed—and you minimized the damage done by those attacks you could not avoid.

Croy's shield took a glaive blade in a glancing blow that sent the weapon up and away. His shortsword parried the axe blade of a halberd, the two weapons grinding together until the halberd was mired in the shortsword's quillions. Croy threw his hips to one side, and a third attack—this one from behind—just grazed his side.

The fourth hit home, and six inches of iron buried themselves in his side.

Croy gasped in pain, but he knew the blow had missed his kidney. Which meant he would not die from the wound. At least not right away. That meant he still had some time. Time to counterattack.

The glaive his shield had deflected was pointed up in the air. The man who wielded it was changing his grasp on the haft, trying to bring it back under his control. Croy put his head down and rushed toward the man, while twisting his right hand around to free his shortsword from the halberd that fouled it.

He felt the sword slip free, but it was his shield that smashed the face of the glaive-bearer. That man went down with a grunt. Croy swung around and suddenly he was facing three opponents head on, rather than being surrounded by them.

A halberd red with Croy's own blood came swinging at his face. He slapped that attack away with the shortsword's foible, then swung his shield around to block a glaive blow that came sweeping up at him from the ground. He no longer saw the men who held the weapons—he was too busy watching the movement of the halberd points and axe blades and the curved, glinting cutting edge of the glaive.

A halberd drove point first toward his left leg. Croy brought the shield down and the point slammed into the oak, piercing it so he saw the point come through the inner side of the shield. Ignoring the pain in his back he threw his left arm wide, pulling the halberd out of the guard's hands. He pressed his attack and brought the shortsword around to slice at the front of the disarmed man, cutting his tunic open and drawing a line of blood across his chest. The guard twisted to one side and fell away.

That left him with two opponents, both of whom stood with their weapons across their bodies in defensive positions. Croy pointed at one, then the other, with his shortsword.

"How much does Hazoth pay you?" he asked.

"Not enough," one of them answered. He threw his halberd on the ground and ran. The other was not long behind him—though he took his glaive with him.

# CHAPTER SEVENTY-EIGHT

Malden stepped through the doorway and into the trapped corridor, careful to test his footing before he put his weight on the floor. It did not give way. He closed the cover of the hand lamp and closed his eyes tightly, then opened them wide again to adjust them to the darkness. He had expected some small amount of light in the corridor— surely at least a little would spill in from under the door or through the keyhole. Yet his eyes swam with the complete absence of light.

Well, almost complete.

The hallway was pitch-dark save for a blot of orange light high off in the distance. His eyes couldn't seem to adapt to the gloom otherwise. He pulled back the hatch of his dark lantern, trying to see anything at all. A pale glow emanated from the lamp, but only for a moment before the candle inside the lantern sputtered and died.

Malden cursed silently and reached into his tunic to find his tinderbox. Before he could reach it, though, the distant orange light flared up and he looked toward it. What had been a shapeless glow was now a fiery orb with a black center, surrounded by a burning ring of gold. It looked a great deal like the eyeball of some enormous monster.

It looked at him. It looked into him. It looked through him. And then madness swept through him like a wind howling out of the pit.

Malden staggered and clenched his eyes shut. He dropped the dark lantern but didn't hear it fall. He clutched at his head with his hands.

*'Ware the eye*, Lockjaw had said. And nothing more. What had the old thief known? Had Lockjaw broken into this villa once and fallen afoul of the same trap? Or had he only heard tale of it from someone else? Malden had realized long ago that Lockjaw's silence didn't only serve to guard his secrets. It made other people feel it was safe to tell him their own. Lockjaw was a great treasure trove of gossip. Yet if only he'd been a bit less stingy with it this time . . . well. What hadn't Lockjaw told him?

Malden shook himself as if he were cold, though in truth he felt like he'd been singed by a firestorm. He opened his eyes, but shielded them with one hand so he wouldn't meet the gaze of that hellish thing again.

He needn't have bothered. The eye was gone. So was the darkness.

He was standing in a corridor perhaps twenty-five feet long. Tall windows stood every ten feet or so down its length, and moonlight spilled in to form pools of silver on the wooden floor. Between each patch of light lay impenetrable shadows. It was as if the hall were one column of a game board with alternating spaces of light and dark.

He turned around and saw that the door he'd come through was gone. The wall there was smooth plaster and wood.

A corridor lined with windows, letting in moonlight—he knew this place. He'd been here before. It was the same corridor he'd crossed to reach the tower room where the crown slept, guarded by its tentacled horror. It was the twin of the moonlit corridor from the palace. A place of traps that he had bested through his skills, and this its perfect double, as if a team of dwarves had worked at copying that hallway down to the placement of each dust mote, the angle of every beam of light. It was as if he'd been transported bodily back to the palace, back to the place of his greatest success—and worst blunder—as a thief. He could almost believe that this was exactly what had happened.

Except—it couldn't be. That hallway had been severely damaged in the demon's magical enlargement. That hallway probably didn't even exist anymore. Surely the Burgrave had no reason to rebuild it exactly as it had been. Which meant he was still in Hazoth's house. Yet there was no way such a hallway could exist in the villa, in this particular location.

There could be no windows in this hallway. The trapped hallway in Hazoth's villa was surrounded on both sides by thick-walled chambers. There was no way the moon could come into this place.

So the moonlight, at least, was an illusion. A phantasm conjured by Hazoth's sorcery. And yet—why did it look so maddeningly like the corridor in the palace? Why would the magician choose to make this place the replica of a corridor that only a handful of people had ever seen? It made no sense.

At least he knew the secret of the hallway. The shadows between the pools of moonlight would hide pressure plates that caused spring-loaded spears to shoot down and impale anyone foolish enough to step on them. The final patch of moonlight would have a collapsing floor, which opened on a shaft that led to the Burgrave's dungeon, or its fell equivalent in the villa. Or—would it? Malden reviewed the plan of the villa in his head. The hallway lay at the center of the third floor. Below it was the gallery that overlooked the grand hall on the ground floor. So the shaft at the end of this hall would drop an unwitting thief onto the iron sphere.

Perhaps there were other differences, too. Perhaps that was the point.

Ah.

*'Ware the eye.* Malden thought he understood a little now. The eye had seen into his mind, and made this place from his memories. That was the only explanation for how it could look so exactly the same. It was a subtle spell, and a shrewd one. It could have made him think he was standing in a field of flowers, or at the bottom of the ocean, or in the pit itself. But he would have known instantly that those were illusions. The eye knew he expected to find a hallway full of traps—so it provided one. The illusion was so complete, and so convincing—the color of the moonlight was a wan silver, the air smelled of old stone and the clean air of Castle Hill. If he had not known better, he might have thought that the disorientation he felt was simply his eyes adjusting to the moonlight. He might have believed utterly in the hallway before him. Without Lockjaw's warning, he probably would have thought all those things. The old man might just have saved his life.

The hallway was based on his memory of the place. There was no reason it would play fair with those recollections. He looked around him for his dark lantern but could not find it. Perhaps it was still there but the illusion concealed it.

In a pouch at his belt he had three of Slag's most reliable creations. Leaden balls, wrapped in leather to keep them from clinking together. He drew one out of the pouch and hefted its weight, then tossed it down the hallway. It landed in a patch of moonlight with a dull thud, then rolled into the darkness beyond where he couldn't see it. If this hallway obeyed the rules that Malden remembered, a trio of brass spears should drop downward from the ceiling like a portcullis and impale the ball in place.

Except that wasn't what happened at all.

Instead the darkness opened wide, and enormous white teeth flashed in stray moonlight. The teeth crashed together on the ball and shredded it. Then the teeth flew open again. A tongue as thick as Malden's arm, forked at its end, flopped out of the mouth/pit and licked at the floor around the teeth like a hungry dog searching for a stray morsel of food. When it found nothing, it flicked back inside the teeth, which closed together and disappeared until only darkness remained on the floor.

Malden thought of the teeth inside the lock he'd just picked, which had chewed at his rake and wrench. Those teeth had disappeared as soon as the lock opened, but they'd left very real marks on his tools. So whether this set of teeth—many, many times larger—were illusory or not, they would certainly make short work of him should he fall into their grasp.

He didn't like the look of that tongue either. If he jumped over the dark sections of the hallway floor—a tactic that had worked admirably in the palace—could he be sure the maw wouldn't open anyway? That tongue could grab him out of the air and pull him into its teeth before he reached the next spot of light.

This was going to take some care and thought. He knew he didn't have a lot of time left. He would have to be quick about this. But if he was too quick, it would be his doom.

He wanted to see just how close he could get to the maw in the floor without causing it to open. Keeping near the wall by the windows where the light was best, he walked out into the first patch of moonlight. He watched the darkness beyond quite closely, looking for any sign that it was aware of him. Thus, when his feet started sinking into the floor, he thought only that he was walking on a thick carpet.

He didn't notice that the moonlit floor was not solid, but as yielding and viscous as porridge, until it had already sucked him in up to the ankles.

# CHAPTER SEVENTY-NINE

The floor did not ripple or shimmer like liquid. It looked as solid and flat as stone. Yet it sucked him downward, little by little, and Malden could feel its substance filling his shoes and sticking to the hairs on his legs.

He tried to pull his left foot free of the floor and found only that this threw him off balance—his right foot had nothing to brace against. He kicked and flailed, but that only sped his descent until the floor sucked hungrily at his knees. He started to fall backward, and knew that if he didn't stop himself he would be sucked down into the floor until his face was covered, until the silvery moonlight stuff filled his nose and mouth and he drowned.

Up and down the hallway the patches of darkness between the pools of moonlight came alive, toothy maws opening and quivering with laughter while long tongues snaked and licked at the air. The hallway was mocking him.

Malden refused to let a patch of floor think him a figure of fun. He had no real honor, as he'd told Croy, and he'd never let pride get in the way of a job before. But no gods-damned inanimate object was going to laugh at him and get away with it.

Desperate for anything to hold onto, his hands shot out and his fingers latched onto the sill of the window. He was embedded in the floor up to his waist, but he could hold himself up if he used all the strength in his arms. That strength was not, unfortunately, enough to haul him free.

He was stuck facing the window. He looked out through the glass and saw the palace grounds—the wall of Castle Hill no more than a hundred yards away, the moon high in the sky. A thin finger of cloud was nearly bisecting the full moon. As he watched, though, Malden saw that it never moved. The stars around the moon never twinkled.

This was all an illusion. The moon, the viscous floor,

the mouths that gibbered and guffawed. All created by that orange eye he'd seen in the darkness. It could affect him—it could kill him, he was certain—but none of it was real.

Heaving, pulling with all his might, he managed to lift himself a few inches. Enough to get his right elbow up onto the windowsill. He braced himself there, resting most of his weight against the wall. Then he released the fingers of his left hand from their death-grip on the sill. He nearly fell back into the liquid moonlight, but just managed to keep steady. The window, he saw, was made up of a dozen long panes of glass leaded into a frame of solid wood. He reached up with his left hand and bashed at the closest pane. It did not shatter (for which he was somewhat glad—he'd worried the breaking glass would shred the flesh of his hand), but instead splashed away from him, as fluid as the floor. He reached through the opening he'd made and felt the air outside. Except it wasn't really air. It felt the same as when he tried to shake Kemper's hand. Cold and clammy, a nothingness that could not exist according to his other senses. His mind could not accept that absence and thus made of it a presence, gave it texture and sensation where none existed.

For all the misery and misfortune he'd experienced since agreeing to steal the crown, Malden was grateful then for the education those misadventures had given him. Most thieves, he knew, avoided magic and the supernatural like the pox, and for good reason. A common man no matter how deft or agile had little chance against even the simplest wizardry. But he was a fast learner, and because he'd had no choice, he learned something of magic in the last week or so. He learned it operated by rules. Not—by definition—the same rules the natural world obeyed. Magic was a perversion of those fundamental laws. Yet like any perversion, it must mirror the original, if only in a distorted fashion. Magic was never just arbitrary, though it could seem that way. There had to be an inherent logic to it, a set of boundaries beyond which it would not pass. Light and glass might act like liquids here, but they would always act like liquids. Solid objects here seemed as strong as steel. For the nonce, at least, he thought he had the hallway's measure.

He reached up through that wet nothingness and grabbed at the wooden frame that held the panes of glass in place. Another pane splashed and dripped away from his touch and his hand closed on the wood, which thankfully was as solid as it looked. More so—it felt as solid as iron in his palm. He thought it might hold his weight.

Thus anchored, he carefully brought his right hand up to grab at the frame as well. He pulled himself up the frame as if climbing a ladder. Little by little his legs came free of the floor. The moonlight did not stick to them or hang in droplets from his breeches, nor did the moonlight shift or flow as he pulled free of it.

In time he climbed up onto the frame of the window altogether, and got his feet up on the sill so he could stand there and let his legs take his weight. Then he looked down.

The floor below him looked as solid as ever. The mouths in the shadows had shut themselves again and showed only darkness. The hall was exactly as it had been when he first entered it. He had progressed about six feet down its length.

Well. That was something. He also had the measure of the place now. He knew its rules—at least some of them.

The next patch of moonlight was ten feet away. He needed to cross over a maw of darkness to get there, and when he arrived he would have to deal with its floor trying to swallow him whole. He thought he might know a way to handle that. Taking the rope from around his waist—the same one he and Kemper had used to get inside the villa, with its end dipped in silver—he tied it to the highest part of the window frame. He gave the rope a couple hard tugs until he was sure it would not come unknotted when he put his weight on it. Then, holding to its silver end, he leapt back to the featureless wall behind him, where the door had been when he came in. The floor there was solid and did not have teeth. It was perhaps the only patch of ground he could stand on safely in the entire hallway.

He rubbed his palms on his breeches to wipe the sweat away, then tied the silver end of the rope around his wrist. Getting a good running start, he dashed forward to the patch of liquid moonlight and then jumped up onto the rope.

It swung him far out over the moonlit floor and up over the darkness beyond.

Beneath him teeth snapped at the air and a long pink tongue shot out to grab him the way a frog seizes a fly. Malden pulled his legs up and tucked them against his chest, and the tongue barely tickled him as he passed.

The end of his arc came fast and he crashed against the second window. The glass there made no sound as it splashed away from him. He was able to grab the frame with one hand before anything more than his toes had sunk into the moonlight beneath him. He scrambled up onto the windowsill halfway down the corridor.

It had worked.

Malden let himself gasp for breath for a while. The hard part was still ahead of him. He had another patch of moonlight—and another wizardly mouth—to cross before he reached the end of the hallway. His rope was still tied to the window behind him. When he recovered his wind, he wrapped one leg through the bars of the window frame and took a strong grip on the rope. With all his strength, he heaved.

The window frame creaked and groaned where the rope was tied to it. The sound was enormous in the otherwise silent hall, but Malden was past caring about making too much noise. He pulled and grunted and sweated as the muscles in his back burned—but then the rope came free, dragging a broken piece of window frame with it. The knotted end fell toward a patch of moonlight, but Malden hauled it in before it could get fouled.

Untying the knot with shaking fingers, he picked broken bits of window frame out of the rope and made another knot, tying the rope to the top of the second, unbroken frame. It would be difficult to repeat his swing from before—he had no room to get a running start this time—but if he failed, he would die.

Malden refused to fail. He kicked off hard from the windowsill and swung for the next window. He didn't get as far out or travel as fast as the previous time, but he made it far enough to get the toes of one foot on the sill of the third and last window. Beneath him a toothy mouth bit and chewed at the wind of his passage, but it couldn't touch him and its long tongue couldn't reach him.

He repeated his trick again—pulling his rope free, tying it off, swinging desperately as the corridor tried to devour him—and suddenly he was at the end of the trapped corridor. He reached down tentatively with one foot and found the floor there was solid. Leaping down, he found himself face-to-face with a statuette of the Bloodgod—just like the one he'd seen in the palace, save one difference. Its eyes were glowing orange.

He ignored their stare as he pushed down on the statue's hinged arm, the one that held the arrow. In the palace, that triggered a section of floor to pivot and transport him into the tower room. Here it had a different effect.

The hallway went black—instantly. Malden's senses reeled, and when he could see again he found the hallway lit well by burning cressets. It was the same length and width as before, but largely featureless now. Just a stretch of unadorned hall with no windows. A normal door stood at either end.

The illusion was gone.

Above Malden, on the wall above the door to the sanctum, was a glowing orange eye mounted in a brass plate. It stared down at him for a moment, burning with hatred. Then brass lids closed over it and it went dark.

The door before him was unlocked. He opened it carefully, then stepped inside Hazoth's sanctum. Now nothing stood between him and the crown.

# CHAPTER EIGHTY

Croy took a step forward and nearly collapsed. The wound in his side was deep and bleeding freely. The wound in his back had reopened, and though it was only oozing blood, the muscles there were painfully stiff and the wound sent jolts of agony through his body every time he moved.

He took another step. It cost him.

The five remaining guards watched him with awe. Two of them had dropped their polearms and looked ready to run away. The rest weren't moving. Their captain kept glancing back at the villa, as if he expected reinforcements to arrive at any moment.

If they rushed him now, Croy knew he was doomed. He could not fend them all off, and Gurrh couldn't help him. The ogre was wounded himself and kept blinking blood out of his eyes.

Croy took another step. Sometimes courage was what mattered, not the strength of your arm. He'd learned that lesson countless times. Courage.

Even if it was empty bravado.

There was an element of showmanship in swordfighting. Bikker had taught him that. A battle of arms was often really a battle of wills, and sometimes brag counted more than bravery. A man with a savage grin on his face could look more dangerous than one with a sword in his hand. He was wounded, exhausted, and ready to slump to his knees. If he showed any sign of weakness at this point—and Lady, how he wanted to just wipe his brow or take a deep breath— he would be finished, and the guards would fall on him in a pile. But if he could just put on a brave face and keep standing, just maybe he still had a chance.

He lifted his shortsword, which was clotted with gore. Brought it up as far as his arm could reach and clanged it against the side of his shield.

"Which of you is next?" he demanded. His voice was hoarse with fatigue but he could still shout.

The two guards who had already divested themselves of their weapons ran off across the grassy common, into the night. Another started shouting for the barrier to be lowered. He ran toward the gate of the villa, but when he passed through was caught up by the magical barrier and lifted into the air. He struggled in vain as his polearm was ripped out of his hands by invisible claws and thrown away.

"He's bleeding," the captain said, then wiped at his mouth with one hand. "He's injured. Look at him! He can barely walk!"

The two remaining guards looked to each other. Then they dropped their weapons and fell to their knees. One of them started praying to the Lady for deliverance. The captain clouted him across the ear, and he fell over on his side.

"What's wrong with you curs?" the captain demanded. "He's just one man! I don't care if he's the king's own champion, one man can't stand against us all. Not if we fight together!" He grabbed at the arms of his charges, trying to drag them forward through sheer willpower.

Croy felt a burgeoning respect for the man grow in his breast. Had things been otherwise, if he had fought beside the captain on some battlefield, he might have called the fellow a hero. If he could avoid it, he very much wanted to keep this man alive, if only for the sake of honor.

But that meant convincing him to shirk his duty, now.

"They don't want to die," Croy said. He pointed his sword at the captain. "Do you? Do you feel such loyalty to the sorcerer that you'll die for him?"

The captain tried to sneer. He failed. "I think I'm more than a match for one bleeding fool," he said. But even he didn't sound convinced.

Gurrh reached down and helped one of the kneeling guards to his feet. The man screamed and ran off. Apparently that didn't violate the terms of the ogre's curse. The other guard, the devout one, crawled away as if too terrified to run.

"Come no further, Sir Croy," the captain said. He looked

toward the villa, where the trapped guard still writhed in the grip of the magical barrier. "Bikker!" the captain shouted. "Bikker! You are needed!"

"Bikker's a faithless coward," Croy said. He took another step toward the captain. He lifted his sword and made his shield ring. "If he was going to help you, he would be here already."

The captain brought his halberd up. Swung it around so the point faced Croy.

Croy stepped closer. Close enough. He brought the short-sword around in a wide arc. The forte of the blade caught the point of the halberd and knocked it away. The captain had no strength in his arms and couldn't hold his weapon still. Its iron fittings rattled as it shook in his hands. That happened to men in the extremes of fear, Croy knew. Their muscles turned to water.

"Hold that thing properly," Croy said to him. "There's no honor in slaying a man who can't fight back."

The captain bit his lip and closed his eyes for a moment. "If you kill me, what do you gain? The barrier is still up. Even your fancy sword won't bring it down."

"No," Croy said, "that's true. But you can lower it with a gesture, can't you?"

The captain stared.

"Lower the barrier," Croy said, "and then walk away from here."

"My lord and master has tasked me to stop you," the captain said.

"I serve your true lord, the Burgrave. I do the Lady's work here. In every man's life a moment comes when he must choose to serve good, or to do evil. What choice will you make? What profit will evil bring you?"

The captain closed his eyes again. It would be effortless to step forward and strike him down, Croy thought. It would be the easiest thing in the world.

The captain raised his hands in the air. He made a complicated gesture with one hand bent in half, the fingers of the others splayed.

The night air on the common fluttered, as if a great flock

of birds had all lifted into the air at the same time. The barrier was down. The guard who'd been trapped by it fell to the gravel with a thud and lay still.

"Thank you," Croy said, turning to look the captain in the eye. But the man was already gone. His halberd lay abandoned on the grass.

Croy breathed deeply. He was badly hurt, and he knew it. But now the barrier was down. His path was clear.

"Hold," Gurrh said. Croy whirled to face the ogre. It was a bad idea, as it aggravated his wounds. For a moment he could see only blood, and his breath caught in his throat.

"Into that place, goest thou must. But not yet," Gurrh told him. The ogre had torn the tunic off one of the fallen guards. He ripped it into bandages and stanched Croy's wounds. "Now, thou art ready."

Croy grinned. There was less humor in his smile than he would have liked, but at least it didn't hurt to move his mouth. "Thank you, Gurrh. You know what you must do now, don't you?"

"I do," the ogre said. He walked over to a point about twenty yards before the gate of the villa and sat down once more in the grass, to wait.

Croy strode up to the gate and hesitated only a moment before walking through. On the far side the gravel crunched under his boots. The main door of the villa stood before him. He started toward it, walking as fast as he could.

But of course he would not be allowed to enter the house, not yet.

Bikker was leaning against the side of the building. His arms were folded across his massive chest. Croy could see the cowl of a chain-mail hauberk emerging from inside his tunic. The big swordsman's face glowed with ruddy health.

"Croy," Bikker said, and stepped away from the wall. "Might I have a moment of your time?"

# CHAPTER EIGHTY-ONE

Hazoth's sanctum was a long room with high vaulted ceilings shrouded in darkness. As Malden entered, the only light came from the rose window at its far end, a massive round piece of stained glass that cast long ribbons of red and blue illumination across the floor. After the gloom of the corridor and its dark illusions, it was almost enough light for him to see clearly by—he almost welcomed the eerily hued light that streamed into the room. Peering forward, he sought what he'd come for, though he wasn't sure what it would look like.

Vague shapes of furniture and magical equipment were all around him. Every corner of the place was cluttered with gear and apparatus, and he was careful not to step forward until he was sure he wouldn't trip over something baleful or disgusting. Once he'd taken a few strides, he began to make out more distinct shapes. He could vaguely see the silhouette of a tree in the middle of the room, its branches raised high like the beseeching arms of a woman in distress.

That must be the witch Coruth. Cythera's mother, who had transformed herself into the shape of a rowan tree, to avoid torture at the hands of the sorcerer.

Malden took a step toward the tree—and the room erupted in light.

Red fire leapt up all around him, from braziers and cressets and dozens of candelabra on high stands. The flames danced wickedly—these were no normal flames, but tongues of fire summoned straight from the pit. They lit up every detail of the room but gave the place a ruddy cast that made everything look stained with blood.

The walls of the room were lined with bookshelves—he had thought Hazoth's library on the first floor impressive, but here there must be ten times as many books, scrolls, palimpsests, and fragments of stone tablets. Standing before

the bookshelves were worktables covered in magical implements: athames, compasses and calibers, goblets, wands,
styli of bitumen, silver chains, bundles of herbs tied together,
ready to be cast into the magical flames. Incense burned
from a dozen censers. The mummified body of a lizard with
a long, toothy snout hung in chains from the ceiling.

On one of the tables stood a glass dome on a carved
wooden trivet. Inside the dome a thing perhaps nine inches
tall scratched at the glass with tiny pincers. Its face was
almost human but its body was . . . not. Malden chose not to
study its form too carefully. Looking away, he saw that on
another table stood a bowl full of what looked like quicksil-
ver. When he walked past it, its substance stretched upward
until a cluster of argent eyes stared at him, mounted on a
thin stalk of liquid substance. It made no attempt to molest
him, so he showed it the same respect. A third table held the
body of a small demon, pinned to the boards with long iron
needles, its lights and guts exposed to the air. The demon's
seven eyes blinked and quivered, and Malden knew it was
still alive. He shuddered as it beseeched him with its alien
gaze, begging him to free it. For all of its alien form, he
might have done just that if he hadn't known better, and if
not for far more pressing errands waiting him. He looked
away again and scanned more of the room.

Skulls inscribed with tiny writing sat in a heap. Charts
of the heavens, with the constellations picked out in gold,
lay half unrolled on the floor. A thing like a clock made of
brass lay in pieces across one table. Its numbered face did
not measure time in any fashion Malden recognized.

A scholar of the arcane might spend a lifetime catalog-
ing all the oddments in the room. Malden had so little time
he barely bothered to glance at the assembled paraphernalia. He moved quickly to the magic circle in the center of
the room, where Coruth stood imprisoned. The circle was
merely a diagram in chalk inscribed on the floor, a double
circle with runes and sigils drawn between its concentric
lines. It looked like a child's scrawl on a pavement, not like
an inescapable prison for a powerful witch. Then again,
Coruth's appearance was deceiving as well.

In the red light she looked far less like a woman and more like a normal tree, though she lacked foliage even now in the height of summer. There was a vague suggestion of a face in the bark of the rowan, but it did not open eyes or whisper secrets to Malden as he approached. If he had not known otherwise, he would have thought it a perfectly natural tree. It was strange, perhaps, that its roots were driven into the wooden floorboards of the room, or that they spread to fill the circle to its full extent but never edged outside the chalk lines inscribed on the floor.

Far more important, and thus absorbing all of his attention, was the leaden coffer half tangled in those roots. It was a simple box traced with a few simple runes, four feet long and two feet high and wide. It had been sealed with great heat so that its lid was fused closed.

Malden knelt down just outside the magic circle and reached tentatively toward the coffer. He knew he had to free Coruth, but the crown was in there! He could almost hear it speaking inside his head, and it demanded to be released. His fingertips passed over the outermost chalk mark of the circle and—

—he pulled his hand back instantly. He had expected the circle to burn him, or perhaps to grab him and hold him like the magical barrier outside. Instead, it only deflected him. He felt no resistance, suffered no pain. His hand was merely repelled, gently, without apparent force. Just enough that he could not have overcome the resistance no matter how hard he tried. He could tell it would be physically impossible for him to reach across the circle and touch the coffer.

There must be some way to break the circle. There had to be some tool for that in this room, some combination of herbs that, when burned together in a flame, would release the circle's captives.

Before he could find them, however, the red flames that lit the room jumped high, and burned a furious white so bright they overwhelmed his vision and blinded him completely.

# CHAPTER EIGHTY-TWO

Bikker made no move to draw Acidtongue from its glass-lined scabbard. Croy left his own swords in their sheaths.

There was an etiquette to these things. When two swordsmen met in single combat, the resultant duel was known as a conversation. Typically it began with exactly that—a verbal back and forth, designed to test the will of the opponents. Such contests could often be resolved long before the first sword was drawn. Croy knew better than to think he could drive off Bikker the way he had frightened the guards or reasoned with their captain. No, it would never be that easy—for Bikker knew about bravado as well. Yet he could score some points against the man with a clever quip or a daring taunt. He might infuriate his hirsute opposite number and goad him into an ill-timed attack. He might chip away at Bikker's confidence, and convince him to spend more effort on defense and thereby avoid a devastating attack. Or he might simply gain some honor by calling Bikker the cur that he was.

"Hello, old friend," Croy said. "I don't suppose you've come around and regained your honor, have you? Care to apologize to me, offer a prayer to the Lady, and be on your way?"

Bikker laughed. "Oh, and is it that easy for a dog to change his spots? I suppose I should make some act of contrition as well. Some penance for my evil ways. Yes, I suppose I *could* give in to your outmoded notions of honor and chivalry. Or I could just kill you—crush you like a gnat that buzzes in my ear, and then go back to my debauchery. Like any sane man living in the real world would do."

Croy smiled, though it pained him. "You know, in some strange way it's good to see you again. It takes me back to better days. You remember, back when you were young and you were at your best."

"I'd like to say it's good to see you, too. Except that you don't look well, Croy," Bikker said, frowning as if this saddened him. "How much blood is left in you?"

"Enough yet to boil, old friend," Croy said. Enough to keep me standing for perhaps a moment or two longer, he hoped. "Enough to best a dozen men, just now."

Bikker nodded in respectful appreciation. "Yes, you certainly showed those dogs how a real man fights. By feint and bluff, mostly."

Croy bowed low. "Perhaps I've been taking lessons from the master of deception," he said. "You taught me much of that style."

"Just as I taught you how to hold that piece of iron you call a sword." Bikker took a step toward Croy. "Tell me. Why are you here? For Cythera, truly? I daresay right now she could fight better than her champion."

"I've come for the crown you stole. The one you paid to have stolen, rather, at the behest of the man who holds your leash."

Bikker shrugged. "Perhaps. Perhaps that's why you came. But you must know you won't leave here with it. I think you came for another reason, though. I think you came to apologize and beg my mercy. To make amends for the time you impugned my honor."

"Do you mean when I called you faithless, because you sell your sword to any man with a purse?" Croy laughed. "A gross insult indeed. Though how, may I ask, did I besmirch your honor—when I spoke nothing but the truth? You were sworn to defend the Burgrave, just as I was. Now you've received a better offer and you work for the man who would unseat my lord."

Bikker's face darkened with rage. "Wake up, Croy. Put away your dreams, your naive ideals. We are Ancient Blades! The Burgrave doesn't deserve our service."

"It isn't a question of merit. It's a question of loyalty. Of duty. You may call those things fancies, but I will not. I believe in them and I will fight to prove it."

"When you die by my sword, what will that prove?"

"That honor is immortal," Croy replied.

Bikker's hand went to his scabbard, and Acidtongue leapt free. Its pitted and corroded surface glinted wet in the moonlight. A droplet of acid formed on its tip and fell to the ground, where it smoked and bubbled. "Draw your sword," the big swordsman said. He held Acidtongue almost straight out at his side.

Croy bowed his head. He uttered a short prayer to the Lady, that She might strengthen his arm in Her service. Then he reached behind him and drew his shortsword, bringing it down over his shoulder to point directly at Bikker. Ghostcutter remained safely in its sheath.

"You bastard," Bikker said. "Draw your real sword."

"Ghostcutter is for killing demons," Croy said, "or worthy opponents. You are neither, only a churl whose blood will befoul even this length of simple steel."

It was a harsh insult indeed, but it had the desired effect. Bikker's wrath bubbled over and he slashed wildly with Acidtongue, bringing the blade up high and then driving it down toward Croy's quillions.

That might have been enough—that one blow could have carved right through the dwarven steel of the shortsword and had enough momentum left to drive Acidtongue right through Croy's body. It could have been the stroke that killed the knight.

But he still had his shield on his left arm. He brought it up high and took the blow hard on his forearm. The acid-wet blade burned through the oak shield and cut through its iron boss as easily as it cut through the air, but Croy rolled his arm under the cut and sent Acidtongue driving down into the grass and dirt between his feet.

Bikker leapt backward, pulling his blade free and out of range of a counterattack. He laughed maniacally. "Very good, Croy. *Very* good." The rage drained out of his countenance. Had it been a ruse? It had looked real enough. "You might survive five minutes if you keep fighting defensively. Will that be long enough?"

"Long enough for what?" Croy asked.

"For your friend Malden to reach the crown. After all, the real reason you're here is to distract me, isn't it? To keep me out of the house while your pet thief robs the place."

Croy could not help but let his face show his surprise. How could Bikker know that?

"You didn't think we would leave the crown unguarded, did you? How very foolish of Malden. Hazoth is a *sorcerer*. He has many ways of watching what goes on inside his own house. He knows that Malden is in there right now, and he knows what Malden is trying to do. Ah! There, look!"

Bikker pointed up at the rose window on the third floor of the house. Multicolored light burst from inside the glass.

"Hazoth is greeting his uninvited house guest even as we speak," Bikker announced.

"No," Croy breathed. "No." It could not be. If Hazoth caught Malden red-handed and killed him as a trespasser, then who would retrieve the crown? Who would free Coruth, and by so doing, Cythera?

"No!" Croy shouted again, and ran at Bikker, his short-sword flashing up and around for a desperate cut.

# CHAPTER EIGHTY-THREE

Malden scrubbed at his eyes with the balls of his thumbs, trying to clear away the burning smears of light that flickered in his skull. His eyesight returned very slowly—whatever caused that flash of light had been strong enough to blind him. He could only hope it wasn't permanent.

His hearing was unaffected. He could sense there were

other people in the sanctum now. He could hear them walking around him. And he could hear someone applauding.

"Very impressive indeed. I thought it was a clever trick that a gutter ape had learned to read! Now I see that animal cunning can evolve to handle basic problem-solving as well, given an adequate stimulus. Though of course, I should not be surprised. Last summer we had a mole that burrowed into the garden, coming through the barrier from underneath the ground, where I never thought to extend it. Vermin will always find a way."

"Good evening, Magus," Malden said, because the voice belonged to Hazoth. Fear washed down his back like a spill of icy water, but he tried to keep his voice level.

"Did I say you could speak? No. Still. You're a bold rodent, aren't you? Courage is admirable, even in lower orders of life. So I'll forgive that breach of manners. I'll forgive your insolence, if only once." Hazoth strode over to stand before Malden, who was hunched over, still rubbing at his eyes. He could see nothing in detail, just vague shapes and shadows.

"You bested the Eye of Klaproth," Hazoth said, as if he couldn't quite believe it. "I wonder—did you somehow see through its illusions, or is it simply that your simple mind was incapable of providing the imagery it works with? Either way, your primitive brain has served you quite well. You might have actually succeeded—I was preoccupied, and I might have remained ignorant of your presence if Cythera hadn't warned me."

"Wh-What . . . ?" Malden managed to ask.

*Cythera?*

"Even a fool of Sir Croy's caliber would not think he could cut his way into my house, not with the magical barrier in place. It was a noisy diversion you had him make out front, but I could not figure out why he was doing it. So I summoned Cythera and demanded she tell me everything. Every detail of your ambitious little plan. And she did, without much hesitation."

Cythera had betrayed him? Malden could scarcely credit

it. She had so much to lose—but then he supposed Hazoth had ways enough to get information from her. He moved one hand down toward his belt, inching it toward the hilt of his bodkin.

But . . . no. He could barely see. Striking out blindly now would be foolish. He fought down his immediate reaction, the rage at being discovered, the terror of what was to come next. It wasn't useful to him. He could deal with it later, if he lived through this.

"Interesting. Look, look at this, Cythera. You can see his thoughts as they grow ever so slowly in his head. Watch his hands, and his mouth. They give him away. Fascinating, really."

Malden held his tongue.

"You're a rodent, my friend, and nothing more. A verminous little animal. Yet you do amuse me, after a fashion. I thank you for bringing a bit of excitement to my tedious routine. Here. You shall have a reward—I will return to you your eyesight."

Instantly Malden's eyes cleared. He blinked a few times and then looked around him. The room had changed little. The flames burned a healthier hue now, and the light was better so he could make out more of the sanctum's contents, though he saw little to recommend the improvement. Hazoth was exactly as Malden remembered him, though now he was wearing a nightshirt and a fitted leather skullcap.

Cythera stood behind him, her eyes downcast. She looked as lovely as ever, even if Malden knew she'd betrayed him. She met his gaze and mouthed an apology, though she did not speak out loud. She looked so piteous, so sympathetic, that he wondered if he could summon up real anger at her betrayal.

He found he could not.

She had pinned her hopes to Croy's star and been disappointed. She had hoped Malden could help her, and that appeared to have failed, too. Her life—and that of her mother—were bound in unholy union with Hazoth, and she could not free herself. She needed help so she had turned to anyone she could get, even a poor thief like him. He'd done his best, and she had helped him to the full extent of her ability. But they had both known it was a long shot. A suicide mission. No, he could not blame her now. Had she maintained her innocence, if she'd held her tongue, Hazoth would have taken out his rage on Coruth.

Malden knew Cythera would never let that happen, if she had any choice at all.

He glanced over at Coruth and the leaden box that held the crown. They were unchanged.

"Quite safe," Hazoth said. He walked over to the magic circle and bent to inspect the chalk lines on the floorboards. While he was thus busy, Malden looked over at Cythera, trying to think of what signal to send her.

All he could do was shrug.

Cythera turned her gaze on the tree that was her mother. A single tear rolled down her painted cheek. Malden's heart went out to her. She must have dared to hope when she saw how close he had come to rescuing Coruth. The plan had gone so smoothly, and now . . . Well. Things had changed.

He longed to speak to her. To reassure her, perhaps, though what words he would use to do so escaped him. Hazoth had not given him permission to speak anyway, so he kept silent. He tried to communicate with Cythera using just his eyes, but she would no longer look at him.

"One thing," Hazoth said, rising to his feet again, "escapes me. I would like to have an answer before I decide what to do with you, little rodent."

He came back over to Malden and stared down at him with unquiet eyes.

"What you are doing here is quite clear. You came to steal back that which you were paid for," Hazoth said. "Why you would do so is no mystery. I imagine you think that if you can recover the item you will be able to bargain for your life with those who seek it. A logical conclusion, though there is one fallacy in your reasoning. The players in this game outstrip you in power and in intellect. They would be glad to have the thing back, certainly. But they would not let you live once they had it. Don't you see? You've learned too much. An animal in possession of a secret is a dangerous animal. They would slaughter you even more readily than I."

Malden bit his lip.

"You may speak," Hazoth told him. "In fact, I insist. Tell me who sent you, and what they want from the crown?"

Malden frowned. "Surely you know the answer. The Burgrave wants what was stolen from him. He will be embarrassed if he appears tomorrow in the Ladymas procession without his crown."

Hazoth smiled. "The Burgrave? Do you mean Ommen Tarness? I really don't think he was the one who employed you." He laughed at the thought. "No, not Ommen."

"Why should he not?" Malden asked.

"Because Ommen Tarness is an idiot," Hazoth answered.

# CHAPTER EIGHTY-FOUR

"A fool, perhaps, but—"

Hazoth's face clouded with anger. "I did not say you could speak!" he thundered.

Inside Malden's chest his heart stopped beating. Pain lanced through his limbs and he dropped to the floor in a quivering heap. He could not draw breath, could not move, and every sound in the room was a distant echo—

—and then he recovered. He sat up carefully, unsure if he was still alive or had passed into the afterlife.

Hazoth went on as if nothing had occurred. "I do not use that word as a casual insult. Ommen Tarness is mentally an infant. He has been since he was thirteen years old, when his father died and he became the Burgrave—his brains stopped growing, even as his body developed. He can barely feed himself. I understand that getting him dressed each morning is a tiresome chore—he doesn't like to wear state clothing, and throws fits of tantrums when the castellan tries to put a robe over his shoulders."

Malden frowned in confusion. He'd seen Ommen Tarness in public many times, and the man had always struck him as highly intelligent and composed.

"Ommen's father, Holger Tarness, was the same. And Holger's father, and his father's father—the line of Tarness is corrupted in the blood. There hasn't been one of them that could wipe his nose properly in centuries," Hazoth said. "It really isn't proper to call Ommen the Burgrave at all. He is like a horse that carries a rider, and that rider is the true Burgrave. Who is currently sealed into yon leaden box."

Malden turned to stare at the coffer tangled in the rowan tree's roots.

"Tell me, rodent. Are you bright enough to know who I speak of? You may answer me, if you think you've worked it out."

Malden considered the puzzle carefully. "I think perhaps I can work out your meaning. I have enough clues to piece together now. The crown spoke to me, when I held it. It possessed an air of command, as if it was accustomed to people accepting its orders without question." He shook his head. He could still remember how it called to him—and how desperately hard it had been to ignore its commands. It wanted him to place it on his own head. He thought he understood now exactly how foolish that would have been.

He considered his second point. "Further, I saw the chamber where it resided when not in use, and that room was full of campaign banners and the trophies of war. Mementos of a military man, placed where no one would normally see them. Yet clearly they were treasured by someone. There is only one man I can think of who fits the bill."

He nodded to himself. "Finally, I know that no other crown will serve Ommen Tarness. Bikker initially suggested that when the crown was stolen, the Burgrave could simply have a replica made and that he would not even come looking for the original, for fear of embarrassment should its theft be discovered. Since then, however, certain . . . others have told me that only this one will do. That it cannot be so simply replaced. But why not? No one ever heard the crown speak, except for me and presumably Ommen Tarness. A nonspeaking replica would be accepted by the people without question. So it must be that Ommen requires the crown to function as Burgrave."

He met Hazoth's gaze directly. "Based on these elements, I believe I have a conclusion. Are you saying that Juring Tarness lives on, eight hundred years after his supposed death, imprisoned inside his own crown?"

Hazoth's eyes flashed with excitement. "Wonderful! You have it precisely. Juring Tarness, the first Burgrave, who founded the Free City of Ness. The general who handed his king a country, and asked for a cesspool as reward. Yes! But you have one subtle detail wrong. It is not Juring who is imprisoned by the crown—it is Ommen."

Malden thought he understood the distinction, but he said nothing rather than risk Hazoth's displeasure with his rudeness.

"Juring and I were fast friends, eight centuries ago. He came to me one night at the end of his life and begged me for my aid. He had a son at that time, an heir who would take up his crown and his title when he died. Sadly, the boy was a wastrel—all his energies were given over to petty entertainments, wine, and whoring. Anyone could see the son would never be a fit ruler. Juring loved his city and worried what would happen to it when his son took power. He had built a fiefdom for himself and ruled it ably. Perhaps his people thought him just and wise. Perhaps they only obeyed him because they knew what he was capable of when angered. His son could not command such respect. More importantly, the boy was incapable of holding onto money. He was a gambler and a drunkard, and Juring knew that if he was given free rein, he would bankrupt the city in a year. The king at that time feared Juring enough to stay out of his business, but once Juring was gone, the king would surely see the son's weakness. One way or another it would end with the city's charter being revoked, and everything that Juring had worked for would be lost."

Hazoth's eyes grew bright as he remembered the long-lost past. Malden was not so foolish as to think the wizard distracted enough to give him any chance of escape. "When he came to me, Juring was at the end of his tether. He could see no solution. If only there was a way for his wisdom to survive his death, some method by which he could continue to advise his son—and to command him, should it come to that . . . He thought perhaps I knew a way to help. I considered the problem from all angles, and eventually I found the answer."

Hazoth grinned. "Juring's body was fragile, like all human flesh. It would perish and decay. His mind, however, could live on, through cunning applications of magics known only to me. It needed something to hold it, however—his mortal brains would rot away, so his consciousness had to be imbued into a vessel that time could not corrode . . . something of gold, which unlike other metals does not rust or tarnish or turn to verdigris. Gold has other qualities that make it ideal for such an enchantment as well—but you would not understand if I listed them. The object in question must also be something that his son would not like to part with. The crown was the obvious choice.

"Juring wanted the crown to speak with his voice, even after his death, and I made it so. Every time the son placed the crown on his head, he heard his father's voice whispering in his ear. He could no longer enjoy his carousing and his ruinous wagers. When he consorted with low company or dealt poorly with his subjects, he was plagued by terrible headaches and by a need to atone. He could only ever be at rest when he was ruling the city with the judicious pragmatism of his father, and so he grew to be a very capable Burgrave. When he grew old, he worried very much what would become of the city under his own son, who was capricious and cruel. But the crown served Juring's grandson well, and his great-grandson, and so on."

Hazoth shrugged. "Even I, however, have difficulty understanding how magic changes over time. It is an unpredictable force even in the short term, and I did not know that the enchantment on the crown would only grow stronger with every passing year. The soul in the crown maintained Juring's brilliance, but its hold on those who wore it made them weaker. The brain is like a muscle of the body. If it does not get proper exercise, it atrophies and eventually dies. Each successive Burgrave was a bigger fool than his father had been. Juring, inside the crown, had to exert more and more control over them, and more and more often had to block out their own misbegotten thoughts and replace them with his own. His character, his intelligence, was imposed on them more frequently, and they suffered for it. Now they can barely speak or count on their fingers without his consultations." The sneer on the sorcerer's face showed how little pity he had for the House of Tarness.

"For a very long time there has been only one Burgrave in this city, and that has been Juring Tarness. It is an unnatural situation, and one some people would like to see changed. Juring was my good friend, and I have always been pleased that he, like myself, survived when so many of our contemporaries grew old and died. But now, perhaps, it is time for new blood to rule this place."

"You betrayed him," Malden said, forgetting himself.

Hazoth seemed not to notice this rudeness. "You speak of loyalty? The man I knew has been corrupted by eight hundred years of stealing someone else's body. He was never meant to live that long. No man was meant to live in that fashion. The enchantment I placed on that crown was meant to last for one generation only. Say instead I am fixing a mistake I made when I was young and foolish."

Malden stared at the sorcerer. He could scarcely credit what he'd heard.

Yet . . . the crown had spoken to him. And he did not doubt it had used Juring Tarness's voice when it did so.

It must be as Hazoth had described. And yet, that meant—

He was not allowed to finish his thought.

"I think the crown will remain here, with me," Hazoth said. "I considered letting you have it. Letting you take it and go free—just to see what would happen. I have a theory, you see. I have a theory that the blood of the Tarness line doesn't matter. That Juring could control anyone who wore the crown. And I am certain you lack the power of will necessary to resist its entreaties. It would convince you somehow to place it on your own head eventually. I wondered if Juring could take some mortal clay—even such a pitiful specimen as yourself—and over time mold it into the stuff of a great leader. I do believe he could. In a span of a few years, I think, you might become king of Skrae."

He looked down on Malden with laughing eyes.

"Imagine that, hmm? A whoreson made into a king. How amusing!"

The sorcerer laughed wildly then, his tongue flapping in his mouth as he gibbered and cackled. It was not a laugh of sanity.

Malden shivered, but not simply because of Hazoth's lapse of lucidity. He considered what would have become of him if he had put on the crown, as he'd wanted to so badly. He didn't doubt that Juring would have given him power in return, knowledge and advice and courage. But he would have been enslaved by it. His greatest fear, that he should lose that little shred of freedom he possessed, would have been realized.

His heart thundered in his ears. It had been a close thing. He barely heard Hazoth when the wizard spoke again.

"But when I tell this tale out loud, I am reminded exactly why I chose to be part of this scheme in the first place. I can't afford to let you become king, you see. Nor can I afford to let the Tarness family—ha ha ha—tell me what to do. I can't afford to have any rivals. No powers must remain that might conscribe me. Do you understand? I think, in fact, you might. How astonishing! How clever! And so tragic, now. No, I'm sorry, rodent. You can't have your prize. And you can't leave my house. Not alive, at any rate."

Hazoth lifted one hand, the third and fourth fingers tucked into the palm, the others outstretched. He began to lift his arm high over his head.

"Malden!" Cythera shouted. "Cover your eyes!"

Malden did exactly as he was told. He also grabbed the hilt of his bodkin and got ready to draw.

# CHAPTER EIGHTY-FIVE

Drops of acid hit Croy's arm and seared right through his leather jerkin. He shouted as the acid burned through his skin as well. Pain lanced up to his spine, while his lungs heaved against the stink of sulfur in the air. Croy couldn't help but cough as the fumes seared his throat and eyes.

It was the sign of weakness he had put off as long as he could. He'd finally broken. Bikker took it for exactly what it was—a call to attack, which he executed with a flurry of devastating blows, one after another. Croy managed to parry them, but not without cost. He had to stagger backward, away from the fight, and wince as the pain threatened to overcome him. He forced his eyes to stay open, to keep watching, to keep assessing the situation.

His shield was reduced to a few sticks of sizzling oak held together by a melting boss. Far worse, the shortsword was etched and notched each time it parried Acidtongue's attacks. Croy could feel his sword growing weaker and less stable with each passing moment.

The weapon was still in better shape than the man, though, and that was the real problem. Already weakened by multiple wounds and loss of blood, Croy's endurance was reaching its end very quickly. Just lifting his sword arm took a great effort and he was gasping for breath. Sweat rolled down into his eyes and he could taste the salt when it trickled across his lips. Proper swordsmanship was as much about the legs as the arms—he could hear Bikker's voice in his head from back when the bigger swordsman had taught him how to fight. *You need to* move *when a sword comes at your face, boy,* lunge *forward with your knee when you riposte,* dance *if you want to stay alive.* His legs felt like they were made of solid wood. He could barely get his feet off the ground without falling over.

A sweeping blow came at his injured side, Acidtongue spitting as it burned through the air. Croy barely brought the shortsword down to counter. Acidtongue flew back to recover from the parry and then whistled over Bikker's head as he brought his corroded sword up for a high slice. Croy shoved the fuming remnants of his shield up into the blow but lacked the strength to hold it back completely. Using Acidtongue like a club, Bikker knocked the shield into Croy's teeth. Croy's entire skull rattled and he felt his brains slosh back and forth.

So tired.

Parry. He tried a riposte but found the shortsword tangled in Acidtongue's withdrawal.

His body was failing him.

Parry. Step back, away from the lunge, one foot behind the other to make his body a narrower target. Acidtongue jabbed past his face, and he batted it away like a cat batting at a piece of string—and just as effectually.

He was going to collapse.

Yielding parry—catching Acidtongue just before it cut his throat, taking Acidtongue's foible with the shortsword's forte. A classic parry perfectly executed, which should have given him an ideal chance to counterattack. By the time he saw the opportunity, however, Bikker was dancing away.

Croy knew he was doomed.

Acidtongue came rushing toward his shield. It might be a feint, which he should ignore. He lacked the strength to turn into the rush. Acidtongue picked apart the shield, scattering its pieces. Croy's left was suddenly exposed and undefended. Bikker howled in joy and twisted around, whipping Acidtongue about and building to a slash that would cut open Croy's belly and spill his guts on the ground.

One last shred of strength remained in Croy's body. He

used it up stabbing downward with the shortsword, driving its point into the ground to make a wall against Acidtongue's slash. The shortsword wobbled, good dwarven steel pushed past its limits of flexibility. Acidtongue cut through it like a ribbon. Fragments of steel flew everywhere, one of them cutting through the skin of Croy's cheek. The sword that remained was nothing but a hilt with a jagged inch or two of blade sticking out of it. He dropped the hilt, then closed his eyes and sank down on one knee.

He couldn't lift his head. His neck was perfectly exposed. Acidtongue could cut through flesh without resistance when it was hot and singing with battlelust. One cut and Bikker could take his head off.

Croy couldn't lift it. He was just too tired.

Cythera, he thought, I love you. I am so sorry.

The blow didn't come.

Croy opened his eyes but still couldn't move. He looked down at the grass beneath him. It looked very soft, and he thought it would be nice to fall, face forward, into its green embrace. One shard of his broken sword lay on the ground there, etched but still shining with polish.

Bikker still hadn't killed him. What was he waiting for?

"Look at me, Croy."

Slowly, painfully, Croy lifted his head and met his foe's eyes. Bikker's face was wild, his eyes mad. Froth flecked his lips.

"Good," Bikker said. "That's taken care of. Draw Ghostcutter. Playtime is over. Now we'll fight like men."

# CHAPTER EIGHTY-SIX

M alden kept his eyes shut until he was sure the hellish light of sorcery had drained from the room. His hand clenched tight at the hilt of his bodkin, and he started to draw it, careful not to make a sound.

When the glare faded from the inside of his eyelids, he opened his eyes again and saw Hazoth still before him. Something had changed, something he noticed only in his peripheral vision, but he focused entirely on the sorcerer. Hazoth was breathing heavily and his hands were down by his sides. Malden bent his legs like springs and then jumped, thrusting the bodkin before him so it would cut right through the sorcerer's belly and come out the other side.

He fully expected Hazoth to turn and glare at him, eyes blazing with some spell that would tear his flesh from his bones. Or perhaps Hazoth would simply vanish before he could reach him. Instead he caught the magician completely off guard. He felt the point of the bodkin part the fibers of the sorcerer's nightshirt, felt it sink into the hated flesh, felt it scrape on bone. He pushed and shoved with all his might until it broke free from the sorcerer's back. He did not feel hot blood pour over his hand, but that surprised him less than the look on Hazoth's face.

The sorcerer simply looked disappointed.

Malden fell backward, pulling the bodkin free. He stared down at the length of iron in his hand and saw no blood on it, nor ichor nor living fire nor any of the things he supposed might flow through a sorcerer's veins. He looked up and saw the hole he'd cut through the nightshirt . . . but the flesh underneath wasn't even scarred.

"A violent response to a threatening stimulus. The hallmark of an unenlightened being. Rodent, you have surprised me so many times tonight—now you prove that there is a limit to what a primitive creature can do with cunning. Ah, well. I suppose even the most advanced of the species must eventually revert to rodentlike behavior. Oh, and now look at what you've gone and done."

Cythera cried out. Malden looked over at her and saw her staring at the palm of her left hand. The ink there looked like it was boiling. Flowers bloomed and their petals fell away, driven up her arm by a howling wind entirely contained within her skin. Vines circled around her wrist so tight they looked like they would constrict her pulse. On her face a hundred snowdrops wilted, while roses erupted in blossom across her shoulders, their thorns gleaming with painted poison.

It would seem the link that bound Cythera to Hazoth wasn't just for inimical magic. It could absorb physical damage as well.

"Cythera!" Malden shouted. "No—please, forgive me, I didn't know—"

"It's . . . all right, Malden," she said, straightening up. "It doesn't pain me. It just startles me a bit when it happens, that's all."

Hazoth looked from one of them to the other. Then he clucked his tongue and faced Malden again. "You interested me, briefly. That's why I've let you live for so long. But not for your animal passions, rodent. For the way you seemed to exceed the limitations of your upbringing. But now I see you've only been so clever, so brave, for one thing—that prize Cythera keeps between her legs." He shook his head sadly. "Pathetic. I'm afraid that attacking me was the last mistake I can permit you."

Malden's blood curdled in his veins. He knew he'd never been closer to death than this exact moment. His brains turned over in his head, desperately trying to imagine what to do next. He could think of only one thing: obfuscate. Stall for time. "I beg to disagree," he said. His mouth was so dry he had trouble forming the words. Hazoth had not given him leave to speak, but he knew it no longer mattered. Silence at that moment would have been his death warrant.

"What's that, rodent?"

"You suggest that my logic was faulty in some way. That I made an irrational decision by attacking you. I would say instead that my information was merely incomplete. I did not try to stab you before, when you caught me. I did not try to do so when your back was turned. I waited until your magic had drained you and distracted your attention to the point where an attack might logically succeed. You see, I thought very carefully before I struck that blow."

Hazoth looked upward, as if consulting a higher power. "Almost clever," he said. "There is one flaw, however. One place where your logic falls apart."

"Yes?" Malden asked, in the tone of a scholar asking for a gloss on a particularly thorny text.

"You," Hazoth said, "are the human equivalent of a cockroach. I am a being of extraordinary power. You should have recognized that someone like you could never, under any circumstances, harm me. The intelligent thing to do in this situation would have been to curl up and die. It would at least have saved you from what comes next."

Hazoth walked a few yards away from Malden and looked up again.

For the first time, Malden saw what had changed. When the sorcerer had cast his spell, Malden did not know what effect it might have. Now he understood. He had been transported from one place to another, without traversing the intervening distance. He was no longer in the sanctum.

Hazoth had delivered the three of them to his grand hall. They stood in the shadow of the iron egg.

"Now, I'll ask again. Who sent you here?"

Malden looked away. "I came on my own—this was all my plan," he insisted. Why implicate Cutbill? It wouldn't save his own life, and it would only make trouble for the guildmaster of thieves. If he could spare Cutbill that, then perhaps he could earn a little something with his death. "I need the crown or Anselm Vry is going to kill me."

Magic buzzed through the air toward Malden like an angry insect. An invisible stinger jabbed him in the chest, causing a bright blossom of pain to stretch its petals all the way around his rib cage.

"Impossible," Hazoth said. "You lack the will for something like this."

"I . . . swear," Malden said as the pain radiated outward, toward his extremities. Red blood stained his vision. "It was wholly . . . my own . . . notion . . . I—"

"It was Croy!" Cythera shouted. "Croy paid him to help me!"

The pain left Malden as quickly as it had come. He dropped to the marble floor, still writhing with the memory of it.

Hazoth turned to face Cythera. "Truly? I suppose I can believe that." Hazoth looked almost disappointed. "I had thought I might discover the name of my fellow schemer. Hmm. But yes—yes, Croy would be foolish enough. Very well."

He shrugged and came over to where Malden had curled up on the floor.

"So. We have reached the end of our experiment. The subject has failed to justify the hypothesis. There remains nothing to say," Hazoth said. "And there are other matters that require my attention. There is a knight errant on my lawn, brawling with the hired help. I think I need to go boil him in his own blood."

"Croy," Cythera said, one hand to her mouth. "No—you can't . . ."

Hazoth looked over at her. "You know perfectly well that I *can*," he said. "And now, by telling me he was behind this intrusion, you've given me every reason to do so immediately."

She went pale beneath her tattoos. "I meant—I meant to say—you may not," she said. "I won't allow it, Father."

Malden's eyes went wide.

"Father?" he said aloud. "He's your—"

"I did not say you could speak!" Hazoth screamed, and Malden's voice was lost.

It didn't matter. His own thoughts were louder than anything he might have said.

*The demon is his child*, she had said. *It is not his first.*

He had assumed she meant he'd sired other demons.

*Not all of his protections are magical*, she had said.

He'd assumed that meant the very human retainers he

kept to guard his gate. But perhaps she'd meant, instead, that he had a hold on her that was more complex than a mere contract of employment. She had betrayed him, Malden, and now he knew why.

In truth, he had never trusted her completely. Even when he'd kissed her, he half expected her to destroy him with her stockpile of curses. He had made sure she only knew half of his scheme. Now he understood that he could not expect her aid any longer. That she was not going to rescue him at the last minute.

He had, in a way, expected this.

It still hurt. It still cut him to the core.

"I will do as I please," Hazoth said, as cool as an autumn day. "As for you, rodent, I'm afraid you have to die. I know your simple brain will have trouble accepting this fact. You'll think there must be some way you can defeat me, no matter how desperate it may seem. I can assure you you're wrong. Please try to think of it philosophically. You had, what, a few decades left to live anyway? Eyeblinks, compared to my life span. The tragedy of your death will last as long as it takes a single tear to roll down Cythera's cheek."

"Very well," Malden said, thinking, Not quite yet. "And how shall I die? Are you going to curse me to death, or open up a crack in the earth and send me down to the pit?"

"Wasteful, and quite beneath me," Hazoth said. "I'm going to give your existence a purpose, albeit a small one. I'm going to feed you to my son." He reached up and slapped the iron egg with the flat of his palm. It rang like a bell.

And then it began to crack.

# CHAPTER EIGHTY-SEVEN

"Glorious! When it is finally born, there will be no power in this world that can stand against me," Hazoth said.

Red lines of infernal fire appeared on the surface of the iron sphere as a cascade of rust fell to the floor. The egg rocked slightly on its stand as the demon inside hammered again and again at its shell, trying to break out.

"The Ancient Blades will stop you," Malden insisted, more for his own benefit than to intimidate Hazoth. "They know how to slay demons."

"Luckily for me I have one of their number on my side," Hazoth pointed out. "Bikker will gladly slay all his old comrades, if I pay him well enough. It's important, rodent, to consider every angle of a problem. That's where you failed. You made a clever try of things, but you just didn't think them through *deeply* enough."

"And you have? This is madness," Malden said. "To release a demon on the world . . ." He thought of the beast that nearly killed him in the palace tower. Unless it was kept wet it grew at a furious rate and would never stop. "It is a creature not natural to this world," Malden said. "What will it do, once released? Will it eat every man and woman in the city? Or will it burn us all with hellfire?"

"Nothing so dramatic," Hazoth said. "Perhaps, when he is fully grown, he will have the power to do as you say. But my son is not ready to be born. When he emerges he will know nothing but pain—and there is only one way to quench that agony. He must devour the first living thing he encounters. Please, don't get any foolish notions. Cythera and I will be perfectly safe, as the demon will know his own blood. But he will swallow you whole, and that will give him strength to return to his egg and resume his gestation."

A thin shard of iron slid free from the shell and clattered to the floor. Red light shot out of the gap thus made.

"He will not rest until he has devoured you," Hazoth went on. "Night and day he will chase you. He could follow your trail for hundreds of miles, even if you do manage to escape this room. I don't think there's any reason why Cythera should have to watch you die. She seems quite taken with you. So I'll leave you to your fate."

Malden shrank back from the egg as it rattled and shook and more shards of iron fell away. "Hazoth!" he shouted. "You said that after eight hundred years, magic had corrupted the Burgrave, yes?"

The sorcerer frowned. "I suppose."

"What of the enchantments on your own self? After so many centuries, what have they done to your soul?"

Hazoth lifted his hand in the gesture that would transport him and Cythera out of the room. "An interesting question, but one that seems quite moot. You'll never learn the answer, I'm afraid."

Malden threw his arm across his eyes as light burst all around him. When it faded he was alone in the great hall.

Though not for long.

The egg continued to hatch as he watched, horrified. For a moment he couldn't move, so transfixed was he by the spectacle of the demon's birth. Then the thing inside the egg howled in utter pain, and he found his feet once more.

Many doors led away from the great hall. The obvious choice was the massive portal that opened onto the front lawn. If he could get out there he could get a head start before the demon came in pursuit.

That would, of course, only delay his doom. Besides, he had another scheme in mind.

He hurried to a door on one side wall, between two statues. It was the door that led eventually to the library, the same way he'd been taken on his first visit to the house. The door was locked but the mechanism was quite simple and perfectly ordinary. Malden hurriedly unwrapped his picks and wrenches from the hilt of his bodkin.

Behind him a clawed hand emerged from the egg and stretched raw flesh in the cold air. The demon started hauling itself out of its prison.

Hands shaking in fear, Malden stared at the rakes and hooks he held. Then he dropped them and kicked at the door until the flimsy lock shattered. When the door swung free he turned and glanced once more at the cracking egg, for a spare fraction of a moment.

What he saw made him yelp in terror.

# CHAPTER EIGHTY-EIGHT

Bikker was sweating. He wiped his brow with the back of one hand.

That was the extent of what Croy's best efforts to kill him had achieved. His tunic was cut in a number of places, but that only showed that the mail shirt he wore underneath it was unbroken. Croy's arm hadn't been strong enough to pierce the chain mail, even with the good dwarven steel of the shortsword.

"Get up," Bikker spat. "Come, now. I trained you to put up a better fight than this."

It was all Croy could do to keep his eyes open.

"Damn you, a good stiff breeze could kill you right now," Bikker insisted. His voice was not so hard as his words. "Croy, you don't have a chance. I could have cut you down a dozen times just now. Don't you want to live? Don't you want to win?"

Somehow Croy managed to find a little breath, which he used for forming words. "I've already won, Bikker. I kept my faith. I kept to my beliefs. You can slay me now, certainly. Doing so won't make you more of a man."

"And letting you live will?" Bikker snarled.

"No. There's nothing you can do to regain your honor. I understand that now. I had hoped to heal the wound on your soul. But it's too late."

Bikker growled then, or perhaps he shouted. It was an inchoate, wordless noise that came out of him as he clawed at the air with his free hand. He stamped his foot in rage. And then, little by little, he regained his composure. He came back to Croy and stood over him and looked down on him with something approaching calm.

"Draw Ghostcutter. Do me the honor of dying on your feet. Come!" Bikker seized Croy roughly under the armpits and hauled him upright. He held Croy there until the knight had his feet underneath him. He could stand, if he braced himself perfectly. But he couldn't lift his arms. The mere effort of standing took all his wind.

"This is folly," Bikker said. "You should learn from it, Croy. *Sir* Croy. You need to be woken up from your dreams of nobility and honor. Did I not teach you that even a mighty lord dies the same way as a humble villein? Apparently you weren't paying attention that day. A shame—if I kill you now you'll never learn. You'll go and sit by the Lady's side still thinking that heroes bleed a different color than the rest of us."

"I kept my faith," Croy whispered. "I lived that dream. I do not fear death."

A mischievous light crept into Bikker's eyes. "Interesting. Because it absolutely terrifies me. That's why I trained so hard, learned to be so strong. Because I knew that the only thing standing between me and the pit is my right arm and whatever iron I hold. But perhaps—perhaps there is something more to life."

"Yes."

"Perhaps," Bikker went on, "it's all true. All those pathetic slogans and vows of sacrifice you made, perhaps they mean something after all. Shall we see?"

"What do you mean?"

Bikker leaned very close until his face was only inches from Croy's. "Let's perform an experiment, like Hazoth in his laboratory. You'll be my test subject. I'll give you a simple choice and we'll see how much you believe your own fancies. Hmm?"

Croy was too tired to reply.

"I'll make you a promise. You can go free, and I won't chase you. After all, killing a weakling like you isn't going to be any fun. I'll let you live the rest of your life unmolested. All you have to do is turn around and walk away from me, without another word."

Croy frowned. This seemed unlikely.

"There is one proviso, however," Bikker said. "You must leave Ghostcutter here."

He looked very satisfied with himself for having devised this bargain. Croy's lips drew back from his teeth and he snarled.

"'My sword is my soul,'" he quoted. "You taught me that."

"Exactly," Bikker said. "So choose. Give up your soul, or forfeit your life."

He said no more.

Croy shook his head, disbelieving. Bikker was an Ancient Blade, same as himself. How could he make such an infernal demand? It was counter to everything Croy had ever believed, everything he'd ever learned. A Blade died with his sword in his hand, or only after passing it on to someone who could make better use of it in the endless war against demonkind. That was the law of their existence. The most important rule of their order.

But of course, that was the point. Croy had called Bikker a faithless coward. That oath only meant something if Croy could prove he, himself, was otherwise. If he accepted the bargain, he would make his insult meaningless. But he would live.

Croy could never accept such a fate. Except—

If he died now, he would never see Cythera again. She and her mother would remain in bondage under Hazoth's rule, forever. If he surrendered now, there would be another chance. Someday. Another possibility of rescue.

Croy made his choice. He lifted an arm that felt like a bar

of lead and placed his hand around Ghostcutter's hilt. Inch by inch he began to draw it from its scabbard.

# CHAPTER EIGHTY-NINE

The demon howled in agony, and Malden had to hang on to the door frame not to be knocked down. It was a hideous thing to look upon, but he could only imagine its pain. It—Malden could not bring himself to think of the thing as a "he"—must have experienced every instant of its new life as an eternity of suffering.

As Hazoth had said, it was not ready to be born. It had no skin on its stringy muscles and it oozed pus every time it stretched. Steam lifted from its back in great white coils, and where its feet touched the marble floor, the stone grew slick with its blood. In shape it was not unlike a horribly deformed hound, though it had seven legs—none of them the same length or shape. Sprouting from its shoulders on long thick necks were a row of human skulls with wicked fanged jaws. The eye sockets were filled with wet red membranes that throbbed and sucked at the air. Malden assumed that was how it scented, and that this was the only sense it possessed.

When it screamed, the sound issued not from the clacking jaws of the skulls but from a gaping mouth in its chest filled with round half-formed teeth.

It pawed at the floor, stumbling like a newborn foal. Every footfall made the entire house shake. Its skull heads wove through the air at the end of the clumsy necks, and its nostrils squeezed shut, then shot open again. One by one the skulls turned to point directly at Malden. How it could smell anything through the thick reek of brimstone in the air was an open question, but he had no doubt it was quite aware of him.

Malden shrank back as far as he could, yet it was as if he were transfixed, so horrified by the thing's appearance he couldn't move.

The demon took a tottering step forward, its multitude of claws clacking on the floor.

Time to run.

The paralysis of horror left him in a rush of blood to his legs. Malden slammed the door behind him, only to hear it splinter and crack as the demon rammed its way through. By that point he was well down the hall beyond, nearly at the door of the library. The demon squeezed into the hall-way and came galloping toward him, no longer so awkward or graceless. It was fast—far faster than he was—and it would be on him in a second if he didn't move. He flung himself at the door to the library and, thank the Bloodgod, it flew open.

Inside the library he leapt over a divan just as the demon smashed through the doorway, shattering the door frame with its odd number of shoulders. It reared up and swung two of its legs through the air, an instant away from crush-ing Malden beneath one foot that looked like a hoof and another like the paw of a wolf.

Malden threw his arms across his face, knowing that if the thing struck him even once, it would be his end. He rolled back and away from the beast as it came lurching for-ward—

—and then stopped in mid-attack.

Kemper, I hope you made it this far, Malden thought. He'd given the card sharp strict instructions to include the li-brary on his itinerary as he made his way around the house, but Malden also knew that if there had been any danger of being caught, Kemper might have cut his circuit short.

Yet now the demon sniffed and sucked at the air, and its skull heads craned around the room, searching something out. Malden edged away slowly, crawling backward on his hands so as not to make any noise, in case the thing had ears hidden somewhere on its body.

One of the skull heads fixated on a particular glass-fronted bookcase. It brought a second head around to sniff as well, as if making sure it had the right scent. Then it threw all of its considerable mass at the case, pulverizing the glass, sending the books flying, smashing through the thick wooden shelves. It savaged the case with its jaws and its huge wet mouth, striking again and again with its claws and hooves and talons until it battered through the wall behind the case as well.

A lone playing card, the six of acorns, floated out of the wreckage and drifted to the floor. The demon stamped on it, tore it to shreds with its teeth, and swallowed the bits of paper that remained.

By the time it was finished, Malden had already broken for the next door, and the next hallway.

# CHAPTER NINETY

Croy gritted his teeth.

For my lord the Burgrave, he thought. For honor. For the code of the Ancient Blades. For the sake of my immortal soul.

*For Cythera.*

Every fiber of his being was in agreement. He would not surrender his sword. He would not turn and walk away. If he died in the next moment, he would die as he had lived. The sacrifice was acceptable.

But he didn't intend to die.

As he drew Ghostcutter free of its scabbard, warmth flowed down his arm. His heart was giving up the last of its strength, all in the service of one final battle.

Bikker smiled, as if this was exactly what he wanted. "You'll fall quickly enough. But you'll die on your feet," he said. "Do you see what honor is, now? Honor is something that exists between men like us. Strong men! The weak of this world, the peasants, the little people—they know nothing of it."

Croy thought of Malden and Kemper affirming that there was no honor among thieves. Maybe Bikker was right.

But—no. Malden had risked everything to help Cythera. Malden had gone into Hazoth's villa, uncertain of what he could achieve, but willing to try.

"You were wrong earlier," Croy said.

"What? What are you prattling about?" Bikker demanded.

"Earlier. You said I thought my blood was a different color from yours. You were wrong."

"I think you're feverish, Croy. Your wounds would certainly warrant it. Speak clearly, man, or just be quiet and let us finish what we've started."

"I don't think I bleed a different color than you," Croy said. "Blood is the same in every man's veins. But there is something in me you can't match."

He thought back to when Bikker had trained him, to one day in particular. They'd been going through postures for hours, Croy learning every way there was to hold a sword. They'd practiced hundreds of parries, thousands of lunges. Bikker called a halt when neither of them could see for the sweat in their eyes. Then, when Croy put Ghostcutter away for the day, Bikker picked up a wooden practice sword and knocked him into a pigpen with one solid whack to the back of his knees.

"Fencing is something gentle folk do," Bikker had said. "You can train a lifetime to master it. But never forget—anyone, even a peasant, can bring you down with a single, solid blow. It only takes one cut to kill a man."

So now he faced Bikker with Ghostcutter gripped in both hands, the point aimed directly at Bikker's heart. Bikker took his own stance, with Acidtongue at an angle across the front of his body.

If he was focused and committed enough, Croy thought, he might strike one more blow before his body gave out completely. He would have to make it the one that brought Bikker down.

The two of them nodded at each other in way of salute.

And then they began.

# CHAPTER NINETY-ONE

Malden hurried down the long corridor at the back of the villa that opened on the dining room and its preparatory. The door there would provide another chance to escape into the night—but he wasn't done yet.

Behind him the prematurely born demon howled and raged and clawed at the walls. An ornamental table stood in the hallway, a delicate piece of turned rosewood. The nine of bells lay on its surface like a calling card.

With a cry of rage the demon smashed the table to flinders, then beat at the wall and floor where the table had been with an unquenchable will and a strength a hundred times greater than a man's. The card was obliterated, but still the demon smashed and clawed until the plaster wall exploded in a cloud of white dust and the wattles behind it burst like matchwood. Malden hurried down the hall, breathing heavily now. Surely it wouldn't take much longer.

Behind him he could hear the demon clawing at the walls, pulling down timbers from the ceiling. The house shook and danced, and he was nearly thrown from his feet with every step. The demon was taking the place to pieces in its search for him.

Half the house was in ruins now, torn apart by the beast

as it sought out his scent. It must be horribly confused, he thought, because it smelled him everywhere—everywhere Kemper had left one of his cards.

Cythera had told him that the demon hunted by smell alone, and that it could follow its prey's scent through any obstacle or diversion. It made him think of someone else who worked miracles with his nose—Kemper, the card sharp, whose cards were not visibly marked but who knew the stink of every one of them so well that when he dealt them, they might as well have been faceup.

With all that in mind, for the past three days Malden had carried those cards inside his tunic, through all manner of exertions. He had rubbed them on his armpits and his groin, on the sweaty back of his neck, on any part of his body that might imbue them with his smell. He had not lacked for exudation—fear made him sweat copiously.

When he gave them back to Kemper, the card sharp was most displeased. Malden had ruined them for gaming by changing the invisible markings Kemper knew so well. But for the purposes of this scheme, the card sharp had been willing to make the sacrifice. While Malden worked his way into the sanctum, Kemper had moved around the house as only an intangible man could, walking through walls and locked doors, keeping out of sight, and placing his cards here and there, one under a fine mahogany dressing table, one in a closet full of crockery and plates.

The cards served the purpose of slowing the demon down. It had to investigate each card, and its method of investigation was to destroy whatever it smelled. The time it took the demon to smash Hazoth's finest furniture was all the time Malden needed to get a head start on it and keep clear of its jaws.

Hopefully, the cards would serve another purpose.

Malden had known it would be impossible to steal the crown back without alerting Hazoth to his presence. The man was a sorcerer, after all, and this was his own house. After hundreds of years in it he must know its every nook and cranny better than Kemper knew his cards. So Malden's scheme to retake the crown had been constructed, by necessity, around the knowledge that eventually he would have to face the demon.

Malden turned in a doorway and looked down a long hall lit only by a single cresset. Halfway down the hall the demon roared as it pulverized a linen press, searching destructively for the card Kemper must have hidden at its bottom. Shreds of cloth and fibers of the best linen floated in the air as the demon beat and flailed at the walls with its mismatched legs.

Malden stepped through the door and slammed it behind him. He was no longer worried about making any noise. Especially when the house had begun to creak and moan all around him. He could hear its columns and its boards shifting on foundations that had stood for as long as there was a city around it. The wood was strained by the damage the demon did to its walls. Malden pricked up his ears as he heard a series of popping noises like thunder cracks. Nails giving way above his head, one after the other, bursting from the beams and rafters they held together.

It was time to flee, definitely. Behind him the demon raged and threw itself at the door he'd closed, desperate to get at him, needing to devour him so it could return to its egg and resume its long sleep. The wall around the door shook and split, as a wide crack opened in the plaster and went racing toward the ceiling.

Get out now, Malden thought, and raced toward a solarium at the far end of the house. A door there stood between him and the garden. It was locked, and far too sturdy to knock down with his shoulder. He cursed as he reached for his bodkin and the tools woven into its grip. He needn't have bothered, though. Before he could get his first pick free, the entire house leaned over to one side, the walls and ceiling seeming to careen right toward where he stood. The door before him, warped out of its frame, went spinning off into the night.

Behind him the demon crashed into the solarium. Its skull heads circled around in the air, its red nostrils pulsing. Malden ran through where the door had been and out into cool night air, the demon hard on his heels. It got one of its skull heads and two of its legs through the doorway before the second and third floors of the house collapsed all at once on its back.

The noise was beyond imagining, like the earth opening wide to suck the entire city down into the pit. Debris was everywhere, tumbling and arcing through the air, entire rafter beams dancing end over end across the Ladypark Common. A rolling cloud of plaster dust hit Malden like a tidal wave and he was knocked down by the shock wave. A piece of glass jagged as a knife blade cut across his forehead, and blood made red tracks through the dust that covered his face.

Choking and heaving for breath, he got back to his feet and surveyed the destruction. It looked like a storm had loosed every lightning bolt in its quiver at the house, all at once. The villa had become a chaotic hell of rubble and wreckage, with barely two boards still standing attached to one another. In the mess, a few small fires burned, while dozens of small animals, freed from their cages in the ruin, burst into flight or went howling away on long legs or only crawled or slithered out of the cataclysm.

Malden could hardly believe his eyes. This had been his plan all along, of course, but even so—the damage was immeasurable. The destruction utterly complete.

He started to dust himself off, but stopped when he saw something moving inside the debris. A massive board was heaved clear and then a snowdrift of plaster went sliding into a cavity in the heap. A pink, raw arm reached up from inside and hauled at a crossbeam that was still mostly intact. Little by little the demon pulled itself clear of the remains of the house. Its skull heads lifted clear of the wreckage and its mouth began to howl once more.

"Bloodgod take my eyes," Malden cursed.

The demon had survived.

# CHAPTER NINETY-TWO

A minute earlier, outside:
  Bikker took a step toward Croy's left, but did not advance.

Croy stood where he was. Ghostcutter's point tracked Bikker as he moved. Croy had lived with the sword so long it took no effort at all to keep it pointed at the bearded swordsman.

This would all be over in a moment.

One strike—and Acidtongue would carve Croy like a chicken. The vitriol on its blade would sear through his flesh and he would be undone.

One thrust—and Ghostcutter would drive through Bikker's shirt of chain, pierce his vitals, and leave him gasping in his own blood. Assuming Croy had enough strength left to complete the stroke.

"Are you ready?" Bikker asked.

"There is no such thing as readiness," Croy said. "One fights, and lives, or one prepares, and one dies. You taught me that."

"Do you regret it has come to this?" Bikker asked.

"Yes."

Bikker sighed. "As do I, to be honest. Shall we count to three, and then strike?"

"One," Croy said.

"Two," Bikker responded.

"Three," they said together.

Acidtongue whirled through the air, coming down hard and fast from Croy's left, his weak side. Croy tried to lean out of the way but knew he wouldn't be fast enough. Ghostcutter shifted in his hand and came upward to parry. The two blades met with an awful grinding, sizzling noise. Acid bit into Ghostcutter's silver edge and notched the iron underneath. Bikker pushed forward suddenly and Croy went sprawling, his left hand out to catch him as he fell.

Not enough, not nearly enough—Croy had wasted his one cut—it was the end—in a moment Bikker would remise, following through on the stroke Croy had parried, bringing the blow home, and—

—Ghostcutter broke free of the engagement, ringing clear of Acidtongue. The acid had made the blades slick and unlocked them. Croy turned at the waist as he fell, trying to catch himself before he fell on his back, and Ghostcutter whistled through the air in a tight arc. Croy used every bit of control he had over the weapon and brought it low and inside Bikker's guard. Busy gaining leverage for his remise, Bikker had his arms up, and that left his side unprotected.

Ghostcutter was a heavy blade. Its own momentum sliced through the chain-mail shirt over Bikker's hip and deep into the flesh beneath. It didn't stop until it had sliced halfway through Bikker's spine.

Bikker gasped and took a step backward, and Ghostcutter came free of his midsection as easily as it was pulled from its own scabbard.

"Sadu take you," Bikker shouted, and lifted Acidtongue again for another stroke. He lunged forward, but before he was halfway to Croy he stumbled and blood came vomiting out of his mouth.

Acidtongue dropped to the grass. It was dry by the time it landed—it secreted vitriol only when held by a strong arm. Bikker dropped to his knees beside it and then fell face forward into the earth.

Croy crawled toward his old teacher and rolled the man over on his back. Bikker's face was congested with blood and his eyes weren't focusing. His mouth moved but the words that came out were inaudible whispers. Croy bent his ear over Bikker's lips to hear what he said.

"When you find an heir for my sword," Bikker told him, his voice no louder than the breeze that ruffled the grass, "teach him that stroke. It's a good one."

Croy closed his friend's eyelids, and wept.

He was not given time to grieve, however.

The grass was blown back by a flash of light more bright than the sun at midday. Hazoth and Cythera were suddenly standing over him. He looked up into her eyes but didn't like what he saw there.

She might have spoken—but just then, behind Croy, the villa fell in on itself with a mammoth crash.

# CHAPTER NINETY-THREE

"Croy! Croy!" Malden called, racing around the side of the house where the debris was not so thick. He jumped onto a fallen rafter beam and leapt into a drift of plaster dust that billowed up around him like a cloud. He managed to sidestep a pile of broken glass but still came down hard on a plank of wood that shifted under him and sent him sprawling forward.

Behind him the demon's skull heads bit at the air. It was almost upon him.

"Croy! Kill it!" he screamed as he came around to the front of the house, where the rose window had fallen in a million shards of colored glass.

He took in the scene in an instant, though he liked little of it. Bikker looked dead, which was a good thing, and Croy was still holding his sword. The knight was sitting down in the grass, however, with his knees up to his chest, and he looked as pale as a sheet. Had the two fools killed each other?

Cythera and Hazoth were there, too. Both of them were staring at the pile of rubble that had been their home. They seemed too paralyzed by surprise to react.

"Demon!" Malden shouted, his feet slapping against the grass. "Croy!"

He raced up to the knight and then jumped over Croy's head. The demon was right behind him, snatching at his heels with one clawed foot.

Ghostcutter was pointed at the sky, suddenly. Croy did not rise, or call out a threat, or even shift from where he sat, but his sword pointed upward. The demon couldn't see it, having no eyes, and as the blade bit into its belly, at first it seemed not even to notice.

Then the cold iron blade pierced it through, and the point came out through the demon's back. It fell on Croy hard enough to crush any man, and scratched at the ground with every one of its mismatched legs, but it couldn't seem to get free.

Cythera shouted for Croy, but the knight was completely covered by the demon's body. If he heard her, he could make no reply.

"Malden, he was already gravely wounded—if we don't get him out of there soon he'll smother," she said, beseeching the thief.

Malden started to shrug. What could he do? His bodkin was useless against the thing. He was no Ancient Blade to fight a demon. But then—

He saw Acidtongue on the ground next to Bikker's body. Like Ghostcutter, it was made for fighting demons. Malden grabbed it and found that he could barely lift it. He'd never used a sword in his life and realized instantly that it wasn't just a matter of swinging it around like a stick.

But then drops of vitriol appeared along the blade's length like sweat. Grabbing the hilt with both hands, Malden rushed toward the demon, holding the sword straight out from his body. He jabbed it into the demon's back and leaned on the pommel until it sank deep into the demon's vitals.

The skull heads reared up and screamed at the stars as the demon redoubled its thrashing. Malden let go of the sword's hilt then and staggered back, trying to get clear of its flailing legs.

Eventually it died, and lay still. Its flesh fumed and liquefied until its bones stuck up through its raw musculature. Its claws curled and withered like paper in a fire. Soon it was no more than wisps of foul-smelling smoke and a pool of vile liquid. Underneath its remains, Croy struggled to pull Ghostcutter free of the infernal thing's rib cage.

Malden stared at the beast in utter incomprehension. He couldn't believe what he had just done. He had killed a demon. He—the puny thief, who had never even cut a human being before—had killed. Of course, it had been pinned and immobile, and— But he had killed it—

Malden started to whoop in joy. But then an invisible hand grasped his heart and began to squeeze.

"My son . . . my house," Hazoth said. "You destroyed my house."

Malden dropped to the ground, unable to move a muscle. The sorcerer leaned over him.

"I was going to allow you a quick death, rodent," the sorcerer said. "No more."

# CHAPTER NINETY-FOUR

Malden rolled on the ground, his body coming to pieces from the inside out. Pain gripped him like iron tongs as Hazoth twisted one hand in the air, and his guts tied themselves in knots. He could barely see anything—his vision had turned the bright red of arterial blood.

Then it cleared, just enough for him to look up into Hazoth's face. "I want you to see me while you suffer," the sorcerer told him. "I want you to feel everything. The pain I'm about to inflict on you would normally drive a rodent unconscious. It might even kill one outright. Your primitive brain would rather die than live through this agony. But I won't let it. You are going to suffer for what you've done to me. And I know more than anyone about what suffering means."

Malden gasped for breath, but every ounce of air he inhaled felt like he was swallowing knives. His arms curled around his chest, constricted by pain, but still he could see the magician staring down into his eyes.

So he could see it very clearly when a red blotch appeared on Hazoth's cheek and burst through the skin as an ugly boil.

It was such a surprise he almost forgot the pain. Almost.

"Your spells are . . . slipping," he wheezed.

"You know nothing of magic. Save your breath for the screams you are about to utter," Hazoth told him.

Yet even as the wizard spoke, pimples erupted near his hairline. Hazoth reached up to feel the bumpy skin there and something miraculous happened.

The expression on his face changed. He started to show real fear. He even cried out as one of his eyes grew thick with cataracts.

On the ground, Malden wanted to laugh. He wanted to crow for joy. The pain he'd felt disappeared as Hazoth reared back and clutched at his ear, which had begun to drip blood. "What is this?" Hazoth demanded. He turned to stare at Cythera.

"The link between us is fading, Father," she said. The vines and flowers on her face writhed and bloomed wildly. "He did it. The thief did it—Coruth must be free. When the house came down it must have broken your magic circle. She has undone the connection she once made between you and I." Cythera looked like she could hardly believe it herself. As if she didn't dare believe what was happening.

But it was real. The curses Hazoth had avoided so long, the inimical magics cast on him by the demons of the pit in revenge for all he'd done to them, were getting through. Instead of being deposited on Cythera's skin as painted flowers, they were appearing on his own skin as blossoms of blood and corruption.

"Damn that woman," Hazoth said, his voice thick with phlegm. He shook himself and spoke a few words in some ancient language. Instantly, the sores on his face stopped weeping and closed again, until his countenance was as unblemished as before. "She's weak, though. Too weak to resist. I'll find her and prison her again."

"No, I don't think you will," Cythera said.

Then she grabbed him by the arms and mashed her lips against his cheek in a brutal kiss. "Farewell, Father."

Hazoth's eyes went wide. Green sparks lit up his hair and his chest.

On Cythera's left hand an oleander flower curled up and withered. A vine retracted around her wrist, shrinking back on itself.

"Malden," Cythera said, quite calmly, "you should go now."

The thief scrambled to his feet and ran. Behind him he heard Hazoth start to scream as the skin of his back split open and demonic arms reached out to grasp at him with shredding claws.

Every curse Cythera had stored on her skin for decades came loose at once, and they lashed out at Hazoth with interest. As the magician's protective spells came apart, the demons he had exploited and enslaved sensed the release down in the pit, and sought every crack and crevice in the universe through which they could reach his side, intent on having their vengeance before the curses could undo Hazoth entirely. The people who lived on Ladypark Common closed their shutters and hid under their beds, but could not escape for the next three hours the screams of a dying sorcerer and the bellowing rage of the Bloodgod's children, denied this prize for so long. They took their time destroying Hazoth. They savored it.

# CHAPTER NINETY-FIVE

Witchly light filled the sky over the common, and the gruesome sounds of Hazoth's demise made the air shiver. Malden did not look back over his shoulder, as much as he might have enjoyed watching Hazoth meet his sticky end. He had places to go yet tonight, things to achieve, or all could still be lost.

He could see his path easily in the weird illumination as he broke for the streets beyond the common, intending to lose himself in that maze and make good his escape.

He was not to be so lucky.

Ahead of him on the Cripplegate Road, a score of men in cloaks-of-eyes were waiting with weapons in hand. They moved quickly to cut off any avenue of escape, circling around him should he even think to return to the ruined villa. When Malden was completely surrounded, one of them came forward and held out an empty hand. "Give it over, thief," he said.

"I beg your pardon?" Malden tried.

"We know you've got a dagger at your belt. Give it over or I'll run you through and take it from you."

Malden stared at the man with pure hatred. But there was nothing he could do. He drew the bodkin from his belt and handed it over. "I'll want that back, now."

With a chuckle, the watchman tossed the knife over the wall of the Ladypark.

Malden's heart sank. The message was clear. He wasn't going to need the knife anymore. He would not be given another chance to use it.

The rank of watchmen parted and someone came through the gap. Anselm Vry—with an expression of annoyance on his face.

"You really couldn't do it with less fuss?" he asked.

Malden blinked in feigned incomprehension. "Do what,

children of the Ashes. Tipped off by Malden, they arrived early and made quick work of sorting through the wreckage. They carried away books and tapestries and valuable pieces of unbroken glass. They carried off magic wands and shards of rusted iron that someone would buy. They took the bits of gold they found, some melted in the fires, some still in the shape of broken jewelry and dented goblets. Malden had told Croy that a rousing story of bravery would not change the children's lives, and the knight thought the thief was just being apathetic, that he did not care for their welfare. He saw now that Malden had arranged for this—he must have given the children notice of what was to come. The quality of life the children enjoyed would be enlarged tenfold overnight, and Croy was glad. One of the children, a little girl in a dress made of an old sack, came over and stared at him for a while. He smiled at her, and she pressed a tiny treasure into his hand. A single glass bead, blue in color, quite valueless, but pretty. He thanked her with all the courtly politesse he could muster before she shrugged and ran away.

Nearer to dawn the dwarf Slag arrived with a team of four horses and a massive wagon. He stared out into the darkness with alert eyes while a crew of human workers made their way through the wreckage with pry bars and block and tackle. It was not easy, but they were able to shift the half of the demon's egg that remained unshattered. Rolling it on its side, they managed to get it into the wagon, and Slag hauled it away before anyone could see. What he wanted with several tons worth of pit-forged iron Croy could not imagine, but he was certain the dwarf would make good use of it.

Others came, people Croy did not know. The news must have spread quickly that Hazoth had fallen and his treasures were up for grabs. Footpads, rogues, and bravos combed through the wreckage and took away what they desired— loot and weaponry, mostly. A papermaker and his apprentices came and carried off great sheaves of scorched and torn paper and cloth, which they would pulp down for raw materials. Half of the chandler's guild came and took all

milord? I was only walking on the common, something I often do at night. I find it calms my mind. I'm not sure what's going on over there," he said, pointing at the green fire dancing on the other side of the common, "but I think you should definitely go investigate."

Vry sneered at him. "What's that on your belt, then?" he asked.

Malden patted his belt as if he couldn't guess what the bailiff meant. Then he said, "Oh!" and unbuckled his belt to remove it. "You mean this." The belt had been threaded through the golden crown he'd hidden under his cloak. He handed it over to Vry, who snatched it away from him.

The bailiff closed his eyes and held the crown up in both hands. His eyes snapped open for a moment and he stared at Malden, but then looked away and nodded. "Yes, of course, milord," he said, as if talking to the crown, not to Malden. "You," he said, to one of his watchmen. "The bag." A velvet sack was brought forth and the crown placed carefully inside. "Very good, thief," Vry said.

Malden bowed low. "So, may I inquire if there is a reward? I prefer it in gold, but will take silver if I must."

"I'll count it out in steel," Vry said with a short, nasty laugh. "You—kill him. Then form a detail and carry his body to the Skrait. Make sure you weigh it down so no one ever finds it."

A watchman with a halberd came lunging forward, but Malden had expected this and was already moving. He scurried up the wall of the Ladypark and dropped into a stand of bushes on the far side. There, he lay still and held his breath.

A half dozen faces appeared over the top of the wall, including Vry's. They peered into the darkness for a long minute before withdrawing.

"It makes no difference. Let panthers and wolves fight over him now," Vry said. "If he lives through the night, we'll just find him in the morning."

And with that they left.

Malden stayed still for a while longer, and then, when he was sure no one was watching, he got up and started looking for his bodkin.

# CHAPTER NINETY-SIX

"Lay easy," Cythera said. She held Croy's hand tight. His other hand still clutched the hilt of Ghostcutter. He looked at the blade and saw a bad notch in its silver edge, a wound it had taken when it blocked Acidtongue's attack. He wondered if a dwarf could repair that damage, or if he should leave it there forever, in memory of Bikker.

"It's over," Cythera said again. "Hazoth is dead."

"Hazoth?" Croy said, confused. "No, it's Bikker, that's— that's Bikker there. I killed him. It had to be done. In the end I think maybe I was getting through to him, but—but it had to be done." He struggled to sit up, and she pushed him back to the grass. He could not resist her hands.

Her hands! She had touched him, and not been very gentle about it. But that could only mean one thing. He looked to her with wild eyes. Her face was . . . was unpainted. The curses that had ornamented her skin were gone. All of them.

She was even more beautiful than he remembered. Her skin was clear and fair, her eyes dark pools of calm and wisdom. Her slender arms were unadorned by so much as a painted leaf.

She was free.

"Over there," she said, and pointed at a pillar of what looked like charred wood standing in the grass a dozen feet away. As Croy watched, it collapsed in on itself, like a log burned down to charcoal and ashes. "That's all that's left of my father."

"What of your mother?" Croy asked.

"I am here as well, but in far better condition." Coruth was suddenly standing at Croy's feet, looking down on him.

She was exactly the way he remembered her. Wild and unkempt hair the color of new-forged iron. A nose as thin and sharp as a halberd blade, and eyes that saw everything. She wore no pleasant countenance, but for that she could

hardly be blamed. She'd spent the last ten years impr[...] in a magic circle. Of late she'd been a tree. Now she[...] a simple black robe and had one arm in a makeshift[...] but he knew that if the kings and queens of the world[...] see her, they would bow their heads in respect. There[...] an aura around Coruth that anyone could sense, an au[...] power.

"I will heal your body," she said. "That shall be y[...] reward. For the thief, perhaps, there will be someth[...] more."

"I thank you," Croy said.

Coruth looked away and nodded. Then she turned herse[...] into a flock of blackbirds and flew away, chattering to her self with many voices.

"She'll be back for you, don't worry," Cythera told the knight. "And I'll stay until she returns."

He reached out his left hand and she took it again.

Together they sat and watched the ruined house. Its fallen timbers smoldered and settled through the night, with occasional rumblings and groans, and now and then a loud report as a broken rafter collapsed or another piece of glass snapped under pressure. The wreckage was full of sharp barbs and unstable piles of masonry, leavened with heaps of broken glass that would shred any foot that tried to walk through them. Occasionally a bolt of green or red or blue discharged as some arcane energy was loosed from long confinement.

The ruin did not look safe at all, but that didn't mean it was left undisturbed.

The first figure to crawl over the pile was that of Kemper. The intangible man cackled and clanked as he picked through the fallen house. His tunic was stuffed full of silver: knives, spoons, plates and dishes, actual coins, buckles, fittings and ornaments. The house had been a treasure trove of the stuff, and he was given the right to first pickings. When he finally left, barely able to walk for all the silver he'd stuffed into his clothes or carried in his straining arms, he was carrying a fortune.

The next visitors to the fallen house were the beggar

the broken glass away, and sawyers took those beams and wattles that had not already been ground to sawdust in the collapse. Just before dawn gleaners from the Stink came and carted away that which no one else deemed valuable.

It seemed impossible that anything would remain, yet one last looter did come. Gurrh the ogre, who had been sitting on the grass outside the gates the whole time, rose at dawn and made his way into the ruin. He picked through the debris until he found a leaden coffer, still sealed and barely dented. He tucked it under his armpit and then headed west, toward Swampwall and his home.

All according to plan.

As the sun came up, Cythera and Croy greeted it together, alone again. "It's Ladymas," Croy said, and Cythera kissed his cheek. "We prevailed," he said, because he couldn't quite believe it. "We won."

Meanwhile, inside the Ladypark a wolf snarled and snapped at the air. Behind it a dozen more circled, waiting their turn to attack. Malden held his hands out toward the beast, trying to calm it. He wished it didn't look so hungry. He wished he'd kept Acidtongue as a prize, so he wouldn't have to rely on his laughable bodkin. He wished so many people didn't want him dead. He wished he knew better how to fight.

He wished he could go home and go to sleep.

Instead it looked like his short career as a thief was going to end with him being devoured by a pack of wolves. All this for nothing, he thought.

The wolf took a step forward, its paw patting at the ground as if it were afraid of something, afraid to lunge. A hundred birds cawed and squawked behind Malden then, and he nearly jumped out of his own skin.

Then an old woman in a dark robe stepped around him. She held one hand down low where the wolf could sniff at it. The animal licked her palm, then laid down in the grass and rested its head.

"I think I know you," Malden said to his rescuer. "I've seen you before."

"Yes," the woman agreed.

"Of course, at the time your complexion was more . . . barky." He put his bodkin away. "You're free, then. It worked."

"Yes."

"So . . . it's over," Malden said, because he devoutly wished that could be true.

"No," she said.

"No," he repeated. "No, I don't suppose it is. Not quite yet."

# CHAPTER NINETY-SEVEN

Market Square was thick with crowds, people of every station and profession crammed together into the wide cobblestoned space, with cheers and prayers going up from every lip, with banners unfurled from every high place and gold or brass or tin cornucopias pinned to every hat and tunic. Since dawn the priests of the Lady had been out ministering to the faithful, leading long liturgical plainsongs and invoking the Lady's blessings on the people, the city, and the king. They had to pick their way with care through streets so crammed with people there was no room to move freely. The citizens of Ness and all the pilgrims who had come for this holiest of days were all abroad, moving back and forth across the city as best they could, paying visits to each other or simply walking, taking in the fine weather while they uttered their prayers and thanks. In a riot of color and noise they praised the Lady.

It was the kind of crowd that could move mountains if it chose. It was the kind of crowd that could, with the slightest push, be inspired to riot. To tear up the city in its excitement.

A little wrath, a little shocked surprise, and the whole Free City of Ness could erupt like a burst dam.

The throng gathered thickest and most fervent directly outside the Ladychapel, the great spired and vaulted church where the day's grand procession would begin. The massive wooden doors were still closed, but men of the watch had to form a double cordon outside to keep the faithful from rushing in and seeing the icons before their proper time. With quarterstaffs and ropes they pushed the crowds back again and again. A few young devotees tried to climb up the heavily carved exterior of the chapel but were knocked down with long poles.

One climber, however, had the brilliant idea to ascend the back of the chapel, where the guards weren't watching. Of course, he was not one of the faithful overcome by religious zeal. He didn't want to fall prostrate before the Lady's altar, nor did he wish to break in and steal the cakes and sweetmeats loaded in the giant golden cornucopia inside either.

Malden clutched at a gargoyle and hoisted himself up to one of the clerestory windows high on the side of the church. The window had been cranked open to let in some air—this close to midsummer, it was already hot just two hours past dawn—so he slipped inside and hid himself in the holy images mounted around the chapel dome.

The acoustics of that place were such, and his senses so sharpened by nervous dread, that he could see and hear everything that took place in the nave below. A red velvet carpet had been unrolled from the altar all the way to the massive doors. Anselm Vry was down there, dressed in a cloak of state. It had the repeating eye motif of a watchman's cloak, but was brocaded with silver wire. It looked very heavy. The Burgrave was there as well in full regalia, though his head was bare. They stood surrounded by a clutch of green-robed priests who prayed and wafted holy smoke around the Burgrave, while young acolytes went about lighting hundreds of candles and dozens of censers until the icons shone like the sun.

"I said, leave us!" Vry shouted.

"Milord bailiff," one of the priests insisted, "this is a holy precinct, and your authority here is—"

Vry established that authority by drawing a long dagger and pointing it at the priest's face. "The Burgrave is not well. I must administer his physic before the procession begins, and I will not have you watch me do so," he said.

The priest had turned deathly pale when the knife came out. Now he nodded and gestured at his fellows and the acolytes. They streamed out of the nave quickly enough.

When Vry and the Burgrave were alone, the bailiff sheathed his dagger and then turned to look at the Burgrave with disdain. Ommen Tarness was weeping softly, a horrible sound well-amplified by the dome of the chapel. Up on his perch, Malden peered down with unsympathetic interest.

"I don't want to wear it," Ommen said, his voice thick with snot. "I won't! I'm free, finally free. Anselm, I feel . . . smarter today. I feel like—like I'm waking up from a very long nap, and I'm still groggy, but I feel—"

Vry slapped the Burgrave hard across the face. Then he drew the crown from inside his silver cloak-of-eyes. "We discussed this. You will put on the crown. You will go out there and make your speech. I have an archer standing ready to cut you down if you start to babble. When you're done speaking the words I gave you, I will emerge and announce that you have been ill and are no longer fit to serve as Burgrave. Then I will take you away from all this, and you'll never have to wear the crown again."

"You . . . promise?" the Burgrave asked. He sounded like a naive child being promised a candy if he was good during a court ceremony. "Never again?"

"Just this one last time. And anyway, this isn't the crown you're afraid of. This one doesn't talk." He lowered it over Ommen's head, and the Burgrave bit his lip and mewled but didn't stop him.

Ommen squeezed his eyes tight as the crown made contact with his scalp. After a moment, though, he opened his eyes wide in surprise. "You're right! It's lost its power. I'm still—still me!"

Vry smiled without humor. His expression changed drastically, however, when the crown lifted off Ommen Tarness's head and started to float away.

Up in the dome, Malden reeled in his line. He held the hat-fishing pole that Slag had made, the one the dwarf meant to be used under the arch of the Royal Ditch. The line strained under the weight of the crown, but Malden brought it up quickly and soon held the crown in his hand. Or rather, the false crown. Slag had made it as well, out of lead coated in gilding metal. It looked very much like the real crown, and had been polished until it shone like gold, but under close scrutiny the cheapness of its manufacture was obvious. Malden had carried it with him throughout his sojourn into Hazoth's villa. He had known that Vry would show up at the last minute and seize the crown, so he made sure he had something to give the bailiff.

"You! Up there! Thief!" Anselm Vry shouted, peering up into the dome. "That's a funny jape you've made. Now give the damned thing back."

"Or what, Anselm? You'll have me killed?" Malden spoke at a normal conversational tone, but the dome amplified his voice until he was sure Vry could hear him. "If I give it back, will you let me live?"

"Give it back! Give it back! I like this one, it's not as heavy," Ommen cried.

Vry silenced him with another slap. "Thief, let's be reasonable. We both know I can't let you live. I can kill you now, though, quickly and almost painlessly. We can spare you the agony of torture and the embarrassment of being drawn and quartered in public. Surely you'd rather avoid that."

Malden laughed. "Perhaps you'd be willing to fight for it. Of course, that's not your style. All your men are outside. You even sent the priests away. You'd have to face me alone."

"That's not going to happen. I am curious to know, however, what you thought you could achieve here."

"I'm going to save my life, and Cutbill's as well."

"So you think you can escape," Vry said. "I suppose

it's possible. You could flee across the rooftops, while my men would have to push through the crowds to give chase. I'll grant you might make it as far as the city's walls. What would you do then? You're no landowner. Once outside the gates, you would become a simple villein. A peasant. Little more than a slave. You would save your life but lose your freedom. I know your type, thief. You don't want to spend the rest of your days laboring on a farm."

"Hardly. All right, Vry. I'll make you a deal. I think you'll find it a bargain." Malden swung the crown back out on the end of its line and started to lower it again. "I only wish to assuage my curiosity. Answer a few questions truthfully, and we'll end this."

Vry looked around him, as if to make sure no priests were hiding in the corners of the chapel, listening. "Very well."

Malden unreeled a bit of line. The crown descended a dozen feet, then stopped with a jerk. He must be careful, he thought, not to let the line snap. "You were Bikker's employer, weren't you? The theft of the crown was your idea from the beginning."

Vry's face clouded with rage. "I'll admit nothing under this duress, you—"

He stopped talking when Malden started reeling the line in again.

"Yes," Vry said, balling his fists in anger. "Yes, it was me."

Malden paid out a dozen more feet of line. "But not you alone. You formed a conspiracy of three to make this happen. I'm impressed, honestly. The chance of such a plot working out is inversely proportionate to how many people know of its existence. You did all this—you may still bring a city to its knees!—with only three people. You promised Hazoth safety for his services. You hired Bikker because as an Ancient Blade he was likely to notice there were more demons about than usual, and he might feel the need to stop you and Hazoth. When Croy returned to town you must have been very worried."

"Sir Croy? Indeed. The Ancient Blades don't have any

more demons to fight, so they wander the land righting wrongs and helping people." Vry sneered at the thought. "They're always poking their noses in where they don't belong, and since Croy technically outranks me in the peerage, I had to find a way to neutralize him. Juring always had a soft spot for that fool. It took real cunning on my part to have him banished—and then to force the Burgrave's hand on his return, to enforce the penalty of execution."

"And when that didn't work out—when Croy got away— you came up with another scheme. You played him like a fish on a line, pretending to do everything in your power to find the crown. But Croy is a simple man and he doesn't suspect treachery until it's proven to him. I myself was nearly fooled by your performance in Cutbill's lair. It seemed you really *wanted* to find the crown. Even when you sent your men to Hazoth's home and had them search the place—even when they left empty-handed, we both thought you were just an overly officious bureaucrat. That you were hampered by rules and laws, and thus ineffectual. You've played this game well. I wasn't entirely sure until I handed you the false crown last night. You acted as if it was talking to you— though we both know it was false. That was when I became certain. You didn't want the crown back. Even while you made a good show of looking for it, in fact you were making sure nobody could get to it."

"Very clever of you. Yes," Vry admitted. "You have the gist of it."

"I am still not certain why you did it, though," Malden said. He lowered the crown farther. "What benefit will come to you? When Ommen walks out there and makes a fool of himself before the entire city—the repercussions will be dire. The people will realize they're being ruled by a fool, and they won't stand for it. They'll riot in the streets— especially when you spur them on."

"No one likes being hoodwinked," Vry said when Malden paused. "The people of Ness have so much freedom, they love to gripe and grumble about the slightest stricture. If I show them their master is a half-wit, they'll refuse to obey even his just laws. And when the violence does not stop, when the gutters run red with blood, the king will know that the Burgrave is incapable of running the city. He will surely revoke the city's charter. Every man in Ness will lose his freedom."

Malden shrugged. "Every man who does not own property," he said, and let out more line. "Such as yourself." The crown was barely six feet above the head of the Burgrave now. "But the free men of Ness are its heart's blood. Their labor creates wealth. That was Juring Tarness's brilliant idea—and it worked. It worked for eight hundred years. Free men will work to make something of themselves. What do you stand to gain when they are enslaved?"

"Power, obviously." Anselm Vry reached up his hands to snatch at the crown. Malden jerked it away from him. Sighing deeply, Vry said, "You don't understand anything. When the charter is revoked, this city will be plunged into chaos. The only force for law and order inside the walls will be me, and my men of the watch. It will be up to us to keep the city from erupting into mutiny. And when we do—when we suppress revolt, and reestablish the king's rule here—how grateful do you think he'll be? He will need someone to rule the city then. Obviously, he will choose me."

"Thousands may die," Malden said. "Shops will shut down, entire guilds will go out of business. The city you inherit will be half dead."

"But it will be mine. To rule as I see fit—by fire and iron. No longer will I be constrained by the laws of the charter. No longer need I answer to the moothall and the guildmasters who control it. It will all be mine, and mine alone. The first year will be hard. There will be little money coming in and people will starve, yes. The second year they will pay me any price I ask for bread. They will accept much higher rates of taxation, in exchange for their lives. It's a long game I'm playing. But in the end I am guaranteed to win."

"I can see the appeal," Malden said. "And I salute you."

"Oh?"

"You're far more crooked than any thief I know. You have my respect. Very well. Here's what you wanted." With a flick of his wrist, Malden sent the crown dancing through the air to come to rest on Ommen's head. He cut the line that held it and collapsed his pole. "I wish you much joy of it."

And then he laughed.

"Watchmen! Priests! Get in here now," Vry shouted. Doors around the nave flew open and the summoned ones came flooding in.

Ommen Tarness straightened up, his posture improving instantly. "Hold," he said, and everyone froze. There was something in his voice that commanded attention—and imposed his will on every listener. "I have heard enough," he said.

Or rather, Juring Tarness said it.

# CHAPTER NINETY-EIGHT

Earlier—just at dawn—Gurrh the ogre had brought the leaden coffer to Swampwall, his home for so many years. He laid it down in the soft soil and then started bashing at it with his massive, hairy fists.

Eventually it came open. The true crown was inside, just as expected.

Malden had been there to see it emerge. Coruth the witch flew him through the air so he would not be late. He thanked Gurrh, who bowed deeply and then returned to his pipe. Then Malden approached the crown, his hands shaking it a little. He lifted it carefully and heard its voice begin to command him. Before he could be overcome, before it could make him put it on his own head, he shoved it into a burlap sack and slung it over his shoulder. Still, it continued to speak to him, made imprecations and promises and outright threats—until Malden explained to it what he had planned. Then at last, thankfully, the crown became quiet.

Later, when Malden drew the false crown to the dome of the chapel with Slag's fishing pole, it was a simple matter to switch it with the true crown—the crown he had lowered once more onto Ommen's head.

The transformation in the Burgrave was instantaneous. Juring Tarness resumed his control of his imbecilic descendant, and heard everything that was said within the chapel.

"You would depose me, Anselm?" Juring asked then. He looked down at the bailiff. Standing straight, he was many inches taller than his servant. "You would go to such lengths to take what is mine?"

"Milord," Vry said, bowing low. "This was a tale, only, a fabrication spun to appease the thief when—"

"No more lies," the Burgrave shouted. The priests and watchmen around him all drew back. Juring drew a jeweled dagger from his belt. It was one of his symbols of office, mostly for ornament's sake. The blade was kept sharp, though, to represent the keen insight the Burgrave brought to his office. "Kneel," he said.

Vry turned to face his watchmen. "The Burgrave is ensorcelled!" he cried. "Seize him—we must perform an exorcism at once. You, high priest, fetch the appropriate vestments and the holy thurible and—"

"I said, kneel," the Burgrave said again. Neither watchmen nor priests moved from where they stood.

Vry tried to run. The Burgrave grabbed the back of his cloak and pushed him to the ground. Then he grabbed the bailiff's hair and pulled his head back. "No more lies," he said again. Then he pried the man's jaw open and cut out his tongue.

Anselm Vry gasped and choked on his own blood. The noises he made were horrible. Even Malden flinched.

"Now," Juring Tarness said when it was done, "someone bring me a rag. I don't want this traitor's blood on my hands when I lead the joyous procession of Ladymas. You, watchman—take this fool away. Lock him in my dungeon. We'll give him a trial and see how well he speaks in his defense now. Then we'll find some way to execute him more horrible than any we've tried before. Maybe we'll force him to eat his own entrails. To swallow his own excrement, as it were."

The captain of the watchmen did as he was told, with a bow, a salute, and no words at all. The priests cleaned the Burgrave's hands and wiped off his dagger. While it was done, the Burgrave looked up into the dome.

"As for you, thief. Go and tell your master Cutbill that I would speak with him. Eventually. I have a long day ahead of me."

Malden supposed that it was too much to expect thanks. He climbed back out the window in the dome and hurried away across the rooftops of the Spires.

# CHAPTER NINETY-NINE

Coruth, her own arm fully healed now, muttered to herself as she mixed herbs together in a stone mortar, then ground them together with a copper pestle. She sang a little song as she painted the resulting foul concoction across Croy's broken ribs and the acid wounds on his arms. Whenever he tried to speak, she shushed him severely. Throughout it all, Cythera sat by his side, smiling, her face unbesmirched by sorcery. Her eyes glittered with mischief to see him almost naked in the bed, only his nethers hidden by a cloth.

If you had to lie abed for weeks and heal what should have been mortal injuries, Malden supposed you could pick few finer places to do it. Croy had been moved just across the Ladypark Common to the house of his friend, the rich

merchant. There was no secrecy about the move, and had
the Burgrave wished to seize Croy (for violating the terms
of his banishment, if nothing else), little resistance would
have been offered. Yet in the six days since Ladymas, no
one showed up at the door with a writ of arrest.

It was possible that the Burgrave was only afraid this
would displease Coruth. With Hazoth gone, the witch was
now the most powerful user of magic in the Free City. Already old clients and new were showing up daily to ask if
they might consult with her, but she refused all comers. She
had much to do, she said, and once Croy was healed, there
would be quite a reckoning of accounts. More than one powerful personage in the city had begun making discreet in-
quiries, looking to hire any magicians capable of deflecting
curses.

When the witch finished her ministrations for the day,
she went to the window and flew off as a flock of blackbirds
again. No one knew where she went, and there was no way
to follow her. Even Cythera could only shrug when asked.
"Perhaps she goes to fetch medicinal herbs. Or maybe to spy
on the city, and learn how it has changed in her absence. She
has never kept counsel with me, even before Hazoth imprisoned her."

"Milady," Malden said, "you'll forgive me if I say you
have a strange family."

Cythera smiled knowingly. "We can't all come from
noble lineages full of great heroes and comely ladies," she
said, glancing at Croy.

The knight was too busy to notice what she said. He
was scrawling something on a parchment with a quill pen.
"Here, Malden. Your prize. As promised."

The thief took the paper he offered and studied it. When
Croy had first come to him, looking for his help in freeing Cythera and Coruth, Malden's first instinct had been to
sweat the knight for gold. Then it occurred to him that Croy
had something else in his possession, something of infinitely
more use to him. The scrap of paper in his hand was what
he had asked for in lieu of money. It was a grant of land, in
the amount of one eighth part of an acre, in the northern

part of the kingdom near the fortress of Helstrow. A very small piece of Croy's ancestral lands. It named Malden as its new owner.

"Is it a pleasant spot?" Malden asked now.

"A rocky field, completely useless for cultivation. It overlooks a dismal bog, and in the summer it is swarmed with flies. May you find much happiness there."

Malden laughed out loud, long and heartily. "Maybe I'll never see it. It matters not. Croy, for this—for everything. I thank you."

Cythera looked confused. "What would a thief want with a desolate patch of ground, not even large enough to put a house on?"

"Freedom," Malden said. "With this parchment, I am a man of property. It makes me a landowner—with the full rights thereunto pertaining. I can go anywhere now. I can leave the city walls and not be enslaved. Here in Ness I can go to the moothall whenever I choose, and stand before the masters of all the guilds, and demand my right to speak. I could even go to Helstrow and request an audience with the king."

"Do you want to do any of those things?"

"No!" Malden laughed. "None of them. But the power to do them—the right to do them—means I am no more a prisoner in the place where I was born. It means I'm free! I imagine you can appreciate that."

"Oh, yes," Cythera said, her eyes far away.

Malden kissed the paper. "My heart's desire. One of them, anyway."

Cythera favored him with a warning smile. Then she looked down at Croy's scarred leg. "You should rest," she told the knight. "Mother says if you don't sleep twice as much as normal, the treatments will be inefficacious."

"You are my lady, and I obey your command," the knight said. He closed his eyes and in moments began to snore.

Malden shook his head. "Like an infant, he sleeps."

"He believes that he has done a man's work," Cythera whispered. "He sleeps like the just. Come with me, Malden. I wish to speak with you."

The two of them headed out onto the room's balcony. It looked out over the remains of Hazoth's villa. There wasn't much left but a pile of ashes and a few scraps of useless lumber—the people of Ness had taken away everything of value, and their definition of value was quite broad.

"Tell me," Cythera said when they were alone, "what reward has Kemper claimed?"

"I had Slag make him a new deck of cards," Malden said.

She frowned. "But with his curse—the only way he could even hold the old deck was because it was so immured with his own essence. He had possessed those cards so long they had become parcel with his being."

Malden nodded. "Aye. So the new deck had to be special. They're made out of pure silver, beaten thin and etched with vitriol for the pips. They're probably worth more than most of the stakes he plays for, but he can hold them easily, and even slip them up his sleeves or down his tunic."

Cythera smiled. "And Gurrh, the ogre? What price did he charge you?"

"None at all. He wished only to serve the Burgrave. If every man had the nobility of that ogre in his heart, we would all live in Croy's world."

Cythera leaned out over the balcony. "Then it seems we all have been repaid for our trouble, and each of us came out of this nightmare better than when we began, and all unscathed."

"All but one," Malden said, his brow furrowing. "I did something, Cythera, that I am not proud of. I took away a man's freedom. It's the greatest sin I know."

"You mean Ommen Tarness?" she asked. "He was a simpleton. And anyway—you saved his life. Had he appeared before the procession in his natural state, Vry would have had him killed afterward."

"I know," Malden said. That wasn't the point, though. In the last moments before the crown was returned, Ommen had said something that struck Malden to the core. He was getting smarter, he claimed. The imbecility was wearing off. He had not been born mindless—only the crown stole his wits, and without it he was becoming himself again.

And he had stopped that process before it could properly begin.

But that was his burden to bear. He decided not to share it with Cythera.

After all, there was one other thing to discuss.

"Come away with me," he said without warning.

She turned around very fast as he put an arm around her waist. He leaned forward and kissed her. Hard.

"I don't have to stay here anymore," he said. "I can travel the world. Come with me, and be my wife."

Cythera glanced into the room, toward where Croy lay in bed.

"Forget him. You broke off your betrothal already."

"Not in so many words."

Malden grimaced. "I was the one who freed your mother. Not him."

"And you think that means I must marry you now?" she asked. "That's how the stories end, isn't it? The hero slays the dragon, and the damsel throws herself into his embrace. Who lives in old stories now, Malden? Isn't that something you always despised about Croy? This is the real world."

"And here, now, I love you," he told her.

She closed her eyes and breathed deeply, and for a moment he thought she would say it in return. Then she leaned her head against his chest. "Malden, you're a thief. A man of property now, but still—a thief. You must understand—you have to understand—that people in the real world do what they must to survive. To make their lives better."

"And that means you will stay with him," Malden said.

"You have a strip of land unfit for human habitation. He has a castle. Servants and retainers. A title. My children will have all those things, too. Do you understand why that matters? Look at my life. Look what my parents gave me. Can you accept that I would do anything not to pass on that inheritance?"

Malden let her go. He strode to the far end of the balcony and looked uphill, toward the palace. All around him the city lay in its unalterable tiers, with the poorest people at the bottom and the rich up top. So it would ever be.

She started to go back inside, to the sickroom. He stopped her by calling her name.

"Do you love him?" he asked.

"What a silly question," she said, and then went inside.

# CHAPTER ONE HUNDRED

Cutbill made a single notation in his ledger, then crossed out two lines. "There," he said. "You are now a journeyman in the guild, with all rights and privileges of that rank." He glanced over the edge of his book at Malden. "There is, of course, the question of the money you owe Slag. And I expect you to start earning right away, to keep my good favor."

And that was it. No thanks, no reward. Fair enough, Malden thought. He'd expected nothing more from Cutbill. He had caused a great deal of trouble for the man, but now he'd repaired the damage. They were even.

And he was in the guild. Croy's deed had made him a man of property, and now he was a man of profession. He could start earning money for himself, having ransomed his place in Cutbill's organization. He was beholden to no one, his own master. He was truly free.

"You may go," Cutbill said. Then he held up one hand, rescinding that. He looked to one corner of the room, where a tapestry was shimmying as if blown by a wind Malden did not feel. "Wait. Use that door, over there."

Malden looked at the indicated door and frowned a question, but Cutbill offered no explanation. Malden stepped through the door and closed it behind him. Beyond lay the spy room, where one could observe what happened inside Cutbill's office without being seen.

Malden bent his eye to the spy hole and watched as a tall man wrapped in a plain brown cloak walked over to Cutbill's desk. The newcomer sat down behind the desk as if he owned the place, then pulled back his hood.

It was the Burgrave. He wore his golden crown and his eyes were very sharp. What was he doing there, unaccompanied?

"Milord," Cutbill said.

The Burgrave was silent for a while. Then he said, "It seems I am once again in your debt. I don't like owing you things, thief."

"Then allow me to say that the debt is all mine," Cutbill responded. "You permit me to exist, and to carry out my operations. If those operations are occasionally to your benefit, I consider it my honor to serve so great a man."

"Honeyed words never sound right in your mouth." The Burgrave got up from the desk and stormed around the room. "I never doubted Anselm Vry. I always thought he was a clerk, and nothing more. Someone gifted with moving numbers around on a page, but wholly incapable of treachery."

"You make him sound like me, milord," Cutbill suggested. He continued to work at his notations.

"Hardly. You—I've never trusted you. But you saved me from a rather unpleasant fate, and you'll have a reward."

"Many thanks. Tell me, milord, have you decided what to do with the two heroes of the day? I speak of Sir Croy and of Malden."

The Burgrave shrugged. "Croy proved his loyalty well enough. I don't suppose I'll make an issue of him. I'll leave his banishment intact but not enforce it. That way, if he crosses me again I'll have legal standing to hang him. Who is Malden?"

In the spy room, Malden cringed. He rather wished Cutbill hadn't used his name at all—it could only lead to trouble.

"The thief who stole the crown. And returned it. One of mine, though he was not acting under my orders in the first instance."

"Oh," the Burgrave said. "Well, he'll have to be killed, of course."

Malden nearly cried out.

"He knows my secret. I can't have that."

"Indeed." Cutbill made another notation. "Understandable. Though . . ."

"What is it?"

Cutbill looked up from his ledger. "You said you would grant me a reward."

"Yes, yes. Gold, jewels, what will you have? It can't be anything official, of course. Nothing on paper."

"Malden's life. Spare it."

Malden's jaw fell open.

"Oh, come now! What do you care about one thief? You have dozens. Many more circumspect ones, at that. This one nearly got you killed."

"But he didn't. He proved far cleverer than he should have been."

The Burgrave let out a curt laugh. "Enough reason I'd think you'd want him dead. Don't tell me you're getting sentimental, Cutbill. I admit, I'd like to let him live myself, but reality is often unfair. You know that all too well."

"Do not mistake me. I don't ask out of a sense of justice. I have none. I ask because he could be an excellent earner, if I keep him under my thumb. He could make me quite a bit of money in the long run."

The Burgrave studied Cutbill shrewdly. "You'll keep him quiet?"

"I'll sew his mouth shut if he threatens to speak out of turn."

"Very well, then." Then the Burgrave left the room, shaking his head in disbelief. He headed through the door that led back up to the Stink.

When he was gone, Malden stepped out of the spy room.

"I don't know what to say," he said, staring at Cutbill in gratitude.

"Say only that I won't regret this," Cutbill told him. "Now. You may go. Don't come back until you have some money for me."

Malden nodded and headed out, into the city that was his home.